Eve Devon writes sexy heroes, sassy heroines and happy ever afters.

Growing up in locations like Botswana and Venezuela gave her a taste for adventure and her love for romances began when her mother shoved one into her hands in a desperate attempt to keep her quiet during TV coverage of the Wimbledon tennis finals.

When she wasn't consuming books by the bucket-load, she could be found pretending to be a damsel in distress or running around solving mysteries and writing down her adventures. As a teenager, she wrote countless episodes of TV detective dramas so the hero and heroine would end up together every week. As an adult, she worked in a library to conveniently continue consuming books by the bucket-load, until realising she was destined to write contemporary romance and romantic suspense. She lives in leafy Surrey in the UK, a book-devouring, slightly melodramatic, romance-writing sassy heroine with her very own sexy hero husband.

Eve loves hearing from readers, so if you'd like to get in touch you can find her at one of these places:

🐦 @EveDevon
f https://www.facebook.com/EveDevonAuthor
www.EveDevon.com

Also by Eve Devon

Her Best Laid Plans
The Love List
It's In His Kiss
The Little Clock House on the Green

Christmas at the Little Clock House on the Green

EVE DEVON

A division of HarperCollins*Publishers*
www.harpercollins.co.uk

Harper*Impulse* an imprint of
HarperCollins*Publishers*
The News Building
1 London Bridge Street
London SE1 9GF

www.harpercollins.co.uk

A Paperback Original 2017
1

A catalogue record for this book
is available from the British Library

ISBN: 9780008253226

Set in Birka by Palimpsest Book Production Limited,
Falkirk, Stirlingshire

Printed and bound by CPI Group (UK) Ltd, Croydon, CR0 4YY

For Dad. For teaching your children that the world is full of amazing places and that life is for living.

'If adventures will not befall a young lady in her own village, she must seek them abroad'

— *Jane Austen*

Chapter 1

The Grandfather of all Clock-Ups

Kate

Kate Somersby upended the contents of her handbag over her desk and watched the hundred or so fluorescent pink post-its flutter to the surface like confetti.

Any moment now she was going to get to grips with the bullet journaling system her cousin, Juliet, raved about.

Yep ... any moment now, she thought, staring down at all the vitally-important, equal-priority To Do notes that had come to her in the early hours of the morning.

In the meantime, she reasoned, her portable, flexible filing system was practically the same thing only without all the pretty panda stickers.

Shoving the roll of stickers and the actual bullet journal Juliet had gifted her into the top desk drawer, Kate pulled out her chair and plonked herself down.

It completely boggled her mind to think that a few months ago she'd been working abroad, pretending she was okay with living out of a suitcase, and now she was back in her home village of Whispers Wood, the proud owner of The Clock

House and on schedule to get it open for business before Christmas. Of course, it immediately un-boggled when she thought about the insane number of hours everyone was putting in to keep them on course and ensure it was going to happen.

Hopefully by the end of the week, Juliet would have her hair-dressing stations in place for Hair @ The Clock House.

Daniel, Kate's boyfriend, had nearly finished setting up Hive @ The Clock House, the co-working space he was going to manage, and all the treatment beds, pedi-chairs and nail station tables were arriving today for Beauty @ The Clock House, the day spa that had been her and her twin, Bea's, dream for so long.

What do you think, Bea? Is this how you pictured all of this when we used to dream about opening our day spa in this building?

A swirl of excitement ran head-first into the wall of sorrow that was acknowledgement of Bea's death and bounced backwards in confusion. She felt the conflict inside her like a cramp and tried to breathe through it.

And then on a shaky breath she imagined Bea snorting with laughter, and offering a '*Hey – I'm still trying to get over the fact that you think you'll get to grips with bullet-journaling,*' and the cramp eased.

Bea would have loved everything that was happening at The Clock House and she, Kate, was nearly used to not searching for confirmation she was doing the right thing every time she walked through the front doors.

Feeling steadier, her hands went to open the first of the

letters that Sandeep, the postman, had handed her on her way in and her heart started beating faster as she stared at the official-looking envelope. Opening it, she pulled out the crisp formal headed letter paper and halfway through the first paragraph she let out a 'Whoop' and twirled in her chair.

They'd only been given their licence to open Cocktails & Chai in the main reception room opposite Juliet's salon. The room with its gorgeous, gigantic chandelier was the *perfect* setting for a tearoom/bar.

'Could this morning get any better?' she laughed and immediately opened the second envelope.

'*No-el, No-el.*'

'Wowsers, Kate,' Juliet shouted up the main staircase of The Clock House. 'It's a bit early to be singing Christmas carols, isn't it?'

'That's singing?' asked Oscar, Kate's brother-in-law who, after being known as The Young Widower of Whispers Wood for years was happily getting used to now being known as Juliet's boyfriend.

'Someone's really murdering that carol,' Daniel commented as he walked into the foyer. Spying the boxes of balance ball chairs that had been delivered, he gave an excited 'Yes', and walked over to inspect them.

'That *someone* is your girlfriend. And if she doesn't stop I'm not sure I can be held accountable.' Oscar pointed to the drill he was holding because he was also known as Whispers Wood's resident builder.

'That's definitely not singing,' Daniel said with a frown.

'I've heard her sing. Or have I? That's really her singing? And what's with the carols in October? I guess I'm going to need you both to promise me you'll never fill out an application for *The Voice* on her behalf.'

'Why would we?' Oscar asked. 'Because that's not singing. In fact, I'm pretty sure Will.I.Am would correctly call it Kitty-Kat Kate Caterwauling.'

'If only she was from Wales,' Juliet lamented, 'she might still be in with a shot.'

'We could move the whole of Whispers Wood to Wales and she'd still hurt ears,' Oscar said. 'It's worse than when Melody went through the *Frozen* sing-a-long sleepover phase and I had to cope with ten five-year-olds thinking that singing mostly involved squealing high enough for dolphins to hear.' Oscar's daughter, Melody, had recently had her ninth birthday. She'd been only four when her mother, Bea, had died and Oscar had had to learn fast how to help his daughter through the grieving process while going through it himself.

'Come on, guys,' Daniel cajoled, 'let's cut Kate some slack. She's under a lot of pressure to get this place ready for the grand opening.'

'*No-el, No-el.*'

The three of them stared up the stairs.

'Okay,' Daniel said, rolling up his sleeves, 'I might just see if I can get her to sing a different carol.'

'Thank you,' Juliet sighed. 'Oscar and I appreciate you taking one for the team.'

Abandoning the yoga ball chairs, Daniel headed for the stairs. 'Right, then. Off I go.' He looked at Juliet and Oscar from the third step. 'Upstairs. To gently explain ...'

'We're right behind you,' Juliet said, grinning as she made a shooing motion up the stairs.

Kate looked up as the man who had been rocking her world for months now stepped into her office.

He'd popped out to get himself a key cut to her place, Myrtle Cottage.

No big deal – if he'd taken her casual suggestion, and for casual, read, extremely well-rehearsed monologue, at face value.

Darn.

It would probably be better, if on his return, he didn't then immediately see her crying.

With a big sniff she realised Oscar and Juliet were hovering in the doorway behind him. Two more excellent reasons to pull herself together. Ever since she'd come back to Whispers Wood she'd tried to show Oscar he could trust her to stick around and get involved in her niece, Melody's, life, and Oscar had tried to show her he didn't blame her anymore for staying away for so long after Bea had died. But maybe the person who had worked hardest to get them to see each other as family, not enemy, was sweet, kind, heart-as-big-as-a-mountain, Juliet, and the fact that Melody and Oscar looked so happy these days was testament to how much they'd fallen in love with Juliet this summer.

Looking at the three people who were helping to make The Clock House a reality, Kate felt the pressure to get everything perfect rise up and shaking her head in dismay, whimpered,

'No-el.'

'The angels, are in fact, genuinely crying, Katey-Did,' Daniel said softly and then hesitated and swallowed. 'Hang on – are *you* crying? What's happened? Why are you sitting here crying Christmas carols?'

'Not singing carols,' she hiccupped miserably.

'See?' Oscar whispered to Juliet, 'I told you that wasn't singing.'

Kate stared at them all as she picked back up the invitation she'd opened and flapped it about manically. 'No "L",' she tried again and when three faces stared back at her uncomprehending she banged her head on the desk and wailed, 'No "L", No "L".'

'Is it possible the stress of opening this place has made her regress to some sort of primitive communication?' Oscar muttered.

Daniel took the invitation from her and began reading aloud: 'This Christmas, you are cordially invited to the grand opening of the—' his eyes got round. 'Holy—'

Juliet and Oscar came to stand over his shoulder.

Kate's head came up from the desk, pleased to have finally made herself understood.

Juliet gasped as she finished reading. 'Oh my God, the letter "L" is missing the whole way through?'

A throaty laugh rumbled out of Oscar.

'It's not funny,' Kate insisted.

'It's a little funny,' Oscar said, grabbing the invitation to check for himself. 'Cock,' he exclaimed. 'I love it,' and at Juliet, Daniel and Kate's raised eyebrows added, 'Wait – that didn't

6

come out right.'

Kate snatched the invitation back from him. 'This is going where it belongs, in the round file,' and with dramatic flair she slam-dunked it into the bin, then, with a pout, moaned, 'It never misses in films,' and fishing it up from the floor, she stuck it in the bin. 'I don't know why you're laughing,' she said to Daniel. 'Or have you always wanted to run your business out of a *cock* house?'

'See when you put it like that ...' Daniel moved behind her to pluck the invitation out of the general waste and move it into the recycling bin.

'You do realise we're going to have to kill Crispin for this,' she muttered. 'I'll need a plan on my desk by the end of the day.'

'How about we don't but say we did,' Juliet offered soothingly.

Crispin Harlow, head of the Whispers Wood Residents' Association believed whole-heartedly that it took a village to raise a village. He put the "e" in pedantic, the nosy in parker and could also be completely sweet and terribly caring, but for the purposes of allowing herself to get justifiably riled up, Kate was going to ignore that. 'As if I have the time to sort out this kind of error. I should never have let him badger me into giving his friend the order.'

'He didn't badger you,' Daniel reminded her. 'He didn't even needle you.'

'Didn't need to, did he, when he can do the whole,' she waved her hand about wildly over her head, 'wig-mesmerising thing.'

Another laugh rumbled out of Daniel. 'What, you think Crispin sort of "*hair*-brained" you into placing the order via the magical mesmerising properties of his wig?'

'I really do,' she sulked, a little shocked to find herself still so close to tears. Maybe it was that she'd spent so much time thinking about the moment when all the invites went out. That excited-nervous, no-going-back, what-did-we-do-all-this-for-if-it-wasn't-to-actually-open-our-doors-to-paying-guests moment that had seen her through all the other completely scary times this last couple of months.

'We'll just have to trust this guy to make the correction,' Juliet suggested.

'But what if he does it wrong again?' Kate worried. 'I don't think Crispin and my relationship would survive it. Honestly, I think I'd rather start from scratch.'

'I suppose we're only losing our deposit,' Daniel said.

'And on the bright side,' she ventured, feeling a little of her earlier joy creeping back in, 'We just got our food and alcohol license ... so we could add that to the invites. Even if we get the spelling corrected, Cocktails & Chai wording won't fit on the existing invitations and what's the betting if we correct the spelling, something else will go wrong with them. We're cutting it close to get the invites out in time as it is.'

'But that's brilliant we got the licence,' Juliet said. 'We're really going to add one more business to the mix, then?'

'I think we'd be passing up a great opportunity if we didn't,' Daniel replied. 'To try opening up Cocktails & Chai once we're already open would be really disruptive. What about it, Oscar? Do you think you could finish up the building work

8

in time?'

'Sure,' Oscar said. 'It's quiet at this time of year and I can give some of my other projects to my team for the chance to build that custom-made bar.'

'I was hoping you'd say that,' Kate said. 'So now we just need someone to do the new invites, choose new card-stock, get them to the printers and then—'

'You could always send an e-vite,' Daniel said.

'Actually that's not a bad idea,' Kate said as possibility roared to life.

'I do have them occasionally,' he murmured with a wry smile. 'We could ask Jake Knightley's sister, Sarah to design it for us.'

Kate considered. 'So you think she's still doing graphic design, then?'

'She had a baby, not a lobotomy,' Juliet laughed.

Kate's gaze shot to Juliet. The way she'd said baby. All dreamy and ... Kate's insides did a sort of double-tuck, full lay-out, gymnastic thing. Were Juliet and Oscar thinking babies? Already? Juliet had only moved in with Oscar and Melody five minutes ago. How would she manage a new business with a baby? And Kate didn't know anything about maternity employment law! Nervously she reached for her pile of sticky notes and then paused. Maybe she should actually check with Juliet before she immortalised or even italicised the words 'Juliet' and 'Preggers???' on neon pink.

'So,' Daniel said, grabbing her attention again. 'We give Crispin's friend of a friend the swerve and ask Sarah to design the e-vite, and we announce the opening of Cocktails & Chai along with the other businesses?'

God, he was good for her, she thought. He was never frightened of the dramatic streak that ran through her and was perfectly trusting that she knew when to let logic over-rule emotion in business decisions. He totally had her back. And she'd never felt more able to be herself...

'*I love you*,' Kate said.

The words came out super-naturally considering it was the first time she'd said them, but as Daniel inhaled sharply, tears made glistening pools of her eyes, which was why she didn't see Oscar swiftly pulling a goggle-eyed Juliet out of the room to give her and Daniel some privacy.

'Sorry,' Kate started babbling. 'Totally the wrong time to drop the L-bomb. At work of all places. I couldn't pick some-where romantic? All the times you've said the words to me and I haven't said them back. Oh—,' she broke off as Daniel closed the distance in one easy stride, swept her up into his arms and kissed her.

As his mouth sealed across hers, a familiar buzz lit across nerve-endings and ignited to spread through her veins. As his lips rubbed, coaxed, *revered*, she felt more of the slippy-slidey, twisty-tangled conflict inside of her settle.

'Wow,' she said.

'Wow,' he echoed with a grin. 'And then there's also this,' he held up the key he'd had cut to Myrtle Cottage.

He'd given her the key to his place, Mistletoe Cottage, weeks ago. Presented it as a point of practicality and with his matter-of-fact tone that she found so sexy, how could she refuse? Even as she'd worried exchanging keys was moving fast, she'd still taken that key and let herself in with it that night and stolen into his bed to surprise him.

Yesterday she'd found herself buying his favourite brand of bread. The one with the sixty-three different types of seeds that dropped down the grill of the toaster and worked their way into the strangest of places. The one he liked to wolf down when he returned from his morning run before he got into the shower. Before then getting back into bed with her, claiming he was the perfect wake-up call.

He was, but that was beside the point.

The point was they were leaving more and more bits of themselves at each other's places ... and, well, what did that all mean?

Only this morning she'd realised that the coat she'd been vaguely thinking of wearing today, was probably still at his place.

Had he hung it up?

Did he care that it was there?

Did he want to move in with her?

Wait! What?

This past summer had been a crazy spectacular rollercoaster of competing with Daniel for The Clock House while falling for him, hook, line and sinker. There was still so much they were finding out about each other and now – already – to be thinking about moving in together?

Kate swallowed and stepped out of his arms. It was enough they had keys to each other's cottages.

Moving in together would be, well, three words: Way, *way* too soon.

Okay, that was four words, but you get what she's thinking, right?

To cover her pounding heart, she reached for her pen and her ever-present pad of post-it notes.

She'd be totally cray-cray adding more pressure to their relationship. They hadn't even opened The Clock House yet.

Leaning down she forced herself to concentrate on what she should really be thinking about, and proud that her handwriting didn't show any sign of "moving-in-together" shakiness, she wrote: *Find someone to manage Cocktails & Chai*, and underlined it four times.

Chapter 2

Crouching Dragon, Hidden Bartender

Emma

Emma Danes blew a strand of rapidly frizzing blonde hair out of her eyes and looked on in horrid fascination at the human pretzel facing the class.

'... And as you bend your body down to the earth,' the yoga instructor drawled, 'bring your palms to the floor, squeeze your triceps against your inner thighs, and tip your body forward until your feet leave the ground and your body-weight is resting on your hands.'

Um ... yeah ... no way was she attempting that balancing pose Emma decided as the butterflies fluttered wildly inside her. She attempted that, pee was probably going to come out!

Honestly, of all the yoga-joints in all the world, you'd think she'd have noticed that the one half a block from her apartment had a super-advanced class at eleven thirty on a Monday morning. Then again, normally at this time on a Monday she was taking an acting class.

Or at an audition.

Or knocking on her agent, Penny's, door, calling out 'Penny' three times in rapid succession.

Poor Penny. She must be so over everyone going Sheldon on her.

Thinking of Penny, she stared hard at her lucky bag crocheted in raspberry, denim and sunshiny yellows that she'd casually tossed at the foot of her yoga mat.

Just imagining the phone inside ringing with the news had her heart bouncing down to her stomach and getting caught up in the excitement swirling there. It was as if she'd swallowed a giant ball of tangled-up Christmas lights and someone had plugged them in to test out the *techno*, *techno*, *techno* light setting.

But she'd deal with the reduced-to-jelly nerves all day long because she hadn't got this wrong.

Today was the *diem* and she was going to *carpe* every last drop out of it.

She'd nailed the audition and the call-back. The screen-test couldn't have gone better and all the great feedback she'd received surely meant that finally the hard work, the sacrifice, the rejection, ahem, *rejections*, were going to be worth it.

Planets had aligned.

Unicorns had gathered.

And after years in La La Land, Emma Danes was finally getting the lead part in the rom-com of her dreams.

Filming on location in England, here she came.

She bent her head to hide the proudly joyous grin spreading across her face and decided to attempt the yoga pose after all.

Halfway through rearranging her body she heard the buzz

from her bag and looked up to see it gently vibrating. With a soft yelp, she leaped upon it and uncaring of where she was, fished the phone from out of her bag, and whispered, 'Penny?' into it.

'Sugar Bean? Are you sitting down?' There was a short silence and then, 'I've just heard back and I don't know what to tell you. I'm so sorry.'

The earth's gravitational pull came to a clattering halt.

That was surely the only reason Emma could possibly be sinking to her yoga mat in a tangle of disbelief. It couldn't possibly have been Penny's greeting, her tone, her actual words or Emma's amazing powers of deduction that was very definitely suggesting…

Emma squeezed her eyes shut.

No, no, no.

She hadn't got the part?

Really and truly?

'I know this wasn't what either of us was expecting to hear,' Penny said, her usual nasal tone enhanced now that it was laced with sympathy.

'It's fine,' Emma whispered, too shocked to process how very much not fine it was as Failure danced onto the stage of her heart and took a flourishing bow.

'I'm just as pissed as you, Pinto Bean. You were perfect for that part.'

She'd really thought so too.

Damn it.

Slowly she looked around her at the rows of exceedingly bendy people all having contorted their bodies into crouching poses with minimum effort.

She didn't do minimum effort. She did maximum effort.

And still came up short, it seemed.

Bitter disappointment and a strange sense of embarrassment became besties, holding hands as they rushed through her veins, stealing her energy. Stealing her joy.

She held her bag out in front of her like it was poor Yorick's skull and stared accusingly down at it. So much for being lucky.

With her phone still pinned to her ear, she pulled herself upright, shoved her feet into her shoes and then fled the yoga studio with its mirrors shamelessly reflecting her dazed expression for everyone to see.

Outside, as she made her way back to the sanctuary of her apartment, the bright sunshine, gentle breeze and ridiculously cheerful Christmas music from one of the Prius' in the endless parade of traffic combined to mock her for daring to assume it had finally been her turn to get the big-break.

'Did they say why?' Emma asked, picking up her pace, eager to escape the feeling that she was being followed by one of those giant arrows with stupidly over-sized light-bulbs illuminating the words 'Not Good Enough'.

'Only that someone unexpected expressed interest and after reviewing her tapes, they decided to go with her.'

'Tell me it's a name, at least.'

'Oh, A-lister, for sure,' Penny stated in solidarity.

Emma let herself into the apartment she shared with two other actresses, her smile perilously close to wobbling.

'Take a couple of days then come see me,' Penny instructed.

'Keep the faith, okay? There's always traditional pilot season coming up.'

Emma supposed it was. If you discounted that it was October and that the month that signalled the start of the season was at the beginning of a whole different year to this one. Tossing her keys onto the sofa, she wandered over to stare at the fridge, aka the shrine where she and her flatmates stuck scribbled notes to each other.

Em, I got that audition and Jacinta's on set all day otherwise we'd be here to celebrate with you. Moo Shu Pork and a bottle of cheap bubbles inside. Congrats! Lily xx

Emma sniffed.

'Lima Bean? Are you crying? There's no crying in baseball,' Penny said, channelling her best Tom Hanks.

Emma opened the fridge and stared at the celebratory feast wondering how many other beans Penny could call her and with her appetite no longer amounting to a hill of them she shut the door and turned around to head into her room.

'I don't think I can do another pilot season, Pen.' People probably thought it was easy to play a corpse. It wasn't like you could get a note that you were too wooden. But do you know how hard it was to lay on concrete, caked in fake blood, staring into the distance unmoving/not breathing while the actress that actually *had* lines kept pausing to ask what her motivation was?

It was hard.

Especially when the actress asking about her motivation was playing a zombie!

Needless to say that pilot hadn't been picked up.

'Of course you can do another pilot season, Jelly Bean. This is how we do. You're an actress. Says so on your ID, right?'

Ha!

Nope.

Actually, it didn't.

Under the heading of occupation she tended to go with what paid her regular wages.

Bartender.

That's what she wrote on any form that needed her to state her occupation.

Said it all, Emma thought, unable to even summon the energy to cry.

With her spirit whimpering: my moxie, my moxie, my kingdom for my moxie, she shucked her bag off her shoulder, pushed open her bedroom door, pulled back her duvet, and tired beyond all reason, climbed in to bed.

Muttering a quiet, 'Bye Penny,' she hung up and closed her eyes on the day that sucked harder than a sucker fish in charge of sucking clean all the *Sea Life* aquariums in all the world.

Chapter 3

Pity and Pitiful

Emma

Emma had no idea how long she slept for, but she awoke to a dark room and the remnants of a weird dream about fifty-seven varieties of bean auditioning for the lead part at Bar Brand – the bar she'd been working at for three years.

Pushing herself upright she reached for her phone.

Five missed calls.

None of the numbers belonged to Penny, so she guessed she knew what she could do with the absurd hope the actress the studio had decided to go with had caught a sudden case of really bad numb-tongue.

She texted her flatmates to tell them she hadn't got the part, but that she was okay (greatest piece of text-acting ever, right there) and that neither needed to rush back because celebrating had been replaced with one of the greatest comforts known to woman: a long soak in the tub and a re-run of *Pride and Prejudice*.

If she dragged her armchair over to the bathroom door, piled up all her books and set up her laptop at the right angle, she could watch Darcy-Colin emerging from the lake, while she submerged her aching heart in the bath.

The next message turned out to be from her mother. With a curious detachment that belied the usual trepidation she felt when listening to messages her mother left, she got up and padded out to the kitchen to open the fridge. Her mother was on a cruise with – actually Emma didn't want to think about what number boyfriend this was. She knew she quite liked this one though. For a start, he was age-appropriate. Fingers crossed he'd last the distance, or at least the length of the cruise, because no way could she deal with her mother having nothing else to focus on but her and how she Had Not Got The Part she might have bragged was in the bag.

Reaching into the fridge she grabbed the Moo Shu pork, a carton of noodles and the cheap champagne.

'Hi,' she said, turning around to greet several imaginary people, 'so glad you could make it. Welcome to my pity party, help yourself to drink and canapés ...'

Pretty convincing, she thought, as she opened a kitchen drawer to grab a pack of chopsticks. Who wouldn't want mad-skillz like hers on the set of a rom-com?

She uncorked the bubbly, debated drinking straight from the bottle, and then put her voicemail onto speakerphone while she hunted up a glass.

'Hi Emma, enquiring friend from across the pond is dying to know if you got the part? Can't wait to post pics all over social media of when I knew you, back in the day.'

Emma shoved a mouthful of cold noodles into her mouth. 'Back in the day' had been three years ago when Kate Somersby had walked into Bar Brand to write a review of the place. It had been Emma's first day on the job and she'd been busy acting her way through her shift, doing the whole fake-it-'til-she-made-it routine until she got familiar with everything. Emma had immediately recognised the actress in Kate. Not the showy, this-is-who-I-be kind of acting, but more the, this-is-how-I-get-through-the-days face that she showed the world.

She'd wondered what had happened to make Kate so eager to try on any other face that wasn't her own. Plus, Kate's British accent and it's reminder of a home she hadn't visited for years, had got her good. They'd become good friends, keeping each other up-to-date with their lives ever since.

Taking a gulp of fizzy wine straight from the bottle she listened to the second message from Kate:

'Me again. Did I get the day wrong? Hope I haven't jinxed anything. Oh, are you busy rehearsing a) a love scene b) a love scene or c) a love scene. Tick all that apply. And call me or text me or email me or send smoke signals or something because clearly our telepathic link is down.'

It was going to have to be a non-verbal communication, Emma decided, swapping phone for laptop so that she could compose better. If she had to actually use her voice, Kate was going to know right away just how devastated she was that she hadn't got the part.

As she munched on more food she emailed:

To: Kate Somersby
From: WritingHerOscarAcceptanceSpeech
Subject: Won't be giving up my day job after all.
I didn't get the part ☹

Emma xx

There, she thought, pleased with her honest, to-the-point and most importantly, no-sobbing-to-be-heard composition.

Minutes later she got a reply.

To: WritingHerOscarAcceptanceSpeech
From: Kate Somersby
Re: Won't be giving up the day job after all.

Oh, EM, G! No coming to the UK to practise your British accent a la Renee Zelwegger??? Waaah—I'm so sorry, hun. I know how much you wanted that part. You would have been bloody brilliant. You ARE bloody brilliant.

Kate xx

Emma searched for the crying emoji and sent a whole line of them back and then immediately felt pitiful so followed it up with: *Feeling sorry for myself will only last one millennia and then I'll be all good.*

Minutes later she got back:

You'll be back to lighting up the sky-line with flames in no time, I know it! (((Hugs))) Kate xx

Tears pricked as Emma replied: *Well, back to bartending at Bar Brand, at least. Rent's due in a couple of weeks. No rest for the wicked-ly untalented. Emma xx*

She was more than halfway through her food when she received her reply:

Hey, if they ever do a remake of Cocktail, Tom Cruise doesn't stand a chance. Seriously, a better part will come along. You just have to believe (and work your arse off) but the part in brackets I know you already do, Kate xx

That produced a half-smile but then Emma flexed fingers

eager to type something else. Picking up the laptop and the bottle of champagne, she headed back to her room to hop back onto the bed. After taking a thoughtful couple of gulps, she wrote: *You sound like my agent, Penny.* Emma's hands paused on the keyboard and then she typed: *Maybe it's time I let the dream go! Emma, xx*

She pressed 'send' and raised her gaze to the dressing table under the tiny window. Sitting prettily on top were various photo frames containing affirmations she'd printed out. Why didn't looking at them spur her on the way they used to?

Over the last year, when her faith in her ability to land a good role had started slinking off to play hide and seek, Emma had seriously considered moving to New York or back to London to try the stage. She'd thought that perhaps the change of scene would herald a change of luck.

If it wasn't for the sly fear she'd end up doing the same thing – going to audition after audition without actually getting a part – except if she moved she'd be doing it in the freezing-cold, maybe she'd even have got on that bus or plane.

She'd been in LA since age nine when her parents had divorced and her mother had taken Emma's 'One day I'm going to be a famous actress' and run all the way to Hollywood with it. LA felt like home now but eighteen years was a long time to try and make it.

She'd had some successes when she was younger.

Trouble was as you got older, straddling that line between wanting more and getting desperate, was becoming increasingly harder to stay on the right side of.

At least bartending was simple, honest work. People came

in to get a drink. She provided them with the drink.

Simples.

Adding a smile and lending an ear if they wanted to talk seemed like fair exchange and came easy.

The thought of finding herself in ten years time, with no good acting projects under her belt, no man in her life, no children ... Her only true achievements a killer-flexible yoga body and a face that didn't move, shook her.

If she didn't get her big break soon she really did have to call time on this dream and go find another. One that didn't eat away at her psyche until she ended up like her mum – hard-wired for what was over the next horizon – never enjoying what she had.

She glanced down as an email dropped into her inbox.

To: WritingHerAcceptanceSpeech

From: Kate Somersby

Subject: NOT LETTING DREAMS GO

Eat a gallon of ice-cream, down some cheap cocktails, watch a ton of tat TV in between pulling shifts at Bar Brand but then go to an Improv class, okay? Kate xx

Emma stared at the screen. Letting dreams go was something Kate actually knew about. So was *not* letting them go, which was why her friend had audaciously risked returning to her home village of Whispers Wood to set about making one come true. Now, not only was Kate's dream coming true, she'd also fallen in love.

Emma reminded herself she was in love too.

With acting.

But as she reached for the bottle she wondered what would

happen if she really did let the dream go?

It shocked her when she wasn't brought to her knees by the thought.

Instead, it felt strangely as if someone was standing outside the front door to her heart and like *The Walking Dead* guy in *Love Actually* showing her large hand-written notices that said things like: 'I'll tell you what you want, what you really, really want ...' 'You want Peace', 'Serenity', 'And ... zigazig ha'.

With a deep breath she hit 'reply' and typed: *Confession: I think I've been awful tired of this acting-gig for an awful long time now...*

There!

She'd said it.

Out loud.

Well, not out loud, but you know what she means.

She waited for a reply.

Waited some more.

Maybe she shouldn't have put that out there into the universe.

Because honestly? If she gave up acting, who was she?

Chapter 4

Think Positivi-tea

Kate

Kate stared at the screen in front of her, feeling bad for her friend, Emma. She knew what it was like to feel as if the path you'd chosen was leading nowhere. All those years she'd been footloose and fancy-free, going where the next work assignment took her and never having to really unpack – either her belongings or her feelings. Never being in one place for long had started off being something she'd needed to do but how quickly had she led herself to believe that it was something she *wanted* to do.

It had taken Old Man Isaac selling this place to get her to change direction and she was so thankful he had because despite feeling a tired she hadn't known existed, it was very definitely a happy tired.

Stifling a yawn she reached over and crossed-through number twenty-seven on her To Do List.

As large hands came around her mid-riff to hug her from behind, she gasped, 'Hey, mister. I know the owner of this establishment.'

'So do I,' Daniel's voice trickled into her ear. 'In fact I'm pretty sure I have a meeting with her in about—'

'Thirty minutes,' Kate smiled, spinning in her chair to face him. 'I have this office booked until then and I'm determined to get through at least fifteen more emails.'

'Just wanted to check how the interview went?'

Kate grimaced. 'Complete dud.'

'Really?'

'Trust me.'

'Are you sure you're not being too …'

Kate raised an eyebrow in challenge.

'Fussy?' he stated bravely. 'Only we're running out of time to find someone to manage the place.'

Kate was very aware they needed to find someone to manage Cocktails & Chai @ The Clock House ASAP.

One of the conditions of buying the building had been to provide space the whole community could continue to use, but with the toddler group moving into the newly-built huts at the local school, that only left Trudie McTravers and her am-dram group using the communal space. Kate had promised Trudie the space would always be available for rehearsal and productions but she'd wanted to add something more.

She'd wanted everyone in the village and anyone booking a spa treatment with her, or having their hair done by Juliet, or booking office space with Daniel, to be able to grab a cuppa or a glass of fizz too and when she'd talked over her plans to add a tearoom/bar in the reception room opposite Juliet's salon she'd been overwhelmed by how much everyone loved the idea. Of course that probably had a little something to do with socking-it-to the neighbouring village of Whispers Ford because there were still a few residents who hadn't got over the hotel opening and the village stealing 'Best in Bloom' out from under them. But she'd got the go-ahead and now with the last licence coming through, it was all systems go to organise staff before they opened.

'So what was wrong with this candidate?' Daniel asked.

'Besides looking twelve?'

'I'll admit he did look a little young, but his C.V. said he was qualified.'

'He asked me if I'd be fact-checking his previous employment.'

Daniel mouthed the word, 'Wow,' and shook his head.

'And, you know, his name was Harry Stiles,' Kate added as if that explained everything and when Daniel looked at her as if that meant nothing, she rolled her eyes. 'I can't handle the disappointment when people realise the real Harry Styles hasn't, in fact, given up his incredibly successful world tour to run a bar and tearoom in a quaint little village called Whispers Wood.'

'You can't not employ someone on the grounds they have a similar name to someone famous.'

'So fortunate that he kept right on hammering in more nails, then,' Kate replied. 'When I asked him what he thought made him most qualified for the position, he responded with "Um, I like to drink?"'

'He didn't?'

'Oh yeah and not even "I like to drink, ha-ha, only joking, sorry that was wildly inappropriate, I'm just really nervous, here's my actual answer," oh no,' Kate went on, 'He said, "Um, I like to drink" ... with a question mark at the end of it. Like he wasn't even sure.'

Daniel rolled his eyes in sympathy. 'Yeah. Okay. Good call.'

'How difficult can it be to find someone who knows how to make a martini as well as they make a matcha latte or a good old-fashioned cup of tea, not to mention someone who actually likes talking with people?'

'We have to think positive. Quick, do your thing.'

'Thing?'

'Your positivity rain dance, thing.'

'Ugh. I'm too tired.'

'Nonsense. This is important. You want the next candidate to be the one, don't you?'

Kate gave a tired smile. 'You do realise how dangerous it is to pander to my quirk?'

'What can I say, I live for danger.'

Biggest fib, right there, Kate thought because while she knew Daniel thought nothing of taking calculated risks, she also knew the chaos he'd grown up with. Living for danger was not what he was about at all but she loved making him laugh and so she rose to her feet and did some over-the-top stretching motions.

'Remember you asked for this,' she warned and wafting her hands up and down like she was trying to take-off, she turned around in circles clockwise and then counter-clockwise chanting nonsense about positivity under her breath in a poor imitation of the dance she'd made up after one too many honey martinis had made her feel invincible. At the end of it she plonked herself back down in her chair, knackered. 'That's the next candidate for the job sorted, then,' she said, trying not to worry that she didn't actually have anyone lined up. 'By the way, thank you for letting me book an office. Mine's got a massage table in it that I'm certain wasn't in there last night.'

'So what's the verdict on the tech?' Daniel asked, with a nod to the set-up she was sat in front of.

Kate swung her chair back to the computer in front of her and sighed appreciatively. 'I'm appropriately jealous. Everything up here seems higher-spec than we put in downstairs.'

'You don't need clients geeking-out over the I.T. downstairs. You want them sighing with pleasure over treatments. You were right to keep the set-up on the lower floors unobtrusive. Doesn't mean I don't appreciate the compliment though.'

Kate grinned with pride for him.

He'd done a fantastic job of matching the aesthete of the spa and hair salon without making Hive @ The Clock House feel too girly. The attic rooms had been beautifully converted so that they now housed an open-plan area for hot-desking, a kitchen area with a long table in, and five meeting rooms with full conference facilities. The original oak flooring had been sanded and re-varnished, so that it set off the white furniture to its best. The clock mechanism had been encased in thick glass walls and formed the centre-point of the cleverly-thought-out space. Throughout, Daniel had added potted trees to soften the look. He'd married the country-chic feel of downstairs with the industrial-loft look perfectly.

'I thought the demented pigeon dance would get rid of

some of these knots,' Daniel said, lowering his hand to her shoulders to start rubbing at the tension. 'But you need a good massage. Smooth out some of the stress-kinks.'

Kate purred. 'The problem with learning all these new skills is I can't do them on myself.' She thought of the half a dozen workbooks on her bed back at the cottage. Was she completely mad to be studying for her diploma in beauty therapy while opening her business? And, yet, she thought, taking Daniel's advice and determinedly channelling positivity, the sooner she completed her qualification, the sooner she could add those skills to her business degree and ensure the spa ran as smoothly as possible.

Daniel leaned down to whisper in her ear, 'Hey, you know we've got time until our meeting. Forget those emails. I've an idea or two of how we can work out some of these kinks.'

'You have?' Kate's grin turned sultry as she spun around in her chair again and lifted her arms to lace around his neck. 'Oh,' she said as her ever-working mind remembered something else she'd written on her list. 'I meant to ask you, don't you think maybe we should have put in some of those standing desks up here?'

Daniel reached out and cranked a lever under the desk, laughing as the desk Kate was sat in front of, rose smoothly up into the air.

'Wow, that's—'

'Impressive?' he said knowingly. 'Now this,' he said picking her up with an ease that she found exciting and lowering her onto the higher surface of the desk, 'is a much better height for what I have in mind.'

'You mean for not putting your back out,' she said with a laugh.

'Practicality—'

'Looks so sexy on you,' she finished for him.

'Thank you.'

'Oh, did you decide what you wanted to do about asking your mother down for Christmas?'

Daniel lifted his head. 'Wow. Did you just ask about my mother while I was getting ready to unbutton your blouse?'

'God, I think I did. I'm sorry. I've got too much stuff going on up here,' she said pointing to her head. 'As soon as I stop thinking about one thing, the next comes to the surface.'

Daniel tilted her jaw and rubbed the pad of his finger across her bottom lip. 'Perhaps if I occupy these for a while, the message that you've got to stop stressing about absolutely everything will get through.'

She pretended to think before replying, 'I suppose we could give your plan a go,' and then her grin turned into a wince of regret as her phone alarm went off with another reminder that she should be doing anything else but sneaking a little time with the man who could make her heart beat crazy-fast. 'We'll have to wait until later.'

The pout on Daniel's face was comical. 'Why did I have the feeling you were going to say that?'

Kate's mouth turned down to match Daniel's. 'Because I always seem to be saying that, lately? I know. It'll get better.'

Daniel chuckled. 'You do know it's actually going to get worse, right?'

'I know. But—'

'We'll always have after hours.' He leaned in to kiss the hollow of her left cheekbone.

'Yes.' Although to be fair, with all the work they both still needed to do to ensure they opened on time, the nights were getting shorter as well.

'My place or yours tonight?' he asked, playfully nipping at her lower lip.

Kate hesitated and distracted him by kissing the underside of his jaw. His place was right next to hers so technically what did it matter? They both had the exact same size bed – the only ones that would fit into the size rooms their side-by-side cottages had. But hers…

She really liked waking up in hers. Liked taking comfort from being unpacked and seeing her things carelessly dotted around.

'Mine, I think. Is that okay?'

'Hey, I'm happy anywhere you are.'

Kate smiled. Of course if they moved in together he could be with her all the time.

'You think we'll still have the energy for "after hours" when we're working even longer hours?' Daniel asked.

'We'd better. I refuse to let Mum and Big Kev outshine us in the romance department.' Her mum had been seeing Big Kev who ran the corner shop for months now. Although for some reason she refused to give out the confirmation memo, so everyone still had to pretend he wasn't romancing her after hours amongst the bakery goods. Oh, that reminded her … Kate still needed to ask her mum if she'd be interested in doing the baking for Cocktails & Chai when business slowed down at the B&B which she ran.

'Rain-check, then?' Daniel asked.

'Til tonight.'

'Tonight. Your place. And to tide us over—'

'Kate, you up here? Oops. Sorry,' Juliet apologised as she reached the top of the stairs and spied them mid-clinch.

'Don't be silly. It's fine,' Kate assured.

Daniel cleared his throat and smiled. 'Kate and I were just testing out the system.'

'Right,' Juliet gave a knowing nod. 'Oscar and I need to do some of that.' A blush formed across her cheeks. 'Not *your* systems, obviously. What I meant was—'

Kate grinned. 'What you meant was that you're both feeling the strain of working long hours and hardly ever seeing each other, as well.'

When Oscar had discovered, this summer, Juliet's plans to work so closely with Kate, he'd gone into full protective mode, making it impossible for Juliet to hide her feelings for him. The sparks between them had got the whole of Whispers Wood noticing and even though Juliet had moved out of her beloved bijou Wren Cottage and into the barn that Oscar had converted within weeks of them finally getting together, Kate was willing to bet that between Juliet setting up her salon and Oscar finishing up all the building renovations around here, they probably hardly got to see each other outside of work, either.

'Anyway,' Juliet said, 'I wanted to tell you I talked over that other thing with Oscar and he agrees that Jake would be the perfect choice.'

'Jake?' Daniel queried.

'Jake Knightley,' Kate explained. 'I thought I'd ask him to take a look at the courtyard. Come up with some plans for re-landscaping the space come spring.'

Daniel frowned. 'Will he have time now he's taken over the running of Knightley Hall?'

'I think he's looking for all the work he can get,' Juliet said. 'Knightley Hall is kind of expensive to run.'

'Okay, I'll try and set up a meeting. Let me write it down, or I'll forget. As you're here and Daniel's here, shall we start the meeting now?'

'Works for me,' Juliet said. 'Have notebook, will meet. So, are we employing Harry Stiles or what?'

'Nope.'

'Melody's going to be so disappointed.'

'Trust me, she really isn't,' Kate said.

'Hey, why don't we show Juliet what we put up in reception, before we start the meeting?'

Kate jumped off the table excitedly. 'Oh. Yes. Perfect. Juliet, come with us,' and grabbing her hand before she could sit down, she steered her down the two flights of stairs until all three of them were standing at the reception desk in the main foyer of The Clock House.

'What do you think?' she asked, pointing to the newly placed vintage photo frames that she and Daniel had put up behind the reception desk the night before. 'I thought it would be nice to have them up,' Kate explained, looking at the three postcards Juliet had sent her at the beginning of the year, explaining that The Clock House was going up for sale. 'You know – a permanent reminder.'

Juliet nodded. 'So when we're super-successful and absolutely rolling in it we can look at these and think: Jennifer Lopez, 'Jenny From The Block'.

'What? No, so we can—'

'Oh, I get it,' Juliet interrupted fist-bumping her heart and then pointing her hand up to the sky and launching into Take That's 'Never Forget'.

'Oh my God. Stop that. I just meant I wanted a lovely reminder of how this space came to be. Of where we started. Of all the hopes you had. All the hopes I had. Of how you tapped into that and started this whole thing.'

A soft smile formed on Juliet's lips as she stopped teasing. 'I didn't really start this whole thing you know.'

Kate nodded. 'I know. Bea did.'

'Yes, Bea did. But it's perfect and I love it. And having them framed for everyone to see, it's like we're paying the sentiment forward.'

Kate turned to stare at the postcards, a huge smile forming on her lips. 'Hey, what would you say if I told you I'd just thought of the perfect way to pay the postcards forward and find someone to run Cocktails & Chai?'

Chapter 5

Geeks Bearing GIFs

Jake

J ake Knightley rounded the corner, took in the sight before him, rolled his eyes, and sticking his fingers into his mouth, produced an ear-splitting whistle.

Bingley the bichon stopped his investigation (chomping) of the lowest border of herbs Jake had been in the process of protecting from winter frosts, and cocked his head at his owner's brother.

'Damn right, you'd better be afraid,' Jake told the dog, trying and failing to sound stern. 'In about one hour from now it isn't going to be rainbows you're sh—' he broke off as he saw his toddler nephew come tottering around the border. 'Pooping,' he said instead, with a stare of exasperation at the dog.

Eighteen month old Elton squealed, 'Bad doggy, Bingey' and catching sight of his favourite uncle grinned like he needed to let some of the sunshine inside of him free. Jake actually suspected each of his three brothers was Elton's favourite uncle but he'd be lying if he didn't get a kick out of seeing the adoration on the kid's face. Smiling back indulgently, he bent and scooped his nephew into his arms. 'Where's Mummy, then?'

Elton flung an arm out, narrowly missing Jake's chin, and pointed behind him.

'Let's go, Bingley,' Jake commanded, and made sure the dog was at his heels.

With his nephew in his arms and the pup at his feet, he wandered through the kitchen garden of the Tudor mansion that had been in his family for generations and which he'd finally been allowed to take over from his parents last year. After studying horticulture and then spending several years working for a garden design firm in London, returning to run Knightley Hall and restore the gardens so they could be opened to the public felt like the realest thing he'd ever done and the place he was supposed to make his mark.

He'd been fortunate enough to work on lots of magnificent gardens, but restoring the ones in his ancestral home was what he'd wanted to do since he'd been a teenager.

Carrying Elton effortlessly, Jake crossed the main patio leading to the terraced gardens that ran the back of the house and walked around the side of the building so that he could get to the front drive.

His sister, Sarah, was busy bumping her car door shut with her hip while she tried to juggle a large cake box and her laptop.

'Sorry, Jake,' she mumbled around the set of car keys in her mouth. She opened her mouth so that the keys fell onto the top of the cake-box she was holding and groaned, 'Little tykes both got away from me.'

Jake reached her side and grabbed the keys that were just about to slide off. 'Tyke number two found a dinner of sorts within seconds of arriving. Expect the distinct smell of parsley when you're cleaning up after him later.'

'Oh Christ, really?' A look of tired resignation came over her face and then suddenly she was smiling. 'Perhaps we'll stay with you for supper and Bingley can have the roam of the gardens.'

'I don't need compost that badly,' Jake laughed, walking with her back towards the rear of the house. 'And you can stay, but I won't be around. I was just organising cloches and cold-frames before I pop over to The Clock House.'

'But I brought food. Well, cake.'

Jake eyed the box suspiciously. 'No.'

'No?'

'No way is cake going to make up for you hatching that evil, twisted plan with Mum, last week.'

'Oh come on. How was I supposed to know the woman mum was talking about was Gloria Pavey.'

Jake shuddered. He was sure Gloria Pavey was perfectly nice. At least she would be once she got over the bitterness of her husband Bob leaving her for a male model called Bobby. 'Thanks to the both of you, she's been round twice, asking if I can pose in her charity calendar.'

'That doesn't sound so bad.'

'Mowing the lawn.'

Sarah winced. 'Going for themed, is she? Well, I suppose mowing is kind of connected to what you do.'

'Naked.'

'What the—' she broke off as she looked at Elton. 'I miss swearing so bad,' she confessed. 'So, Gloria's putting together a *Calendar Girls* but with boys?'

'I think that's the gist. To be honest, I tried not to pay too much attention.'

'Is it possible you've got this all wrong?'

'I don't think so. Lady Chatterley was mentioned. She even asked me to wear my hair down.' He tugged self-consciously on his man-bun because he knew it was only a matter of time before his family started referring to him as Pirate Pete from *TOWIE*. He should have got his hair cut months ago. One more thing he hadn't had time to do. As soon as Juliet opened up her hair salon, the better. 'Both visits were awful. Just awful,' he said. 'No cake is going to make up for what the two of you have started.'

'Are you sure? It's lemon drizzle. Sheila Somersby made it.'

Jake paused because as well as running Whispers Wood B&B, Sheila baked really nice cakes. He deposited Elton on one of the kitchen chairs and, unable to resist, lifted the lid of the box. 'Okay, this can stay. You can leave it with the one that Mum dropped around yesterday.'

'We just care about you, Jakey.'

Jake snorted.

'Ever since—'

Jake held up a hand. 'Unless you bought ear-defenders for Elton, we're not talking about "ever since". And to show me you really care how about putting a halt to the endless parade of women. It's ridiculous, completely unnecessary and did I

40

mention ... ridiculous?'

'Okay, okay. No more women. Promise.'

Jake wasn't going to be stupid enough to believe her. He knew his family meant well but ever since he'd taken over this place and ever since – well, last Christmas – discovering they didn't think he could run Knightley Hall without a good woman by his side was too much. Hadn't he been working his arse off all year to show everyone he could manage the place on his own?

'Have you got time to show me which part of the gardens you've been working on?' Sarah asked, with a grin that said, 'See, I can change a subject with the best of them.'

'Why?'

'I thought I'd bring a photographer friend down to take some shots.'

Jake stared at his sister, his eyes narrowing. 'Is your photographer friend female?'

'Yes.'

'Single?'

'Yes.'

'For God's sake, Sarah.'

'No, it's not like that. She works for *Rural Rooms* magazine and I was thinking if we got some shots of the gardens through all the seasons then you could use them for publicity.'

'Wouldn't she need shots of the house, too?' Because he really didn't have the time, not to mention the money, for a large feature article which was only going to expose how rundown the place had become since he spent every penny he made on restoring the gardens to their former glory.

'The fam can tart up a couple of the main rooms for you, but I've stressed it's the gardens that you're going to be opening up to the public, not the house.'

'As long as the focus isn't on the inside. When can she come?'

'Soon, hopefully. I'll show you some of her work in a minute. Oh, and I have something else to show you.' She held up her laptop and grinned determinedly. 'If you don't love it, tell me you do anyway, because it took a gazillion number of hours and it's probably the best thing I've done in ages.'

'Hey, you always do good work.' Jake knew his sister struggled to feel like she was back at the cutting edge of her work since she'd had Elton and he'd seen on more than one occasion glimpses of how shocking she found motherhood. She was a brilliant mum but both she and her husband were way more used to their tech than a little person who didn't behave like one of their designs, even though, technically, he was. 'I wish I could pay you for doing the brochures for this place when we're ready.'

'Please. Are you planning on charging all of us whenever we come to you for advice?'

'Maybe if any of you actually took it …' It still befuddled him that any of the Knightley brood, of which there were another three brothers and a sister, came to him at all, for advice. Particularly as he wasn't the eldest.

He guessed he was the one best able to cope with no longer having the family's money to fall back on though – probably because the estate had never been about money for him. Out of all of them he was the one who carried this place in his bones, his heart, his soul. And maybe having those roots so deeply embedded represented a familiarity – a stability – that the actual Hall couldn't because even when he'd been in London and his siblings dotted all over, they'd been drawn to him whenever their lives got chaotic.

Sarah sipped her tea. 'Has Seth been around since the split?'

Seth was their youngest brother and had been married to Joanne for two years, yet they seemed to be happier apart than together. 'I think he knows that if he does, I'm just going to send him straight back to her.'

'I don't know, Jake. It sounds sort of final, this time.'

'As opposed to the other times? If it's all so bad, why did he bother marrying her in the first place?' An uncharitable anger kicked against his insides wanting to get out.

'Maybe if he stayed with you for a while,' Sarah suggested.

'No. Way. I've got enough to do without babysitting a grown man with zero interest in what I'm trying to do here.'

'But maybe a little hard work would make him see sense.'

'No.'

'Is that a, "No", no or a—'

Jake simply stared at his sister.

'Okay so that's a real and actual no.'

Elton chose that moment to chase Bingley around the table with a marker in his hands. As Jake reached out to grab the marker, Sarah took her son in her arms and settled him on her lap. 'So, what's all this, then?' she asked, indicating the plans that had been spread out on the large kitchen table.

'I found them in the library last night.'

Jake watched her turn her head to look at the plans and

found himself holding his breath for her reaction.

'It's the rose garden you've been working on, right?'

Jake nodded. 'Notice anything unusual?'

Sarah leant forward to stare at the plans, making sure she captured Elton's sticky hands in her own so that they couldn't reach the age-spotted foolscap drawings. 'This looks bigger somehow.'

'I know. I don't know why this area was never finished, but finally I've found the missing part of the puzzle.'

'All this time there's been a missing part of the garden?'

'Mmmn. Every time I've worked in that area I've kept feeling as if the perspective was off. And I was right. Look,' Jake said, pulling out a kitchen chair and shoving his mug down on the end of the plan to stop it rolling back up. 'This looks like the same wall that divides the kitchen garden from the rose garden, but it isn't. There's another small private garden that extends down from a doorway that's been bricked up.'

'You mean, like a ...' her nose scrunched up. 'Secret garden?'

'Exactly. A secret garden.' Jake grinned, trying and failing to keep the excitement from showing in his voice. 'Yesterday I broke through that part of the wall. Next step is to dig out some of the foundations and see what I unearth.' At least he would, as soon as he had the time. 'Actually, can you tell me what you think of this?' Getting up from the table he walked over to the dresser, pulled out a drawer and took out some sketches. 'I drew them up last night. It's how I think it should look when finished.'

Sarah stared at the watercolour sketches. 'Oh, I love these. You've made it into a sort of garden chapel.'

'Actually, that's not a bad description.'

'It's stunning. A private oasis beyond the rose garden.'

'So you can see how it should look in bloom?'

Sarah nodded. 'It's a shame you can't finish it straight away. With The Clock House opening up in a few weeks, Crispin's going to start bringing up your plans at the village meetings.'

'If Crispin wants me to open earlier, then he can raise the tens of thousands of pounds needed to finish this project off.' Jake wasn't rushing anything. If it was worth doing, it was worth doing well.

'Maybe if you did Gloria's charity calendar – joking,' Sarah added, as soon as she saw his trademark scowl hit his face. 'You know if you're going for the chapel look, you could hold weddings here.' She pointed to his sketches and the plans. 'Set up a marquee on the back terrace, or have a picnic down by the lake, but the ceremony should be here under this main connecting arbour. Can you imagine the scent? So romantic.'

Jake winced.

Yes, okay, the thought had trickled in, along with the puzzle of why his great-great grandfather, George, had added a plan for this area but never had it made.

George Knightley had started his career in theatre construction so it wasn't that surprising to Jake he'd shown a true gift for design. What was surprising was why something that would have worked so well on the estate had been bricked up?

George's designs had been fascinating Jake since he'd stumbled across them while poking about in one of the potting sheds, looking for a bottle of beer or a cigarette when he was fourteen.

After overhearing yet another conversation about money between his parents, he'd been in need of a distraction. They'd all found ways to deal with the stress and reality growing up on an estate the size of Knightley Hall but he'd been the only one to put that energy back into the land and that had been down to Sid, the head gardener at the time, taking him under his wing. Showing him a different way of dealing with pressure and showing him George's designs so that his passion for restoring the gardens had sparked.

Years later and Jake knew his plans to get the place to pay for itself were going to work. He just needed to be done with winter and for spring, summer and autumn to last about twice as long as it usually did.

'Sorry. Shouldn't have mentioned the "R" word,' Sarah said, getting up to plonk her mug into the cheap-as-chips stainless steel sink before turning around to walk back over to the table and switch on her laptop. 'So, about what I brought to show you ... the thing is, I kind of wanted you to see it first so that when you receive your invite, you're not too shocked.'

'Invite?'

'Mmmn. It's for the opening of The Clock House.' She brought up the gif she'd been designing and said, 'Okay, press "Play" and tell me what you think.'

Intrigued, Jake reached forward and set the gif in motion. As the envelope opened up on screen, he grinned. 'Now this is what I call an invitation to a grand party.'

'You like it?'

'I do. More to the point, I think Kate, Daniel and Juliet are going to love it.'

'I thought it was good. I mean, you know what I mean.'

Jake's gaze snagged on the date of the party as it flashed up on screen.

Sarah bit her lip. 'And now I'm guessing you've realised the date of the opening was going to be your—'

'It's fine,' Jake said, cutting her off.

'Is it?'

'Is this really why you came here, to tell me about the date?'

Sarah looked at him with what looked suspiciously like sympathy. He tried a warning scowl and the sympathy in her eyes only deepened. Damn siblings. They saw you running around in a pair of dungarees made from curtains when you were younger and there was just no way they could ever be scared of you again. Gentling his voice anyway, he ran a hand absent-mindedly over his hair. 'I don't have dibs on dates, Sarah.'

'Well, no but—'

'Like I said, it's fine. But I won't be able to babysit Elton for you that night.'

'Of course you won't. You'll be at the party.'

'Actually I won't.'

'Jake, you can't mope around here on your own.'

'I won't be.'

'Okay. That's good. Wait — are you saying you're going to be moping around somewhere else?'

'That's exactly what I'm saying. I've rented a cottage in Cornwall over Christmas. You lot are always on at me to take a holiday, so I am.' And if that happened to mean he was also going to be far away from pitying glances and memories of last Christmas, how very handy.

'What are you talking about?' Sarah demanded. 'You disappeared on Christmas Day last year and all we got was a text saying you weren't coming back until the day after Boxing Day – and we totally understood after what happened,' she rushed out, 'but you know Mum's hoping we'll all be together to do the family Christmas celebration, thing.'

Jake bit back a grimace. If he had his way no one would ever find out where he'd ended up on Christmas Day.

'You really won't be in Whispers Wood this Christmas?' Sarah asked.

'Correctomundo.'

'And you don't think everyone will worry when they hear about this?'

'It's just a holiday, Sarah.'

'Bull. You're running. In fact I'm changing your name to Running Bull.'

He could tell the moment she realised he wasn't going to change his mind. That she could call up the family and get them all to call him Running Bull but that nothing could get him to change his mind from vacating Whispers Wood over Christmas.

Chapter 6

Season's Greetings

Emma

'Em, heads up. Incoming.'
    Emma looked up from concentrating on measuring out a shot of tequila and just managed to catch the bottle of water being thrown at her.
    'Take the water and grab five minutes.'
    'Are you kidding?' Emma looked at Bar Brand's manager, Rudy, like he was insane and then jerked her head pointedly at the three-deep throng at the bar.
    'Not actually kidding,' Rudy confirmed. 'You haven't had a break since you got here and this is your third double shift of the week. DiNozo's going to cover you.'
    Emma felt *Tony* (DiNozo's actual name) bump her hip as he reached over to grab the jigger from her hand. He flashed her one of his trade-mark grins. 'What are we making?'
    'Looks like *you're* making a Mulholland Drive,' she said, whipping off her black apron and stepping back. 'Apparently I'll be seeing you in five.'
    'Make it thirty,' her boss threw over his shoulder as he

49

loaded a tray of drinks.

Thirty? Rudy was certifiable if he really thought she was going to be able to sit upstairs for thirty whole minutes on a busy Friday night.

But as if he knew she was about to argue, he added a, 'That is a direct order, Danes.'

'Sir, yes Sir,' Emma shouted back, giving him a mock salute as she backed out of the bar doors into the kitchen.

'Jeez, Emma, is there any chance you could come through the doors and not nearly knock me over?'

'Sorry, Jade. You're going to have to direct that stellar sarcasm, we've all come to know as wit, at DiNozo for the next few.'

'Sure thing, shirker. Nothing I like better than having to repeat an order eleven million times over to the guy who can't think for smiling at the *ladeez*.'

Emma grinned because the way DiNozo was looking at Jade it really wasn't going to take too much more of her wince-worthy wit for him to decide that the best way to silence that mouth of hers was probably with his. And once they locked lips...

With a happier heart than a few moments before, Emma walked through the busy kitchen and headed up the steep staircase to Rudy's office.

Flinging open the door she took two steps and flung herself down on the fake leather Admiral's chair. If she lowered her aching limbs to the equally fake Chesterfield sofa shoved along the wall beside the filing cabinet she was pretty sure she'd fall asleep and sleeping on the job?

Yeah.

Tended to be thought of as one of those things you didn't do.

Moving a crate containing a new brand of vodka off the desk, she decided thirty minutes was enough time to check Rudy had added all the forms for Christmas parties to the spreadsheet she'd set up for him.

She got so engrossed that when the office door opened and in walked Rudy, she turned in surprise.

'Relax,' he said, holding out his hands. 'Break's not over. I couldn't take the chemistry down there any longer.'

'Jade and Tony? It's True Love, Rudy. Can't stand in the way of it.'

Rudy groaned. 'You and your match-making. Why can't you let Tinder take care of all that?'

Emma shuddered. Dating via an app took all the romance out of it. She knew because she had the unbroken heart to prove it. Dating in the movies was a whole lot different to dating when you worked in the movies. In Hollywood it was virtually impossible to even get a date without using an app and once you did, if you wanted anything more than a casual hook-up, then anyone from within the industry tended to only be interested in what you could do for each other's careers and anyone from outside of the industry tended towards petty jealousies or secretly wanting into the industry anyway.

'Tinder takes care of one thing and one thing only, Rudy. When it comes to matters of the heart, human intervention works best.'

At least it did for others. If only she was as good at matchmaking herself as she was her friends. It was like when you saw an outfit in a shop window and knew instantly who it would look good on, but when it came to choosing one for yourself, you just couldn't see it.

Maybe she was just blind to 'Eligible Guy Reveal Yourself', because she only had eyes for, 'Let The Actress See The Role'.

'What am I going to do if they discover that the path to true love doesn't involve working together?' Rudy asked.

'They'll be fine. Trust me. Think of it this way, won't it be nice to be around Jade when she's singing like Cinderella instead of spitting nails?' She grinned, and then gestured to the screen, 'You need to order more glassware if you're really going to say yes to this number of private Christmas parties.'

'Yeah, yeah. Danes, listen up.'

'It should be okay,' she continued, not really listening-up. 'As long as you don't double book anyone.'

'Stop about the holidays for a moment. Look, you keep running around here like you're indispensable, I'm going to start wondering what I'd ever do without you.'

'What are you talking about?' She turned towards him and blinked. 'When I get The Call, you'll just hire someone else.'

Rudy gave her a long measured look and then shrugged. 'Okay. Yes. This is what I would do. But would they be as good as you? Would they practically run the place when I'm not here?'

Emma's heart skipped a beat. 'Are you planning on going somewhere?'

'Maybe. This place is doing well. Makes me think I might like to open another one.'

Terrific. Was everyone moving onto something except her? 'Where?'

'New York.'

Huh. If only she'd actually made the move to trying theatre. She'd have been in with a shot of getting a job to pay rent while going for auditions.

'I guess I'm asking what you want more,' Rudy said. 'Your name in lights? Or, maybe, your name above this door?'

Emma started shuffling the pile of party requests. He wanted her to run this place for him while he scouted out and set up a bar in New York? 'I want my name in lights, Rudy. You've known this from day one.' Her heart felt heavy because, okay, day one had been three years ago and she hadn't been able to make it happen.

Rudy looked at her shrewdly and then got up and headed for the door before pausing and saying, 'You don't have to answer now but think about it will you?'

Left alone in Rudy's office once more, Emma didn't know what to think. Could she really manage this place for Rudy? Could she really give up chasing The Dream in favour of being surrounded by people who were pursuing that very same dream? Every night, could she watch happily as one by one they started their new adventures and made it in the industry, or would it make her bitter?

Not much of an adventure for her, she thought and immediately felt awful because sweet, sweet Rudy was offering her more options than she'd given herself for the last three years.

With a huge sigh she pulled up her emails hoping to distract herself.

She was young and single with talent.

When did she get to start her adventure?

Idly she clicked on a new email from Kate:

To: WritingHerOscarAcceptanceSpeech

From: Kate Somersby

Subject: Season's Greetings

Attachment: Invite

Emma, Hi!

Beyond excited to show you the mock-up of the invitation we'll be sending out.

Can you do me a massive favour and give me your honest opinion? We've been working on these for so long I've got analysis paralysis!

Oh, can you pay particular attention to the last business and give me your thoughts?

Intrigued, Emma clicked on the attachment and was hopelessly enchanted when an old-fashioned cream-coloured linen envelope, whizzed across her screen and came to a stop, looking like something straight out of a Jane Austen novel. It had her name and address written on it in flowing script, like it had been written with fountain pen and sent by messenger to end up on a silver tray, waiting to be sliced open with a beautifully engraved letter opener.

A second later and it was turning itself over and opening up right in front of her eyes.

The flowing script in the middle read:

This Christmas you are cordially invited to the grand opening of The Little Clock House on the Green…

Oh, wow. Emma squinted past the cursive script. Was that

the actual Clock House in the background? It looked so stately, so fabulously and so quintessentially English, that she felt an unexpected pang of home-sickness.

Which was completely ridiculous, since LA was her home, not England.

The envelope closed up again and divided into four triangles with a number and a 'play' symbol in the centre of each one. Charmed she clicked on the top triangle of the invitation and as it 'unsealed' itself to open up, she read:

Beauty @ The Clock House
Day Spa
Manager: Kate Somersby.

Smiling, Emma clicked on the second leaf and with a smile on her face watched it magically open up to read:

Hair @ The Clock House
Hair Salon
Manager: Juliet Brown

She clicked on the third:

Hive @ The Clock House
Rentable Co-Working space
Manager: Daniel Westlake

And then she clicked on the last one:

Cocktails & Chai @ The Clock House
Tearoom/Bar
*Manager: **Emma Danes***

Emma stared at the screen in shock.

Absurd excitement shot through her, exploding like fireworks. Reaching out she quickly clicked back onto the email to make sure she wasn't imagining things.

How about it, Emma?

*Fancy coming to Whispers Wood and setting up Cocktails &
Chai?*

p.s. I can help out with airfare.

*p.p.s. On days off you could finally get to visit where Jane
Austen lived.*

Ooh, that was sneaky.

Kate knew she'd wanted to do that for as long as she could
remember.

*p.p.p.s. And as Jane Austen once famously said … If adventures
will not befall a young lady in her own village, she must seek
them abroad.*

Chapter 7

Making Cow Eyes

Emma

Emma adjusted her grey wool beanie to a more attractive angle and wrapped her dusky-pink pashmina more securely around her shoulders as she wrenched open the front door of Wren Cottage.

She was late.

So very late for her first day at The Clock House.

She hated being late. Stupid jet lag. Now she was going to feel on the back-foot all day as well as feeling nauseous from the butterflies hurling hand-grenades at the walls of her insides.

Quickly she bent down and shoved her feet into the pair of boots sat outside the front door.

Holy moley, they were beyond freezing. Why in God's name did people in this country leave perfectly good footwear outside? It was barbaric.

Honestly, mid-November in Whispers Wood could not be more different to mid-November in LA.

That was it, she thought, her toes curling and clenching

inside the boots. When she got in tonight she was bringing these puppies inside and shoving them by the fire – once she'd plucked up the courage to ask again how to switch the fire on, that was.

Quite sure her toes were going to drop off if she didn't get moving, she half-shlepped, half-slid along the icy path and came to an abrupt halt at the front gate.

'Wow. Cow.'

Master of the understatement. That was her all over. Because, excuse me, but what the hell was an actual four-legged, real-life, black and white, *farm* animal doing standing in front of her, plain as day?

Emma closed her eyes and then opened them again.

It was still there.

And it wasn't moving.

Oh God. Why wasn't it moving?

Was it dead? Did cows die standing up?

And why was it staring at her, with those ... cow eyes?

Slowly, Emma reached out and unlatched the little wrought-iron gate separating her from the cow and tugging it over the frosted tufts of grass, pulled it open enough to slip through.

The cow looked at her as if to say, 'Hi there, it's all good. Wanna chew the cud with me?'

Emma shook her head because, you know, Day! As in, she had one. Had places to be and people to meet and she really didn't fancy her first phone call to Kate to be along the lines of a sickie that went, 'I'm sorry I can't come to work today, I'm trapped in my house by a cow.'

'Shoo,' she whispered, watching her breath turn misty as

it left her mouth. When nothing happened she mustered her courage and, feeling brave, flung a hand out from under her shawl to make a shooing motion.

Her actions had zero effect.

'Hey, you? Mr Moo? Please shoo,' she tried again a little louder, totally wishing she was eating Moo Shu pork, or doing anything that felt in any way familiar to her old life in LA.

She wasn't sure this really fulfilled the 'adventure' brief she'd sold herself on when packing her case to make the move back to the UK, although, she'd only been here one whole night and one whole day so perhaps she should give it more time.

Or maybe the jet lag was screwing with her reasoning?

She blinked again in case it really was jet lag that had her imagining a cow had come to visit the tiny cottage Kate had helped her settle into when she'd arrived in Whispers Wood.

No. It wasn't her imagination.

The cow was still there. Filling up her entire view because, as it turned out, cows were genuinely fear-for-your-life enormous close-up.

As an antidote to not getting her dream role, not being able to get out of the wrought-iron starting gate wasn't quite the look she'd been going for.

Wisps of frosty fog wrapped themselves around her, and as the damp air seeped deep into her bones she was closer to admitting she may have misjudged this opportunity. What would Rudy think if he could see her now?

She'd thought this would all be so very quaint, hadn't she? *How could you have been this wrong, Ems? This, So.*

Completely. Wrong.

All it was, was freezing, she thought, wondering if she could get out of the back garden of the cottage and find her way to The Clock House, thus avoiding the cow-staring scary start to her rural adventure.

Emma looked around helplessly and then, leaning closer, risked cricking her neck permanently to check out the pair of feet she could see approaching.

'Is someone there?' she asked.

'Whack it on its arse,' said a male voice.

'What it on what?' Emma asked.

There was a sigh, and then, 'Give it a good slap on its hind rear and it'll move right on by.'

Emma stared suspiciously at the cow's rear-end. The instruction sounded a bit *Fifty Shades Darker*.

'Thank you but I'm not into that,' she said, not quite under-her-breath enough.

'Look, do you want it to move, or not?'

She did. She really did. It was time to swap out her What Would Bridget Jones Do for a more kick-ass What Would JLaw Do? She licked her lips and stared again at the cow. 'So ... just sort of ... hit it?'

'Sometime today would be appreciated.'

'And you know to hit it because?'

'It's Gertrude.'

'Well.' Emma folded her arms. 'I have to tell you that I am none the wiser.'

'But you are getting older. And so am I.'

A head popped around the rear of the cow and to Emma's

surprise it had a face belonging to it that stopped the breath in her lungs.

Maybe it was the fact that she faced imminent death by cow, but Emma's powers of observation all narrowed down to one impressive: Valhalla-lujah.

The man was all dark and dangerous with Viking hair and beard and eyes the colour of the pints of Guinness that Bar Brand served up on Paddy's night.

Eyes that, despite being framed by lashes that could compete with Gertrude's, she could see were now drawn into a deep scowl.

'For heaven's sake,' he said. 'Hold these will you and *I'll* move her on.'

Without thinking, Emma held open her arms and allowed Mr Heart-Wrecking Handsome to deposit a weighty pile of magazines, what looked like rolled-up plans, a laptop and a tape-measure the size of a dinner plate in them.

The next thing she knew she was staggering against the sudden weight, her feet sliding across the ice in opposite and modesty-mocking directions.

She hit the ground with an audible bump.

Oh, my, God.

Years of yoga, Pilates and dance and who knew all it was going to take for her to finally be able to do the splits was a British country lane, a cow, and a Viking!

She blew a strand of blonde hair out of her eyes and looked up just in time to watch Gertrude walking off down the road, bovine hips swinging like Jessica Rabbit.

'Sorry. Are you all right? Here, let me help you up.'

Emma righted her beanie so that she could get an even better look at the Viking. 'Oh, I think you've done more than enough under the circumstances,' she harrumphed and then thought that on the bright side at least the heat in her face was bound to trickle down to her toes.

'It's not often these days that a man gets to rescue a woman from the perils of nature.'

Was he kidding?

'It's not often these days that a man expects a woman to hold his papers for him while he wades into danger,' she muttered.

'Quite. Well,' he muttered all very Mark Darcy. 'As it happens they're important papers and I didn't see you getting it done.'

Emma felt her bottom lip protrude. 'So I did a little *cowering*. Excuse me for being surprised to find I was trapped in my own home by the bovine beast of Whispers Wood. I'm sure I'd have worked out how to get her to move—'

'Eventually,' he replied with a slight twitch of his lips.

Her gaze stalled on his lips. Until she saw him notice. Then, with another rush of red to her head, she glanced at her watch and stammered, 'Oh. Help me up will you, I need to get to The Clock House.'

'The Clock House? Really?' He hauled her to her feet as if she was as light as a leaf floating in the breeze and she tried unsuccessfully not to be impressed.

'Yes. Really.'

'That's where I'm off to. We might as well walk together, I suppose.'

Don't do me any favours, she thought and then tried to

remember how to get to the village green. As compasses went, she had an excellent moral one. As for working out which direction to take to get, well, anywhere … not so much.

'So you must be the famous Holly Wood,' came the rich dark-roasted coffee voice.

'Huh? Oh. No, my name is Emma Danes.'

'Not Holly Wood? I could have sworn—'

'No. I'm *over* from Hollywood, and I'm definitely not famous,' she replied feeling a little funny that she might have been talked about before she had even landed. 'I'm here to help Kate open Cocktails & Chai @ The Clock House. And you must be… ?' *Apart from a rural Viking God with super-sexy British accent, appearing out of nowhere to save me from cows named, Gertrude, that was.*

For one awkie mo she worried she'd said rural Viking God with super-sexy British accent out loud because there was another quirk of his lips into a smile that made her heart sort of descend into her stomach like someone had snapped its strings.

And then he was introducing himself Bond-style, with a, 'My name is Knightley. Jake Knightley.'

Chapter 8

The Art of Conversation

Emma

'So if your name's Knightley, have you come from Knightley Hall, then?' Emma said, as she set off down the country lane beside him.

When he didn't answer she thought he hadn't heard her all the way up there where the tall people hung out, so she said a little louder, 'That huge black and white building surrounded by all that precision-cut hedging on the other side of the village?'

'Topiary,' he murmured.

'Huh?'

'The hedging you're referring to is called topiary,' he corrected helpfully.

Ignoring the dictionary lesson, she said, 'I thought it said it was called Knightley Hall when I passed it yesterday on my walk. That's where you live?'

'I do.' He increased his speed as if he hoped she wouldn't have enough breath left to chat.

Which bugged her because it was him who'd invited her

along on the journey, not the other way around. 'And your name is Knightley?' she asked, trying to keep pace with him in boots that were at least two sizes too big for her.

'It is.'

'But your first name is Jake, not—' *Oh, God, don't say George, Emma. Or My Mister Knightley. He probably gets that all the time.* 'Not ... George, then?' Damn, she'd said it.

'George was my ancestor.'

'Well, of course he was,' she answered as if that made the most perfect sense in the world.

They walked together in silence until she decided that the best way to take her mind off the nerves that had reappeared was to engage in chit-chat, and the only person around to do that with was him, her reluctant Knight-ley. 'With a name like Knightley, I'm guessing someone was a real Jane Austen fan, huh?'

'Or Jane Austen was a real Knightley, fan,' he answered.

Ha. Cute.

'So, what are you, like, the owner of that huge estate?'

This time when he shot her a quick look she swore she could see the edge of caution in his frown. 'I am,' he stated.

'But you're quite sure you're not Succinct of the world-renowned Succincts?' she asked, puffing out a breath.

Jake turned to look at her again and then shrugged. 'I talk. When it's warranted.'

'But do you make conversation?' she quipped back and felt him doing the staring thing again.

'Rescuing you wasn't enough? You want conversation from me now as well? Interesting.'

'It could be, yes. If you had anything to say, that is. Is there some sort of law that prevents us from—' Emma came to an abrupt stop as a sudden thought occurred. 'Oh, shit. I mean, sugar.' Knightley Hall had looked all huge and stately, hadn't it? All landed gentry, heritage-old. 'Am I supposed to address you as Sir Jake or Sir Knightley, or something?'

Jake stopped and regarded her for a heartbeat before, with yet another shrug, saying, 'Either is fine.'

There was that heart-spiking lift of his lips again before he resumed walking along the path and Emma realised he might possibly be playing with her. But on the off-chance she'd be causing some sort of international incident on her first full day as manager of Cocktails & Chai, she decided not to call him out on it, and really, how hard could it be to have a conversation without observing the traditional naming conventions?

As she scurried after him, layers of wool flapping in the wind, she tried to think of something to say but all she could come up with was, 'I'd love to look around your home some-time.'

'Really? And why is that?'

Um … *Good one, Ems, invite yourself over to the gorgeous stranger's house, why don't you?* Scrabbling around for some-thing to add, she tried, 'Because when I walked past it yesterday I thought that it looked absolutely beautiful.'

'Beautiful?'

The white plasterwork separated with a grid of black wooden beams and the brown twisted fairytale vines running all over it, which she fancied was wisteria that would look stunning in the summer, was maybe more imposing as a structure than beautiful.

'Handsome, then,' she amended.

He cocked his head as if to weigh up her description and as they entered a wooded area, deigned to slow his pace a little. 'Looks can be deceiving,' he told her softly. 'Trust me the inside of Knightley Hall is neither beautiful nor handsome.'

'And it's what's inside that counts, right?'

He gave her an assessing look as if she'd surprised him and then nodded. 'Not a polished concrete surface or a cinema room to be seen.'

'I guess if your taste runs more to modern, then you probably can't class it as beautiful, then, but surely it gets extra points for standing the test of time? There's a beauty in that, isn't there? Or is it not actually old at all? Maybe it's one of those clever kit houses, that come flat-packed, and take only a team of four ten-year-olds to erect?'

'What the... ?' Jake offered her a horrified look. 'No it is not a kit house,' he said with a derision that had her wondering if he was channelling the late and great Alan Rickman.

'When was it built, then?'

'The original Tudor frame probably goes back to early sixteenth century.'

Emma's eyes widened. 'I guess the oldest houses in Hollywood were probably built around 1870.'

'That's close to when my family took over the Hall.'

His family had been in Knightley Hall since the 1870s? Emma couldn't even imagine a family home existing since the *1970s*. Her experience of family was that they often crumbled at the simplest of hurdles.

She snuck a look at her walking companion. All that time, one family, living in one place. Making history. Generation after generation. Maybe he was entitled to the slight odour of smugness that wafted off of him.

Oh, who was she kidding? The scent wasn't smugness so much as it was cedar wood mixed with a hint of lemon and trying to ignore the way it kept teasing at her, making her want to keep pace and move in a little closer, she looked about the woods.

The smooth white bark on some of the trees had her wanting to reach out and rub her hand over the surface. They looked magical against the milky blue sky. She would have if she was alone, but she didn't want Jake to think she was some weird tree-hugger.

'So,' he said, 'I'm guessing you were in Hollywood for the same reason every other beautiful woman is there?'

'Hark,' she exclaimed to the woods, 'for he initiates conversation,' and then with a grin and a flutter of her eyelashes, looked up at him and said, 'You think I'm beautiful?'

The eyelash fluttering didn't go down quite as hilariously as she'd hoped, but she decided to think of the dull flush across his cheekbones as a blush rather than a rush of annoyance.

'What I meant was, you're obviously an actress?'

'I am,' she answered finding pleasure in being able to mimic his short, closed answers of earlier.

'So then what are you doing here?'

Good question. 'Resting?'

'You don't sound sure.'

Emma glanced down at her borrowed boots. 'No, I don't, do I?' Why on earth had she said she was an actress when the whole reason she'd travelled thousands of miles was to prove she was capable of doing something she secretly suspected was far more difficult: managing a tearoom and bar? 'I guess I need to see how this is going to work out first.'

'Hedging your bets,' Jake said with a grim nod.

'You make that sound like a bad thing?' It felt sensible to her. She'd put all her eggs into one basket before and hadn't *egg*sactly got hit with the success stick.

'Pardon me for hoping for Kate's sake that you make it work out. I guess it's too much to expect people will actually commit to something these days.'

'Hey. I resent that. You don't know anything about me.'

'Apart from that you just admitted you had commitment issues.'

Emma stopped in her tracks. Her hands went to her hips in full-on umbrage-taken mode and she could feel the heat of embarrassment form two huge circles on her cheeks, making her wonder if she could look any more of a cliché. 'Kate knew exactly what she was doing when she invited me here. I appreciate her faith in me and you can bet your "arse",' she added, swapping to full British accent, 'I'm going to work hard. I intend to give this my all. I certainly don't believe in only giving pieces of myself.'

'Wow. When you use a British accent like that you sound so much more believable,' he said, turning on his heel and walking away, his pace brisk.

Emma's mouth opened and closed a couple of times like a guppy coming up for air. Thank God he had his hands full with all his 'stuff' because otherwise she was pretty sure he'd have added a slow hand clap.

'Again, you don't know me, so I'd appreciate it if you didn't talk to me like I'm some sort of flight risk. What?' she called after him, 'I have to have done something since the sixteenth century to be considered committed to a cause? You know what,' she said scurrying to keep up with him again when he simply carried on walking, 'maybe we shouldn't speak to each other. Let's flout society's rules about polite conversation and not converse.'

'Works for me.'

Emma started muttering under her breath about people who copped-out when a conversation wasn't going their way.

'Call me an idiot,' he huffed out.

'Idiot,' she shot back and got a roll of his eyes for her effort.

'But I assumed that your plan for not talking would actually involve less of this,' he held up his hand and opened and closed his fingers to mimic a mouth talking, 'and more of this,' he said, finishing with keeping his fingers closed.

'Oh, believe me,' she hissed out, unwilling to let him have the last word, 'the thought of respite from your incredible smug-self is definite motivation to stop talking.'

'And yet ...'

She delivered her most fierce death-glare and strode ahead of him.

He caught up with her in five steps and thank goodness,

because she could see they were nearing the end of the woods and was she supposed to turn left or right at the end of them? He had her so flustered she couldn't even think.

They'd taken maybe twenty steps in silence before he shocked her by saying, 'You know if you really want to see something beautiful while you're in Whispers Wood, you should take a look around Knightley Hall's gardens.'

'Really?' She glanced up at him. 'I'd be allowed to do that? What are your opening times?' Darn. So much for not speaking to him.

'The gardens aren't open to the public – well not yet, anyway. I suppose I could give you a tour though. When I have time,' he added, making it sound like he actually wouldn't have the time any time soon.

She was just contemplating this when they cleared the woods and stepped out onto the village green. Without thinking she reached out and laid her hand on his arm to stay him and was quietly charmed when he instantly moved protectively in front of her.

'What's wrong?' he asked, his gaze wandering across the village green.

With a sigh she stepped around him. 'Nothing. This is my first real look at The Clock House, is all.'

And, oh, it was wonderful.

Three storeys of red brick house standing in regal Georgian fashion, its sparkly clean windows glinting invitingly, beckoning her closer.

She could almost hear the horse and carriages of old, driving up the gravel path.

'It's like something out of a regency romance,' she whispered. 'I can't believe I get to work here.' She couldn't help herself. Feet no longer as cold as they had been, she went straight into a Happy Dance.

Jake stared at her. 'You were first in line the day they held auditions for Pharell Williams' *Happy* video, weren't you?'

'Ha-ha. And I suppose you've never busted out a few moves, have you? Or is rolling your eyes at the world your signature move?'

Instead of looking at the huge great big clock, he glanced at his watch and then back at her pointedly, 'Are you going to celebrate the outside all day, or might you eventually want to go inside?'

'Oh, I can't wait to get inside. If it's half as beautiful as the outside,' she slid her gaze sideways to his, 'and it's what's on the inside that counts, right? Well, then prepare for more dancing.'

'I'm pretty sure Kate's going to frown at you salivating all over the parquet flooring.'

'I'm embarrassing you? Simply for gushing a bit about a building? Not a romantic bone in your body, is there?'

Those full lips of his pinched tight. 'To coin a phrase I recently heard: Hey, I resent that. You don't know anything about me.'

'I know enthusiasm is anathema to you.'

'Not at all. But not everything has to produce a larger than life and slap-you-about-the-face instantaneous Oh my God, Oh my God, Oh my God, reaction, either.'

She realised he didn't believe or trust her reactions were

real and opened her mouth so that the flames she so badly needed to shoot him down with could come out, but all that came out was a huffy-hoity, 'Your American accent is atrocious.'

His hand went to his heart. 'You wound me to the core,' he said in a way that left her in no doubt that she couldn't possibly. 'Now are you coming or not? I'm not sure Whispers Wood is ready for you to dab your way across the village green, so you might want to save the celebrations for when you get inside the building.'

'Hey, you know what would be great?' she muttered, in hot pursuit as he set off across the village green.

'What?'

'If you didn't provide a sarcastic voiceover in my ear as soon as I voice any kind of pleasure.'

'Fine.'

And suddenly they were at the front doors and Jake was gallantly gesturing for her to precede him into the entryway.

Emma strode through the double doors and gasped, a huge grin forming as she took in the polished parquet flooring, the sweeping staircase, with the elegant antique writing desk tucked underneath, forming a welcoming reception area. As she lifted her head she took in the balustrade balcony area that must lead to the spa treatment rooms and co-working office space. Looking to her right two double doors had had their wood panels replaced with glass that had 'Hair @ The Clock House' etched in swirling white and gold lettering across them. Through the doors she got a brief, delightful, glimpse of chandeliers hanging over ornately framed floor to ceiling mirrors with elegant tables in front of them. The room was obviously still in the stages of being finished but, oh, wow.

'It's like out of a film set,' she said, turning again in a slow circle.

She saw Jake shake his head at her. 'Could you be more awe-struck?'

American, she thought he meant, but she was too happy to be offended. 'Probably not. Oh, I love it. It's like I'm in an actual real-life Regency Pump Room.'

And then she was turning her head to the left because that was where the tearoom had to be...

Oh, shoot! The double doors were closed so that she couldn't see in.

'All you need is an empire-line dress and you'll be all set,' he murmured. 'It's like you've found your people, only they're not people, they're old things.'

'Hey, you said you'd be quiet.'

'Did you know when you're piqued you get this little wrinkle on the bridge of your nose? Maybe they have a treatment for that here?'

Her hand instantly came up to brush at her nose and she opened her mouth to speak but no words came out.

Honestly, either he had her speaking like something out of a turn of century – the *last* century – novel or, he was making her feel like she needed the safety-net of a script to follow.

She clicked her fingers and said, 'Oh my God, I've just realised who it is you remind me of.'

He looked at her as if he expected her to say some famous

actor.

So her smile was extra-wide when she nodded and said, 'Yep. Also lives in a wood. The Hundred Acre Wood.'

When he frowned she made an uncanny braying noise.

'You are referring to Eeyore?' he spluttered.

'Well, what do you know, not just a hat-rack,' she said pointing to his head.

She watched with satisfaction as his jaw dropped open and then in the next moment he was pulling in a breath and announcing loudly in a voice full of boredom, 'Hello? If anyone cares I brought Hollywood with me,' and just like that he was walking away from her.

Unbelievable!

Insufferable!

'My name is Emma,' she called out to his retreating back. 'And thanks for the asinine conversation.' With a mock curtsey and an embarrassed look around to check no one had seen her so easily dismissed, she headed off in the complete opposite direction to Sir bloody Mr Knightley.

Chapter 9

And the Fairy-Light Dawns...

Jake

'Hi, Jake, did you say you've brought Emma along with you?' Kate looked up expectantly from the tower of towels she was stacking in an ornately painted white and gold armoire.

'I left her downstairs,' he said, feeling a tad bad for abandoning her. He bent his head into an open box of bottles of lotion and instantly inhaled the heady scent of honey. It was calming which was good but then made his stomach rumble which wasn't. Should have had a sneaky slice of Sheila's cake before he'd come out. Or, maybe he should have brought the cake for them all to share. You couldn't really call it a bribe if the baker was related to the client, could you?

'Oh, hi there, Jake,' Juliet said, entering the large storage room with more boxes, 'is it meeting time already?'

'I can wait if you need to get this done now?' he automatically offered. 'Or I can help?' He glanced down at his hands. Okay, they were probably the last things Kate and Juliet wanted around their nice-smelling, beautifully packaged bottles and soft-looking towels but anything to get some breathing space from the pint-sized acting mixologist with eyes the colour of silver-grey brunia berries.

He wasn't quite sure why she'd made such an impression. But from the moment he'd peered around Gertrude and seen her, it had been all he could do to keep his tongue in his mouth.

She was like a beautiful blonde woodland fairy blinking back at him.

Of course then she'd opened her mouth ... and kept on opening it ... In the category of chatting there was little doubt she could give head of the am-dram society, Trudie McTravers, a run for her money.

And he'd reacted to a little sass by behaving like a complete and utter arse.

What the hell?

It made no earthly sense.

Aside from the realisation he was close to getting sucked in by what was on the outside and then getting slapped upside the head with her unending enthusiasm for her surroundings that was. Oh, and that undeniably seductive life-energy that was practically vibrating out of her.

It was all very thought provoking, he decided.

Alluring? Maybe, he conceded.

Suspicious? Definitely, he concluded.

Because seriously, there had to be a little guile lurking in there somewhere, right? Where was the 'what's in it for me?' And why was she really here in Whispers Wood? Who went from acting to managing a tearoom?

Then, suddenly, it was all making sense.

She had to be straight out of the Marlon Brando school of method acting and was obviously here to learn the ropes and soak up the lifestyle for a part in a film.

Okay.

So with that sorted there wasn't any need to be any more curious, he decided.

Soon as she nailed how to pull a pint or how to perfect a British accent, which with her melodious voice already halfway to charmingly clipped when she'd said 'arse', wouldn't be long, and then she'd be off.

Not that he was going to be around anyway, he reminded himself.

Phew.

Analysis and compartmentalisation complete.

'We shouldn't leave Emma on her own on her first day. I could give you both a quick guided tour at the same time,' Kate decided. 'I know you've probably come up with designs for our courtyard already, but maybe this would help give you an idea of how to tie in the aesthetics?'

'Sure. Daniel not around?'

'No, he's out picking up some extra fairy lights,' she explained.

'Fairy lights?'

'You can never have too many, I think. Especially with Christmas coming up.'

Right. Christmas. Fairy lights. Christmas lights. They all equalled one thing.

Celebrations.

Jake stared at a bale of towels. 'I have a few boxes you can have,' he offered without thinking.

'Yeah?' Kate closed the armoire doors and began flattening the cardboard boxes as Juliet unpacked them.

'Yes. Two dozen to be exact.' He grabbed a couple of the boxes and made short work of deconstructing them. 'They're all white though.'

'That would be—oh,' Kate broke off as the fairy-light dawned on why he might possibly be in possession of a small town's supply of stringed lights. 'No. It's all right. You don't have to do that, Jake. Honestly.'

The shrug was hard to pull off when he could hear the sweetness in her voice. 'It's not like I need them anymore,' he stated.

'Oh, but, you might want to decorate Knightley Hall anyway? You know, for Christmas,' Juliet added, her voice super-kind, making Jake's shoulders stiffen. This was exactly why he couldn't wait to get out of Whispers Wood.

'Bit tricky on a Grade I listed building,' he insisted. 'Seriously, now that they won't be going up in the gardens, you'd be doing me a favour. One less thing to store.'

Kate smiled gently. 'Well, let's see how many Daniel finds, before I give you a definitive answer.'

'Sure.' He pushed the word out and tried to leave it nonchalantly hanging as he followed her and Juliet out of the room.

'It'll probably take him about half an hour to get back. You okay waiting?'

Jake thought about how if he nipped back home he could pick up the boxes of lights, get them out of the house and still get back in time to have the meeting proper. Then he thought about how getting this job might provide enough funds to fix the leaking roof before it suffered another year's worth of winter damage and decided that a little oohing and ahhing over a full-ticket price tour was the better option. 'Absolutely. Lead the way,' he told Kate.

They found Hollywood in what was going to be her 'office'.

She was gazing up at the crystal chandelier hanging from the ceiling rose in the centre of the room. The expression of magical delight on her face was the same one his nieces got when he remembered to re-arrange the fairy furniture in the stumpery before they visited.

'Is this light an original fixture?' she asked when they walked into the room, self-consciously removing her beanie and running a hand through her hair.

'Depends what you mean by original,' Jake muttered, as he watched the pale gold swathe of her hair swing free and settle gently around her heart-shaped face.

Kate threw him a worried frown and mumbling, 'It's absolutely gorgeous, isn't it?' walked over to hug Emma. 'Welcome to your new home away from home. What do you think?'

'Oh, only that it's fabulous,' Emma laughed, her eyes sparkling. 'I mean, I don't know exactly what the place looked like before, but the space you have now is amazing.'

Jake had to admit Emma's enthusiasm was justified here. He'd worked on garden designs for some of the houses Oscar Matthews had renovated so he knew his friend did good work, but to be honest it was hard to believe this was the same room the village congregated in whenever Crispin Harlow called a Whispers Wood meeting.

Oscar had installed a stud wall at one end of the room, presumably so that a small kitchen area could be included behind it. The new wall was now kitted-out with dark-stained oak cabinetry that could give the hand-crafted mahogany bookshelves from the library at Knightley Hall a run for its money.

A couple of feet in front of that there now stood a stunning oblong bar. Oscar had mimicked the traditional Georgian design of the windows by making simple rectangular panels inset into the base at regular intervals and then painted it in thick cream gloss to match the architraving. The bar's surface was a polished mid-tone marble that picked out the cream of the base and the darker stained oak of the wall shelves. A sturdy kick-bar and hand-rail in burnished copper had been fitted along the outside, and suspended above the bar was a series of small chandeliers surrounded by a glass and copper-piping racking system. A fresh lick of eau de nil paint on the walls and all the original features had been buffed, shined and polished.

The large reception room also now housed a selection of wooden tables and chairs that looked stackable for meetings or for Trudie's am-dram productions.

'I hope it's okay I got started already,' Emma smiled. 'I wasn't sure if you'd like refreshment for your meeting, but there's already a pot of breakfast tea brewing or, I can make coffee, if you prefer.'

'Tea would be gorgeous. Hi, I'm Juliet,' Juliet said, reaching over with a warm smile to shake Emma's hand. 'Sorry I wasn't around to meet you when you got here. It's my cottage you've moved into. Did Kate show you where everything was? How it all worked?'

Jake watched the tiniest hesitation hover behind those brunia berry eyes and then Emma was smiling warmly and gushing, 'Everything is perfect.'

'You're sure?' Juliet queried maybe seeing the merest hesitation as well. 'Heating's a bit temperamental and I meant to warn you about the cats.'

'Ah. I think I met one of them this morning. I woke up with the weirdest feeling like I was being stared at. Turned over, and discovered I was.'

Juliet laughed. 'If it was a ginger Tom it was probably Aramis getting a quick look to report back how stunning you are. If it was a Persian and staring at you like he'd never met a stupider human, then it was Catty McCatface.'

'It was definitely the second one.'

'Sorry about Catty. He knows we've moved house, but,' Juliet sighed, 'well he'll do anything to maintain his ornery rep.'

'I probably shouldn't try to make friends, then?'

'God no, it'll only make him laugh at you more. The best way to win him over is to pretend he doesn't exist.'

'Treat him mean, keep him keen, huh?'

Jake watched Emma's bee-stung lips form a quick smile. It occurred to him that she didn't look like she had a mean bone in her body, but then looks could be deceiving, couldn't they?

'So you two have already met?' Kate asked looking between

Emma and Jake.

'We certainly have,' she replied, and then with a huge wink, added, 'He thinks I'm beautiful.'

'She prefers to call me, Sir,' he quipped back.

'Sir?' Daniel asked as he walked into the room carrying one small box of lights. 'That's a new one. Hi, I'm Daniel,' he said, offering his hand in introduction to Emma, 'and I'm pretty sure this one,' he said with a nod to Jake, 'actually answers to Oi, You, as well, okay?'

'Good to know,' Emma said and looking at him added, 'I actually tried him out on Eeyore.'

'Eeyore?' Daniel threw his head back and laughed. 'Priceless.' And then made the mistake of looking at Jake, and correctly interpreting the glint of murderous violence in his gaze, cleared his throat and said, 'Um ... that doesn't sound like him at all.'

Emma gave Jake a look suggesting she wasn't often wrong and it annoyed the hell out of him that he should care what she thought. 'I'll probably come up with a few other names for him while I'm here,' she added.

'Depends how long you're here for, I suppose,' Jake replied, and if she wanted to infer from his statement that he didn't think she'd last five minutes, he had absolutely no problem with that.

'Unless I decide to bar him on opening night, that is,' she said with another grin at him.

'What the hell could you bar me for?' he asked with a frown.

'Oh, I don't know ... maybe cruelty to cows?'

He opened his mouth but before he could say anything

she turned and asked, 'Daniel, what'll you have to drink?'

'Cappuccino please.'

'Coming right up.'

'And I'd like a Cortado, please,' Jake decided, thinking he might cope better with the bar between them.

'Sure,' she said, walking up to the machine that had been installed behind the bar and then busied herself pressing buttons and pulling leavers, giving every impression she was the new Doctor getting the TARDIS started.

With Juliet making a call on her phone and Daniel and Kate talking about the scary non-existence of Christmas lights on the shop shelves, Jake had no choice but to stand at the bar waiting for his coffee.

'You might want to remove some layers,' he said, disliking that he'd noticed that the dusky pink wrap gave her skin a warm glow. 'We have this thing called central heating now.'

'How modern,' she threw over her shoulder, before casually unwinding the pashmina to reveal a soft grey v-neck jumper.

She tossed the pashmina at him and he caught it automatically, his hands clenching around the soft wool. He could still feel her body heat. Any moment now he'd sniff it like a horny teenager.

Thank God she was behind the bar so that the glimpse of long legs, despite her height, encased in skinny jeans that had probably once been black but were now so faded and silvery-soft, was mostly barred from his view.

'Oh, guys,' Emma said, looking over at Kate and Daniel. 'Did you get the footstall ordered?'

'Yep,' Kate said. 'It's out the back in the kitchen.'

'Great.' She popped back in front of him to pass him the coffee she'd made for him. 'It's such a chore being short,' she confided.

Jake refused to allow his eyes to wander any lower than hers and took a careful sip from the glass of coffee she'd given him. 'You've done this before,' he murmured, taking another sip.

She leaned casually on the bar. 'I thought everyone knew that actress is actually short for barista?'

'Well, Hollywood, you make a pretty good short barista.'

'Only pretty good? Hmm. Wait 'til you see my acting,' she said with a waggle of her eyebrows.

He studied her for a few minutes, before saying quietly, 'I thought I already was.'

Chapter 10

Grand Designs

Jake

Jake watched wariness and hurt flood Emma's eyes before she quickly turned and began efficiently setting out tea on a tray.

Damn.

Briefly, he wondered if there were as many words for 'idiot' in Eskimo as there were for 'snow' because even though she might be some Hollywood actress who was going to take off the minute it got cold proper, that didn't mean he had to behave like he was counting down the minutes until she did.

He watched as with practised ease, she shoulder-pressed the heavy round tray with one hand and strode confidently over to one of the largest tables.

If he were the fanciful sort he might think she looked like some Nordic warrior, striding across the room with purpose, her pale gold hair flowing down her back.

Thank God he wasn't.

And right there he was hit with the realisation of exactly why he'd been behaving like an arse.

Being called Eeyore aside, it was actually because she'd accused him of not having a romantic bone in his body.

Why the hell he should care if she was right, he didn't know.

Life was altogether a lot more bearable if he didn't go around acting and feeling like some bloody poet in love.

Been there. Done that. Not to mention been given the billowy shirt by his comedian brothers as a joke.

In his family, when they'd all been vying for roles growing-up, the minute he'd expressed more than a passing interest in the gardens on the estate he'd been labelled 'The Romantic' of the family. Ironic, really, considering he'd been the only Knightley not to labour under the idyll that the family money would never run out.

As soon as he'd started adding girls into the mix, his brothers and sisters had absolutely no problem referring to him as the Heathcliff-bloody-Rochester of the Knightley clan.

Actually, that wasn't technically true. Lately he'd been known as the Uhtred of Bebbanburg-Knightleys', but that was completely his own fault for not getting his hair cut.

Which reminded him...

'Hey, Juliet,' he walked over to the table they were obviously going to hold their meeting at, put down everything he'd brought to pitch his design, and shrugged out of his jacket. 'I don't suppose you could cut my hair before you open the salon to the rest of the hordes, could you?'

'Are you sure?' Juliet tipped her head to the side as she regarded his 'do'. 'The man-bun is definitely working for you. If you're desperate I could see if Mum's available?'

Aware that Emma was listening as she fussed a cloth over the pristine bar, he said, 'Don't worry, I'll figure something out.' Juliet's mother, Cheryl Brown, grew exceptional dahlias and roses and she'd been a hairdresser for as long as Jake had known her. And it was precisely for that reason that he thought he had it in him to wait until Juliet was ready.

'Right then,' Daniel said, pulling out a chair at the table, sitting down and reaching for his coffee. 'Jake, are you all set to pitch to us?'

'What? Oh, yep. Born ready,' Jake replied, efficiently setting his laptop up, so they could all see what he was going to be describing.

'Emma,' Kate called over to the bar, 'come and grab a seat and a cuppa, you should be in on this meeting too.'

She should?

Jake busied himself opening his notebook to stare at the loose pitch he'd prepared while she settled herself at the table and poured herself a cup of tea. It was weird, he thought. He wasn't usually nervous before presenting a new garden design, but what with Hollywood watching…

'So,' he began, with a subtle clearing of his throat. 'There are a couple of options for revamping the courtyard, but I want to start with what I feel follows the brief you provided and then pushes the boundaries a little.' Jake indicated his laptop screen. 'If you like what I've come up with, I have a quote already drawn up. But this should be a collaborative process, so if we need to adjust for budget, or if there's something we need to add, we can do that as well.

'Kate, you mentioned wanting to match what you've done

inside, but I've actually taken inspiration from outside. At the moment when you look out of any window onto the courtyard all you see is patio before your gaze is drawn straight to the moon-gate in the far wall.'

The moon-gate had actually been his starting point, because even though he loved that your eye was drawn straight to it and the romance of it had you wanting to know what was on the other side, with The Clock House opening up as a business, he didn't think Kate would want people from outside the village, who didn't know the history to what was on the other side of the moon-gate, to go get curious and start disturbing the beehives that were kept in the wild meadow beyond.

'I've zoned the courtyard to provide each window with a unique vista, creating mini gardens to reflect what you do here. Providing relaxing and enchanting views will add to customer experience. It'll mean building walls to divide the space but we can match the original brickwork. In each wall I've created a round aperture to mimic the moon-gate. It would work really well if we could use the same wrought-iron design work. The round gates also subtly mimic the face of a clock. Planting will be soft to counter the architecture but won't require a lot of maintenance. I know you'll be using honey in a lot of your treatments and that got me thinking about planting herbs for you to use in the tearoom and bar as well. I can go into specific planting detail once the design is approved, but take a look at the preliminary sketches,' he said, moving the laptop to rollout some sketches he'd drawn of the courtyard from different angles. 'And tell me what you all think?'

Kate, Daniel and Juliet all started talking at once and Jake breathed a quiet sigh of relief at the excited tones of their voices. Right up until he noticed Hollywood frowning down into her mug.

What the hell?

He'd honestly only ever had positive reactions to his designs before.

Probably because he spent time getting inside a client's head so he could produce something he knew they'd like.

'Is there a problem, Hollywood?' he asked.

She looked up. 'Oh, it's really not my place,' she said, bringing her cup of tea to her mouth as if it would help stop her from voicing her opinion.

'You were invited to sit at the table and participate,' he said tearing his gaze from hers to stare down at his sketches. He couldn't see anything wrong with them. He'd created gardens within a garden and different views according to where you were inside The Clock House, each taking into account where the sun rose and fell. He'd designed access paths, chosen an easy-to-maintain planting scheme, and most importantly, the three people he'd come to present to didn't appear dissatisfied.

In. Any. Way.

Obviously picking up on the growing tension, Kate carefully placed her teacup back in her saucer and said calmly, 'What did you want to say, Emma?'

'Well, if you're sure you'd like the feedback?' she asked, only she wasn't looking at Kate, she was staring up at Jake with challenge set on her face.

'Yes, of course. I'd welcome it,' he answered uber-politely.

'You're sure?'

Impatience sparked. 'I just said so, didn't I?'

'All right, then.' Her gaze fell on his design as if she was gathering herself and then her gaze bounced back up to his. 'So what you've designed is stunning.'

It was so completely unexpected that Jake felt his chest puff out with pride.

'It's sophisticated,' Emma continued, 'It's contemporary...'

When she paused, a pulse ticked in his jaw. 'And yet?'

'And yet, well, it's not very practical, is it?'

'Practical?'

'Yes. I know that word is probably a designer's bugbear. You've created a space everyone inside can enjoy, but I imagine, during the spring, summer and autumn months the courtyard will get more footfall. I also imagine that if the tearoom and bar is successful,' she quickly glanced at Kate in askance, 'you might want to give customers the option of eating and drinking out there?'

She was right, Jake realised.

Why hadn't he thought of that?

Why hadn't they?

Or had they? In a mild panic he started going through the original notes he'd made. He knew he'd been spinning a few too many plates over the last year.

Ever since...

He breathed in sharp.

Had he totally dropped the ball on this one?

'Jake, I must apologise,' Kate said, interrupting his search through his notes. 'I completely missed telling you about this. I'm so sorry. I've had so much on.'

'It's not a problem at all, Kate. Honestly, I can relate.'

'I know you can.'

What he needed to do now was think on his feet and come up with a workable solution that didn't dampen the creativity of the project either.

'This is only a suggestion,' Emma inserted into the conversation, 'but what if you were able to make the walls not solid, but more, sort of, moveable partitions somehow?'

Intrigued, there was only time to be mildly surprised by her insight while feeling sickened at his oversight. Out came his pencil and he started sketching out the gridwork that would be needed. It would be expensive. Really expensive. Would Kate go for it? She'd already sunk so much of her own money into the place.

While being given the guided tour, it had been impossible not to recognise what you could do when your budget was so large. Jake's budget for Knightley Hall, on the other hand, was miniscule. His life a constant juggling act of form-filling and grant-obtaining to help with the up-keep.

He knew he was still at the setting up part of the whole process at the Hall and that once the gardens were open to the public, he'd be able to make money for the estate. He'd already thought about reserving an area for local schools to learn about gardening, about holding gardening weekend retreats and about selling produce from the kitchen garden further afield than the local village markets.

Basically he'd been thinking and dreaming, dreaming and

thinking about how to make the place pay for itself for as long as he could remember but he couldn't help wondering if life would be different had he been able to act on his plans sooner and show Alice a glimpse of what their life together would have been like.

Annoyed at where his thoughts were taking him he concentrated on adding a few more lines to his sketch, determined to capture what he thought Emma had been suggesting. Then, holding out his sketch for her perusal, his gaze bored into her while he awaited her reaction.

Chapter 11

Heart of Glass

Emma

Emma wanted to squirm.

It was seriously hot and seriously intense under Jake's unrelenting gaze.

And, oh, didn't he just know it was.

She shouldn't have said anything.

Despite the fact she'd been fuming before she sat down because what was worse than being caught being nervous?

Yeah – being called out publicly for being nervous.

So what if she'd been acting more confident than she felt? Whatever got her through, she'd been thinking.

Right along with wondering whether she'd ever met a more arrogant jerk in her life.

But then he'd started presenting his ideas and, darn it, because she'd joked that he didn't have a romantic bone in his body but as he'd talked about his vision, she'd heard the story he wanted to tell with the garden he was creating.

She'd been seriously impressed and it had made her want to show him how committed to doing a good job at The

Clock House she was. How serious she took this opportunity. That she wasn't some starving actress who'd just pitched up to have a laugh, do a little sight-seeing, and grab a pay-cheque at the end of each week. So she'd taken his idea and given it a good outing.

The shock on his face when she'd actually ventured her opinion though.

But instead of going apoplectic, he'd done a total one-eighty on her and listened.

Proper listened.

Which she'd found proper sexy!

No.

Wrong word choice, she told herself.

She was not in Whispers Wood for proper sexy!

She was in Whispers Wood for an adventure.

No ... not *that* kind of adventure, she cut herself off before her imagination could take itself out for a spin again.

She hadn't realised how much she'd needed to feel as if she was heard.

Really heard.

That was all, she assured herself.

All those years of keeping the faith while getting one knock-back after another, she'd obviously started to feel invisible. That what she had to say and every way she tried saying it at auditions, was irrelevant.

Jake's reaction had made her realise he wasn't so arrogant, after all. Not if he could take feedback on something that was obviously the most important thing in his world and rise above criticism to take the good out of what she'd voiced.

Then he'd grabbed a pencil and rather than stab her in the eye with it, he'd started sketching. Long, sure lines, and oh my God, how cute was it that the tip of his tongue poked out in concentration? Making her squirm for an altogether different reason.

A couple more lines and then he was shoving the sketch in front of her and asking her, 'You mean something like this?'

She took the sketch with hands that were trembling, very aware of Kate, Daniel and Juliet leaning forward to get a good look at what he'd drawn, too.

She looked down at the sketch, drew in a breath that felt funny and then gazed back up at him slightly star-struck because it was like he'd created exactly what she'd been imagining.

'Um, yes,' she said, looking back down at the sketch because looking up at him had her completely unable to concentrate. 'Maybe make these site-lines wider for wheelchair access and so that you can bring tables and chairs into each segment.'

He nodded, walking around the table to stand behind her and stare at the sketch. 'Need to figure out a way to make the walls the gardens and so that everyone could see each one. I don't know – maybe turntables?'

Excitement sparked and she nodded. 'Then you could turn them to get the best of the weather, and to change each view. Ooh, could you tie in each movement to the clock?'

'Great idea,' he mumbled, leaning over her so that she felt surrounded by him. 'Yes,' he breathed out softly and she felt the caress of his breath against her cheek.

Actual squirming ensued.

As if finally realising he was in her personal space his gaze flew to hers and as her tongue came out without her permission to slide over parched lips, she watched mesmerised as those dark brown eyes of his tracked the movement. One, two, three slow thuds of her heart and then Jake was jerking upright and taking a hasty step back.

Able to breathe again, Emma inhaled and stared back down at the sketch.

'So what do you guys think?' Jake asked everyone around the table.

As Kate, Daniel and Juliet all agreed it was a wonderful new design, Jake began packing up. 'I might need to see if Oscar's free to handle some of the building work on this. Are we still shooting for having it ready by spring? I could start end of January?'

'Yes. That would be great. About the noise?'

Jake smiled at Kate. 'And the dust and the access, yeah, I'm not going to lie, there's going to be some, but I'll try to minimize it. If we could build the structures off-site, would that help?'

'That would be amazing.'

'Well, it's not like I don't have the room at my place. So we'll start with that as a plan. I'll get back to you with a revised quote ASAP,' Jake said, moving towards the exit doors.

'There's no rush. I trust you,' Kate laughed, getting up from the table to follow him out.

'Actually, the reason for the rush is … I hope you don't mind but Sarah showed me the invites for your party.'

'She did?'

'Normally she'd never do something like that, it's just that she realised that the date was the same as—'

Emma watched Kate's eyes grow large as she brought a hand up to her mouth.

'Oh, crap, it's not?' Kate asked.

'It is,' Jake replied, 'but it doesn't matter. Truly.'

'Of course it does.'

What mattered, Emma wanted to know? And what was so important about the fourteenth of December, which was the date of The Clock House opening?

'No. It really doesn't,' Jake stated emphatically. 'Look at it this way, most people around here are already going to have that date blocked out anyway, so you'll probably get more people to come.'

'But not you?' Juliet asked, her tone sad as if she immediately understood what Jake had been trying to say.

'No. I'm sorry, not me,' Jake confirmed. 'I won't be in Whispers Wood at all over Christmas—'

'Oh.'

'—and I'd really appreciate it if you didn't make a big thing about it,' he asked, looking from Kate to Juliet.

'No. Fair enough,' Juliet said.

Emma watched as Kate touched Jake's arm briefly and said, her voice quiet and gentle, 'If anyone gets what it feels like to want to disappear for a while ...'

Emma saw the flash of pain before Jake blinked it away and replied, 'Thank you. I knew you'd get it.'

Get what? Why did he need to get away?

Darn it, she had absolutely no reason to feel disappointed

that he wouldn't be around for Christmas. It wasn't like she'd be here on the actual day, anyway. Not if her Dad did what she was pretty sure he would do and invited her to spend the day with him and his wife and children.

Jake was just disappearing through the doors when she realised he'd left his jacket on the back of the chair.

Gathering it up, she called out, 'Hey, Sir Knightley.'

She watched him pause at the doorway, stiffen slightly, and then turn around.

Wow, he really wanted to leave, didn't he?

'Your jacket,' she said and performed a little curtsey. She'd meant to make him smile but felt silly when he strode back to her and took it without looking at her.

A tinkling sound could be heard as something fell onto the floor between them.

'Oops, I think something's fallen out of your pocket.' Automatically she bent down to pick up the sparkly bead of glass. Holding it out in her palm she watched Jake frown down at it.

'That's definitely not mine. It must be from the—' he broke off and glanced up at the chandelier.

There was an audible gasp as Kate and Juliet glanced from the chandelier to the droplet of glass and then to Jake and Emma.

'It's like a sign,' Kate exclaimed and then shut her mouth quickly and after a strange look at Juliet carried on an entirely non-verbal conversation with her cousin.

With more head-turning than a tango on the *Strictly* final, Emma asked, 'What's a sign?'

'Forget it. It couldn't be less of a sign,' Jake bit out, his expression murderous as he snatched the glass out of Emma's hand and handed it to Kate. 'It's a bit of glass that fell off the chandelier because it was loose.'

'Um, what he said,' Kate mumbled, taking the glass droplet and holding it to her chest. 'I'll reattach it safely.'

'Could have had someone's eye out,' Jake muttered, putting his plans on the floor so that he could shrug into his jacket. 'I'll be back later with the revised quote.'

In silence four pairs of eyes watched him bend down to pick up his plans, turn on his heel and walk towards the doors but before he disappeared completely from sight, Juliet dragged in a breath and called out, 'Hey, Jake?' He paused and didn't turn around. 'Stop by the salon after you drop the quote off. I'll give you a couple of different choices to the man-bun.'

'Appreciate it,' he murmured and walked off.

'What the hell was that all about?' Emma said as soon as she heard his footsteps crunching on the gravel outside.

'I felt bad for him,' Juliet said.

'I think she meant about the chandelier,' Daniel said, grinning as he started loading up the tray with empties. 'Could you two have been more obvious?'

'About what?' Kate asked, doing a really bad impression of appearing mystified.

'What do you mean, "about what"?' Emma asked. 'A bit of the chandelier drops off and suddenly Jake's setting his engines to warp and scarpering.'

'Oh that. That was nothing. A bit of village folklore fun

that is in no way serious.'

'You two are the worst actresses in the world.' Emma eye-balled the both of them until Kate gave in.

'Okay, okay. It's just that Jake is a bit sensitive at the moment.'

'About folklore?'

'About the chandelier,' Juliet said.

Emma looked up at the light radiating sparkly warmth over the room and then looked at Kate.

'And about other stuff,' Kate supplied.

She wanted so, so badly to ask what the other stuff was, but she didn't.

Kate and Juliet were obviously trying to protect Jake and from a couple of conversations and some observation, Jake was a proud and private man and, if that flash of pain was anything to go by, definitely feeling humiliated about something.

She realised she didn't have the right to know.

She was the newcomer and needed to earn that right.

Double darn.

It was going to burn her up inside not being able to ask questions about him without coming across as being 'interested'.

Which she wasn't.

In the slightest.

Chapter 12

Mince Pies on the Prize

Emma

'Sheila, these are so good, they should be illegal.' Emma bit into another of the bite-sized mince pies with the little star and little Christmas tree sweet-pastry toppers and told herself this would absolutely be the last thing she ate seconds of during Sheila's visit.

Kate's mother's face lit up at the compliment. 'Bootleg mince pies. I like the sound of that. Perhaps I should deliver them under the cover of night.'

'We'll set up a code and a secret handshake,' Emma joked alongside her, delighted to discover where Kate got some of her sense of humour from. 'Honestly, I can't remember the last time I ate a mince pie this good.'

To be honest, she wasn't sure she'd had one since she'd left the UK, and as the rich fruit flavours burst on her tongue and the sweet buttery pastry melted in her mouth, the vault containing Christmases past burst wide open.

Suddenly she was six years old again. Valiantly trying to stay awake on Christmas Eve and waking in the early hours

102

with the feel of a pillow case filled with treats, against her feet, signalling that Father Christmas had been. With excitement she'd feel her way past the small wrapped toys, and the dreadfully squishy Satsuma, hunting for her favourite present, a book. Tearing off the wrapping she'd clamber out of bed, read the title by the dull hallway light and rush into her parents' bedroom to climb in between them and fall asleep, happily clutching it to her chest.

As the carousel of Christmas memories sped up there were more books but it was harder to steep herself in the stories with her parents hurling recriminations at each other until her father would inevitably decide to go for a drive.

Feeling a little sick, Emma quickly tugged on the reindeer reins, jumped off the carousel and fled the vault, slamming the door shut behind her. Picking up her clipboard she concentrated on putting another tick in a column.

'Well,' she said, forcing a smile for Sheila. 'These are definitely going on the menu. As is the triple layer chocolate-fudge cake. Also, the Tiffin brownies and, oh, I don't suppose you could do mini Yule-logs with white frosting to look like snow?'

'I think I could do that.' Sheila jotted the request in the notebook beside her. 'What if I dust them with a pistachio crumb in the shape of a holly leaf and add a couple of cranberries for the berries?'

'That sounds yummy. They'd need to be small enough to fit on these cake stands,' Emma said, pointing to the pretty mismatched ones she'd laid out, so that Sheila could get an idea of what would go into each festive afternoon tea. 'Is that going to be possible? I don't want to make your life too fiddly.'

'Oh, I can handle a little fiddly.'

Emma heard the determination in Kate's mother's voice and looked up from where she'd been adding notes to her order sheet. 'Do you not get busy at the B&B at Christmas?' she asked.

'Not during the lead-up. That's why I'm so happy to be doing this.' Sheila fussed with the napkin she'd laid across her lap. 'It's a strange time of year,' she confessed.

'Because of Bea?' Emma couldn't believe she'd come right out and said that and reached a hand out in automatic apology. 'I'm so sorry, Mrs Somersby. I shouldn't have mentioned anything.'

'Actually it's fine. Everyone always tiptoes around it, not wanting to make it harder on me, I know.'

'I remember Kate only ever made flying visits back to you at this time of year. I guess that made it even harder?'

'I'm ashamed to say at the time I hardly even noticed. After Bea died I could never really get myself into a place to celebrate. This year, I'm feeling so much better and so thankful and well, Oscar and Melody should be allowed to celebrate with Juliet and Kate will want to celebrate with Daniel of course,' she rushed out. 'Their relationships are so new and I don't want to intrude.'

'Of course,' Emma said, feeling awkward. She wasn't sure it was her place to reassure Kate's mother that Kate and Daniel, and Oscar, Juliet and Melody were bound to include her in their Christmas plans. She hated thinking the first year she was ready to celebrate since her daughter's death, Sheila was worried about intruding on her other daughter's or her son-in-law's plans. Was Sheila subtly asking Emma to get involved? If she could help then perhaps she should mention something to Kate? It wasn't like she couldn't speak to the feeling of being on your own at Christmas.

'I get the odd guest at Christmas but between you and me,' Sheila said leaning forward in her chair conspiratorially, 'there's this phenomenon in Whispers Wood where even the largest of houses tend to magically shrink at this time of year.'

Emma leaned forward too. 'Between you and me it's not only in Whispers Wood where there's suddenly "No Room at the Inn". Perhaps the greatest gift family can give each other at Christmas is space. Everything seems to work better when no one is under each other's feet.'

'You're probably right,' Sheila said but Emma could see the tinge of sadness in her posture and decided it wasn't meddling if she could help her not to feel alone. 'How about you? What's Christmas usually like for you?'

Emma sat back in her chair. 'Usually my mother and I spend Christmas Eve at a spa and then we open our gifts to each other.'

'So she spends Christmas day on her own – I mean – you both spend the day apart?'

'No. My mother never spends the day alone. She always spends it,' Emma held her hands together to form a heart and added in a thick French accent because somehow, to her, it sounded less judgey, '*avec l'amour du jour.*'

'Oh.'

'It's perfect really. She gets to do what makes her happy and so do I.'

'And what makes you happy?'

'Being in my apartment where it's usually quiet because my flatmates have gone home to their families,' Emma confided, bringing up the memory she'd created and filed under "How Not to Feel Alone at Christmas". She'd spent a good few Christmases honing her skills so that now she always associated spending that particular day of the year on her own with happy thoughts. 'I've usually stuffed myself silly at Thanksgiving, so I lay off a huge lunch and enjoy a few little treats. Nothing as nice as these though,' she added, looking again at the finger sandwiches and baked goods Sheila had brought along to the afternoon tea tasting session. 'Then I sit in my favourite chair and read. It's bliss. Truly the best Christmas present I could give myself.' Infinitely better than being invited to spend the day with people who were all coupled-up, or get herself a Tinder date and discover the guy didn't want to be out with her, so much as he didn't want to spend the holiday alone.

Sheila looked as if that was the saddest thing she'd ever heard. 'It sounds lonely. Do you and your mother not get along?'

'We do,' Emma laughed a little self-consciously. There was absolutely no need to mention the bitter disappointment followed by the endless links to auditions for panto season, when Lydia Danes had discovered her daughter was coming back to the UK. Or the strange relief Emma had felt in ignoring them. 'But I guess the pressure on Christmas being perfect can bring out the worst in everyone, so we switched to going big on Thanksgiving when we moved to the States.'

Now Emma realised with a start that Thanksgiving wasn't far away. A pang of home-sickness hit and she felt caught. Her loyalty divided between two different celebrations. Maybe if she asked everyone over for a meal on Thanksgiving? It might be a nice way of fitting in. Not that she should really be let loose cooking and only if she could get the cottage to warm up, that was. As the hurdles started mounting up, she lost her confidence. Who'd want to have a Thanksgiving celebration so close to The Clock House opening up? Everyone would surely have their own plans.

To prove to Sheila she didn't have some weird penchant for being on her own at Christmas, she found herself admitting, 'Anyway, this year is all change. I expect to be at my Dad's on Christmas Day, spending it with him and his family.' Nervous as she was about that, and worried she'd be crying out for down-time and solitude after having worked so many hours at The Clock House by the time the big day came around, she was also looking forward to breaking with tradition.

It was all part of her new adventure. And, anyway, she and her Dad would get better at chatting on the phone with each other so that by the time they actually met up it would be less stilted.

She was nearly sure of it.

Eager not to let her mood flatten she changed the subject. 'I also have another favour to ask.' Standing up, she pulled a piece of paper out of her pocket, unfolded it and slid it across the table to Sheila Somersby. In a careful whisper, she asked, 'Is there any way you could make these out of gingerbread?'

Sheila took the piece of paper and unfolded it. 'Oh, how lovely,' she said, looking up at Emma with a soft expression on her face.

'And could you not tell anyone about it? I want to create little scenes and put them under the glass domes so that they look like giant—'

'Snow globes,' Sheila said on a delighted sigh.

'Exactly. Do you think you'd have time to get them done by opening night?'

'Yes. I think I could do that.'

'Wonderful. I thought it would help Christmasify the theme, I'm glad you like the idea.'

'I do and Kate will love it.'

'Love what?' Kate said wandering into the room.

'It's a surprise,' Emma and Sheila answered together and Emma was pleased to see how happy Kate looked that her mother might willingly be in on a surprise for her daughter.

Chapter 13

The Holly (wood), and The Knightley

Emma

By the end of the week an exhausted Emma gave Big Kev a wave and a smile as she exited the corner shop. The bell above the door made that tinkling sound that made her think of sleigh-bells and reminded her The Holidays were coming. Her smile grew wider.

She hoped she'd done the right thing asking Big Kev how he was going to be spending Christmas. She was fairly sure mentioning Sheila in the same conversation had been the right thing to do as well because if they were both going to be in the same vicinity, then she couldn't see why they shouldn't spend some, or all, of the day together.

No one should have to spend the day alone if they didn't want to.

She, on the other hand, couldn't wait to have a little down-time this evening. She'd been working flat out, getting to grips with the new equipment, and setting up contracts with suppliers. She and Kate had worked out a set of opening hours that complied with their licence and complimented when the spa, salon and co-working spaces were open.

All that was left to do was agree on which style of Christmas decorations to put up and they'd be ready for the grand opening.

Of course first she had to get through hosting her first ever Whispers Wood village meeting, but she was kind of looking forward to the experience.

Tonight though, she had crumpets, a tin of luxury hot chocolate and a pint of milk, packed away in her bag and she was going home to Wren Cottage to curl up and read.

After she'd gone to war with the heating and won, that was.

It was either finally work out what she was doing wrong, or work out a way of enticing Catty McCatface onto her lap to keep her warm.

Of the two she thought she knew which she was in with a shot of achieving.

With a glance up at the clock on The Clock House, she saw that it wasn't quite six-thirty in the evening and already the sky was inkjet black behind the fast-moving wisps of cloud. Soon that cloud would unveil a few sparkly stars and getting to look up at them would more than make up for the cold.

She'd developed a routine of standing in the garden of Wren Cottage each night, wrapped in coat and gloves and hat as she lifted her face to the sky to gaze up at those stars.

Not wishing on them exactly...

More, choosing to think about all the ways they were better than a Hollywood star with her name underneath.

Was she awful for continuing to self-check her decision to

take a break from acting? And is that what she was doing, then, or was this all a big lead-up to her finally getting comfortable with being able to use the word 'former' in front of the word 'actress' when asked what she did for a living?

She hadn't been able to make a living from acting, so could she even call herself an actress, or was it enough to know that because she'd lived, breathed, and slept that life, she was. And if she genuinely thought she was, why wasn't she out in the world, acting?

She sighed.

She couldn't be happier in Whispers Wood but was that because she wasn't getting turned down, passed over, and rejected at every turn?

As the end of her scarf fell across her shoulder she shoved it back, and at the sound of footsteps close behind her, instinctively picked up her pace, moving so that she was under the glow emitted by the lampposts.

The lamplights had been fitted with white LED bulbs. That titbit had come straight from Crispin Harlow himself and how she could have coped one moment longer without that information she didn't know! Feeling safer, she walked along the edge of the village green towards the woods. Crispin had come into The Clock House yesterday to introduce himself and give her a few pointers for setting up the room for the village meeting he'd called for later in the week.

The number one topic to be discussed was to be the Whispers Wood annual tree-lighting ceremony. Apparently there was going to be carols on the green beforehand and Kate had mentioned The Clock House providing a drinks stand.

Emma couldn't wait for a proper taste of the village community all coming together.

She wondered if Jake would be there.

Not that it should matter either way.

Although wouldn't it look a bit strange if the owner of the largest estate in the village didn't attend?

She supposed it was possible he'd have left Whispers Wood by then anyway and then she was calling herself all sorts of idiot because she'd been doing so, so well not bouncing up and down with questions about him. In fact she hadn't been thinking about him at all.

Well, hardly, at any rate.

If she wanted to get the best out of her time here she really didn't need to be thinking about a certain brooding bachelor. All she should be doing was thinking about how to ensure she did a good job running Cocktails & Chai.

The sound of heavy footsteps was right behind her now and without pausing to think, she reached into her bag and whirling around, commanded the invader of her personal space to, 'Back off if you want to keep your dignity because I'm trained in krav maga.'

'Whoa – backing off.'

Emma blinked up at the very person she'd just been congratulating herself for not thinking about.

'Jeez, you nearly gave me a heart-attack,' she accused, absolutely sure that the super-bright white light of the lamplight was capturing the heat suffusing her face beautifully.

'I see that,' Jake said, lowering his gaze to what she was

holding in her hand, 'and if it makes you feel any better I'm completely certain you could have taken me down with that packet of crumpets.'

Emma looked at the now slightly squashed crumpets she'd been brandishing like a can of mace, and lowered her arm back to her side.

'Sorry,' she said, a bit glum because maybe the tin or the pint would have wiped the smile off his face. 'You shouldn't creep up on people, though.'

'It really wasn't my intention to scare you. I'm sorry. Just as a note though, this is Whispers Wood, not Hollywood,' his grin got fuller and his voice gentled, 'Hollywood.'

Impossible man.

Being all nice to her, slowing her world down to it just being the two of them under the lamplight, and giving her time to get her heart-rate back to somewhere in the normal range. Not that her heart appeared to be listening to either of them the way it continued to skip about.

Emma cleared her throat. 'Yes well, I'm not used to this walking everywhere thing that you all do. In LA everyone drives everywhere.'

'I really thought you'd heard me call out to you.'

She had. She'd just thought she was imagining that gorgeous voice of his.

'You heading back to Wren Cottage?' he asked, as she put the packet of crumpets back in her bag.

She nodded. 'You heading back to Knightley Hall?'

'Yep.'

Neither of them moved and she scrabbled around for something to say that wasn't, 'What was up with the way you left The Clock House the other day?' So of course what came out was, 'You've shaved off your beard.'

He grinned. 'Nothing gets past you, does it, Detective Danes.'

She guessed not. Which was why she was able to make the observation that without the facial hair, his lips looked even more ... she bit down hard on her lip because she wanted to say sensuous. But if she did that would mean admitting how easy she found it to focus on that mouth of his.

And focusing on Jake Knightley?

Exactly. So was not the point of being in Whispers Wood.

'Aren't you cold without it?' she asked, annoyed with herself for not letting it go. 'You must feel so naked.' Quickly she lowered her chin until her mouth was cut off by her thick woolly scarf because even to her own ears her voice had sounded disproportionately loud and accusatory. How had they gone from assault with a deadly crumpet to talking about nakedness?

Actually let's make it a little more mortifying and admit that it was only her talking about nakedness. Not him. Which then made her will him to start talking about nakedness so that it wasn't only her.

'Actually I do feel a bit naked without it,' he admitted.

'Well, thank God. I'd hate to be the only one in this place that feels the cold.'

His gaze tracked over her ridiculous scarf and he laughed and the deep, rich earthy tone, did something very peculiar to her knees, in that they sort of giggled, making her feel unsteady on her feet.

'So you've been thinking about me naked, Hollywood?'

She had only one way to go with that and so she went there really fast. 'Oh, completely,' she said, nodding her head vigorously so that her scarf loosened. 'Utterly. Yep. *Barely* been able to think about anything else. Consumes my every waking moment.' She stepped forward as if to let him in on a secret. 'So tiring ... bordering on boring.'

'All right. I get it. If you *must* know I thought going for slightly shorter hair and no beard would make me look less—'

'Less?' If anything it made him look *more*. Darn it. There she went with her noticing again when she was supposed to be focused on doing work she was good at and that made her happy and in the process restoring her confidence in herself.

'I thought it would help someone see me in a less Lady Chatterley's lover light, that's all.'

'Do you mean me?' she asked, without thinking.

'No.' His laugh this time was one of genuine bemusement and Emma wanted to swallow her own tongue. 'Why would I care what light you saw me in?'

'Absolutely no reason at all,' she said, absurdly peeved to find that since they'd met she'd occupied not one corner of his mind. 'It's all this unpolluted fresh air,' she complained, hoping he didn't hear the slight breathless note in her reply. 'It's giving me brain-freeze.'

'Let's walk, then. It'll warm you up.' And just like that they were walking towards the woods together. As if they'd been getting on famously from the second they met. But then, ever since their eyes had connected over his designs for The Clock House courtyard...

'So how's it going at The Clock House?' Jake asked.

'Good,' Emma answered. 'Kate wants me to interview for a member of staff. You know, to help out if it gets busy. To be honest I'm not sure it's going to be necessary.'

'Of course it will be. Have you ever managed a place like Cocktails & Chai before?'

'Sort of.'

'For real, or for acting real?'

'For real,' she said with a roll of her eyes. 'Why on earth did you think I'd come here?'

'Honestly? To learn the ropes for a part you wanted.'

'You thought I was here to Christian Bale myself into a role?' she risked a quick glance up at him and realised he wasn't totally convinced she still wasn't. 'What, you think I've adopted some sort of character for the duration I'm here? Is that what everyone thinks?'

'Probably.'

So the residents she had met already thought she was second-best to a real bar manager. 'Well, I'll just have to convince you all otherwise,' she promised. 'How do you think I met Kate?'

'I assumed while she was travelling.'

'I really want to say the thing about when you assume but I suppose, technically, you're right. She came in to write a review of the bar I worked in. A few years on and I knew enough so that I could run the bar when the owner, Rudy, went out of town.' You see, she wanted to point out. I'm hardly a stranger to commitment.

'Then you already know you can't do everything on your own. Unless you want to let everyone down when you keel-over from burnout?'

'I've no intention of letting anyone down. And I've no intention of burning out. Tomorrow is my day off and I'm going to—' she hesitated.

'Going to?'

'As it happens I'm going to spend the day in Chawton.'

'Chawton – sounds as if I should know it.' His hand came out to rub over his clean-shaven jaw. 'What's in Chawton?'

'Jane Austen's House Museum.'

'Right. More old things.'

'Is there something wrong with doing a little sight-seeing on my day off? Soaking up a little culture? Getting away from Whispers Wood for a while?'

He had the grace to look embarrassed as he mumbled, 'No, no, and no.'

She was content to let his acknowledgements rest in the air for a moment as they walked through the woods.

'Are you driving there?'

'No way. I've seen *The Holiday*. I'm not even attempting driving on the wrong side of the road in a shift-stick Mini or something equally small. Kate has to go into town anyway so she's dropping me off at the station. So what do you do on your days off then?'

'I spend time in the gardens.'

'That doesn't really sound like a day off.'

'Only to you. To me, it's great. Peace and quiet and some

manual labour.'

'Mindfulness 101.'

He nodded. 'Putting your hands in the earth does give you that zen-like quality of life that's so elusive when you're constantly plugged in.'

'Have you lived that life then, the one where you're constantly plugged in?'

For a moment she thought he wasn't going to answer and then he was saying softly, 'Once upon a time.'

'And you fell out of love with it?'

'Maybe it fell out of love with me.'

She waited and when he didn't elaborate she huffed out a breath. 'Are you this cryptic with everyone, or is it just me?'

'Oh, definitely just you.'

'Right. Don't trust the imposter. I get it.'

'Are you pouting, Hollywood?'

She didn't answer and after a moment, he surprised her by confiding, 'When your family has lived in a place like Whispers Wood, generation after generation, you get used to everyone already knowing your life story. You fall out of the habit of volunteering personal information.'

'And?' she asked.

'And?' he mimicked, one eyebrow shooting up.

'Oh, come on. There has to be more to it than that.'

He was silent for a moment and then added, 'I guess I sort of forget how to talk to people sometimes. Comes from working on my own a lot.'

'Working too much on your own can make you a little paranoid.'

'Hey, just because I'm paranoid, doesn't mean they're not out to get me,' he said with a laugh.

The way he said it definitely made her think he'd been burned. 'What happened to make you believe every newcomer is here to personally shake you down?'

He turned his head so that she couldn't see his expression and his tone was mild when he said, 'Nothing happened.'

Too mild. She felt the spike of sadness that he obviously didn't trust her.

'So do you not have anyone to help you with the gardens?' she asked.

'I can't afford to take on anyone at the moment.'

'And what are you going to do if you keel-over from burnout in those gardens of yours? Who's going to come to your rescue?'

'Are you kidding? This is Whispers Wood. If someone from the village doesn't work it out in five minutes, I'm pretty sure one of my five brothers and sisters would stumble across me.'

'You have five siblings? Do they all live around here?'

'No, thank God. At the moment I only have to worry about Sarah and Seth popping in every five minutes.'

'I'm finding it hard picturing you as someone from a large family. You must be the oldest, right?'

'Nope. Middle.'

'Ah. The peace-maker.'

He looked at her in surprise.

'With that many siblings someone has to be. So maybe Sarah and Seth are popping around to get advice and be listened to. They probably love having you nearby.'

'They hate it. Because after the listening and the calming

everyone down, invariably comes the lecture.'

'I'd start calling it "advice" – at least in your own head. Sounds better, doesn't it?'

'You seem to know an awful lot about family dynamics. Do you come from a large family?'

'Nope. Only child.'

'Actually, that makes total sense.'

'It does?' She looked up at him. 'Explain, please.'

'The acting.'

She walked a couple of paces and then trying very hard to take the ire out of her voice said, 'Do you think I went into acting to get attention because I was an only child?'

'No, I think you might have been lonely.'

She tripped over a tree root. At least that was what she told herself as he automatically put his arm out to prevent her falling. 'Okay?' he asked, that super-intense gaze seeking out hers.

She nodded, and glanced away. After pausing to shove her scarf back, she said, 'You couldn't be more wrong. I had lots of friends and a perfect childhood.'

'No one has a perfect childhood, Hollywood.'

'Well, I did.' Even as she said it she wondered what it was about this man that made her speak without thinking. Someone so completely comfortable in his own skin should make her feel comfortable too, right? Why on earth was she pretending to be perfect for him? He didn't care either way. Worse, he saw right through it.

It must just be because she was getting nervous about seeing her dad again after such a long time. Nervous she'd take one look at him being perfect with his new perfect family and wonder why it couldn't have been that way with her. 'So, what's your plan for not keeling over with overwork then?' she asked, determined to bring them back onto safer ground. 'I take it you do have one?'

'I do. It's called a holiday.'

'The getting away for Christmas? I got the impression that wasn't so much of a holiday as an escape.'

'Eager to see the back of me, Hollywood?'

'Couldn't care less!'

He stopped and turned to stare down at her and vaguely she realised they'd arrived at Wren Cottage. As his eyes searched hers he must have seen something she'd been hoping to hide because his voice was soft and thoughtful when he said, 'Huh. Turns out you really are a good actress.'

'Turns out you have an ego the size of a—'

She didn't get the rest of the words out because suddenly he was reaching out and tugging on the end of her scarf and for one insane moment she genuinely thought he was going to close the distance between them and stop her mouth with his.

Instead those lips of his twitched as he swung the ends of her scarf in opposite directions around her neck, nearly knocking her out as the giant pom-poms at each end bounced off each side of her head. ''Night Hollywood. Enjoy your day off tomorrow,' and whistling *The Holly and the Ivy*, he sauntered off down the road.

Chapter 14

Lights, Camera, Action: Scything!

Emma

'That feels amazing,' Emma said as Kate removed the last of the honey facial mask from her face so that she was free to run her fingertips over smooth and refreshed skin.

'I told you it would,' Juliet said, collecting up the bowls and towels from her dining-table, where the three had been sat, enjoying a bit of pampering during an evening off.

Well, not an evening off exactly. But it was much more fun going through Christmas plans for The Clock House, when it came with facials, manis, pedis and scrumptious food provided by Juliet.

'Kate sold shampoo, conditioner and skin moisturiser using Bea's natural organic recipes at the village fete this summer and sold out within hours,' Juliet said proudly as she cleared away. 'Right, who's for some Christmas popcorn?'

'I'm in,' Emma said, figuring she could call it healthy because it was popcorn. Getting up from the table she followed Juliet and Kate over to the kitchen area of the gorgeous barn-conversion home that Oscar had renovated. 'So the facial scrub was from one of Bea's recipes?' she asked Kate, leaning against the large breakfast bar.

'Yes. There's heaps to do before we'd be allowed to use Bea's Bee Beautiful products in Beauty @ The Clock House but one day I hope to stock a full range and then sell to other spas and shops. For now I'm just pleased you both agreed to be my guinea-pigs. Hopefully my skills are getting better. I nearly poked someone's eye out at college the other day.'

'I don't know how you both fit everything in,' Emma said. She'd thought she'd been busy in LA, going to class, auditioning and working at Bar Brand. Thought she'd loved it all but it hadn't been like this. She'd hardly ever seen her flatmates for a start. They all got on but there wasn't the camaraderie. Their world was too competitive. Being in Whispers Wood felt like she was working towards something with friends – that they were all equally invested to make The Clock House work.

Kate grinned at Emma. 'It helps we have you on the team.'

'Agreed,' Juliet said, reaching up into a shelf to get what looked like a huge canister of sugar.

'I'm loving it,' Emma confessed. 'I know we haven't even opened yet, but it's so much fun it doesn't really feel like work.'

'You're not missing your City of Stars?' Kate asked.

'Apart from feeling cold most of the time? No. God, is that awful?'

'Depends,' Juliet said. 'Is it LA or acting you're not missing?'

Emma thought for a moment. 'I guess I don't know. This – being here – doesn't feel like a novelty, maybe that's why

I'm not feeling homesick?'

'And at least you have family over here, too. Have you arranged to meet up with your dad, yet?' Kate asked.

Emma nodded. 'I'm going the day after the tree-lighting ceremony.'

'When's the last time you saw him?' Juliet asked.

'My eighteenth,' she answered without missing a beat. 'Either Mum organised it or he was over on business, I don't know. Anyway, he stopped over and took me out to dinner. It was ...' she tailed off, unsure how to describe the happiness of seeing him with the disappointment of not seeing her friends and going to the party they'd organised for her. 'Very grown-up,' she finally decided upon. 'He's not the most gregarious of men. He's more serious. Likes numbers. Doesn't approve of what I do. Did,' she corrected.

'He didn't like you acting?'

'I'm not sure he thought it a viable career option. You know, not stable enough.' She guessed he'd been right, hadn't he?

'So what does he think about what you're doing now?'

'I guess I'll find out.'

'You haven't told him?'

Emma shook her head. 'I didn't want to tell him on the phone.' She hadn't wanted to hear the confusion followed by the bemusement in his voice and feel even more unrelated to him. 'I'll tell him when I see him. What about you, Kate? Does your father know what you're doing with The Clock House?'

'Nope. And even if he did, I doubt he'd have an opinion on it either way.'

Emma searched her friend's face to see if she was trying to hide her feelings. 'Don't you miss him?'

'How can you miss what you never really had?' Kate replied and Emma realised she really was reconciled to not having the man in her life. 'The small number of years he was in my life was really an illusion anyway. I tried to pretend he really wanted to be there, but he really didn't. I'm over it.'

'And at least you have your mum,' Emma waited a heartbeat and then decided to just ask, 'Will you be inviting her over for Christmas Day?'

'I need to find out what Daniel's doing about his mum, first. I haven't met her yet and it feels a bit too much asking them both to spend the whole day together. God, when did Christmas get so complicated?'

'I think it happens the moment you get your own place and have to decide who you're having over for Christmas,' Juliet said.

'Let's cheers to that with a honey martini?' Kate asked, efficiently setting out the ingredients.

Emma eyed up the size of the glasses Kate had got out. 'It's nice having someone make me a drink for a change, but so I can pretend the correct amount of outrage, are you *trying* to get me drunk?'

'You deserve to let your hair down after the crazy hours you've been putting in, which don't get me wrong, I thoroughly appreciate, but, sooner or later it really is going to feel like hard work and I don't want you thinking coming here should be all work and no play. If it makes you feel better think of the drink as mostly medicinal.'

Emma laughed. 'And why do I need medicine?'

'It'll warm you up,' Juliet insisted. 'You think we haven't noticed how cold you always are?'

Emma watched as Juliet next put a glug of oil and a knob of butter in a large pan and tipped in the popcorn kernels before covering the pan with a tight-fitting lid. 'I really do have to get a handle on the heating situation,' she admitted, thinking about how she should have asked Jake to show her how to work it again but somehow feeling cold had been the furthest thought from her head when they'd been sparring. Chatting. Flirting...

Whatever the hell it was they'd been doing.

'I'm going to write it all down for you again,' Juliet said with a smile, taking a gloriously misshapen bowl with hideous blue and orange squiggles all over it from a cupboard and setting it down on the counter-top.

'*What* is that?' Emma asked, clapping a hand over her mouth when she realised what she'd said.

'It's a bowl, of course,' Juliet said with a sniff.

'You kept it,' Kate said, clutching her heart and smiling. 'This,' she said, pointing to the sunken clay receptacle, 'is proof Juliet isn't perfect at every craft she tries. I dared her to keep it so that the balance of those who can craft and those who can't was restored.'

'It doesn't go with anything,' Juliet said, looking forlornly down at it. The glazes all came out wrong. I think I was going through my displacement activity of "I'll never get together with Oscar" phase, otherwise I'd have mastered the art of the throw-down better. If it wasn't so big, I'd wrap it up and give it to you as your Secret Santa present.'

'It's so ugly it's beautiful,' Kate declared.

Emma definitely agreed with the first part, and reached tactfully for the canister. She opened it and inhaled. 'Oh my God.' The scent of vanilla pod, cinnamon, lemon and orange peel filled the room. 'It smells like—' she was going to say home but realised with a start that it actually smelled like the set of a Christmas movie she'd worked on when she'd been thirteen.

'Christmas,' Kate supplied with a nod, picking up the cocktail shaker. 'I know. Juliet is the best at making things look, taste, smell and sound perfect. Except when it comes to a pottery throw down. Not a bit of Molly Jensen/Emma Bridgewater to be found and that makes me so happy.'

'Just for that I'm going to sign up for more classes,' Juliet pouted.

'Please,' Kate said shaking the cocktail ingredients. 'As if you'll have the time once we open.'

'Oh, that reminds me! Watch the pan for a moment, will you,' Juliet ordered Emma. 'I've got something for you both.'

Emma could hear the kernels already popping inside the hot pan. 'What do I do when it's ready?' she called out.

'Dump the whole lot into the bowl with the sugar and stir until it's all coated,' Juliet said emerging from another part of the barn, laden with packages wrapped in bubble wrap. 'I made you both something for The Clock House.'

With an excited squeal, Kate put down the cocktail shaker and moved over to the dining table, to tear open the bubble wrap. 'Are they ... oh, Jules, they are and they're so gorgeous,'

Kate said as Emma quickly transferred the popcorn into the bowl and stirred. 'Emma, look, they're signs for the treatment rooms.'

Emma looked at the cute signs dangling from Kate's fingers. Juliet had used large embroidery hoops and in the centre of each one stitched in beautifully flowing script: 'Quiet Please, Treatment in Progress' in Clock House coordinating tapestry threads. The round frame was covered in mini pinecones and mini baubles in antique gold, rose copper, glittery white and a frosted shade of light green.

'Good job you both agreed my colour scheme for Christmas, huh?' Juliet said cheekily. 'These are to hang during the festive period. Afterwards, I'll make some generic ones. Emma, I made you a sign too. It's only a bit of fun, really ...'

Emma walked over to the wooden frame covered in the same Christmas baubles, but inside, Juliet had stitched "How To Tell The Time At Cocktails & Chai" and designed a picture of a tea-cup next to the words a.m. and a wine glass next to the words p.m.

'It's like a Cocktails & Chai clock. Seriously, and again,' Emma put the sign down and bent over waving her arms, 'bowing down to you because it's gorgeous and I don't know where you find time to do all this.'

When she poked her head back up she caught Kate looking at Juliet with a worried frown on her face and Juliet must have sensed a question she didn't want to answer coming because she walked over to grab the bowl of popcorn off the table, saying, 'Speaking of time, one of you pour out the martinis, and we'll get started.'

Kate poured the drinks and Emma swiped the basket full of nail varnishes they were going to test and then followed the two of them over to the huge squishy-cosy grey sofa in front of the TV.

'So maybe this is where I should tell you I haven't seen the first season of *Poldark*. Or even the second,' Emma whispered as she sat down.

'I'm not sure it matters,' Kate said. 'For the purposes of plot, all you need to know is tin mining is a thing.'

'Don't worry. It's not the only thing,' Juliet assured, when Emma looked like she wasn't sure she could find anything interesting about tin mining.

'She's right,' Kate said. 'Mostly the other thing is all about simmering passion.'

'On account of Ross Poldark,' Juliet explained.

'Okay,' Emma accepted, grabbing a handful of popcorn. 'Ross. Tin mining. Simmering passion. Got it.'

'Obviously we only watch it for the intricate plot,' Kate explained, with a grin, as she too dived into the bowl of popcorn.

'Obviously,' agreed Emma.

'And the scything,' Juliet commented, taking a sip of her drink.

'Erm ... scything?' Okay, Emma was nonplussed again.

'Let's forget season three,' Kate said, 'and put it on from the beginning.'

'Or just from the scything,' Juliet decided, searching for it on iPlayer.

'We are so nice,' Kate confided, popping up to look over

at Emma.

'So nice,' Emma nodded in agreement, even though she was really none the wiser about this Poldark thing. To cover her confusion she opted to take a sip of her very large cocktail and as the wonderful taste hit her lips, had an idea. 'Hey, how about if we make honey martinis a special at the grand opening?'

'Ooh, good idea,' Kate said. 'I love the thought of Cocktails & Chai having a signature drink. As long as we have other options too. Daniel and Oscar are complete wimps when it comes to these.'

'So where is Oscar tonight?' Emma asked. 'At Daniel's?'

Juliet shook her head. 'He's at Jake's. With Daniel. Playing poker. It's all very Den of Iniquity.'

Kate snorted. 'Oh, to the joy of Drunk Daniel at about 3am tonight. The front door to the cottage will open. Silently in Daniel's head. In reality there'll be enough clanging to wake the dead. Then there'll be the inevitable repeat while he closes the door and thuds up the stairs until he's standing in front of my bed. That's when the serenading will start. For some reason when he's drunk he likes to channel Sylvester Stallone's *Rocky*, so everything comes out very "*Adrienne*" as he sings, Are you awake, Kate? You're so beautiful, Kate. Kiss me Kate …'

'You love it,' Juliet accused with a huge grin on her face.

Kate screwed up her face. 'Not when it ends with falling out of his jeans face down on the bed, I don't. Maybe I'll stay here tonight, with you.'

'So you can laugh when Drunk Oscar gets in? I don't think

so,' Juliet said. 'That's why I said Melody could stay over at Persephone's. So she doesn't have to wake up to witness the carnage from, "I think I'll make a nice toasted sandwich using every kitchen utensil we own before I go to bed".'

'I wonder what Drunk Jake is like,' Kate asked.

Emma concentrated on a mouthful of popcorn and when she couldn't stand it any longer, asked, 'Have none of you seen Jake drunk, then?'

'Don't think so,' Kate answered.

'I have,' Juliet confirmed. 'The night that—'

'Well that was completely understandable, wasn't it?' Kate said hurriedly cutting her off.

'Actually I saw him the other night,' Emma said, not wanting to feel left out, and strangely unable to tear her eyes from Ross Poldark working the fields on the TV screen in front of her.

'Drunk?' Kate asked shocked.

Emma shook her head. 'Stone cold sober.'

Kate leaned across Juliet to stare at Emma, curiosity filling her huge eyes. 'What did you talk about?'

Emma waved her hand about nonchalantly. 'The only thing two unattached adults talk about these days, of course.'

'Brexit,' Juliet surmised with a sage nod of her head.

'Nakedness,' Emma corrected.

Juliet immediately pressed the mute button on the TV and Kate put her glass down and turned to face Emma. 'Girly night has officially started. Spill.'

'Brexit would have been more interesting,' Emma tried to insist.

Eve Devon

Kate put her hand to her mouth and coughed out the word, 'Rubbish'.

'Really,' Emma said. 'I just commented on the fact that he'd shaved off his beard and that he must be – you know – feeling the cold without it.'

'And he said...?' Juliet asked, making a 'continue immediately' motion with her hand.

'Something about how he hoped changing his look would help someone change their mind about him and then how it hadn't so he might grow it back again,' Emma said.

'What the...? And men go on about how cryptic women are,' Kate said.

'Anyway,' Emma insisted, 'it was all very scything.'

'Scything?' Juliet asked.

'Crap.' Emma fanned her hot face. 'I actually might have meant boring.'

Chapter 15

The Grinch Who Stole Christmas

Emma

Both Kate's and Juliet's heads turned towards the TV. 'Oh my God,' Juliet whispered, her eyes round when she turned back to Emma, 'You're totally thinking about how much Jake Knightley looks like Ross Poldark.'

Emma feigned indifference, while her eyes remained glued to the field in which much scything was now occurring. 'There's really no more than a passing resemblance.'

'You've been thinking about what Jake Knightley looks like without his clothes on,' Kate accused.

'Again,' Juliet exclaimed.

'Again?' Emma asked, reaching for the safety of alcohol.

'Yes again,' Juliet nodded. 'Earlier. Beard – absence of. You – talking nakedness with him.'

'I—'

'It's probably because he works with his hands, isn't it,' Juliet commented matter-of-factly. 'That's one of the things I love about Oscar. It's very primitive.'

'Daniel, too,' Kate sighed happily.

'Daniel doesn't work with his hands,' Emma commented confused.

'Right. He works with his head. It's very … cerebral. Adds a whole other element.'

'I can't believe the three of us, talented and intelligent women, are reduced to fantasising about what men we know would or would not look like scything,' Emma said, taking another huge gulp of honey martini.

'While using their brains,' Kate snuck in.

'Brains and brawn,' Juliet sighed, reaching for her drink.

'Exactly,' Kate smiled chinking her glass against the side of Juliet's. 'Evolution complete.'

'Surely it'll only be complete when they remember to put the toilet seat down,' Emma sighed.

Rising from the sofa, Kate downed the rest of her drink and made 'drink-up' gestures to Emma and Juliet. 'Another round.'

'Last one or I'll start colouring outside the lines,' Emma said, gesturing to the basket of nail varnishes.

'We'll sober you up with Christmas Pudding flavoured ice-cream, which isn't as disgusting as it sounds, because Juliet made it.'

Emma held out her glass and Kate collected Juliet's too. 'So you've been thinking about Jake Knightley?' she asked, turning around to waggle her eyebrows, before walking over to the breakfast bar.

'Maybe we shouldn't encourage her,' Juliet spoke up, with a small frown.

'None needed – what I mean is,' Emma said, 'I am absolutely, unequivocally, not in the market for anything complicated.' And Jake Knightley with his impossibly brooding looks had complicated written all over him.

'But it doesn't have to be complicated,' Kate said from the kitchen area. 'It could just be recreational.'

'I don't have time for that either,' Emma insisted, pushing down the rush of adrenaline.

'Shame,' Juliet murmured. 'You can't deny all the sparks between you two.'

'Sparks?' Emma said, with a quick sip of the fresh drink Kate handed her.

'Impossible to deny,' Kate replied with a grin.

Emma found her resolve wavering, because if it wasn't just her imagination about the sparks, then ... No. What was she thinking? She was supposed to be the match-maker, not them. Of course it would be easier if they weren't already with their perfect partners. 'Just because you two are all loved up,' she muttered, taking another sip of her drink.

'Exactly,' Kate laughed. 'That's how we're able to recognise someone falling...'

'I am *not* falling,' Emma insisted. 'I couldn't be more stationary. Besides,' she added pushing her shoulders back into the sofa. 'I'm not sure Jake is really the recreational sex kind of guy.'

Kate wrinkled her nose in thought. 'Yeah. You're right. He wears "noble" like his winter Barbour. Plus, he has that intense thing going for him.'

Emma tried not to think about how Hollywood was really the easiest place for a casual hookup but that in reality she'd only taken advantage occasionally. Something about Jake acting nobly was way more seductive, knocking 'casual' into a cocked hat.

'And also, ever since—' Kate stopped abruptly and gave a sad smile.

Emma's heart skipped a beat. 'Ever since ... what?'

'Maybe we should tell her,' Juliet said, looking pointedly at Kate.

'Yes,' Emma insisted. 'Maybe you should.'

Kate gave a large sigh and then announced dramatically, 'It's all the Grinch Who Stole Christmas's fault!'

Emma blinked.

'To be fair her name is actually Alice,' Juliet explained.

'Well, who the eff is Alice?' Emma demanded.

Kate snorted into her drink. 'Good one, but now I'm going to be singing that for ages. Alice Grinchfield is Jake's "ever since", isn't she, Juliet?'

Juliet nodded. 'Last Christmas he gave his heart to her.'

'And in an awful turn of events, guess what happened the following day...' Kate continued.

'She only went and gave it away,' Juliet confided.

'So, this year, of course,' Kate explained, 'to save him from, you know what...'

'He's giving it to someone else?' Emma half-sang, half asked.

But Kate was shaking her head sadly and saying, 'He's ... going away.'

'This is the reason he's not going to be around for the grand opening?' Emma asked.

'Yep,' Kate confirmed. 'And why he's all about stuff

Christmas and the sleigh it rode in on.'

'Wow,' Emma's mind jumped from one dramatic thought to the next, but while doing that her silly big heart was thinking of him getting dumped. This Alice must have really hurt him for him to need to get away from the memories.

'She definitely ruined Christmas for him,' Juliet said, turning off the TV. 'But then, breaking their engagement right in front of his whole family, and most of Whispers Wood, would tend to do that, I would think.'

'In front of everyone? But that's just cruel,' Emma said, her mind whirring. 'She must have had a good reason, though, right? Why did she break it off?'

'That's just it,' Juliet added. 'No one knows why and Jake's remained completely schtum about it.'

'Did she,' Emma licked her lips, 'did she break his heart, then?'

'I think she must have,' Juliet said, 'because she'd already postponed the wedding once before due to work commitments. I mean, I feel bad saying it but she wasn't the easiest person to get to know. They weren't around much. They lived in London for most of their relationship.'

Emma felt appalled on his behalf.

Getting engaged was a serious thing. Hardly anyone in Hollywood ever transitioned from Tinder to actual relationship followed by engagement.

'Oh no,' Emma looked down into her now empty glass, 'Please don't tell me the fourteenth of December was going to be his wedding day?'

'Okay,' Kate agreed gently.

'We're opening The Clock House on what would have been his wedding day? I feel a little sick,' she confessed. And sober.

No wonder he didn't want to be around Whispers Wood this Christmas.

Not only the memories, but being on your own at Christmas only ever highlighted the fact that everyone else wasn't.

How was she going to be able to look at him and not let him know that she knew? Because she kind of thought that it would hurt him to know that she knew. Like, not just his pride but deeper. Now she thought she understood why he was so cautious with her. So suspicious. He'd been waiting for the gossip to reach her. Waiting for her to look at him differently.

Here she'd been thinking he'd been looking at her for entirely different reasons.

Embarrassment washed over her.

She should definitely leave thoughts of her and Jake well alone.

She had a job to do here.

And anyway he was going to take himself off to distant shores soon.

Not that she could blame him when she'd run away from her own embarrassing failure. No matter how raw, how stripped down, and how broken she'd felt not getting that part, it was hardly the same as a broken heart.

Into the silence, Juliet's phone went off.

'It's probably Oscar telling me he's won loads of money and asking me what we should do with it, to gloat in front of Jake and Daniel.'

Kate laughed as Juliet got up to answer it. 'Den of Iniquity might have been overstating a bit,' she said to Emma, 'They don't even play for real money. Mostly they do like a co-op system.'

'It's okay,' Juliet said, padding back over to the couch. 'It was Melody asking if I can charge her back-up Kindle.'

'Melody likes to read,' Kate explained and Emma grinned thinking she was a girl after her own heart.

'So what's the betting by the end of the evening Jake will have won back his stake and tomorrow a hung-over Daniel and Oscar will be helping him mend the roof?' Juliet mused as she pulled the basket of nail varnish towards her and pulled out two bottles. One in a pretty pale pink called 'The Nice List' and the other, a dark red, which she passed to Kate, called 'The Naughty List'.

Emma grabbed a bottle of dark glittery green called 'The Holly and the Ivy' because it looked nice, she told herself. Not because she secretly wanted a certain impossible whistler on her hands. 'So is Gloria Pavey Persephone's mother?' she asked, hoping to steer the conversation away from Jake.

Kate paused with the nail varnish brush in her hands. 'Now why did you have to go and mention her when we were having such a lovely evening?'

'She is her mother, yes,' Juliet said, resting her hand on her knee and swiping pale pink varnish over her nails.

Emma carefully painted her left thumb nail. 'I've seen her around a few times and she came into The Clock House with Crispin the other day.'

'Dreadful woman,' Kate muttered.

'Dreadful, *nosy* woman,' Juliet said. 'She's why I've put up paper behind the glass doors in the salon. We've got to leave some surprises for when we open.'

'I thought she seemed a little sad,' Emma mentioned.

'No, no, no,' Kate whined. 'Don't get me all conflicted about her again. What she did to Juliet was awful.'

'Except, her name-calling last year kind of did get me out of a rut and force me to make some changes,' Juliet commented.

Kate frowned. 'Well, that aside, what she did to Daniel in the summer was unforgiveable. We've all been trying to be extra nice to her, but it's like she couldn't find her way out of being a bitch if someone implanted her with a satnav. Someone should tell her she can't use the ending of her marriage to be a bitch forever.'

'They should,' Juliet said with a nod as she started painting her right hand. 'And I'll be right behind you when you do.'

'She was really nice to me,' Emma said.

Kate and Juliet shared a shocked look. 'Bizarre,' said Kate.

'I guess you can't blame her for struggling to get out from under everyone knowing what happened. I mean if someone like Jake feels he has to get away from everyone thinking about his non-wedding, I can't even imagine what it must have been like for Gloria having to stay around for her daughter. Maybe because I'm new she feels she can start from fresh with me,' Emma commented and then sighed a little. 'Can you imagine navigating the fallout of the lie her marriage was? Her husband probably never set out to hurt her like that, but, I swear, sometimes it feels as if no one enters into a relationship with honest intent these days.'

'At the start it's probably easier to think everything is perfect,' Kate mused.

Is that how things had started out with Jake and The Grinch, Emma wondered. It was certainly how her mother started every relationship. Hanging back and patiently waiting for a relationship to develop, wasn't something Lydia Danes had managed to do since the breakup of her own marriage. Nope, she went in heart first so that everything was happy and rushed and exciting, but then...

Sometimes Emma wished her mother could be transported back to times where a little restraint helped you figure out whether you really wanted the person or the 'in love' feeling you thought they represented.

'Everything's always perfect at the start because at the start you both spend all your time together,' Juliet said quietly.

Emma looked at Kate who was looking worriedly at Juliet again.

'It'll get easier when we open,' Kate said.

'Promise?' Juliet asked with a wobbly smile before confessing in a rush, 'Won't we be spending even less time together? If I can't manage a relationship and this job, how on earth would I manage—' hurriedly she lifted her glass to her mouth and drained the whole lot.

'How on earth would you manage what?' Kate asked, obviously not in the mood to let it go.

'Nothing,' Juliet said, and Emma got the distinct impression Juliet was mortified she'd said anything.

'A baby?' Kate pushed.

Juliet stared down into her empty glass.

'Wow, have you both been talking about having kids?' Emma asked gently.

Juliet shook her head. 'We hardly manage enough time together to watch a second episode of whichever series everyone's currently talking about on Netflix, where would we find the time to talk about babies? Besides,' she licked her lips and looked up at them both, shock clearly etched across her fine features. 'It's way, way too soon to be even thinking about babies.'

'But you're feeling broody?' Kate asked.

Juliet looked both baffled and a little embarrassed. 'It's probably only because of Melody. She makes it so easy to love her and share in the parenting of her.'

'Yes, that's probably all it is,' Kate mumbled but she didn't sound convinced and Juliet, being sensitive, picked up on it right away.

'Don't either of you ever feel broody?' Juliet asked, looking like she really needed them both to answer with an immediate affirmative.

But Emma shook her head honestly and said, 'I don't – I mean, I haven't. Yet,' she added when Juliet looked crestfallen. 'But then, I'm not in a relationship—'

'You don't have to be in a relationship to want a baby,' Juliet quickly said.

'Well, no. But, I think for me, I've been so caught up in wanting the acting to come off it was only when I didn't get this latest part that I came up for air and started thinking about anything else at all. Then, sure, I thought about babies.'

'Thank God,' Juliet immediately said. 'Phew. I don't know

what I've been worrying about, then. It's completely normal for women our age.'

'But I should be honest,' Emma said, feeling bad for how panicked Juliet looked. 'I thought about them years down the track, and coming with a man, too.'

'And you?'

Kate looked at Juliet like she'd heard the unspoken 'comrade' at the end of the question and she looked really guilty when she admitted, 'Jules, I haven't. But as we're being so honest, I *have* been thinking about asking Daniel to move in with me and even thinking about it freaks me out, so I can only imagine what you're feeling.'

'You know what?' Juliet said determinedly. 'I think it's probably as well Oscar and I barely have time to talk because I don't want to begin a conversation until I've worked out where I'm going with these feelings.'

'Maybe if you tried less crafting and more talking?'

'The craft doesn't have anything to do with avoiding talking babies with Oscar,' Juliet replied. 'I don't think,' she added with a frown.

'Has Mum been having a go at you?' Kate probed. 'Because if she has and you're not comfortable, you really have to tell her, she'd expect you to.'

'No, she hasn't said anything. I think I'm just being really bloody stupid! It's like I have everything I could possibly want. More than I actually thought I could have, even. So, what, now I want even more?'

'Why not? And why not now?' Emma said, feeling instinctively that Juliet wasn't someone who normally rushed in without thinking. 'You could handle it.'

Juliet looked at her as if she was mad. 'Because it's precisely when you have everything you want that it all gets ripped away from you.'

'Oh, Jules. No, you can't think like that,' Kate said, reaching out to put her arm around her. 'It's okay to want even more than you have. You work hard enough for it.'

'But I shouldn't want *everything all at the same time*. I mean, that's insane, right? Isn't that what's freaking you out about moving in with Daniel – which I totally think you should do, by the way.'

'It does feel really fast and I am worried it would put too much pressure on our relationship,' Kate murmured.

'Exactly,' Juliet said holding up her hands.

'Or maybe it would enhance it?' Emma said.

'Noooo,' Kate moaned. 'You're supposed to be on our side, not playing devil's advocate.'

'I am on your side,' Emma insisted. 'I'm just removed enough to help you with perspective. It's hard when society tells you everything is attainable but then frowns on you for chasing it.'

'Oh my God,' Kate said. 'Do you think that's what we're experiencing? Millenial Guilt – like Catholic Guilt, but without the lightning bolts?'

'Or maybe it's simply the silly season,' Emma continued, 'aka, Christmas, and you're all doing what everyone else is doing and looking about and bumping into the two biggest watchwords of the season: love and family.' That was definitely why she kept thinking about Jake, she decided. She didn't like him looking sad and overcome with unhappy memories at a time of the year when everyone was supposed to be feeling jovial and full of Christmas spirit.

'Okay, the panic I've been carrying around is practically limping off the field in defeat,' Juliet said. 'You're really good at this.'

Emma smiled, pleased to see the deer-in-headlights look had vanished from Juliet's eyes. 'Acting is all about observing motivation and then portraying that through actions, so you learn to question and sooner or later some answers pop up.'

'Oh, is that all?' Kate said. 'It couldn't also be because you're genius at people?'

If Emma was so genius at people she'd be able to work out what had gone wrong with her parents' marriage and be able to put it to bed but she smiled. 'I don't know about that, but I guess listening is the number-one skill for a bar-tender. That and the ability to serve drinks! Seriously though, you and Oscar and you and Daniel,' she said, looking at Kate, 'need to spend some time together talking ... and not about work. Oh,' Emma leant forward suddenly excited as an idea came to her, 'you know what? I actually have the perfect solution.'

She was going to arrange a soft-opening of Cocktails & Chai, she thought.

Just a small gathering.

With no talk about work allowed.

It would give Kate and Juliet some breathing space to enjoy their men without the weight of the world on their shoulders.

And it might just stop her thinking about a certain man with a pre-owned heart.

Chapter 16

Sleigh-bells Ring, Are You Listening?

Jake

Jake could feel the excitement from the open doors of The Clock House. With a swift glance up at the clock to make sure he wasn't too late, he hurried across the gravel drive and in through the double doors, and as he walked into Cocktails & Chai he was met with the biggest turn-out he'd ever seen for a village meeting.

The last time Jake had seen so many people at The Clock House was summer just gone, when everyone had come to see Daniel and Kate present their ideas for themes and fund-raising for the village fete.

He supposed he should be grateful for such a big crowd. Now no one could accuse him of hiding himself away and as soon as Crispin started wrapping up the proceedings, he could leave without having to endure any of the well-meaning conversations about why he should stick around for Christmas.

The question was, he thought as he edged further into the room, nodding his head and smiling at a few people, had everyone come out on this cold evening to get a good gawp at one more completed room at The Clock House?

Or, were they all here to see Emma?

At the far end of the room, Jake noticed Crispin standing on the makeshift stage in prime position by the lectern.

Tables had been neatly stacked against one wall and the chairs had been laid out leaving a central aisle.

From the assortment of colourful coats, hats, scarves and gloves reserving seats, he could tell he was going to have to pick a spot right at the back to stand in.

All the better to sneak out as soon as the meeting ended.

He picked his spot and without anything else to do, his gaze started scanning the room for a glimpse of the woman of the hour.

When he couldn't immediately locate her, a spike of disappointment shot through him and his scan of the room became a little less patient.

Obviously seeing Emma wasn't the reason he'd come.

He'd come to do his bit for the community and support Crispin in the telling of his plans for the annual tree-lighting ceremony. It was his land that supplied the tree, so it was important to be here.

He looked around the room, trying not to wish he was already ensconced in a cosy cottage in Cornwall, sipping a single malt. His sketch book in his hand, the grey ocean stretching out before him and nothing to remind him of where he'd gone wrong with Alice, only the space to think about where he was going with his plans for Knightley Hall.

He was only aware he was frowning when his gaze searched wider and wider into the room and suddenly collided with

Oscar and Daniel's.

Oscar, who was looking back at him and grinning from ear to ear, with a terribly knowing look in his eyes, and Daniel, who, without a shred of subtlety, suddenly started inclining his head and pointing over at Emma, who was chatting to Cheryl Brown, Juliet's mother.

Jake's hand went to pull at the neck of his jumper.

Was it overly hot in here, or was it just him?

Not content with the crazy head-twitching and mad pointing, Daniel then nudged Oscar and they both winked at him, making Jake wish with all his might that an alien ship would appear and hover over the village green, it's tracker beam searching him out and dragging him up to the ship to take him to a galaxy far, far away.

It was his own bloody fault.

So he'd asked a couple of questions about Emma during poker night.

All right, a lot of questions.

Was that any reason for the pair of them to turn one alcohol-infused conversation into a step away from holding up signs and shouting clear across the room, 'Mate, the woman you couldn't stop talking about at poker night is standing right there.'

What happened to the first rule of poker night being not to talk/gesture/infer what happened at poker night? The next time the game got round to being at Knightley Hall, he was introducing a new rule: no women talk.

What was wrong with talking about work, anyway? The three of them all did different things.

Sport.

They could also talk about sport.

He tensed as he saw Emma spot Oscar and Daniel pointing at her, and then watched helplessly as she moved the direction of her gaze so that it bounced right into his, leaving her in no doubt he'd been staring at her.

With a bright grin, she lifted her hand and waved 'hello' at him.

All friendly-like.

All sexy-like.

He gave an infinitesimal shake of his head.

No.

Not all sexy-like for f—

'All right, there, Jake?' Kate said, stopping beside him at the bar.

'What? Oh. Yep.' God, he could do with a drink.

'Thirsty, you say?'

Jake turned to find Kate looking at Emma before suddenly swinging her gaze back to him and looking at him shrewdly.

'Huh?' he managed.

'I was saying that, although we can't serve from the bar until the licence kicks in, Emma made sure to lay out tea and coffee on one of the tables over there.'

'Oh. Great idea.'

'She's great, that's for sure.'

Jake gave an evasive smile and asked, 'So does this mean you'll no longer be bringing along contraband to village meetings?'

Kate laughed. 'How did you know about that?'

'Because one meeting in the summer I was sitting behind you and Juliet and I believe I saw a hip-flask and a jumbo packet of Skittles being passed back and forth.'

Kate laughed again and looked back towards Emma. 'I always had you down for the observant type, Jake.'

He couldn't help following her gaze back to Emma and had a feeling she wasn't just talking about contraband.

Stepping away from the bar, he said, 'Maybe I'll grab myself a quick cup of coffee before the meeting starts.'

'Bring one back for me, too, will you? I'll save you this spot.' She moved slightly so that she was going to be between him and the doors.

Damn.

Now he was going to have to stand next to her for the duration of the meeting, which meant he couldn't easily sneak away.

As he picked his way across the room to the table of refreshments, he could feel a pair of eyes on him and despite ordering himself not to, right when he got to the table he turned and found Emma looking at him.

Her grin had dropped a notch and he realised he might not have smiled back at her after the Weasley twins had done the whole gesticulating, head-twitching, winking, thing.

He felt himself frown.

That warmth that oozed out of her, that radiance ... you couldn't fake that.

Could you?

And why did he find himself so compelled to respond to it?

Rattled, he turned back to the table and with only slightly shaking hands poured coffee for both himself and Kate. He made it halfway back to where Kate was before he couldn't help himself, and swung his gaze back to seek Emma out.

She was busy chatting with Mary, the school chaplain, and careful not to spill coffee, he turned back to Kate and pretended not to notice her keen gaze.

'Testing, one, two, testing,' boomed Crispin's voice across the room, creating an instant moment of silence.

'Dear God, who gave that man a mic and headset?' Jake asked under his breath.

'Do you think it's an early Christmas present from Mrs Harlow?' Kate asked.

'Hey, Crispin,' Ted, the local mechanic pointed to Crispin's head on his way to his seat, 'what's with the Britney Spears setup?'

Kate choked on her coffee, and Juliet, walking up beside her, gave her a helpful slap on the back. 'I just got here, what did I miss?'

'Someone broke the rules and gave Crispin a mic and headset,' Jake supplied, taking a gulp of his coffee.

'Wait a minute, you don't think this was what the urgent meeting with Daniel was for, earlier?' Kate asked, looking at Juliet.

'Where is Daniel?'

'Conveniently absent,' Kate said scanning the crowd for him. 'What's the betting he lent Crispin some of the tech from upstairs. Do you see him anywhere, Jake?'

Jake pointed to the double doors to where Daniel was

hovering, thinking it served him right for being at poker night. He'd been so bloody happy to encourage questions about Emma that Jake had lost all concentration and lost big-time.

At three pairs of eyes staring at him in varying degrees of accusation, Jake watched Daniel grin back sheepishly as he made his way over to them.

'If Crispin starts offering up info-graphics on how much bigger this year's tree is compared with last year's, you are going to be in such trouble,' Kate told Daniel.

Jake grinned because it would certainly explain what Crispin had done with all the stats he'd been asked to provide on how big the tree was and how many lights were needed. 'I bet now you're wishing you bought contraband,' he mentioned.

'Let's get started, then, shall we?' Crispin was saying. 'Thank you all for coming tonight. Firstly, I think we should all give Kate, Daniel and Juliet a round of applause for allowing us to move out of the foyer for our meetings and into what will be our new home, Cocktails & Chai.'

'Oh, he's so sweet, really,' Juliet said as everyone turned around and clapped and cheered. 'It's impossible to stay mad at him for long.'

'Your version of long sounds like it's coming up short,' Kate murmured. 'My "long" is way longer than yours.'

'Ladies, please,' Jake inserted, 'I'm not sure now is the time to have a dick-measuring competition. The meeting's started.'

'Wow, are you seriously talking about your dick right now?' Emma asked, moving to stand on the other side of Jake, a big grin on her face as if this was payback for him not smiling back at her.

Jake's jaw dropped open and his heartbeat went into over-drive as he followed her gaze down to his jeans and then his heart missed a beat entirely as he realised at the exact same moment as Emma, that the entire room had heard her comment and had now turned to watch her staring at Jake's...

'What did you say, dear?' Crispin asked into the silence.

'Way to make your debut, Hollywood,' Jake whispered and then felt awful as humiliation crept into those gorgeous eyes of hers, turning them from sparkling to opaque so that he had no choice but to take pity on her and say loudly, 'She said, she's so nervous, she feels sick, right now.'

'Oh,' Crispin said. 'For a minute there,' he shook his head at the ridiculous notion that male appendages were somehow pertinent to the meeting. 'Are you feeling quite all right, dear?'

'Yes,' Emma squeaked, her face blazing red.

'Good, good,' Crispin said, 'because I was about to offer a very warm welcome to the young lady who's going to be managing Cocktails & Chai. She's come all the way from America to help out at The Clock House everyone, please welcome star of stage and screen, Emma Danes.'

With Crispin publicly announcing her presence Jake figured he could legitimately do some more staring at her now. Her face turned up towards his, some of the embarrassment replaced with a 'thank you' written clearly across her features but he also noticed she'd done something to shore up her defences so that he couldn't see any deeper.

The other night when he'd teased her about thinking of him naked, she'd been able to laugh him off in a split-second and he remembered thinking how lucky she was to have those acting skills to hand because he hadn't been sure he'd managed to hide what thinking about her thinking about him naked had done to him.

As he watched her now, he found himself wondering what kind of actress hated being the centre of attention?

'Now, I know we're all looking forward to the grand opening of The Clock House,' Crispin continued as the applause died back down and people turned to face the front again, 'but let's not divert our attention from the main point of tonight's meeting: the unveiling of the plans for the tree-lighting ceremony.'

As Crispin talked about how the ceremony this year was going to top last year's, which is what he did every year, Jake couldn't help thinking back to twelve months ago, when he'd stood at the side of that exact same stage. Waiting to talk about what a privilege it was to be asked to supply the tree from his land.

It had been one of his first suggestions after taking over the estate and when he'd wanted a small sign strategically placed to advertise where the tree had come from, Crispin had agreed and even suggested Jake supply the tree for the neighbouring village Whispers Ford and why not erect a sign there advertising Knightley Hall in Whispers Wood as well. Anything to one-up the village that had opened a hotel and taken some of their business away from them, Jake had understood.

Of course, he'd still had a sense of humour back then. Despite the fact that Alice had phoned him only one hour before the meeting to tell him she wouldn't be able to get back from London in time to attend.

She hadn't even sounded miffed, he remembered now.

He should have known then, that she'd started to realise she'd confused rural *lifestyle* with actual *rural-life*.

Maybe he had known.

Maybe he hadn't wanted to admit it to himself.

After campaigning so hard to take over Knightley Hall, he hadn't exactly been in the mood to think about any mistakes he may or may not have been on the verge of making.

At least there was no danger of him ever repeating that mistake now.

'Aw, reindeers, how lovely will that be? I can't wait,' Emma suddenly said.

Tuning back into Crispin, all he could think was: Hang on ... Sleigh-rides around the village green?

Didn't you need snow for that?

Chapter 17

Snow Way, Snow How

Jake

Jake looked around the room to see if anyone else thought the idea was impossible but he must have missed Crispin talking about hiring snow machines because everyone was looking delighted by the prospect.

Oh well, let them all volunteer to be part of the 'clearing-up-the-reindeer-droppings committee', if they wanted.

Although maybe he should ask someone for all the proper details so that he could at least mention it to the family. Mostly his brothers and sisters all lived as far away from Whispers Wood as they could. But sleigh-rides around the village green were bound to be something the nieces and nephews would want in on.

He glanced down at Emma and pictured her sitting in a sleigh, tucked cosily under a fleece blanket, her button nose tinged pink with cold, her sparkling eyes connecting with...

Not his, obviously.

Jeez.

As soon as Crispin stopped speaking and everyone stood

up to chat, he'd make his excuses and go.

His mind drifted to coming up with excuses that didn't sound lame, when Emma suddenly let out a delighted gasp.

Between the swoon, the sudden clasping hold of his arm, and her gaze darting from his to Crispin's, Jake finally cottoned onto the fact that Crispin was looking at him as if waiting for him to react to what he'd just announced.

'Sorry, Crispin, could you repeat that last part?'

'I was talking about the exciting news,' Crispin elaborated.

'News?' His heart started beating heavily against his chest wall. Surely Crispin wasn't asking for a full run-down on when Jake intended to open the gardens?

'Crispin wants to present you with a shiny blue plaque,' Kate whispered, helpfully.

'Blue plaque?' he asked, none the wiser, but definitely getting more uncomfortable each second from all the attention.

Sure he'd won some awards for his garden designs. Some of them had even been prestigious. For professional purposes he listed them on his website, but he actually kept them in the cloakroom. And not even the downstairs one, so that people could see. He wanted his work to speak for itself, not a bunch of awards.

To his knowledge there weren't any outstanding awards he needed to be presented with, so what the hell was Crispin going on about?

'I was actually going to pop over tomorrow to talk to you about this, Jake,' Crispin said. 'I didn't expect to see you here tonight because—' Crispin had the grace to stop himself before going any further but Jake still felt a dull blush form across his cheeks and remembered his beard had been handy for something, after all. 'Well, anyway, you're here so I thought, what better time to announce it,' Crispin explained. 'Especially as, in the long run, we'll all benefit.'

'From what, Crispin?' Jake asked, his voice low and gruff as impatience, embarrassment and foreboding all vied for the chance to be seen and heard.

'*As* I just said, it transpires that Jane Austen herself may have stayed at Knightley Hall.'

Beside him, Emma was squirming like an over-excited puppy and Jake tried to focus on the backdrop of animated murmurs from everyone in the room and not on the warmth shooting up his arm from where she still clutched it.

Then the words truly sank in.

Jane Austen had once stayed at Knightley Hall?

Oh, no way, no how.

'Bollocks,' Jake said, clearly.

'No. Not,' Crispin grimaced with distaste, 'what you said, Jake. But actually extremely likely from my source.'

As the ramifications presented themselves Jake could feel knots of tension forming at regular intervals up the length of his spine. 'Is your source a direct descendant of the Austens?' he asked.

'Well, no, but—'

'Is your source a direct descendant of the Knightleys?' he asked, fairly sure they couldn't possibly be, because if there had been the slightest possible chance that the family could have cashed in on a fame connection to raise money for their home, they would have done so, in triplicate.

'Well, again, no, but—'

'No buts, Crispin,' Jake said knowing he had to nip this in the bud. 'I'm sorry but this is all reindeer manure.'

'Now Jake, I am assured of written proof. My friend of a friend was very serious.'

'Oh, well if it's *a friend of a friend…*' he said, his tone as dry as a bone while he looked around the room, wondering why the hell everyone was looking excitedly like they were all one step away from opening up Austen Land and retiring off the profits.

'Obviously as soon as I receive the proof, you'll be the first to know, and then we'll have to get the Jane Austen Society to substantiate it,' Crispin said.

Jake allowed himself to relax slightly. If Crispin's friend of a friend really did have some sort of documentation, it would take months to corroborate. Surely there'd have to be some sort of analysis? If it wasn't laughed out of the society first, that was.

'But if it's legitimate,' Crispin was saying, his voice growing louder with excitement, 'then we need to jump all over it. A blue plaque. A statement on your website. Think of how good it will be for Knightley Hall. Think of the visitors to Whispers Wood. The tourism possibilities.'

Jake snorted. 'Tourists which will end up staying in the hotel in Whispers Ford, so I don't think you've quite thought this through.'

'You might want to think about how you could provide parking for coaches,' Crispin continued, 'because once the heritage sites know …'

Any sense of relaxing and not taking this seriously immediately vanished and he knew he had to shut the absurd notion down.

Because, actually, if any of this turned out to be true it was going to be a bloody nightmare.

No way was he about to find himself in a situation where he could start advertising Jane Austen's favourite Knightley Hall walk, or how visitors to Knightley Hall could buy Jane Austen's favourite rose. What was the betting that if Jane Austen really *had* stayed at the Hall, it had been in the dead of winter and she hadn't stepped foot in the gardens once. All the focus would be on the house.

He didn't have the money to sink into opening up the house so that excitable women could traipse through, gush about how they could 'practically sense her presence' like something out of *Ghost Hunters*, before then whipping out their phones and iPads to film the whole experience.

They probably wouldn't even have time to wander around the gardens before being herded back onto the coach for the next haunt. Probably a footbridge across a boggy field, cunningly disguised as a moor that Charlotte Brontë had once wandered across!

'Perhaps you should spend some time having a look through your family records, Jake,' Crispin helpfully suggested.

'Oh, absolutely,' Jake nodded. 'I'll be sure to "jump" right on that.'

As if he didn't have a million other things he needed to take care of before he dumped a bag in the Land Rover and sped out of here as fast as the accelerator could take him.

And yet, as his jaw locked together, he knew that if he wanted to get ahead of this then he was going to have to search through the family journals. Every single one of them.

'Good, good,' Crispin said and then picked up his glasses to peer through to his notes. 'Now, one last thing I've been asked to mention to everyone. If anyone wants to dress up for the Carols on the Green service before the tree-lighting ceremony, Trudie only has seven Victorian costumes left and they're all size small. Unless you're desperate to spend the next three weeks on the 5:2 diet, or the 4:3 version, or some sort of kale and vinegar affair, just turn up in warm clothes.'

It was all anyone wanted to bloody well talk about, wasn't it?

Not the tree-lighting ceremony.

Of course not that.

Why would you want to talk about Christmas festivities, when you could be talking about who in your family would know if Jane Austen had ever stayed at Knightley Hall.

The one time Jake would gladly talk all things Christmas and no one wanted to.

On his third cup of coffee now, he was feeling distinctly jittery.

And trapped.

Somehow he'd ended up in one corner of the room with Ted and his wife. An innocent bystander in their argument as to whether Ted's ancient Aunt Meryl was a Jane Austen super-fan or an Agatha Christie super-fan.

Thank God for Kate wending her way over to them. 'Hey guys, sorry to interrupt, have you seen Daniel, only I wanted to remind him he can go and re-set the clock to the proper time now that the meeting's over.'

Jake took the lifeline and gazing over the tops of everyone's head located Daniel and pointed to where he was standing talking to Gloria.

Kate followed his gaze and with a downturn of her smile, muttered, 'Now why would he allow himself to get stuck talking with her?'

Jake watched as Gloria leaned closer to speak and Daniel suddenly choked on his tea.

'What is *that* about?' Kate asked.

Jake remained schtum, but thought he had a pretty good idea that Gloria had just asked Daniel to pose in her charity calendar. No doubt she'd pitched it to him as posing with a laptop strategically placed.

'Hey, we should ask Old Man Isaac,' Ted said, and for a moment Jake thought he was talking about Gloria's charity calendar and really didn't need the picture now in his head of Old Man Isaac posing with one of his carriage clocks, but then he realised what Ted meant.

'Yes,' he said, immediately scanning the crowd again. If anyone would know if Jane Austen had visited Knightley Hall it would be Whispers Wood's oldest resident. 'If you'll excuse me, I'll go and find him.'

It figured he'd find him with Emma. The two were talking animatedly, having nabbed two chairs near the front of the stage area.

'Isaac,' Jake greeted, walking up to them.

'Jake,' Isaac offered him a warm smile and immediately started rising out of his chair until Jake gestured for him to sit back down.

'Quite a shock you must have received tonight, eh, Jake?' Isaac chuckled.

Jake couldn't help the answering warm smile. Everyone had time for Old Man Isaac. Depending on your age, he was either every man's Yoda, or, every man's Dumbledore. A retired clock-maker, from a family of clock-makers, he'd owned The Clock House until it had got too much for him and he'd moved into Rosehip Cottage on the green and put it up for sale, right for Kate and Daniel to come along and breathe new life into it.

'You of all people, Isaac, must know it can't possibly be true,' Jake said, dragging one of the empty chairs around so that they sat in a group.

'I must?'

Jake caught the twinkle in his eye and felt hopeful. 'Our families have been close for generations. I'm sure had anyone in my family any evidence at all she'd stayed at the hall, they would have told their dearest friends.'

'Your family's been in Whispers Wood for as long as Jake's has?' Emma asked Old Man Isaac, with an expression of awe on her face.

'No,' Isaac said with a chuckle. 'Not quite as long, but we have been friendly ever since—' he stopped and pointed upwards, and as Jake looked up at the chandelier, it felt entirely probable his evening was about to slide from bad into worse.

Emma followed Isaac's finger. 'The chandelier? Ever since

the chandelier went up?' she asked, glancing back at the old man for confirmation.

Jake could see questions all shaped like little ducks lining up in a neat little row behind Emma's eyes.

He absolutely did not want to talk about the chandelier. In desperation he stood up and caught the attention of the nearest person. 'Trudie,' he said with relief, 'have you been introduced to Emma, yet?'

'Hi sweetie,' Trudie sing-songed. 'I was just coming over.' She held out her hand and Emma stood up to shake it.

As Jake's heart-rate settled back down, he ignored the knowing look in Old Man Isaac's eyes and enthusiastically told Emma, 'Trudie runs the Whispers Wood amateur dramatic society. Trudie, I'm sure you heard Crispin introduce Emma earlier. The two of you must have lots in common.'

Trudie gave Emma a huge, welcoming grin. 'I'm sure we'll discover all our little secrets during rehearsals in the coming weeks. But right now, I only need to check your availability.'

'Availability?' Emma's smile shrunk a tiny bit as her unsure gaze included Isaac and Jake for an explanation.

'For the Christmas show, of course,' Trudie explained with another chuckle. 'I know you'll be busy with opening up here—'

Jake watched as Emma nodded vigorously.

'Yes,' she confirmed. 'Super-busy.'

'But obviously you'll want to be involved,' Jake said helpfully.

'No.' Emma brought a hand up to her neck and Jake noticed the blotchy rash creeping over her collar-bone. 'I really don't think that would be fair.'

'Fair?' Jake asked before Trudie could do it.

'What I mean is,' Emma told Trudie while shooting him daggers, 'I could obviously help out— *will*,' she corrected as Trudie's expression changed from welcoming to merely pleasant in the blink of an eye, 'obviously help out with setting up the room. Kate said you'd be using the room for rehearsal and the show itself, so we've booked all those days and evenings out in The Clock House diary, but other than that, I really won't have time to be, well, *in* the show.'

'Nonsense, I simply won't take no for an answer,' Trudie said, brushing right on over Emma's speech. 'It would be a sin not to have someone with your talents involved.'

Jake looked at Emma and was surprised to see her knuckles had gone white as her hand clenched nervously at the top of the cornflower blue cashmere jumper she was wearing.

She really didn't look impressed.

Probably thought she was way too good for a provincial am-dram group.

'Usually we alternate between Dickens and a pantomime,' Trudie continued, 'but not knowing how much space I'd have once you opened, I decided this year to go ahead with a show.'

'Show?' Emma asked, her voice low and husky.

'Mmmn. Christmas-inspired ensemble pieces. Whatever you want – within reason,' Trudie leant forward to confide, 'I had to take a hard pass on Betty Blunkett's burlesque routine to *Jingle Bells*.'

'Betty Blunkett from T'ai Chi?' Old Man Isaac asked, looking intrigued as hell.

Trudie nodded. 'Let's just say that her arthritic hip doesn't seem to hold her back. Anyway,' she said, turning to Emma, 'you have a good think about what you'd like to do and then let me know. I'm sure it'll be fine but I wouldn't be doing my job if I didn't take a look at it first.'

'You want me to audition for your Christmas show?' Emma asked, if possible her voice even smaller.

'Mustn't show favouritism. And you, you delicious man,' Trudie said, suddenly turning all her attention on Jake. 'I don't see your name on the sign-up sheet.'

'Me? Why on earth would I—'

'Now, Jake, you shouldn't hide a voice like that. So, shall I put you down for a song? Perhaps some Bing?'

'Bing?' Jake was mystified.

'As in Crosby,' Trudie said. 'Ooh, I can see it now, sitting on a stool, one single spotlight,' and then she was gazing off into the distance, hands flinging around dramatically as she painted her scene, 'maybe a fireplace in the background. We'll have to see if we can get someone from scenery—'

'I'd be happy to be part of the scenery – I mean, I'd be happy to be part of stage crew,' Emma interrupted.

'Nonsense,' Trudie told her. 'You can't possibly be expected to open this place and be in the show *and* part of the back-stage crew. Now, Jake, do you know the words to *White Christmas*? I know you own a tux from the bachelor audition that was organised in the summer.'

Emma, he noticed, had gone from looking sick to looking fascinated, while Jake was fairly certain he'd switched from fascinated to looking sick. Just the thought of wearing a tux while crooning the Bublé out of Christmas ... And then he remembered and his shoulders relaxed. 'Trudie, I won't be able to be in your Christmas show—'

'Nonsense,' Trudie began.

'On account of me not actually being in Whispers Wood over Christmas,' he finished succinctly.

He'd expected an 'ah' and a sympathetic yet dramatic hand on his arm at his news. He was even prepared to be half-smothered in one of her comforting hugs.

He wasn't prepared for the gush of laughter at his news.

'Oh, sweetie,' Trudie said, gasping for breath, this time putting a hand on his arm but more to support her shaking-with-laughter frame. 'You're not going anywhere this Christmas.' And with that statement she pointed up to the sky. 'There's a chandelier hanging in The Clock House over Christmas again.'

'I don't understand,' Emma said.

'Well, the last time this chandelier was hanging up here at Christmas, Whispers Wood had the biggest snowstorm on record,' Trudie said.

Jake shook his head at the absurdity.

'Now, Jake,' Isaac said, catching the expression on his face. 'Don't be too quick to pooh-pooh local myth.'

'Right. I'll leave the reindeer to do that when they take a turn around the green,' he said.

'Oh, so you've already heard?' said a voice, joining in on the conversation. 'Hi, I'm Felix,' he told Emma. 'Local dairy farmer on the other side of Knightley Hall.'

'Heard about what?' Jake asked.

'About the snow,' Felix replied with a quick glance up at the chandelier.

'Please tell me you're not talking about the ridiculous urban myth surrounding the chandelier at The Clock House?' Jake asked.

'Which one, the one about the snow or the one about the—'

'The one about the snow,' Jake smoothly inserted. There was absolutely no need to talk about the other one.

'Nah. I assumed you were talking about the long-range weather forecast I watched before coming out.'

'We're going to have snow? Really?' Emma said, her voice breathless, her eyes already glowing with excitement. 'It never snows in LA.'

'Don't go busting out the moves yet, Hollywood. This is the south east of England, not Scotland. If we get any snow at all, it'll be a tiny smattering at the most.'

'No. Honestly,' Felix replied, 'they were predicting heavy snowfall in the next couple of weeks.'

Every part of Jake wanted to throw back his head and shout, 'bollocks' at the top of his lungs because there was just no way he could deal with the possibility of being stuck in Whispers Wood over Christmas.

'Snow at Christmas, followed by a wonderful romance,' Trudie beamed. 'That's what the legend says.'

'Legend? Romance?' Emma asked.

Jake refrained from throwing his toys out the pram but it was the absolute last straw when someone tapped him on the shoulder and he turned to find himself staring at a very determined-looking Gloria.

'Tsk, tsk,' she said. 'I thought we agreed you wouldn't get your hair cut until after the photo-shoot?'

Jake managed to spare them all the head-throwing-back-swearing-at-the-top-of-his-lungs moment, and instead found another way to flout every ounce of good manners bred into him by simply turning on his heel and leaving.

Chapter 18

A Knightley at Pemberley

Emma

It made total karmic sense that Emma would find Jake chopping wood!

All her rehearsed words fell right out of her head as she watched him lift the axe in a practised, smooth arc, and then swing it down on the piece of wood balanced atop the tree-stump.

The wood split in two and Jake bent to pick both halves up and toss them on the growing pile of wood beside him.

Emma reached up to undo the top button of her coat, and, for extra measure, tugged her scarf from its stranglehold around her neck. Every time Jake swung the axe up, a small strip of tanned skin appeared in the gap between his jacket and jeans. It was kind of hypnotising, so it took a few seconds extra to realise that when the axe went up this time, it didn't immediately come back down.

'What do you want, Hollywood?'

Wow. How did he know it was her? 'Sorry, I didn't want to interrupt during actual axe-wielding in case you went all

"Here's Johnny" on me.'

'Sensible. So, what do you want?' he repeated without turning.

She'd been prepared for this and to be honest, without him turning around it was easier to draw herself up to her full five feet and two inches, set her shoulders and lift her chin.

'You really need a wreath for your front door.'

'Excuse me?'

Okay, so she hadn't meant to lead with that at all.

What she'd meant to do was calmly, logically, and confidently express her reasons for hunting him out, here, on his own turf.

If she'd thought walking up to the big door of Knightley Hall intimidating, it was nothing compared with wandering through the gardens and stumbling across him in full-on lumberjack mode.

'Massive front door like that,' she said, forcing some strength into her voice. 'It needs a Christmas wreath to hang from that massive door-knocker.' She saw his hands tighten around the handle of the axe.

'I don't do Christmas decorations.'

'But that's crazy,' she said. 'A place this size is crying out for them. Either traditional or you could go down the tacky illuminated installation route. You know, Santa on a ladder by the chimney, Rudolph and a sleigh on the roof, angels on the front drive.'

Jake swung the axe down on the next piece of wood, effectively silencing her.

Maybe she should say why she was here. Clearing her

throat, she went with the truth, 'So, speaking of massive ... I have this massive favour to ask.'

Jake hesitated as he bent to move the wood to the woodpile, but his answer was perfectly clear. 'No.'

'You don't even know what I'm going to ask yet,' she felt herself pout and stopped, choosing to lick her lips instead, hurriedly shoving her tongue back in her mouth when he turned around to face her.

With one hand resting the axe in the wood-stump, he used the other to shove through his nearly-black hair. Naturally, it fell in perfect waves back from his face. Like something out of a L'Oréal commercial. Emma quietly reminded herself that her plan was 'worth it'.

'No, I will not help you audition for the Christmas show,' Jake said in a bored tone. 'No, I will not be in the Christmas show. No, I will not help organise the Christmas show. In short, no, no, no, no, no.'

'I wasn't going to ask you any of those things,' she said, tipping her chin up higher.

'You weren't?' His eyebrow lifted in doubt. 'Well this wood isn't going to finish chopping itself, what were you going to ask me?'

'I was going to ask you if you'd help me run my lines for the Christmas show. Kidding,' she immediately added, holding her hands out and taking a step back, when he reached with both hands to pull the axe out of the wood. 'Sorry, I couldn't resist.' Her head tipped to the side as she asked, 'Who knew something like a little itty-bitty Christmas show would get you so uppity.'

'Who knew you'd think yourself far too good to be in a village Christmas show?'

'What?' Emma forgot all about her plan. 'That's what you think?' How on earth had he got to that conclusion? Just because she hadn't jumped up and down with excitement the moment Trudie had mentioned ... oh—wait.

'Don't tell me the real reason's because you're scared?' Jake asked, his intense gaze searching hers and making her annoyed that she wasn't near quick enough to hide her hasty swallow of dry air.

'Of course not,' she answered, resisting the urge to look down and check her pants weren't on fire. 'I've probably been to more auditions than you've had roast dinners. What could I possibly have to be nervous about?'

'Exactly,' he said, that gaze of his not letting up at all.

'I'm actually already preparing a piece to show Trudie.' Her stomach bottomed out. What the hell had she said that for when the moment Trudie had introduced herself, she'd felt on the verge of a massive panic-attack.

It just hadn't occurred to her that here in the safety of Whispers Wood, someone would require her to show off her acting skills.

Or that they would expect her to *want* to show off her acting skills.

Or that she would then be *judged* on her acting skills.

'Great,' Jake said. 'So break a leg and all that.' And with that he turned around and picked up the axe again.

'Don't you want to know what it is?' she asked not liking the fact that he'd backed down so easily. Had he seen something in her eyes? If he'd decided to take pity on her because he'd seen some of her secret fears she was going to be irked big-time. She certainly didn't need Jake Knightley feeling sorry for her.

'I don't need to know what it is,' he said over his shoulder. 'I won't be here. You could take over Betty Blunkett's burlesque act and I wouldn't care.'

The axe fell sharply on the wood and her gaze narrowed because she thought, hey, now, maybe he *might* care to see that, but she decided it was time to wade out of murky waters and head for higher ground. 'So, about that favour...?'

'No.'

'Please, Jake, you're the only one I can ask.'

'Highly doubtful,' he murmured and she wondered if it was her plaintive 'please' that had him sighing and turning back around to face her.

'It's not even a favour,' she rushed out. 'It's more of an invite.'

'Invite?'

'Yes.' Her gaze really wanted to track to the serenity-inducing scene of the bare rose bushes twisting up the arbour in the distance, but she determined to hold her ground. 'I'm holding a little soft-opening for Cocktails & Chai @ The Clock House and well,' her hands came out of her pockets and lifted half-way as if it wasn't a big deal, 'you're invited.'

'How little?' Jake asked, suspicion oozing out from every pore.

'Oh, it'll all be very intimate.'

Oops. Completely the wrong choice of words if his frown

and the darkening of his already dark eyes was anything to go by. He was definitely about to say that word she'd taken a dislike to, again, so she rushed on with, 'Before you say "no", it's really more about giving Kate and Daniel and Juliet and Oscar a much needed night off. They've been working so hard and I know they wouldn't have it any other way, but they really deserve a few hours where they won't have to talk "work".'

'But they will be at work,' Jake observed.

She could see she was going to have to pile it on. 'That part can't be helped. I'd really like to do this for them and couching it as a soft-opening was the only way I could get them to free up the time.'

He didn't move and mentally she pushed up her sleeves and prepared to stoke the furnace. 'Okay, I can't pretend it's not going to help me out too. I really want everything to go perfectly for Kate, and opening up for a couple of hours, so that a small group of kind-minded individuals could help me see any kinks in the system, is actually pretty perfect. Not that I expect there to be any kinks,' she added. 'But, please, Jake. They're your friends. You must see how stressed they've been getting with each other?'

For the first time she saw an easing in his stance and decided to give it one more push.

'It would only be for a couple of hours. I can't risk inviting anyone else because if Crispin finds out we might as well open to everyone early. At least this way, if he does happen to notice, I'll be able to explain it away as a last-minute meeting to introduce anyone going to be working at The Clock House to each other.'

'But I won't be working there until next year.'

'Please, Jake. It's for your friends...'

'Okay.'

'And it would mean – wait – did you just say, okay?'

'It would seem so.'

'Great. Wonderful. Oh, you won't regret it.' Her hands came out to clasp together as she beamed.

'Great and wonderful are subjective, and I have a feeling I will regret it, but as I'm out of here in a couple of weeks, consider it my last good deed for the year.'

'Your friends will thank you, Jake.'

'And you?'

'Me?'

'Mmmn. How do you intend to thank me?'

She wanted to lick her lips. She wanted to take a step closer. She wanted to say something daring and provocative. But she remembered her plan and so she searched for something innocent and came up with, 'Um ... by letting you give me a tour of your gardens?'

For a moment she thought he looked disappointed but then he blinked and she knew she'd been fooling herself.

She waited for him to offer to show her around and knew she'd like nothing better because on her way to finding him this morning, it had been really hard to stick to the main areas and not venture down paths she was sure led to more magical vistas.

Her jaw had dropped open a little at noticing the lake sited at the bottom of a huge terraced lawn that looked encrusted with diamonds as the dew sparkled under the watery sun. Tendrils of misty fog floated up from the surface of the water, as if calling to her.

Good job she hadn't thought about what the lake would look like in summer, with Jake Knightley emerging from the water in a billowy shirt plastered to the sculpted planes of his torso.

Nope. She hadn't thought about that at all!

The BBC had a lot to answer for: enhancing its productions so that when she looked at this particular lake all she could see was a Knightley at Pemberley!

She'd had no idea how vast the gardens were and there was excitement bubbling under her breastbone as she regarded Jake, waiting for him to put down the axe, run his hands down his jeans and offer to show her the grounds.

It whimpered out of her like a deflated balloon when instead of downing tools, he said, 'I'll have to let you thank me another time. I have this to do and then I'm having lunch with my sister.'

She supposed it was for the best, she thought, as she promised she'd see herself off the grounds without getting lost.

The more time they spent together, the more she might regret the real reasons for inviting him along to the soft-opening...

The chandelier.

Romance.

And Gloria Pavey.

Chapter 19

Moving Im-PEDI-ments

Kate

'You should come up with a code,' Juliet told her as she helped Kate move the stack of small galvanised steel vintage troughs out of treatment room No 2.

'Won't that confuse him?' With the tubs that were going to be used as country-chic foot-spas moved out to the corridor, Kate concentrated on straightening bottles of essential oils, so the labels were facing forward attractively on the top shelf of the treatment trolley. After a second's contemplation she rolled the trolley to the other side of the treatment bed and stood back to take in the overall ambiance of the room.

'Or you could use a euphemism in place of a code?' Juliet said, turning the dimmer switch so that the chandelier above the massage table emitted only the softest glow.

They were talking about how Kate should broach the subject of moving in with Daniel in order to gauge his reaction because she certainly wasn't going to bring it up until she was one hundred per cent certain he was open to the idea. The only problem with her logic was that if she never brought the subject up, how was she ever going to know how he felt about it?

'A euphemism,' Kate pondered, prepared to consider everything, because after talking it through with Emma the other night, the idea, instead of fading away, had started to take hold. 'What should I use that would make him completely get it without, you know, getting it, so that he then magically thinks moving in together was his idea?'

'That's the part I get stuck. Ooh,' Juliet gave a click of her fingers before reaching out to straighten the sign pointing to the shower. 'Forget euphemisms. Why don't you use the Cosmo technique?'

Kate pouted. 'See? Cosmo has written about a new sexual position and I haven't even had time to read up on it, let alone try it.'

'No. The other technique – the one where you leave a copy lying around, left conveniently open on a page with an article about moving in together?'

Kate screwed up her face. 'Let's be honest, if he even noticed it, he'd just pick the magazine up and turn to the Cosmo-technique pages. I don't know, getting all crafty about asking him doesn't feel right.'

'Unlike this room, which is now perfect, yes?' Juliet asked as she moved to stand in the open doorway.

Kate nodded. At least she felt confident about something. Happy, she looked around the treatment room with its painted walls in the same soothing eau de nil as the rest of The Clock House, its soft polished wooden floors, and the serene white of the furniture with the details picked out in flecks of gold-leaf, giving a hint of sparkle under the crystal chandelier that hung from the centre of the ceiling. 'It definitely looks better with the equipment trolley on that side and the armoire moved to the opposite wall, right?'

Juliet nodded. 'So that's all three rooms laid out just how you want them now?'

'Yes. I went ahead and added another bed and two treatment chairs to room three because it's so much bigger. That way we can have group treatments if someone books a package but they're going to have to be done on days when we're not booked out because I'm not hiring more than three therapists until I know trade can support the cost.'

'You know, you don't sound nervous at all,' Juliet remarked, looking proudly at her.

'About this?' Kate breathed deep and shook her head. 'I really think I've got my head around embracing the madness that comes with opening four businesses at once.'

She'd given herself a bit of a talking to. She had a responsibility to make this work now. Not just for Bea. Or herself, Daniel and Juliet. She had staff to look after as well and you couldn't run a day spa and not be able to chill out. So, now, every morning, no matter the weather, she'd taken to walking through the moon-gate to stand in the wild meadow, amongst the little white beehives.

The wildflowers were non-existent at this time of year, the buddleia straggly and forlorn-looking, and the grass no longer a lush green, but a sea of beige. And although the bee activity was quieter, if she stood still she could hear them working away inside their homes to keep warm.

Being around Bea's bees was proving to be the nectar that kept her focused. About The Clock House at any rate. Every time she had nothing to think about, the subject of moving in with Daniel started tapping her on the shoulder.

'The spa rooms really do look wonderful, Kate. Calming. Sumptuous. Luxurious.' Juliet gave a tired but happy grin. 'We're so close to opening now, I can taste it.'

Kate grinned back. 'Come on, let's take the new pedicure spas downstairs and set them up in the salon.'

Juliet picked up one handle of the stacked tubs and walked them downstairs with Kate because they'd sworn a pledge they wouldn't get lazy and use the lift that had been installed for guests.

'What's the worst that could happen if you ask Daniel about moving in together?' Juliet asked setting her end of the tubs down at the bottom of the stairs so that she could open up the doors to the salon.

'He could say no,' Kate huffed out.

'So if he says no you keep "Rocking All Over the World" anyway.'

'Huh?' Her days of travelling all over the world were packed up in a large trunk, thanks to coming home and laying down roots again.

'You know,' Juliet did a little guitar and box-step dance, 'Keep the status quo.'

'Oh. Ha. But that's just it, could we? Surely it would change everything, because then,' she said, making her eyes crazy-scared, 'it, would be out there.'

Juliet picked up her side of the troughs again and walked

them over with Kate to the back wall of her salon, to where five plush white leather pedicure chairs had been installed. On the dividing wall that separated the salon from the old kitchenette, which had now been made into an area for mixing up hair dyes, Oscar had installed special, custom-built racks to hold Beauty @ The Clock House's vast selection of colours you could choose to have your nails painted in.

'But if he says it's too soon, how is that the end of the world?' Juliet asked, setting out one of the kidney-bean shaped tubs in front of each chair.

'It isn't, really.' Kate automatically pulled out each portable nail bench to check sufficient amounts of towels had been stored. 'It would actually be eminently sensible.'

'And isn't that part of what you love about him?' Juliet checked, standing back to look at their handiwork.

'Yes.' Kate heaved out a sigh. 'Am I rushing to get to the next part when I should be enjoying the now? On the other hand though, by the time we're open, we're going to be so rushed off our feet, it will be too easy to concentrate on business. You were right the other night. Our private life isn't going to get a look-in once we open, is it? Tell me honestly, do you think it's too soon?'

'Hey, when it's right, it's right.'

'Good. I mean I figured since you and Oscar…'

'Are what, perfect?'

The way she said it had Kate whipping her head round to look at her. 'Hey, sorry I didn't mean—'

'No it's me who should be sorry,' Juliet said with a sad smile. 'It's just a lot of pressure.'

'To be the perfect couple. To be the perfect family?'

Juliet wandered over to one of the hair-dressing stations and straightened the chair. 'Don't look so worried. Not all of my waking thoughts are about babies. After the other night though I've been doing a bit of thinking, yes, *while* I was crafting! And you know what I concluded?'

'What?'

'That Emma was right about me hitting the silly season. I really want to wait at least a year before I revisit thinking about babies. I want to get the salon up and running properly. Enjoy the success. Enjoy the madness of running my own business.' She caught Kate's eyes in the mirror and smiled. 'Really, I feel so much better having decided.'

Kate honestly couldn't tell if she'd genuinely decided or simply talked herself into it, and gently mentioned, 'You don't look that happy about your decision.'

'It's not that. It's Christmas. I can't help thinking about how Oscar had it perfect with Bea and—'

'Oh, Jules,' Kate walked over to plonk herself down in the chair Juliet had straightened. The hard act of following Bea was always going to resonate with her. Her twin had had such a knack for getting everything she wanted, in the nicest possible way. 'Oscar was never going to give his heart easily after Bea, but that's how I know he thinks it's perfect with you.'

Juliet gave a nod and a shake of her head as if willing herself not to get upset. Almost absent-mindedly, she turned Kate around to face the mirror and started pulling out the band holding her hair in a ponytail. 'I guess I just need it to be perfect in a different way. In *our* way and well, that's going to take time, isn't it? We're both so busy. And both so practical. It's almost too easy to fall into a pattern, but is it *our* pattern, or is it recycled from his and Bea's?'

'Juliet, I promise you that Oscar doesn't see you as a substitute Bea,' Kate assured, meeting her cousin's eyes in the mirror.

Juliet fanned Kate's long brown waves over her shoulders and then picked up a hairbrush. 'We were at your mum's for Thursday night dinner last week, and she let slip how Christmas Day used to be with Bea and it was all: wakeup and he'd cook breakfast while Melody opened her presents, then it was off to the mid-day service, and back so that she and Sheila could put the finishing touches to lunch, then it was a walk in the afternoon and silly board games in the evening.'

With a sigh, she pushed Kate's hair over to the side, and studied the effect before moving it back to its natural parting. 'It's not that I don't think all that would be nice,' Juliet mused. 'It's just that I was looking forward to starting my own traditions with him and Melody.'

'How about if I invite Mum to Myrtle Cottage for Christmas?' Kate said wanting instantly to make everything better if she could. She'd have to run it past Daniel, but then he still hadn't told her if he was going to invite his mother down. Before she could give herself time to worry about that, she was thinking about how the four of them would fit around the tiny table. Not that the one Daniel had in Mistletoe Cottage was much bigger.

'I don't know,' Juliet said, brushing all of Kate's hair back and pulling it into a neat low ponytail. 'I don't want to deprive Melody of seeing her Gran on Christmas Day.'

'What's *your* mum doing?'

'Oh, she told me in August she'd been invited to Trudie and Nigel's so I needed to "sort myself out" for the day. I made her walk around for an entire weekend with a giant Christmas rosette pinned to her top, for being the first to talk about Christmas plans.'

Kate laughed and then sobered as she thought it was all very well her advising Juliet, when she couldn't drum up the courage to talk to Daniel about their living arrangements, but it was worrying her seeing one of her favourite people on the planet struggling when she should be feeling so happy. 'Don't let this one fester, Juliet. Mention it to him tonight, okay? Have a think about what you'd really like to do and suggest it to him and see what he says.'

'You're right. I should. I don't know why I'm feeling so emotional the last couple of weeks.'

'Let's face it, what we're doing here is pretty big,' Kate said, looking at Juliet and thinking she really did look quite pale. Not that she looked the picture of vitality, either. They just had to get through to opening, she thought. Then all the wondering about was this going to work would stop and the real day-to-day work could begin proper. She and Juliet would be so busy they'd have no choice but to follow their own lead.

'That must be it,' Juliet said. 'I'm actually really looking forward to tonight. Emma must be nervous though. I haven't seen her all morning and I'm dying to see what she's doing in Cocktails & Chai.'

185

'I haven't seen her since eight this morning when she made me promise not to step foot in the room until tonight.'

'Hmmn. It doesn't seem quite right,' Juliet grinned as she spun Kate around in her chair, 'you being the owner of this fine establishment,' and then walked over to the salon doors, 'and not being able to wander freely into each room.'

'Juliet Brown are you trying to get me into trouble?'

'Me? How could little ole me, get *you* into trouble?' she asked, beckoning her over, and then poking her head out to look left and then right.

Kate stepped up behind her, poking her head out above Juliet's. 'What are you doing?'

'Do you want a sneaky-peak on what's going on in there or not?' Juliet whispered.

'Okay, but just to check if Emma needs a hand with anything.'

'Exactly. After all, there's no "i" in "team".'

'Or in "nosy",' Kate whispered.

'Coast is clear,' Juliet observed.

'Roger Bilco.'

'I think it's Wilco.'

'I thought that was a shop that was all about filling up your basket with essentials like extension cord towers, sticker sheets of cute little pandas, lampshades, glittery notebooks, and pic 'n' mix?' Kate muttered as she tip-toed with Juliet across the foyer, up to the doors of Cocktails & Chai.

She'd just put her hand on the round brass doorknob when a voice bellowed, 'What are you two doing?'

'Waaah,' Kate whirled around as Daniel came up behind

them. 'Never you mind,' she said popping a hand against her beating heart.

'Hey,' he said, casting the doors a brief glance, 'if there's a spying mission going on, count me in.'

'Okay, but you have to be super-quiet.'

'Okay.'

'We're trying to see what Emma's doing for tonight.'

'Why? Don't you trust her?'

'Of course we do.' Kate had her hand on the brass round doorknob when she got a tap on the shoulder and a completely unsubtle clearing of a throat.

'Shh.' Kate said, waving her hand about behind her and not connecting with anyone. 'We're nearly in. Damn. She's locked it.'

'If it wasn't for those pesky kids,' Emma said in a perfect Scooby-Doo impression.

'Busted,' Juliet whispered as the three of them turned around.

'It was her,' Daniel immediately said, pointing to Kate. 'She's the ring-leader.'

'Hey,' Kate elbowed Daniel in the ribs.

'Yeah, she made us do it,' Juliet giggled.

'*Hey*,' Kate turned to Juliet her eyes narrowing, even if it was nice to see her laughing.

'Kate Somersby, you promised,' Emma said, folding her arms and tapping her foot. 'Well, what have you got to say for yourself?'

'That it's outrageous your agent didn't get you a part on *Orange is the New Black*.'

When Emma merely raised an eyebrow and waited, Kate was impressed and said, 'We didn't see anything. Promise.'

'And you,' Emma said, throwing Juliet a stern look. 'I'm surprised at you.' Then the tiniest crack appeared and her voice faltered as she looked at the three of them. 'Is it that you think I'm going to mess this evening up?'

'Absolutely not,' Kate said, feeling bad that her and Juliet having a little fun might not feel that way to Emma, who felt she had something to prove. 'In fact we'd just been talking about how much we were looking forward to tonight.'

'But you couldn't wait a few more hours and let yourselves enjoy the surprise?'

'Surprise?' Kate, Juliet and Daniel chorused.

Emma shook her head sadly at the trio. 'Now I'm going to have to come up with some sort of punishment.'

'Yes. We must be punished,' said Daniel, which Kate thought thoroughly deserved another elbow in the ribs.

'But we didn't see anything,' Juliet moaned.

'Doesn't matter,' Emma said shaking her head. 'The intent was there.'

'Ugh, you're not going to make us wash dishes, are you?'

Emma held up her finger as her phone signalled an incoming text. Reading it, she suddenly grinned from ear to ear. 'Well, what do you know? Perfect timing. And perfect punishment.' Emma's grin got bigger. 'Yeah, so, your evening just got extra-special because that was Gloria Pavey confirming that she can come tonight.'

'Oh, sh—' Daniel said, turning to Kate.

'Nooo,' Juliet moaned, also turning to look at Kate's reaction.

'Is this a joke?' Kate demanded.

'Mwahahaha,' Emma evil cackled as she left them standing in the foyer.

Chapter 20

Christmas Cocktails at
The Clock House

Kate

Kate walked into Cocktails & Chai and any nerves she might have had about whether Emma was having a mini breakdown behind the doors disappeared instantly. Emma, dressed in her uniform of crisp white fitted blouse, black trousers and apron with the image of The Clock House printed on it, smiled warmly, looking the very picture of confident host as she insisted on showing Daniel and Kate to one of the tables.

The place looked gorgeous.

And smelled divine.

Looking around at the tables set up for two, Kate saw that Emma had placed long copper trays filled with cinnamon sticks, orange peel, pinecones and candles laced with glitter so that they sparkled under the light from the chandelier.

All Kate needed to do now was relax about sharing her evening with Gloria Pavey.

As tall orders went, socialising with Gloria was going to

be the tallest, but then again, when they opened she'd be actively encouraging her patronage, so she might as well get used to seeing her on the premises.

'What'll you have to drink?' Emma asked. 'I'm doing table service tonight and I've done a menu with some Christmas cocktails and mocktails on.' She passed them one to look over. 'You can actually order whatever you like, but I thought this would be more festive.'

As Kate sat down, she shrugged out of her coat and looked at the menu. All the drinks had been given Christmas names and she was touched and impressed that Emma had gone to so much trouble. 'I'll have a Winter Wonderland, please.'

'Do you have a bottle of Whispers Wrangler?' Daniel said, passing back the menus.

'Of course,' Emma said with a smile. 'I'm trying to stock as much local produce as possible. Back in a mo with your order and a feedback card for later.'

Kate gave Emma a huge grin and two thumbs-up and then turned to look at Daniel who was smiling warmly at her.

Her heart gave a happy little lurch. It had been too long since they'd sat down at a table without her bullet journal or their phones or a laptop in between them.

After delivering their drinks, Emma returned to the front of the bar and tapped a knife against a glass to get everyone's attention.

'Hi everyone,' she greeted. 'I just wanted to say a few words about this evening. Firstly, to thank you for coming along and secondly, I'm sure you've noticed that I've deliberately set up the room for couples-only tables...'

Kate looked around and saw that all the staff was sitting opposite someone with the exception of Gloira, who, thank God, wasn't staff, but who had a strange expression on her face that Kate thought might be nervousness as she waited for her 'date' to show up.

'As a thank you for Kate letting me hold this soft-opening tonight,' Emma continued, 'I wanted to offer something a little different and give my partners in crime here, Kate, Daniel and Juliet,' she said, pointing to the two tables where she and Daniel and next to them, Juliet and Oscar were seated, 'a very well-deserved night off. To that end, and because there's only one of me on duty, I hope you'll enter into the spririt of a small planned activity...'

'Planned activity?' Kate whispered to Daniel, shocked. 'Planned activity is only one step away from, "let's all turn to our left and tell the person sitting next to us a little about ourselves". I started my own business so I didn't have to go on work courses with icebreakers.'

'Icebreakers aren't that bad,' Daniel whispered back. 'It'll be a great way for the staff to get to know each other.'

Kate shuddered. 'I once went on a course where I got slapped on the back with a sticker that said "Fork" and I had to "find my other half and strike up a conversation". I spent the entire allotted time racing around trying to find my "knife" only to discover afterwards that I had supposed to have been looking for a "spoon".' She stopped talking, acutely aware that she'd started babbling. She was babbling because she was nervous. Any moment now she thought he was going to ask her why she was nervous and she was going to respond with,

'Moving in together ... how about we do that ... huh?'

And he was going to respond by...

'I can see that you've been scarred for life,' Daniel said, biting back a smile.

She breathed out. 'So what crappy icebreakers did you have to do, then?'

'Well being that I was in accountancy and not media, we had terribly sensible icebreaker games, like "turn to your right and tell the person next to you a bit about yourself".'

Kate grinned and poked out her tongue at him before turning her head to listen to Emma.

'Tonight,' Emma declared, her voice dropping seductively, 'is all about date-night, not work-night. I'm talking speed-dating with a difference, and the difference is that you'll stick with your partner for the evening. No work-talk. At all.'

Kate frowned. No work talk. Like, at all? 'But what will we talk about?' she asked. 'We've already covered icebreakers.'

'I'm sure we'll think of something,' Daniel said, looking confident.

Kate swallowed. Now that she couldn't talk about work, the only thing on her mind was the one subject she'd vowed not to introduce into conversation until she'd figured out what his response was going to be.

'To help you,' Emma continued, 'on each table, you'll notice a small wrapped present and an egg-timer. The egg-timers are going to be used when we open to help people judge the right amount of time to brew their tea, but for tonight, I think you should use them with your present. So, dive in, and have fun getting to know each other and remember, no work-talk allowed.'

Kate took a sip of her Winter Wonderland cocktail and looked around the room to see that everyone was entering into the spirit and opening the boxes on the tables. Determined not to spoil Emma's efforts, and because it was going to save her from talking about moving in together, she tapped the lid of the box. 'I think you should do the honours and open it.'

'Okay, here goes.' Reaching out he took the box and undid the Cristmas wrapping paper and bow and peered inside. 'Ha. Cute idea.'

Kate craned her neck. 'What is it?'

'It's a stack of cards with the words "Christmas Quiz" stamped on them. The label says we each get to ask a question and the other has to answer before the egg-timer runs out.'

'Oh, that actually doesn't sound too bad.' She watched as Daniel took the stack of cards out and put them in the centre of the table next to the pretty hourglass encased in its wooden cage. With a quick look around she saw that others had started asking their questions.

'Ladies, first,' Daniel said, indicating she should ask the first question.

She took the first card off the stack, turned it over, read the question, and smiled. 'How many milk-maids are a-milking in the song *The Twelve Days of Christmas?*'

'Easy,' Daniel said, bringing his bottle of beer to his lips and taking a chug. 'Five.'

Kate made the sound of the X-factor buzzer. 'Nope, that's

gold rings.'

'That's silly – why would you want five gold rings? Surely you'd only want one?'

Kate felt her drink go down the wrong way. 'One?' she spluttered.

Daniel looked at her like she'd lost the plot. 'Of course, one. One wedding ring.'

'Partridge,' she squeaked out. Here she was vacillating between asking him to move in with her and not asking him to move in with her. And here he was, calmly talking about wedding rings!

'Partridge?' Daniel repeated like a parrot. 'I thought that was two. In a pair of trees.'

'Oh my God,' Kate shook her head at him, feeling on much more solid ground talking partridges and trees. 'It's a *pear tree*.'

'Oh, yeah, partridge in a pear tree.' Daniel grinned at her like he might have known that all along and she felt herself grin back.

This was fun and Emma was a genius for setting up the evening like this.

Kate made a promise to herself that she and Daniel would introduce date night once a week, regardless of how busy both their schedules were.

Everything was going to be fine if she just allowed herself to be in the moment with him and stop worrying. It really had been way too long since they'd kicked back and enjoyed each other's company. She wasn't about to spoil it with deep and meaningful questions that once asked, couldn't be taken back.

Daniel picked up the second question. 'Name all thirty-six reindeers.'

'Call yourself an accountant, there were only eight. Or maybe nine if you count Rudolph, but he was a bit of a late entry because he only appeared in the twentieth century.'

Daniel leaned forward and stared into her eyes. 'Given that Melody is the one in your family with the voracious reading habit, I know you haven't swallowed a Christmas lexicon. There's only one other possible explanation ... You're secretly Mrs Claus.'

'You can find out when you unwrap me, later,' she replied with a coy smile.

He grinned. 'Yes! All my Christmases have come at once!' Signalling to Emma to bring them both another round, he asked Kate, 'So can you name them all?'

'Sure. Rudolph.' To play for time she took the last sip of her cocktail.

'Time's running out,' Daniel laughed indicating the egg-timer.

'Rudolph,' she said.

'You already said that one.'

'Okay, you want a name?'

'I want all eight/nine.'

Kate smiled and leaned forward so that Daniel's attention was drawn to her neckline. 'Rudolph, Donner, Kebab, Blitzen, Shmitzen, Dobby, Bobbly, Twilight Sparkle, and Pikachu.'

Daniel threw back his head and laughed. 'Erm, I'm pretty sure Pikachu was not a reindeer.'

'So I got one wrong? Do I have to do a forfeit?'

'Maybe later.'

'I'm going to hold you to that.'

Reaching forward, Daniel took hold of her hand and linked their fingers together. 'This is really great, isn't it? Want to do it again next week?'

You see, she thought. They were so on the same page. The little devil on her shoulder whispered in her ear that if they were on the same page as this, then maybe ... To cut off any more whispering, she said, 'What? Harden our Christmas trivia skills and take on the pub quiz teams of the world?'

'You make it sound so romantic,' he said, 'so yes! And as well as that, do you want to do this again next week, as in, you and me, no work talk, just date talk?'

Her fingers tightened around his. 'How about we do this all the weeks?'

'You had me at "Fork",' he said, his voice curling around her insides.

'If Emma hadn't gone to so much trouble, I'd have been asking you to get your coat because you'd pulled,' Kate said.

'And even though I usually play coy on a first date,' Daniel grinned, 'I might have got my coat and followed you all the way home.'

Home.

Together...

It had such a comforting sound to it.

But since when had comfort become the new adventure?

She glanced at the man sitting opposite her and had her answer.

Kate put her hand under the table and pressed it down hard on top of her knee to stop her foot from tapping away and the action helped strengthen her resolve.

She didn't ever want him to think she was rushing life – rushing him and what they had now.

'So how long do you think we have to stay for?' she asked.

'I think we have to stay until the last of the staff depart.'

Kate pouted. 'It's so hard being the responsible one.'

Daniel winced. 'Hard is not the right word to be using right now.'

'Oops. Let's cool this down then and go back to playing by the rules.' Reaching out she picked up the next card. 'Favourite place to spend Christmas?'

'That's easy. Anywhere with you.'

Kate's heart got too big for her chest. 'How do you know? We haven't spent a Christmas together, yet?'

'Don't you feel it?' he asked, his blue eyes piercing hers. 'Don't you feel what we're building here?'

Slowly, she nodded her head.

'You know I'm not talking just about this place, right?'

Slowly, she nodded again.

Maybe the shock of Bea's death – the shock of losing half her identity had finally passed. Juliet had allowed her a way of finding her way back to Bea, but it was Daniel who had led her to find herself.

She didn't need to know how he was going to respond to asking him to move in together.

She already knew the answer in her heart.

Ever since she'd come back to Whispers Wood, she'd been

trying very hard not to depend on Bea sending her signs of what to do and she thought that she'd found a better balance. She was learning to find her own way and make her own decisions. Daniel showed her that she could be that brave every day.

So she would ask him to move in with her.

But not here in The Clock House.

She'd ask him on Christmas Day.

In the place they'd first started sharing secrets all those months ago.

Over the garden wall between Mistletoe Cottage and Myrtle Cottage.

Chapter 21

Bar Hygge, Bah Humbug!

Jake

Jake's punishment for arriving twenty minutes late to the soft-opening of Cocktails & Chai, in his opinion, *in no way* matched his crime. Although, rest assured, he thought, being forced to sit opposite Gloria Pavey on a tiny table for two, with a bloody scented Christmas candle between them and an egg-timer – and, no, he absolutely did not get what the egg-timer was for, was going to be nothing compared to the punishment he was going to mete out to Little Miss Match-Making Mixologist.

'*I'm doing a small soft-opening and you're invited*', she'd said, all easy-peasy, informal, he remembered, unravelling his scarf and hanging it over the back of the chair she'd frog-marched him to before offering a full smile and retreating to the relative safety of the bar.

'*It's for your friends,*' she'd said, all plaintive.

'*Please, Jake,*' she'd begged, all husky.

Duped.

That was the word that came to mind.

Not for the first bloody time, either, was it, he thought, as memories of Alice flashed through his head. He reached for his bottle of beer wishing he'd asked for a Boilermaker, because getting drunk seemed like the only sensible answer to the way his evening was unfolding.

'What's your favourite part of the lead up to Christmas?' Gloria asked him.

'What?'

'Oh, hang-on, I'm supposed to turn over the egg-timer.'

Jake watched mystified as her hand, with so many rings on, he wondered if it was a fashion statement or improvised knuckle-duster, reached out to flip over the egg-timer.

'I ask you these questions,' she explained, 'and you have to answer before the time runs out. It's like speed-dating only you stay with the same person. Quite a clever idea, right?'

'Not really.' Was there a man in the world who wanted to perform to an egg-timer?

When it became clear he wasn't into playing the game, Gloria elected to answer the question herself. 'My favourite part in the lead up to Christmas is buying gifts for Persephone's stocking and then working out new places I can hide them. As she gets older I'm having to get more and more imaginative.'

He just stared over the top of her head to where Emma was determinedly avoiding him.

'And ... you're back in the room,' Gloria said, clicking her fingers under his nose and this time Jake finally caught the note of desperation in her voice.

He looked into her eyes and saw that she was busy

pretending not to notice how quickly they'd become the centre of attention in the room.

This wasn't her fault he tried reminding himself, as he eased out the trapped breath in his lungs. Not all of it, anyway.

'Sorry,' he said, feeling bad that while his gut twisted and clawed, Gloria was doing her best to follow the rules Emma had set out for her little soiree. 'You were saying about hiding Persephone's presents? I have to say, I'm amazed she still believes in Father Christmas.'

Gloria tore her attention from Kate's openly curious gaze and blinked a couple of times before bringing out the wide smile he was more familiar with. 'Of course she doesn't, Jake. But some pretence is worth keeping up, isn't it? For the sake of family peace?'

Jake kept his expression carefully blank. When it came to keeping the peace, most families kept secrets. Whether from the world or from each other, he was willing to bet Whispers Wood wasn't different to anywhere else.

Luckily Gloria seemed to sense that a Christmas quiz wasn't designed to expose them and went back to a lighter footing as she added, 'Sometimes it gets to Christmas Eve and I can't remember all my hiding places. I've had to start writing them down. Although as a side note I wouldn't recommend hiding chocolate money in the airing cupboard next to the hot water tank. The laundry smelled really nice but the melted chocolate left a dreadful mess. Also I've learned to wrap her gifts as I go now so I don't have to stay up wrapping them the night before.'

'Clever,' he offered. Looking around at the other tables he

saw Sheila and Big Kev, deep in conversation. Kate and Daniel laughing over their drinks. Juliet and Oscar gazing into each other's eyes. The beauty therapists Kate had hired had pushed their table together with the two hair stylists Juliet had hired and looked to be having a whale of a time asking each other questions while enjoying a bottle of wine.

'Of course this year is the first year that Persephone is spending Christmas Day with her father.'

Jake would have had to be a complete bastard not to hear the naked emotion in Gloria's statement. 'That's got to be tough,' he paused, and then had to ask, 'You're not going to be on your own for the day, are you?' The thought of the trouble she could get herself into if she spent Christmas on her own, feeling all wronged and maligned, sat uneasily in his chest.

'Are you worried about me, Jakey?'

'Absolutely not.' Christ, could this evening be any more awkward? He couldn't wait to think about all the different ways he was going to get Hollywood back for this. 'What I mean is, you're a strong woman, Gloria.' He looked her squarely in the eyes. 'I can't imagine you wanting Persephone to worry about you being on your own.'

To his relief she nodded sensibly. 'You're right. There are some things a child should never have to worry about. No need for you to worry either, I'm not going to be alone, I'm actually spending the day with her grandparents.'

'Good. Good.'

'Worry isn't usually the first emotion I evoke in people. Well, not worry for my safety, anyway,' she added with a small smile, 'so, thank you. And I can see I've made you uncomfort-able again, so let's move right along ... What *is* your favourite part of the lead up to Christmas?'

'Oh-oh, it looks as if time's run out,' he said, staring at the egg-timer.

'Next question then,' Gloria said, picking the next one off the pile and turning it over. 'And this time you have to answer. Ready?'

No, he thought. 'Yes,' he nodded grimly.

Gloria laughed. 'You don't have to look so tortured. Right, here we go: Who was the last person you kissed under the mistletoe?'

'Give me that,' he said grabbing the card to look at it. 'Good grief, is every Christmas about bloody questions?'

'Don't you mean, is every bloody question about Christmas?'

'This is insane.'

'Not into Christmas themed party games, then,' Gloria tsked.

'Not into *any* game-playing,' he bit out.

She raised her eyebrows. 'Nobody's forcing you to sit here, Jake.'

Of course they were.

One was called Hollywood and one was called Pride and he was damned if he was going to give either the satisfaction of walking out.

Jake swung his gaze to the bar area and just managed to catch Emma looking back at him before she looked guiltily away.

Forcing himself to sit back in his seat, he picked up the

beer he'd ordered and drank it straight down. 'You're right. I'm sorry, Gloria. Look, how about I pop to the bar and get us another drink. I promise by the time I come back I'll have sent Scrooge home and popped my civil hat on.'

'But it's so hot in here.' Her gaze narrowed but he detected a softening around the edges of her mouth. 'Do you think you can wear it for the duration?'

'I promise to try.' As he got up he hesitated and looking down at her, quietly said, 'As long as you realise this – you and me – what I'm trying to say is that nothing's going to happen, okay?'

A delighted trickle of laughter fell out of Gloria's mouth, and Jake was very aware that several people turned to look in their direction.

Putting out a hand and resting it on his forearm, she looked up at him and said just as quietly, 'Oh, Jake, don't worry so much. As if you'd be interested in me.'

He felt bad as he stared down at her hand with all the rings glinting in the light. Hands that probably never enjoyed driving into the earth. 'It's not that you're—'

'God. I know,' she said with a trace of her old self-confidence. 'It might have taken me this last year to realise Bob didn't leave me because I'm not good enough – that he left because I'm not a man, but I *do* finally realise it. When Emma asked me to be your date for the evening—'

'Emma asked you specifically to be my date?' he asked, wanting to make sure he got his facts exactly right before he gave Hollywood a piece of his mind. Most probably everyone else got sucked in by those gorgeous eyes of hers and promptly forgot what they'd been going to say. Well, not him.

'Yes, why else do you think I'm here?' Gloria purred. 'Anyway, she didn't exactly have to beg me. I saw it as a golden opportunity to persuade you to do the charity calendar. I've already roped-in Daniel and Oscar for June and July.'

'Gloria,' he leaned down to whisper in her ear, 'are you telling porkies?'

Her nose wrinkled in delight and he thought that when she wasn't acting like she was perpetually stepping in dog-poo, she could be quite fun.

'Okay, I might be. But they'll definitely do it when I tell them you're in,' she said.

'But I'm not in – I'm decidedly out.' He winced as she paled a little. 'Sorry, poor choice of words. But I'm not doing that calendar, Gloria.'

She pouted and he threw back his head and laughed, catching Emma looking at him like an angry librarian as he brought his head back up.

'So then, we understand each other?' he checked.

Gloria nodded. 'Of course. It's as clear as day that your heart is fixed on someone else, anyway.'

He couldn't help it. His gaze shot straight to the bar again, his heart thundering against his chest wall. What the hell did Gloria mean it was as clear as day?

Once again she laid a hand on his arm. 'Everyone knows you're not over Alice.'

'Alice?' Shock silenced him. Of course he was over Alice. Alice had humiliated him in front of his family, his friends, everyone in Whispers Wood. Alice had made it so that he thought he might never enjoy Christmas again. Is that why people thought he wanted to be out of the village this Christmas? Because he had a broken heart? A broken heart that only a naïve newcomer would think could be fixed as easily as putting someone single in front of him?

He looked around the room and saw that Emma was now at Oscar and Juliet's table, chatting animatedly with them. Annoyance that she'd forced him to sit here with Gloria, making it look to everyone like she knew exactly what he needed, fizzed in his veins.

He cleared his throat and looked down at Gloria. 'Right. Alice. Yes. I'm still—' he stopped, unable to force himself to tell the lie. 'So, what'll you have to drink?'

'Oh, surprise me.'

Two hours later, Jake sat at the bar nursing the last of his third tumbler of JD and coke. He'd swapped to the hard stuff so that he could go back to the table and stomach answering questions about Christmas. Somehow he'd managed to admit that the last person he'd kissed under the mistletoe had, of course, been Alice, while hoping to God the admission didn't reinforce to Gloria that he was indeed a man in need of fixing.

Kissing had never been all he and Alice had done under the mistletoe. But then they'd never needed mistletoe to stoke the fire. They'd never needed any excuse. Their passion had, ironically, been the most real thing about their relationship and had been the main reason he'd been so sure they were going to work.

He frowned down into his glass, wishing away the memory

of the last time he'd seen her.

'Thank you so much for coming, guys,' Emma was saying at the door. 'Don't forget about our neighbours and be sure to leave as quietly as you can.'

To be fair to Gloria, she only let Emma serve him after he'd placed his car-keys in her hand. As soon as the clock had struck eleven she'd offered a lift to anyone who needed one. He'd declined, telling her he wanted the fresh air and the walk and now the only guests left in the bar were Big Kev and Sheila who were busy in deep conversation with Kate and Daniel.

As if aware that as soon as they left, she'd be left alone with Jake, Emma didn't look in any hurry to move them along.

If she thought he wasn't comfortable waiting to talk to her, or that he'd get bored and leave, she was wrong.

You didn't work with the seasons and not learn how to be patient.

She'd flustered so delightfully earlier when he'd walked up to the bar to order another round of drinks for himself and Gloria. He'd asked for a JD and coke and when she'd asked what Gloria might like, he'd leaned across the bar, dropped his voice a deliberate octave and said what he really wanted to give her was a Screaming Christmas Day Orgasm. She'd stared at him for a full twelve seconds before carefully, thoughtfully, professionally, composing herself to say, 'Of course, sir. That particular cocktail isn't on the menu but if that's what you think your date would like, I'll whip one up especially.'

With the way she'd emphasised the word 'date' and the ease

with which she'd been able to hide behind her hostess role, he'd quickly decided he hadn't got her hot and bothered enough to make up for her conning him into spending an evening centred around his least favourite subject.

Yes, he'd ended up having an okay evening with Gloria but that so wasn't the point. The point was that Hollywood shouldn't go meddling in affairs that didn't concern her. It was like she'd been pulled aside by someone in his family and told how to annoy him most.

As she passed him to reach for a cloth, he put out his hand to stop her.

She stared at his hand on her arm and then, sucking in a breath, lifted her gaze to his and pasted on her hostess smile. 'Where did Gloria go?'

'Why do you care?' he shot back, willing her to tell him why she'd thought a little meddlesome matchmaking something he might require.

'I planned this event. I wanted to make sure I said goodbye to everyone and—'

'Personally thank them for helping you out?' he finished for her.

'Exactly.'

'Well, she's gone and left me all alone.'

Emma frowned. 'Oh. I'm sorry.'

'I guess your matchmaking didn't quite work out the way you thought it would.'

He witnessed the spark of what he thought was disappointment flare in her eyes and his hand tightened against her arm. What was that saying about keep your friends close and your enemies closer?

Except he got a strange taste in his mouth when he thought of Emma as the enemy.

He swallowed because, of course, he'd really prefer no taste of her at all.

Well, hardly any, at any rate, he told himself, glad there wasn't a sprig of mistletoe in sight and deliberately wiping over any thoughts of tasting Emma with the excuse that he didn't have time to treat her as friend *or* enemy.

'So the two of you didn't hit it off?' Emma asked softly.

'People aren't pawns, Emma. Whispers Wood isn't your stage and this isn't a play where you can direct people to react in the manner you want them to.'

He noted she at least had the grace to look embarrassed.

'I—'

'Gloria is in a vulnerable place at the moment, and to make her even half-start to believe that I, in the place I am at the moment, would be a great person to set her up with, was really thoughtless and totally unhelpful.'

Emma's chin came up at that. 'Gloria's been dating for the past few months.'

Jake snorted. Gloria hadn't been dating so much as trying to get past the fallout of Bob leaving her for Bobby as publicly and as outrageously as she could.

'I've got to know her,' Emma continued defending, 'and I know she's in the right frame of mind to start getting serious about meeting someone.'

'Is that right? And what makes you so sure that I am?'

She went bright red and he found himself caught between

really wanting to know how she thought he was ready to date when the rest of Whispers Wood seemed to think his heart was still broken or frozen or whatever the hell it was they thought when they gave him those pitying looks, and wanting to know why she looked less able to defend her thinking that he was in any way the right person to put together with Gloria.

'I—you—' she stuttered.

'You—me—what?'

She shook her head, well and truly flustered.

'Because, hell, Hollywood, if you're that hell-bent on me getting a date, then come out with me one night next week.'

Wait – *what* had he just said?

No way he could have just asked Hollywood out on a date?

He didn't know who was more shocked.

'Excuse me?' She snatched her arm out from his grip, and looked at him like he was mad and he thought that okay, maybe out of the two of them it was her who was more shocked.

Which actually offended him a little. 'Nope. I won't excuse you. Getting me here on false pretences.'

'Yet you're asking me out? On a date? That's what you just did? You asked me out?'

'That's right.' When she just continued to stare at him as if he was speaking in Klingon, he leaned forward into her personal space and said, 'I'm one of those men who don't actually need the help of a matchmaker or a dating app to function.'

That had her eyes narrowing a fraction and he couldn't

deny the spark that shot through him. 'What's the matter?' he asked. 'Don't you know the proper etiquette when there's no swipe-right function?'

'Ha. How do you know I'd swipe right?'

He just grinned back at her and waited.

If possible she went an even deeper shade of red, except now it might be from anger and he found he didn't mind that so very much because it brought out the pretty flecks of silver in her eyes.

'So how about it, Hollywood? Or when it comes to dating are you all mouth and no trou—oops, sorry, what's the American? Oh, that's right ... are you all mouth and no panties when it comes to dating?'

'P-pants,' she stuttered. 'The American for trousers is "pants". And of course I wear panties. *Will* be wearing panties,' she muttered. 'Which will be staying on,' she stated, no sign of a stutter now. 'For our date.'

He'd only meant to fluster her and get his point across that it wasn't nice to be manipulated into a date but now she was accepting?

As she breathed out, he felt the gentle waft of air across his face, and couldn't help but feel his body tighten as she leaned forward so that they were practically nose-to-nose.

Dimly, he could feel his mind working overtime, trying to get him to a point where he could resist being entranced by the way she demurely lowered her lashes. Resist falling for the sparks when she lifted those lashes so that she was staring back up at him, her voice soft as the first summer rain, when she said, 'As you're so ... experienced, I'll leave it to you to organise what we do and where we go.'

Suddenly she was leaning back, grabbing his now empty glass from him and turning to stack it with the other empties. When she looked back over her shoulder there was no trace of the smouldering she-devil, only the friendly, warm smile of a woman with not a care in the world.

Oh she was good.

She was really good.

And he was possibly never touching a drop of alcohol again.

Chapter 22

The Bauble's in Your Court

Kate

'*Are you kidding me?*' Kate clung to the ladder, dropping a handful of lametta so that it glooped instead of cascaded onto the top branches of the Christmas tree she and Juliet were decorating.

If anyone had asked her she'd have said lametta went out with sherry and charades but Juliet said she wanted The Clock House Christmas trees to look like they were positively dripping in vintage Victoriana jewels. And kudos to Juliet because somehow the silver strands went perfectly with the baubles in shimmering rose copper, frosted pale green and glittery white. Strands of pearls and crystal droplets helped the light bounce from decoration to decoration but Kate's absolute favourites were the antique-jewelled bees, complete with tiny gossamer wings that Juliet had found to represent Bea's bees behind The Clock House moon-gate.

Decorating The Clock House for the grand opening was a lot of work when tasked with hanging each strand of lametta to hang *just so*. Thank goodness Juliet had come up with a

214

handy spreadsheet to ensure her vision could be achieved in the only day they had available before they got busy organising their stand for the tree-lighting ceremony. But even with Juliet's military precision and two trees still to go, she'd been in a really great mood until about thirty seconds ago.

Juliet winced. 'You promised you wouldn't shout.'

'That was before Emma used you to try and kill me.'

'I really don't think that was her intention.'

Kate snatched two of the mini baubles off the top branches of the tree, shoved them into her mouth and giving it her best Don Corleone, said, 'And that she would send you to do the deed.'

'I think you should think about it,' Juliet said, looking up at her. 'And, eew, take those out of your mouth and put them back *exactly* where I told you to.'

Reluctantly, Kate removed the baubles from her cheeks. She was just going to have to be the Don without the chipmunk face. 'And do you want me to have this think while I'm up here placing each bauble that you hand me *just so* because what if I forget to concentrate on placing each decoration on the *exact* branch and facing the *exact* angle that you direct me to?'

'Okay, so trimming the tree makes me a little Martha Stewart. You'll thank me when everyone's saying how good it looks.'

'Are you even going to let Melody near the tree at the barn?'

'Of course. She's old enough to decorate it properly.'

'Because you'll be giving her a spreadsheet to follow too? What on earth are you going to do when you have all your babies and they get old enough to want to see their toilet-roll-Santas on the tree?'

Juliet smiled a smile that suggested to Kate she'd thought about this. 'Easy. I'll have two trees. One they can go to town on, and one I can.'

'Something tells me your babies are coming out with glue-gun attachments anyway!'

Kate thought that once Juliet had a baby she probably wouldn't care how the tree was decorated and again noticed how tired she looked. All Juliet's gorgeous red hair came with a pale complexion but even from all the way up the ladder Kate could see there was now a new translucent quality to her skin.

'Hun, are you sure you're not coming down with something?' she asked, trying not to panic because she so didn't have a plan for if they all got ill right before they opened.

'Positive,' Juliet replied. 'I'm taking every vitamin known to man and I have zero time to be ill.'

After they'd finished decorating today, Kate was going to insist on some pampering as a thank you and work out a way of bringing the conversation around to how Juliet needed to start delegating once they were open.

Spotting movement out of the corner of her eyes, she whipped her head around to see Emma sneaking quietly out of the kitchen area behind the bar. 'Emma Danes, I don't know what you paid for that invisibility cloak but you were fleeced. We can both see you. Come here and explain yourself.'

Emma, looking guilty, sidled up to Juliet. 'You asked her then?'

'Oh my God,' Juliet exclaimed, looking up to where Kate was staring down at the both of them. 'You can't tell by the way she's frothing at the mouth?'

Emma put a hand to the side of her mouth and mock whispered, 'I'm too short to see all the way up there.'

'Well,' Kate informed her, 'let the dribble that's about to land on your shoulder be clue number one.'

Emma reached out to catch a few of the strands of lametta floating down and held them up for Kate to reposition. 'So it's a flat-out "no" then?' she asked, the corners of her mouth turning down.

'Yes,' Kate said, adding an emphatic nod, and tightening her grip on the ladder.

Emma immediately turned her frown upside down. 'It's a yes?'

'No it is not a "yes", oh for— one of you hang on to the ladder, I'm coming back down.'

At the bottom of the steps she popped her hands on her hips and said, 'I want you to explain, in words of one syllable, and possibly via the medium of mime too, why on earth you think I'd agree to such a crazy idea?'

Emma shuffled her feet and mumbled, 'You asked me to hire someone.'

'Someone,' Kate confirmed. 'Not the Wicked Witch of Whispers Wood.'

Emma pouted. 'She just put her name as Gloria on the application form.'

'You gave her an application form, already?' Juliet gasped. 'I thought you were just mooting the idea.' She turned to Kate,

217

a rising note of panic in her voice. 'We have to interview her, for real?'

Emma reached out and poked one of the beautiful antique bee decorations dangling from the nearest branch so that it swung back and forth. 'Come on, guys. Everyone deserves the chance to fly.'

'Hey,' Kate tapped the ladder behind her, 'I've already been defying gravity today. And how is it possible that you've turned into Glinda, the Good Witch of the South? If you arrived here on a bubble this morning, I'm afraid I'm going to have to burst it. Because there's just no way...'

'But why not?' Emma asked.

'Why not?' Kate repeated, shaking her head in wonder. 'Well for a start, I think there's an actual law that requires staff to be human.'

'I think it's only on *S.H.I.E.L.D.* that they're funny about that. Gloria's—'

'Also,' she added, 'staff need to be the right fit and, honestly, how could you possibly think that Gloria would fall into that category?'

Emma straightened as if that extra half an inch would help her stand her ground. 'You gave me a chance—'

'Don't you dare say when no one else would,' Kate shot straight back, hating hearing Emma's voice change from confident to small and hesitant. That her friend could feel she was second-best or some sort of consolation hire when she hadn't taken a step backwards since the moment she'd walked in and made them all feel as if working hard at The Clock House was going to be a pleasure, not a chore, wasn't a nice feeling at all.

The days were hectic in the countdown to opening, but how could she excuse missing Emma feeling so raw still after not getting that part she'd so badly wanted? 'Ems, if you hadn't come here, you *would* have got back up on that horse and landed a role you were perfect for and you would have been the studio's first choice – their only choice.'

If she had her way, Emma would happily stay at The Clock House running Cocktails & Chai, but she had to place the ball firmly in Emma's court.

Her friend had to choose. *Really* choose what she wanted because Kate didn't want her to feel trapped here. That wasn't what coming here was supposed to have been about. 'It's okay to tell me you're missing your old life, you know. I can find a way to work things out here, if you need to go back?'

Emma swallowed. 'Do you want me to go back?'

Kate heard the underlying uncertainty. Her friend never faltered when it came to enthusiasm and positivity and Kate realised it was the highest form of people-pleasing. She didn't want Emma to stay out of gratitude. She wanted her to stay because she felt she belonged.

She'd seemed so happy and confident in her decision to come here but now all Kate could think was how Emma had flown thousands of miles leaving behind her passion and everyone she was close to.

'Do you want to go back?' she forced herself to counter.

Emma shook her head emphatically and, relieved, Kate let out the breath she'd been holding. 'Good. Because the minute you mentioned you were thinking of giving acting up, you became my top choice to run Cocktails & Chai. And it's more than being about you having handy work experience. It's about this feeling I have that you're going to be exceptional at it.'

Emma swallowed and Kate saw her eyes fill with tears. 'Thank you. You have no idea how much I needed to hear that. And, maybe because of that,' she said, clearing her throat and pulling herself up tall again, 'I'm going to push my luck and tell you that I really think Gloria might be an asset to the team. We're all here because we wanted to make a change in our life. A change for the better right?'

Juliet aimed a soft smile at Kate. 'Why do I feel as if we've been hoist with our own postcards?'

Kate thought about the postcards hanging up at reception and heard her resolve let out a whimper as Emma's expression took on a pleading quality.

'I think Gloria's at that stage where she's looking to make a change too,' Emma said. 'At least let me interview her. I've interviewed heaps of candidates before.'

Kate felt one of her eyebrows arch up.

'A few. I've interviewed a few,' Emma said, with a winning grin.

Kate's eyebrow lifted higher. In none of her plans for The Clock House had Gloria Pavey ever featured.

'Okay I've only ever carried out one interview,' Emma confessed. 'But that went really well and she got the job.'

Kate folded her arms and thought that now would be a really, really good time for Bea to give her a sign or whisper in her ear what she should do.

Silence.

Great.

Never around to answer the really tough questions.

'But *why* would Gloria want to work here?' Juliet murmured.

Emma thought for a moment and said, 'She's lonely, I think.'

'We can't give someone a job because they're lonely,' Kate automatically replied, and then swallowed because wasn't that partly why they'd given her mum the baking for The Clock House?

She looked at Emma. Was this why she'd only taken one of her days off? Maybe it was less about having too much to do and more about not wanting to spend the time alone.

The last thing Kate wanted was Emma thinking that if she just kept busy the holes and wounds inside her would automatically fill up. She knew that didn't work because she'd spent years simply going through the motions after Bea had died. It hadn't been living and she didn't want that for anyone. Even Gloria, she admitted quietly to herself.

'Okay,' Kate sighed. 'She can have a trial period. *If*—'

Emma brought her hands together in a clap of glee and broke into a little victory dance.

'—*If* she comes in first for a chat. Tell her she's going to have to eat a serious amount of crow.'

Emma stopped mid-dance. 'How serious is a serious amount?'

'Enough for me to be satisfied our customers aren't going to have to worry they're being served afternoon tea by the woman who accidentally-on-purpose insulted them in the corner shop only hours before.'

'Okay.'

'I mean it,' Kate said putting on her serious boss face. 'I'm not interested in seeing her come through those doors for the wrong reasons.'

'That's fair. That's more than fair. She's trying really hard to put her behaviour behind her. You'll see. Even Eeyore—'

Kate's antenna shot up. 'Eeyore?'

Emma grabbed hold of a couple of bee decorations and scrambled up the ladder as if heading for higher ground. 'I mean, Jake – even Jake seemed to get on well with her.'

'I knew it! You feel bad your matchmaking didn't work and guilty because Jake rumbled your little plan.'

Emma sighed with bemusement. 'Gloria doesn't seem upset at all that Jake isn't interested. But, yes, okay, Jake was a little,' she stopped, dragged in a breath, 'upset at my match-making. I have to go on a date with him as punishment.'

Kate looked from Emma to the chandelier shining brightly from the centre of the ceiling, the glass droplets seeming to wink at her. She'd loved the chandelier since she'd been a little girl and seen it in glamorous black and white photos from the 1920s that Old Man Isaac used to display in the foyer.

When Daniel and Oscar had brought it down from the attic and re-fitted it in this room for the summer village fete it had felt to Kate as if it was hanging once again in its rightful home. But she hadn't really given much thought to the folk-lore surrounding it being back up at The Clock House again until she'd seen Jake Knightley standing under it with Emma, the day he'd come to talk about his designs for the courtyard.

With a huge grin she turned back to Emma and said, 'I don't think you're going to find your date a punishment, and if you're hoping Jake will, I think you're wrong on that score too.'

'Speak of the devil,' Juliet said, looking out the window.

'Oh no,' Emma moaned, running a self-conscious hand over her hair. 'What's he doing here?'

Seconds later they all heard the main doors open and a man's footsteps approach.

'Jake,' Kate announced, swallowing her grin and throwing Emma an innocent look, 'fancy seeing you here?'

'What do you mean?' Jake asked, somewhat grumpily as his gaze took in the large Christmas tree taking up most of the window, 'you phoned me and asked if I could bring all my lights.'

'Oh, yes, I remember now,' Kate said and tried not to react to Juliet's 'please tell me you're not doing what I think you're doing' face as she walked over to him. 'Here, let me take those for you.'

She went to take the boxes but he didn't release them and she grinned in delight as she watched his gaze seem to get stuck on Emma.

'See something you like?' she whispered to him.

'What?' Tearing his gaze from Emma, he shook his head a little, clung onto the boxes, and said, 'I take it you wanted these lights for the outside of the building?'

'Mmmn, Daniel and Oscar have done the front. These will be great for the courtyard.'

'I'll go and give them a hand.'

'Thanks.' When he stayed where he was, she leaned forward and added, 'You'll probably want to move in order to do that.'

'Right, um,' he slid his gaze to Emma again and said, 'While I was here, I thought I'd have a quick word with Emma.'

'Sure,' Emma said.

'In private?' he said.

Oh, no way was he about to tell the girl who went in to bat for everyone and thought of herself last that now he was sober and had had time to think ... With her grip still on the boxes, Kate tugged until Jake was standing more underneath the chandelier and gave him a don't-even-think-about-it-mister stare.

'Juliet and I were just telling Emma how if there was one thing she didn't have to worry about, it was you,' she said.

'You were?' his gaze narrowed and if she'd been anyone other than Kate Somersby she might have felt as if she was wading into dangerous waters.

'No you weren't,' Emma said glaring down at Kate.

'You weren't?' Jake asked again.

'We were about to, weren't we Juliet?'

Juliet's eyes said 'why am I being dragged into this?', but her voice said, 'Oh, definitely.'

'We wanted to reassure her you weren't one of those guys who reneges or,' Kate paused, '*chickens out* on stuff.'

Jake stared back at her like he was only a couple of heart-beats away from telling her exactly what she could do with her meddling.

Kate's gaze didn't waver.

Juliet always understood exactly what she was saying without having to actually say it.

Men!

So incredibly dense.

Jake's gaze filled with a dangerous glint. 'Did you just say I was incredibly—'

Kate had no choice and unleashed her best don't-be-a-dick stare on him and finally must have got through because his jaw slammed shut and she could see the ticking muscle there.

Tough.

To send her point sailing home she said, 'Yes. I mean, we all know it's been a while. Of course the first person you asked out wouldn't be out of pity or anger or alcohol.'

With a deep breath in, he moved slightly so that Kate was out of his immediate sight line. 'Emma, are you free on Thursday?'

'Thursday?' she parroted.

'I thought I'd cook dinner for you.'

'Dinner?'

'You do eat, right?'

'Do you cook?'

'I can handle myself in the kitchen.'

'Great.'

He turned to look at Kate with a 'happy now?' lift of his eyebrows and when Kate made a 'keep going' motion with her hand, he rolled his eyes and turned back to Emma. 'Come early so that I can give you that tour of the gardens while it's still light.'

'About 3-ish?'

'It's a ... date.'

'Fabulous,' Kate said, grabbing the boxes from him. 'Give the man a gold star—oh, wait, I actually have one of those, can you grab it from the crate of decorations and pass it to Emma for the top of the tree? Juliet and I will see how they're getting on in the courtyard.'

A couple of hours later, everyone stood in the courtyard. Technically the big switch on would happen on the tree-lighting night, but they had to test their lights worked and it seemed extra special with only her and Daniel, Juliet, Oscar, Emma and Jake.

As the lights flicked back off and their spontaneous burst of applause died down, Kate suddenly grinned and breathed out a happy, 'Oh.'

'What?' Daniel asked.

Kate inhaled. 'You smell that?' she said, looking up to the sky.

'Smell what?' Emma asked.

'Breathe in,' Kate told everyone.

'I don't smell anything,' Oscar said.

Kate simply looked up at the sky.

Jake snorted. 'You're not one of those weirdos who thinks they can smell snow coming, are you?'

'Just call me Lorelai,' Kate said.

'Never heard of her,' Jake commented and at Juliet's, Emma's and Kate's collective gasp of outrage added, 'What? Is she some famous meteorologist?'

'Lorelai Gilmore?' Emma giggled. 'Yeah, of sorts.'

'From where?' Jake asked suspiciously.

'Hartford.'

Daniel laughed. 'She's not even a weather presenter. She's

an innkeeper.'

'Some friend of your mother's then?' Jake asked Kate.

'She's not even real,' Daniel informed him.

Emma looked like he'd just sworn like a trooper. 'Lorelai Gilmore is so real.'

'Mark my words,' Kate said, looking at Jake and Emma. 'Something special is coming.'

'Whatever it is, it isn't snow,' Jake said under his breath.

Kate laughed.

She had a feeling Jake wasn't about to know what hit him.

Chapter 23

Nightly Haul

Emma

Emma wasn't in the least bit excited or nervous and any suggestion she was, would earn her commentators, in this case a pair of cheeping robins keeping pace with her like they'd been despatched to escort her to her destination, a very stern scowl indeed.

As she walked up the long sweeping drive to Knightley Hall, she wrapped her coat tightly around her and thought about how when she got back home later she was going to have to put away all the clothes lying on her bed because in disturbingly accurate pre-date behaviour – even though this wasn't a date – she'd taken out all the clothes she'd brought with her and sighed over and discarded nearly every option. Though it was a wonder her brain had been functioning enough to evaluate each option, she'd been shivering so much. Note to self: next time figure out what to wear *before* she got in the shower.

'Not that there's going to be a next time,' she assured the robins as they flitted in and out of the holly hedge to her left.

Talk about her plan to fix up Jake and Gloria backfiring. She'd been so sure they'd get on. Positive he'd enjoy Gloria's acerbic wit, what with his being the same, albeit on a grumpier level.

'Okay,' she muttered when one of the robins did a *Top Gun* flyby past her nose. 'I admit it. The whole point of arranging it so that Jake was off limits was so that I'd think about him less.'

The other robin flew past her to settle in the hedge opposite. 'I know,' she sighed. 'So far, that's not really working out for me.'

Maybe she should have called Juliet and asked her what to wear? She had vintage-chic down perfectly. Then she'd thought about asking Kate but reasoned that she wasn't sure she could pull off the daisy dukes and Doc Martens look.

Not that she should be making a special effort.

'Because this isn't a date,' the robins seemed to be singing at her before breaking out into bird-cheep laughter, their wings helpfully stopping their sides from splitting.

Truthfully she didn't know *what* this was.

She only knew what it wasn't.

And it wasn't Jake wanting to spend time with her because he liked her.

He'd asked her out because he'd been angry with her, his pride dented. And he'd looked forward to the experience so much he'd then tried to wriggle out of it.

Good thing she'd gone for her best pair of midnight-blue skinny jeans and black wrap-around top with the sequins that flirted along the edge, then.

Completely casual.

Especially when matched with her black suede over-the-knee high-heeled boots.

Totally practical for the English winter, she decided, clacking up the lane.

Shoving her scarf higher over her mouth she took a last look around for her compadres and spotted them in one of the topiary spirals. With a wink at them, she turned, blew out a breath and rang the bell of Knightley Hall.

When Jake opened the door, the first thing she registered was that he hadn't shaved and that his stubble, once again, made her think: Vikings and Pirates and Lumberjacks, *oh my*.

He moved to casually lean against the door-frame, looking every inch the A-list celebrity in a commercial for aftershave, and her gaze dropped to take in the long-sleeved waffle-textured top in dove-grey that perfectly displayed an impressive shoulder line and chest, before her gaze wandered lower to the fit of his dark jeans.

She knew how long it took stylists to get actors perfecting the casual, sexily rumpled, yet utterly-in-control look. So she could get a little annoyed it had probably only taken him ten minutes of jumping in and out of the shower, before shucking into a pair of perfectly fitting jeans and top.

'You're here,' he said.

'You seem disappointed,' she replied. 'Thought I'd chicken out?'

'And miss getting to see around Knightley Hall? Unlikely.'

So he thought the only reason she was here was because she was nosy? It rankled.

Trying to see past him into the hallway, she asked, 'Are you going to invite me in, then?'

He waited a heartbeat and then pushed the door open wider and stood to the side so that she could pass.

The entrance was stunning.

What she could see of it in the dim light.

All dark wood panelling on the walls and green and white encaustic tiles laid in a geometric pattern on the floor.

And then there was the grand staircase, its apple-green carpet held in place by brass stair rods, inviting her upwards as if it was a yellow brick path to adventure.

She was staring up at the galleried landing, imagining Jake as a boy, pushing toy soldiers through the banisters and watching them parachute down to the ground below when the adult version of him stepped up behind her and said, 'Welcome to my humble abode.'

She turned and found him staring at her like he was waiting for her to not be able to see past the threadbare carpet, or the bare yellow light bulbs, or the draft whispering over her face.

'It's wonderful,' she said.

When he didn't answer, but moved his gaze slowly over her, she fought the need to fill the space between them with awkward conversation and tried instead a smile he could read as warm and relaxed instead of excited and nervous.

Pulling off her gloves and shoving them in her pockets, she moved her hands up to the large buttons on her coat, hoping he didn't see the fine tremble in her fingers.

Maybe he did though because as she fumbled with the top

button she saw his hands automatically lift as if to help undress her. Her gaze shot straight to his and he checked his movement and waited for her to hand him her coat.

As he took it, she started unwinding her scarf and realising he hadn't been able to see the first smile, tried for another.

It must have worked because he stared at her mouth. And when he continued to stare and his dark eyes got darker, pulling her in and making her heart strike against her ribcage, she couldn't fight the need any longer and licked her lips.

He drew in a breath and closed the distance between them and her own breath came out shaky because ... in the name of all that was Jane Austen, *was he going to kiss her*?

At the beginning of their date, not at the end?

How very ... un-date like.

How very ... acceptable.

As he leaned his head towards hers, she felt her eyelids drift shut and for the first time in her life understood that it was her body's natural response to shutting out all other distraction so that it could savour this one pleasure as fully as possible.

But it wasn't the touch of that sensuous mouth against hers that had her sighing again, albeit this time with disappointment. It was his fingertips.

'Sorry,' he said, his voice sounding gruffly intimate, 'you have a fibre from your scarf stuck on your lip-gloss. There. Got it.'

If this was a romcom script she had no doubt she'd be reading the line: Emma realises Jake isn't about to kiss her and *dies*.

Her eyes flew open to search suspiciously for the naked-to-the-human-eye piece of fluff he appeared to be holding between thumb and forefinger and she didn't have to act to know she was completely dying of mortification as her heart raced and her fingertips clenched at her sides and her pupils kept right on dilating.

She wasn't a good enough actress to stop a one of them from highlighting to him she'd not only thought he was going to kiss her ... she'd welcomed the knowledge.

In a sudden need for movement, she yanked her scarf from her neck and held it out to him.

'All g-gone?' she stuttered, brazening it out.

'Yes,' he replied, running his gaze over her again. 'Come through to the kitchen, it's the warmest room.'

Emma looked down to what removing her large winter coat had revealed and with a little self-conscious laugh, slapped her thigh, 'I couldn't decide between Dick Whittington or cat-burglar.'

Jake's footsteps faltered briefly before he continued down the long corridor. 'No man on earth could hate those boots, but if you were thinking cat-burglar in search of a nightly haul, trust me, you won't find anything of value here.'

But then she walked into the kitchen behind him and wanted to call him out for being so wrong.

They said the kitchen was the heart of every home.

And, okay, yes, the dark grey stone tiles on the floor were hard and cold and had three non-matching rugs placed strategically in front of the sink, the Aga, and under the giant kitchen table.

Yes, the heavy oak cabinets that ran under the windows were a hideous shade of olive green and not one of them probably concealed a built in wine-fridge or a commercial-grade dishwasher.

And yes the work-surfaces weren't composite, granite, polished concrete or even oiled wood.

But with the steam fogging up the cold leaded windows and the warmth enveloping her, she felt heart and soul cocooned in simple, earthy, cosiness.

There'd probably once been a fire where the Aga was and Emma imagined that if you were all alone in here, you might sometimes see a flicker of a silhouette ... cooks of yester-year lifting giant copper kettles of water ... scullery maids scrubbing at the stone floor that she was standing on.

The stories these walls could tell.

A privilege to hear them.

'Something smells good,' she said when she could trust her voice.

'Roast turkey and all the trimmings.'

'Like Christmas dinner?'

'No. Like Thanksgiving dinner. I went online to see what was what and, we'll have to see how the pumpkin pie comes out. What would you like to drink? You can have tea or if it's not too early for you, there's a bottle of red breathing.'

'Wine would be great. Thank you. Um ... you're cooking me Thanksgiving dinner?'

'I'm attempting to. I thought you might be missing home today.'

'I don't know what to say.' Partly because her heart had

travelled up to her throat, partly because him talking about LA made her realise it had taken only a few short weeks to fall utterly in love with Whispers Wood so that she couldn't even entertain the thought of leaving. But that Jake had understood that today was Thanksgiving and that she might be feeling homesick, yeah ... more travelling-heart feelings.

'You don't have to say anything,' he said walking around the large kitchen table, to hand her a glass of red wine.

It was like she'd forgotten how to school her features. How to bank the naked emotion swimming in her eyes. And in a bid to prevent him witness the fight in her, she took the glass of wine from him and concentrated on looking around the kitchen in search of more distracting detail.

A giant vase filled with lichen-covered twigs and Chinese lanterns sat on the windowsill. Garlands of ivy swagged along the free-standing French dresser. Green and white patterned tiles the same as the ones in the hallway with thick Church candles planted on them had a scattering of rosehips and sprigs of rosemary at their base and formed a centrepiece on the table. In the corner of the room, perched at an angle on a wooden stool, a small Christmas tree, dripping with strings of mini pinecones and more rosehip.

'Jake, did you put up these Christmas decorations for me, too?'

'Absolutely not. I leave these up all year.' He grinned at her from over the rim of his glass before taking a healthy sip.

Oh my God.

This was *so* a date.

'Happy Thanksgiving, Hollywood.'

235

Absurdly touched, she felt tears spring back into her eyes and knowing he'd be embarrassed, hurriedly blinked them away. 'Happy Thanksgiving back.'

They stared at each other, the giant kitchen table between them and she thought that if she'd been standing nearer she might have done something completely stupid like fling her arms around him to thank him. Maybe even impulsively touch her lips to his.

Some of her thoughts must have showed up on her face because the air turned thick and then, suddenly, he was all movement.

Only not towards her.

Instead he was grabbing a tea-towel and chucking half of it over his shoulder like a celebrity chef and then bending to open one of the oven's doors.

She was just telling herself not to stare at his butt, or that if she absolutely had to, not so openly, when out of nowhere a white ball of fluff came scampering through the kitchen door and jumped up into her arms.

'Oh-oh, bad Bingey,' shouted a toddler, rushing in after it.

Emma burst out laughing as the dog licked her face, opening her eyes just in time to see the top of a head skirting the kitchen table and heading in the direction of the oven.

'Oh, no. Hot,' she called, shooting around the table, dog still in her arms, to stop the little boy from touching the oven.

Thankfully, Jake turned effortlessly and picked up the boy before he could touch the surface. 'Hey, buddy. What are you doing here?'

'Oh, crap,' said a woman, walking into the kitchen and

stopping abruptly as she took in the fact that Jake had company.

'Crap,' said the little boy. 'Crap, crap, crap,' he repeated, making the dog in Emma's arms yip along.

'No, Elton. Do not copy Mummy,' the woman said, walking over to take the dog out of Emma's arms. 'I'm so sorry. I had no clue Jake would be entertaining. He never entertains. Not since—'

'*Anyhoo*,' Jake interrupted. 'Emma, this is Sarah, my sister, Elton, my nephew, and Bingley the Bichon.'

'You're the actress?' Sarah asked, swinging around to stare at her.

'I used to be,' she carefully corrected her. 'Now I run Cocktails & Chai. Are you the Sarah who did the invites for The Clock House, because I have to tell you they're wonderful.'

'Thank you. I—'

'Probably can't stay that long?' Jake asked, shifting Elton again so that he could shut the oven door.

Sarah grinned at her brother. 'Actually I have all the time in the world.'

Jake let out a deep sigh. 'What do you want, sis?'

Taking pity on him, she said, 'I have dates from that photographer. But I can see you're busy so I'll turn around and—oh,' she stopped and stared at the Christmas tree. 'Oh, Jake, you've decorated.'

Jake rolled his eyes. 'It's not a big deal.'

'He told me he left them up all year,' Emma said unable to resist teasing just a little.

'He did? Aw, that's so...' Sarah's hand went to her heart.

'Crap,' Elton finished for her with perfect timing.

'Bad word, Elton. Uncle Jake doesn't want to hear that come out of your mouth again.'

''Kay.' Elton patted his hand over Jake's stubble and then twisted in his arms to stare at Emma. 'She's pretty.'

'Yes.' Jake said, treating Emma to one of those intense smiles of his. 'She is.'

Emma's heart melted.

Because of Elton, obviously.

Not because of Jake.

At least that's what she told herself while trying not to catalogue how completely comfortable he looked holding his nephew.

'So what are these dates, then?' Jake asked his sister, reaching forward to grab his glass of wine and take a casual sip.

'She can do the week before Christmas, or...'

'It's going to have to be "or". You know I'm not going to be around for Christmas.'

Sarah jerked her head to indicate Emma. 'Your plans won't be changing now?'

Jake glowered. 'No. They won't. So don't go getting any ideas. At all,' he added for good measure.

Sarah looked like she wanted to say something but instead opted for, 'In that case the photographer also mentioned the first week in February. I told her about the new bit of the garden you're doing and she was really intrigued.'

Jake pursed his lips. 'You told her about the secret garden?'

'You didn't say it was a secret.'

'I definitely called it a secret garden and said it was something new I was working on and you know I don't advertise unfinished work.'

'But now you have a few extra weeks to complete it.'

'Damn it, Sarah, it's winter. I don't have time to get it ready for then.'

'You'll have to find a way because she loved the sound of it. Said it sounded uber romantic and that would be the best angle to promote. She asked me to tell you to keep that in mind for when she creates her compositions.'

'You never said anything about creating scenes. I want photos of how it really is, not what some stylist got it to look like.'

'She, um, also wants to take a couple of photos of the inside of the house.'

Jake shook his head. 'No way.'

'Look if it's about the money—'

'You'll what?' Jake said, his voice as tight as the line of his shoulders, Elton was happily prodding away at. 'Magic some up from somewhere? There isn't enough time or money before she visits to make this house look loved.'

'We really wouldn't need to do much,' Sarah asserted. 'Honestly, the way you keep comparing the outside to the inside all the time. I know you love having absolute control over the gardens—'

Jake snorted, making Elton giggle and try to copy him. 'Control is just an illusion.'

Emma couldn't pretend to know the subtext to the conversation but she totally got Jake's assertion that control was just an illusion. After all acting was creating just that. A fake reality.

Mostly a better one, depending on the story.

'You worry too much, Jake. I only suggested three rooms: the library, this room, and your bedroom.' Turning to Emma, Sarah added, 'You've probably seen the bedroom already, so you'll know about the—'

'Oh, for f—' Jake stopped, stared down at Elton and with what looked like great effort, said, '*family* sake, Sarah, Emma's not interested in my bedroom.'

Emma raised her glass to her lips and took a ginormous mouthful to make absolutely sure she didn't say something stupid like, 'actually you couldn't be more wrong'!

'We can discuss the interior photos another time. I expect Elton needs to get home for his tea,' Jake said, holding his nephew pointedly out to his sister.

'Bye, Unca Jakey.'

'Bye buddy. Try and be good for your mum, okay?'

'Jake,' Sarah said, her voice full of contrition as she set down Bingley and reached for her son. 'We're really all just trying to help and support you.'

'I know.'

'We may not have wanted this place, but none of us wants you to lose it.' And then, as if realising she was about to discuss family business in front of Emma she stopped and with a gentle smile said, 'So I can tell her first week in Feb for definite?'

Jake nodded.

'Fab.' Sarah turned and smiled warmly at her as Jake edged her towards the hallway. 'It's been lovely meeting you, Emma.'

'You too. And Elton and Bingley. Love the nod to Jane

Austen by the way. Oh, has Jake told you about Crispin's claim?'

Jake hit his forehead with his palm. 'And the hits just keep on coming.'

Sarah planted her feet and looked at Jake. 'What claim?'

Emma totally failed at keeping the excitement out of her voice. 'Crispin says Jane Austen stayed here once.'

'What?' Sarah's eyes went round. 'Oh, wow, that would be great for business. But, hang on, when would that have been?'

'I'm pretty sure it was on the twelfth of *Never*,' Jake replied. 'But I can't wait to put up my blue plaque.'

'Crispin's getting a blue plaque made?' Sarah asked.

'It's going to have to read: Knightley Hall, on this date ... where absolutely nothing happened,' Jake answered sarcastically.

'But what if she really did stay here?' Sarah asked.

'Oh come on. A story like that would have been handed down from generation to generation like the stupid story about the snow and the chandelier. We'd all have heard of it. But now, as well as everything else I need to do, I'm having to go through the family journals just in case.'

'Poor Jakey. So, I'll um, get back to you about what's needed for the photographer?'

'Email, text, write me a letter,' he said, edging her further towards the front door. 'The forms of communication not requiring actual physical stopping-by are both numerous *and* time-saving, these days.'

Emma watched Bingley disappear out the door where it raced to the car and started sniffing the wheels.

'What you're really saying,' Sarah said, 'is now I should knock before I walk in.'

Before Jake could combust from sighing, Emma stepped up to the door, draped her arm around him and answered with a knowing grin, 'Maybe wait for an answer, too.'

Chapter 24

Tour of the Roses

Jake

Jake watched Sarah settle Elton and Bingley into the car and then cursed under his breath when she hopped into the driver's seat and proceeded to root around in her bag and triumphantly withdraw her phone. 'She'll be texting the whole clan before she drives off.'

'But will she be texting them about Jane Austen and the Blue Plaque Affair ... or ours?'

He shot Emma a look as she removed her arm from around him. She looked pleased with herself rather than horrified at how his family took open-door policy to new levels.

'Why did you say that to Sarah?'

'Honestly? You looked like you were ready to implode. I get that this is the old family home but maybe she'll think twice about wandering in now.'

Jake searched her gorgeous eyes for ulterior motive and accepting his suspicion with a small roll of her eyes she grinned and said, 'You're welcome,' before outrageously adding, 'I guess you'll want to give me that tour of the bedroom now?'

To his utter surprise a laugh escaped. 'How about a tour of the gardens instead?'

'Actually, I'd love that.'

He'd had every intention of cancelling their date. But aside from Kate giving him the stink-eye when he'd taken the lights to The Clock House, he'd seen the look of resignation cross Emma's face – almost as if she'd expected the rejection – and it had been that look, more than Kate's, that had had him changing his mind. He'd coerced her into the date in the first place. To cancel would have been a really shitty thing to do.

'I'll grab our coats and we'll head out the back way,' he told her, hoping the fresh air and walking his land would help him feel on more solid ground.

He'd keep it simple.

Give her the tour. They'd eat some dinner. He'd walk her home.

And not once would he think about the way she'd looked at him earlier when she'd thought he was going to kiss her.

Or the fact that he wished he had.

To distract himself from her mouth, he stared down at the worm casts in the grass.

'We'll do the lake another time,' he said, moving them down one terrace, through an archway of pleached hornbeam whose brown leaves clung on determinedly. He'd show her the formal knot garden. 'Those boots of yours won't survive the wet ground, so we'll stick to the paths I've put in.'

As they walked, he watched her out of the corner of his eye. She was busy taking every single detail in. Concentrating so avidly he found himself warning, 'It's not looking its best, but I still think it's beautiful.'

'I can tell,' she replied.

'You were expecting flowers? Not at this time of year. But the formal borders are a riot of colour in the summer. Purple globe thistles, golden rod and crocosmia fill in the gaps and on the other side of this hedge, lavender, roses and hollyhocks.'

'No,' she put a hand on his arm to slow him, 'I meant I can tell *you* think it's beautiful. It adds something to see it through your eyes. When you open up to the public will you be giving guided tours?'

He shuddered. 'Not sure.'

Emma laughed. 'I think it would be great to have an expert explain how the gardens came to be, which was, how, exactly?'

'Why do I feel like I'm auditioning for a part? Isn't that supposed to be your speciality?'

'Just tell me about this place as we walk. Tell me about the history. And then tell me why what was here, then wasn't, and why you want it to be again.'

'You really want to know?'

'I really do. Come on, Jake, take me to your Zen place.'

Making her see the past, the present and what he wanted for the future, was a tall order when areas were left empty and only the structure of established shrubs and trees gave a clue as to what was where during winter, but her plea was seductive and so was the way she listened with open heart.

'To begin with then,' he began as they walked; the cold air somehow unable to penetrate their companionable bubble. 'The estate was originally purchased by civil engineer John Knightley in 1857. I think he described the place as a handsome house in a handsome village, which back then included Whispers Ford, so was much bigger.'

'Good description,' she murmured.

'To make it more handsome he added Tudor wings and renamed it after himself. Watch your step here,' he instructed, beckoning for her to climb onto an observation plinth with him so that they could look down on the whole of the knot garden.

'Wow.'

'Yes,' he said, only he wasn't looking at the gardens, he was looking at her. Her cheeks were rosy and her eyes sparkling, and damn, she looked like she fit.

'It's like a mini Versailles. Is this your design?'

He shook his head. 'I altered the layout slightly to include an exit at the far end. The planting within each section has been replaced over the years but it matches what would have been here in Victorian times. There's an orange tree for the centre that I'll bring back out after the last frost. It gets replaced with a large yew standard over winter.'

'It looks so intricate from up here.' She widened her gaze to the copse at the edge of his land. 'So how much land makes up Knightley Hall?'

'Originally ten acres. There's not much more than four now. As money began running out, more and more of the land was sold off.'

'That's sad. Have you had to sell any?'

'I sold a third of an acre to Oscar Matthews.' It had been hard to see another parcel of land go but he'd needed the seed money for the gardens. Most of the profit he'd made working in London he'd given to his parents. A thank you for paying for his studies, and a way of replacing the retirement funds they'd used up seeing Sarah and Seth through college years earlier. After last Christmas he supposed he could've returned to London to earn more money, but it would've meant going backwards not forwards. He hadn't wanted to bump into his old life with Alice. He'd wanted to let this place heal him. 'Oscar renovated the barn that stood on it,' he added.

'Oh, I've been there. He's done a really wonderful job.'

Jake nodded. 'I knew he could be trusted to build something in keeping with the area and when he said he wanted to remodel the original barn, I thought that was great. He's a good neighbour.' He indicated they should turn around and then he pointed to the fields in the distance. 'Felix, who you met at the village meeting, he rents the last of the land to the west. He's a dairy farmer.'

'That's where Gertrude lives?'

'With the rest of the herd, yes.'

'Hey, Jake?' Emma said softly.

'Mmmn?'

'After we walk through the knot garden can we visit the rose garden?'

When she looked at him like that, he couldn't wait to show her.

'Of course.' Jumping off the plinth he offered his hand. She took it without hesitation and it seemed churlish to let go once she'd stepped down onto the path.

'So who ran Knightley Hall after John?' she asked, her hand pulsing in his, or was that his pulsing in hers?

'That would be his son – also called John, and then came George.'

'Your smile changes when you mention George,' she said perceptively.

'George was my great-great grandfather and he laid the foundations of what you're seeing now. He wanted to show the progression of how the gardens came to be. A sort of living history. Of course later came the Second World War and work on the gardens ground to a halt again.'

'He inherited Knightley Hall when his father died?'

Jake nodded. 'He was twenty-four. It was 1925 and he'd been living in London making a name for himself building theatres for a chain of theatre companies.'

Emma grinned. 'So you have the stage in your blood? How fabulous.'

'Would have been an even deeper connection to the stage if he'd had his way. But then he was a Knightley and traditionally, we're not great at love.'

She burst out laughing.

'Interesting,' he said, glancing down at her. 'I haven't got to the funny part of the tour yet.'

'Sorry, but you're joking, right? This place has been in your family over a century. Your parents had six kids and are still together and you're saying Knightleys aren't great at love?' She stopped at the entrance to the knot garden and watched as he let go of her hand. 'Wow. You're actually not joking?'

He shrugged, a little embarrassed and walked around the outside edge of the geometric box hedging until he came to the exit. 'I'm sure you've heard about Alice.'

She bent to pick up a piece of box clipping and twirled it thoughtfully in her fingers. 'So, one failed relationship and you're not great at love?'

Jake entered the knot garden through the exit and walked a couple of turns through the mini-maze, mirroring her movements. 'If this was a real guided tour, I wouldn't be talking about Alice.'

Emma took another few steps towards him. 'So back to George, then?'

'Back to George,' he nodded. 'I suspect at twenty-four and doing very well in his chosen field, thoughts of ending up here were far from his mind. Especially after meeting an actress called Anna-Rose Banning and becoming besotted.'

'How romantic. And was she besotted back?'

'By all accounts,' he said lightly. 'You know the chandelier that hangs at The Clock House?' He could feel her intrigue from where he was standing. 'George actually commissioned it to grace the entrance of a new theatre he was building for Anna-Rose. It was to be his wedding present to her.'

'Yet it ended up at The Clock House?' She wandered a couple of steps towards him. 'The plot thickens and I'm beginning to worry about Anna-Rose and George.'

'When George's father died he was called back here. Anna-Rose visited of course. And they wrote letters back and forth, making plans for their future. As time went by Anna-Rose began to get plays written especially for her and George got more involved in running the estate and more excited about making Knightley Hall his home. A place he could indulge his love for design in both the building and the gardens.

Anna-Rose loved coming back to see the progress he was making and take a break from the bright lights. They were due to get married the following year, but on the eve of their wedding day—'

Emma's hand went to her throat. 'Oh no. She died!' Her eyes filled with tears. 'Oh that's so sad. She never got to see her chandelier? And he couldn't bear it, so he gave it away?'

'Wow, you went straight to Shakespeare tragedy,' he said, a bit awestruck she could be so open and immerse herself so fully in a story. More awestruck still that she could carry him along in the moment, when he already knew the story.

She'd give wonderful guided tours. Different stories for each season. Tales that would resonate and intrigue and have visitors wanting to come back, time and time again.

'Well you led me there, My Storyteller Guide, with your hushed, grave tone.'

'You took a wrong turn about halfway through the knot garden because she didn't die. She simply changed her mind about marrying him.' The words left his body but didn't leave his heart. Despite the fact that he wouldn't be here today if she hadn't decided Whispers Wood in no way compared to the bright lights of the London stage.

'That's still so sad, though.' Emma reached the centre of the knot garden and put her sprig of yew under the tree he'd planted, as if out of respect for the death of George and Anna-Rose's relationship. 'How did the chandelier end up at The Clock House?'

'George asked Old Man Isaac's grandfather, William, to take it. George ended up spending every penny he made on the gardens. In fact, he went through his entire fortune in one year. Most of it went on the rose garden.' Sudden realisation hit him. In all likelihood there was no big secret about not finishing the secret garden – George probably just ran out of money.

Well, that wasn't going to happen to him, he promised himself.

For a start he was seeing his plans through without the distraction of a broken heart.

He'd already got that out of the way and survived. Remarkably easily as it had turned out. But then he guessed he'd had his entire upbringing to understand that love and Knightley Hall just didn't work together.

'Why didn't George take back the chandelier and sell it to fund the estate?' Emma asked.

There was no way Jake could bring himself to say *because the chandelier had other ideas* so he went with, 'I guess he believed he'd given it to William as a gift.' He glanced at his watch and then up at the darkening sky. 'I think we just have time to see the rose garden before it gets too dark.'

Comfortable with the abrupt change of subject, Emma followed him.

'Can I ask another question?'

'Of course.'

'You said you weren't the oldest in your family, so, this is going to sound crass, but, how did you end up being the one to take it over?'

He led her through the brick archway into the rose garden. As he watched her gaze roam over the bare walls and empty obelisks, he wished she was seeing it for the first time when the buds were on the branches and the heady scent of anticipation filled the air.

'I was the only one who wanted it,' he replied, shoving his hands in his pockets.

'The only one out of all of you?' She walked straight to the rose tunnel he'd constructed out of iron posts to hold the weight.

'Yes.'

'But why would anyone not want all this?' She held her arms out and turned in a slow circle.

'It's not easy being born into this,' he said mimicking her movement to indicate the house and grounds. 'Even your un-ending enthusiasm would wear off if your relationship with this place was predominately based upon how much it all costs to run.'

'Oh.' Her hand reached out to follow a twisted thorny stem.

'Mmmn. When money floods out and only trickles back in, it can all start to feel like a noose around your neck. All this space yet you feel the walls are closing in. Duty becomes synonymous with overwhelming responsibility.'

'But not for you?' Her fingers trailed along branches he'd spent years tying-in, long after Sid, their head gardener, had been let go. It was almost as if she was anchoring herself to the beauty so she could dispel the cold reality of running a place like this.

'Sometimes. The difference is the love affair I have with this land outweighs that feeling every single time.'

'You said you were once plugged-in but that that world fell

out of love with you. Did you not always want to be at the Hall, then?'

'I wanted to be here from the moment I was fourteen and the head gardener caught me smoking and drinking in one of the potting sheds. He decided manual labour would curb any propensity for extending my repertoire of bad habits. He hooked me well and good. Somehow with my hands in the soil I felt—' he broke off not knowing how to explain.

'Nourished?'

'Yes.' God, how was it that she got it? 'I went on to study horticulture and ended up working for a small design company in London. We grew really quick. Mostly because we said "yes" to every opportunity and worked demanding hours without complaint. I always knew that to come back here I needed skills and capital. Mostly capital,' he finished with a smile. 'I racked up both but it was getting to a time where I needed to commit fully to the company or cut ties and come back. There was no halfway-house. I hated all the networking to get more business and the company deserved someone who could put their soul into it.'

'But it was in London that you met Alice?'

'I was invited to do a garden for Chelsea Flower Show and she was the representative from the sponsor.'

He didn't provide any more detail and Emma's usual curiosity and enthusiastic questions seemed to dry up.

Either that or she was inwardly dissecting how similar his path to Knightley Hall mirrored his ancestor's.

In the middle of the rose tunnel, Emma turned to him. 'So when these are all in bloom, what colours will they be?'

He wanted to tell her she'd have to hang around and find out for herself, but instead he said, 'A mix of blousy bubble-gum pink, purest white – so white they'll almost look pale green, and a deep, velvety, plush purple.'

'And they'll trail down in a shower of scent?'

'That's the general idea.'

She sighed. 'It's so beautiful, Jake.'

And then as if too much for her, she picked up her pace, hugging her arms to herself.

'Hey,' catching up with her he gently turned her around to face him, 'what's up?'

'Sorry. Lost in memories, I guess. I rarely think about the house I grew up in over here when my parents were still together. As a kid I thought the garden was endless. As an adult I realise it was an average suburban garden. But there were roses. Lots of roses. I used to pick up all the rose petals that had fallen from the rose bushes.' She reached out as if she was picking a rose, and her smile was wistful, as she admitted, 'and some petals that hadn't technically made it to the floor. I'd pop them in a bucket and add water. Then I'd grab a stick and squelch it all together and with a funnel fill up some old perfume bottles mum let me have. I'd stick on my own labels and make her use my incredible rose perfume.'

The way she set the scene, he could see it all so perfectly. 'That sounds like a nice memory to have.'

'Yes.'

'But?' he murmured when her eyes turned all misty.

With her smile still in place she shook her head as if to say it was nothing and walked a determined couple of steps ahead out of the rose tunnel, and towards the new part of the garden he'd been working on.

He saw her hesitate and then step through the once bricked up entrance.

Eager to see what she made of the space he let her have a few moments to herself and then followed her. When she didn't immediately turn around to face him he reached out to stroke a hand gently down the length of her hair.

'You know,' she said, turning around, 'I'd forgotten it was my dad who used to get me the bucket, and the funnel, and the piece of lint cloth to use as he helped me strain my perfume into tiny bottles.' She shook her head a little as if upset she'd done him some sort of disservice. 'For years I've always thought of him as the unimaginative one of my parents.'

'Maybe you brought out the creativity in him,' he offered.

'Seeing this – well, it's a timely reminder. I've been second-guessing every Christmas present idea I come up with for him but all this has made me think I should go outside the box. That maybe surprising him doesn't always have to be a bad thing.'

'This place has made you think all those things, huh?'

'It's—'

He found himself leaning closer, wanting to catch her praise because she was maybe the only person who seemed able to bring his plans to life in a way that made him feel that anything he wanted to do with these gardens was possible.

'It's enchanting,' she whispered, looking around at the bare brick walls that needed re-pointing and had tiny ferns growing out of cracks. 'Magical. Beautiful.'

'You're very good for motivation,' he told her. 'Already I'm now looking for the first shoots of growth when I know it's way too early.'

'No, I mean, yes, later it's still going to look enchanting, magical and beautiful, but I actually meant it does now. Even this secret space you've unearthed. It would be perfect for small weddings, but right now ... can't you imagine a little café table and chairs, and a patio heater, and lanterns and tea lights and fairy lights and candles? And gorgeous blankets to snuggle into while you drink mugs of hot chocolate and read from your favourite book? A secret family space, private and away from the public. Can't you see it?'

He nodded because she made him see it.

Want to live it.

'You know this is how you could set it out for those photos. You could borrow things if needs be. I'm sure everyone in Whispers Wood would love to help.'

He turned so that she wouldn't see how much her scene creation disturbed him.

At some point Knightley Hall would have to be about family again – it would be criminal to see this land not loved. Not used. Not passed on.

But he wanted a few years first.

Before he had to settle for duty and a marriage of convenience, like his parents, grandparents and great-grandparents had done.

Chapter 25

Deck The Halls, Not Your Family

Jake

How could he stay mad when she was such good company?

As they sat at his kitchen table, a little drunk off sharing the second bottle of red, and with the candles flickering softly between them, he'd spent the meal laughing like he couldn't remember laughing in a long time.

'Okay, are you sure you're ready for this one,' she asked, grabbing a spoon off the table and stashing it in her jeans pocket. 'This was my all-time favourite audition. I have to get up, hang on a sec.' Pushing back her chair, she turned so that she was facing away from him and as she widened her stance she seemed to get taller and sexier so that anticipation shot through him. 'Ready?' she checked, looking over her shoulder.

'Hit me with it,' he said, taking a sip of his drink and then nearly choked on it as she turned around, her face deadly serious, her hands pulling the spoon from her pocket and brandishing it like it was a gun or a phaser or, well, something that put her instantly in charge.

Holding the spoon out towards him like she handled a gun every day of her life, her voice was a hundred-and-ten-per cent commitment as she said, 'Drop your weapon and don't even think of doing anything different, or I will end you, dead.' Her gaze slid to the empty space beside him and her expression changed to concern then dread. 'Commander Dixon? Commander Dixon you get up, you hear me? Your crew needs you. *I* need you, damn it. If we don't fix the engines this ship is going to hit the horizon. We'll burn up on impact and I'll never get the chance to tell you—'

He wanted to hear the declarative lines that were so hammy they could form a whole side of bacon when her face suddenly transformed into a giant grin and she was turning the spoon around and breaking off a piece of pumpkin pie and shoving it into her mouth.

'Commander Dixon?' Jake laughed. 'What was your character's name?'

'Lt. Vixen.'

'Dixon and Vixen, are you serious?'

She nodded and finished her mouthful. '*Star Hike: The Dixon and Vixen Voyages*. I can't believe you haven't seen it over here.'

'Baffling to have seen *Sharknado* 1–4, yet missed this masterpiece! You were beyond awesome though. I don't know who they ended up going with for Vixen but the way you handled that spoon just then? Very ... foxy.'

She batted her eyelashes, pursed her lips, fluffed out her hair.

Their eyes met across the table for a heartbeat and then

they were both laughing again.

'I can't believe you didn't get the part.'

'I know, right?' She looked down and then shoved her hair back behind her ears and couldn't quite meet his eyes as she picked up her wineglass and finished the contents. 'That was so delicious. Thank you,' she said graciously and back in complete control, it only taking seconds to completely wipe every shred of hurt she might have felt at not getting the part. 'So am I going to get a tour of the house too?'

'Maybe the library,' he conceded, pushing to his feet, wanting to give her something to salve the ache she was hiding.

'You don't want to clear up in here first?'

'Later,' he said, with a smile. Right now she needed something she could distract herself with so he gestured for her to follow him out of the kitchen and down the length of the corridor where he turned right into the oldest wing of the house.

Inside the dark room at the end of the hallway, his hand went automatically to the light switch. The central Tiffany ceiling pendant cast a cosy glow and he crossed the ancient Axminster carpet that left a foot wide strip of oak floorboard around each of its edges, and stopped in front of the large regency style rosewood and leather library desk in the centre of the room. Leaning across the round table he switched on the matching Tiffany lamps so she could see the room in all its glory and then turned around to watch for her reaction.

He'd known she'd love the room.

Didn't she love everything new?

Or in this case old?

Soaking up every experience she came across, he swore so that she could summon it for a role later on, but even suspecting that, it still gave him a kick of excitement to see the pleasure on her face.

'If I lived here I might never leave this room,' she whispered, her gaze bouncing off every non-matching chair, card table, footstool, and mini-electric heater.

If he was being honest it was his favourite room in the house too. The heavy mahogany floor to ceiling bookshelves with the ladder fixed to the rail for access to the shelves higher up. The window seat that ran along the width of the window. The armchairs in front of the fire.

He watched her as she walked the room's perimeter, a hand outstretched so that her fingers could trail over the spines of books.

'Have you read all these books?' she asked, pausing every few steps to pull out a title, look at it, and then slot it neatly back in.

'Yes.'

She turned her head to look at him and then the smile he worried he might be getting addicted to seeing graced her face again. 'You've read about ten per cent of them, right?'

'Yes,' he admitted with his own smile.

'Can I tell you my favourite part?' she finally said, clutching her hands together in front of her.

He nodded.

'It's that you've mixed fiction with non-fiction, modern classics with old classics. It's all jumbled up so you can stumble upon a book you might not necessarily have given a second glance.'

'We had to sell some of the rarer books and it was going to be too hard to move them all around to cover up the gaps so I tend to shove in books where there are spaces.'

'Well, I love seeing Child next to Wordsworth and Rowling next to Dickens but what do you think the photographer will think?'

'I really don't care.'

'No.' She glanced at him curiously. 'You really don't, do you?'

He watched her and after a second or two she started searching the bookshelves again, but this time it was with a more determined look in her eyes.

'Yes,' he said taking pity, 'there are Austens amongst the shelves.'

She laughed. 'She probably dropped a few copies off when she stayed. Probably made sure they were all facing forward, so that whoever popped in for a book saw hers first.'

He groaned.

'What are those?' she asked, pointing to the table covered in dozens of leather-bound books he'd taken from the shelves to search through.

'They're the family journals.'

'Do you keep one?'

'I have gardening journals and my design portfolios. I keep those up to date.'

'But why not write about other things as well?'

'Because I'm too busy doing the gardens. The journals stop

sometime in the 1970s. I think it got too depressing when they became lists of what went for what at auction.'

'But generations before took such time to write in them.'

'Probably didn't have anything else to do,' he said.

'You could write about why you're turning this place back into a family home.'

'But that's not what I'm doing,' he said, wondering why he felt the need to keep rapping her romantic streak on its knuckles.

It wasn't like she was going to be staying in Whispers Wood.

Wasn't like either of them should be getting any ideas…

'Of course that's what you're doing,' she insisted. 'You're breathing new life back into Knightley Hall starting with the gardens. Restoring them back to what George was creating.'

He folded his arms. Leant his hips against the edge of the table. 'And what, exactly, is it you think George was trying to create?' he asked.

'A marriage of house and garden, maybe? A way of preparing it all over again.'

A sense of foreboding settled like a dead weight in the pit of his belly. 'Preparing it for what?'

'For new generations.'

'And that's what you think I'm trying to do here?'

She stared back at him one perfectly arched eyebrow raised in question, 'Aren't you?'

Why did he find it so hard to admit? Was it because he didn't want to jinx it or was it because he didn't know if he could pull it off? How would he ever be sure his parents hadn't given him Knightley Hall simply because they'd run out of options? How would he ever know if they believed he could combine artistic talent with good business sense?

His parents were lovely, affable, educated people, but both had floundered as the money started running out. Neither had been able to shoulder the burden fully, try new things and find a way through.

'I guess all that I really am,' he said, slowly, 'is the current caretaker.' A role that surely even she would find unappealing.

Her gaze slid briefly to the journals beside him, then back to study him. 'I think people who get to own homes like this are only ever just the caretaker for a while. But,' her eyes came alive, 'what a great job: to be able to create and take care of something that offers the next generation that sense of stability – of belonging. That's pretty hard to find these days.'

Suspicion flared beneath his skin, because, damn it, she wasn't the one who was supposed to understand.

Or was it all an act?

Alice had said she understood. The long hours he was going to have to work. The sacrifices they'd both have to make. Every single penny being ploughed back into the Hall. Never having anything left for them.

She'd assured him she was looking forward to it.

Couldn't wait to share their lives together.

Until, it turned out, she could.

So of course he'd be stupid to trust Emma, the actress, the one whose very job was to help people escape reality and enjoy fantasy.

Running a place like this was about as romantic as sheep-shearing and as far away from Sunday night cosy TV drama as you could get. But how did you convince the very person who was apt to star in those programmes?

'You make it sound so easy,' he murmured. 'So idyllic. I'm afraid that wasn't to be the case for George when instead of marrying his Anna-Rose, he married a second-generation American heiress called Lillian. She was looking for a husband and by then he was looking for money to save the estate. You only have to read these journals to get the full, extremely unromantic, but mutually convenient picture.'

And he only had to over-hear his own parents to understand how love had had very little to do with keeping the house in the Knightley family.

'Were you engaged to Alice for her money, then?' Emma's voice was stilted and the tilt of her chin suggested she was secretly appalled by the idea.

'No. I wasn't,' he answered steadily, biting back the anger because it was what everyone had assumed.

Relief flashed in her eyes. 'So you're trying to change the pattern?'

'I'm not trying to do anything other than prove I can run this place on my own.'

'Because you're so terrible at love?' she scoffed. 'Why is it so shocking to you to believe you could marry for love and run this place together?'

'Trust me, the reality of running a place like this is a tough sell.'

'Maybe you've been selling it to the wrong women?'

No.

He wasn't having her steal into his soul so that he could

begin imagining her in his garden tending the roses, or in the kitchen teasing him with a ladle full of food, or in his bedroom...

'I haven't come across a woman yet who could fall in love with me and,' he looked up to indicate the roof over their heads, 'everything that comes with me.'

She contemplated him for a moment and then asked, 'You don't think you could make a woman fall in love with you?'

He grimaced. 'Make a woman fall in love with me? Sounds a bit contrived.' A copy of *Persuasion* winked at him from a shelf behind her. 'What do you think Jane Austen was really trying to say in her books? You find it all so sigh-worthy and romantic but wasn't she saying over and over how ridiculous, how unfair, and how unjust it was that women had to play these games so that they weren't left alone and penniless? The times have changed but not the houses they took place in. And the people who live in these places still need fortunes to run them.'

She grinned and took a step towards him, her hands sliding into her tight jeans pockets. 'While I applaud your feminism, I think Jane Austen was actually trying to say that true love can conquer circumstance and that that is eminently worth striving for.'

'A convenient message in order to sell books,' he replied, refusing to get sucked in by her rosy conviction.

Instead of looking insulted, she looked amused as she walked up to the table and took one hand out of her pocket to stroke over one of the journal covers. 'I know you don't believe that. You couldn't design and tend and nurture these gardens if you really believed that.'

'Why couldn't I? Plants don't say one thing but actually want another. They don't feel disappointment. They don't change their mind.'

'You'd be more believable as a cynic if you hadn't flirted with me this evening.'

He wanted to stand up to dispel the energy pulsing between them but he stayed where he was leaning against the table. 'You really think I've been flirting with you?'

Her nod was easy and relaxed. 'I've enjoyed the back and forth. The exchange of ideas. Discovering where we look at the world in the same way and where we differ?'

'That's just pleasant conversation.'

'Could be. So let me ask you, then? Why did you really invite me here tonight, Jake? You didn't enjoy cooking for me? Decorating for me?' her voice wrapped itself around him. 'You haven't enjoyed the way I hold your gaze a second too long?' She closed the distance between them. 'The catch in my breath when you step in closer to me?'

'Technically you're the one stepping closer to me, but okay, yes, I can't say I'm averse to that catch in your voice. And I didn't say women weren't attracted to me. I said to make someone fall in love with you is contrived.'

'So you're definitely not trying to make me fall in love with you?'

'Scout's honour,' he whispered, holding her gaze.

'So this,' she waved a hand between them, 'this is not something to worry about.'

'Oh, it's definitely something – it's just not falling in love.'

'Phew, because I definitely don't have time for falling in love at the moment.'

'Ditto.'

In the blink of an eye, her hand came up to rest against his thudding heart and her lips sealed across his.

Even interpreting the signals he was still a step behind. As if he hadn't quite trusted that she was going to follow through.

And what a follow through it was.

Sweet.

Hot.

And gone before he could respond.

In a second, she was off him and taking a couple of steps backwards, her hand outstretched, a look of embarrassed beseeching that they never, *ever* speak of this again. 'I'm so sorry. I thought—' she stopped, shook her head a little and tried again. 'I shouldn't have—'

In an instant he was reaching for her, dragging her into his arms and covering her mouth with his. Letting her know that her thinking was absolutely fine. That she should definitely have. And that he was a first-class idiot for making her think for one second she'd thought wrong and that she shouldn't have.

Her lips were soft and inviting and when the tip of her tongue touched the tip of his the rush of passion eroded judgement, blanked out rational thinking and had him holding on tightly. His arms wrapping themselves around her slender frame as he turned her to place her gently on the library desk.

This wasn't novelty.

But just to make sure...

Another touch, he thought, as his fingers brushed gently across her cheekbones, collecting her trembles and savouring them.

Another kiss, he thought, as his mouth sought hers over and over.

He was drowning in sensation and any moment he wasn't going to make it back up to the surface for air.

'Jakey? What's with all the food? I thought you were brassic?' The library door slammed back against its hinges and Jake and Emma shot apart.

'What the hell? Seth?' Jake stared at his brother thinking he could quite easily swing for him.

'Oops,' Seth said, as he squinted at the scene before him.

The harder he looked the more he swayed, making Jake swear under his breath at how stinking drunk his brother was.

With an apologetic look at Emma, Jake reached out to gently help her off the table. When he felt her make the move to flee, he took her hand and kept it clasped within his.

None of this was her fault.

Mostly it was his fault for not laying out boundaries when he'd been given the keys to the Hall.

'Did Sarah send you over here?' he asked his brother as he walked towards him.

'God no. The last thing I wanted was another woman getting preachy and telling me what to do.'

'Don't be a dick, Seth.' With another apologetic look at Emma, he let go of her hand and grabbed a hold of his brother to start walking him towards the kitchen, his intention to pour the biggest vat of coffee down his neck imaginable.

In the kitchen, Emma went to fill the kettle with water and switch it on. Turning to him she mouthed, 'Mugs?' and he pointed to the cupboard to the right.

'If Sarah didn't ask you to come, does Joanne know you're here?' he asked Seth.

'Nope. She told me to leave, Jakey. For proper this time.'

'I'm not surprised if you were like this.'

'This came after,' he said, seeing the wine and reaching for it before Jake could stop him. 'So you've been cooking? Must be serious.' He looked up as Emma pushed a mug of black coffee in front of him. 'I'll tell Mum you've found someone to help you run this place. She'll be pleased.'

Jake caught Emma's eye. She didn't look in the least tired, insulted or jaded.

Which was okay, he supposed, because he was feeling enough of all that for the both of them.

Emma was the forever-romantic type, wasn't she? He'd seen it in the way her eyes lit-up in the library when she'd tried convincing him that Jane Austen was all about true love, not social commentary.

And here was his brother, drunk and about to bitch about his wife, basically doing his best to prove how very unromantic the Knightleys could be.

'Is there a bedroom made-up that he can sleep it off in, tonight?' Emma asked, nudging the coffee closer to his brother.

Jake nodded. 'He can use his old room. He's stayed here before.'

269

'I am here, you know,' Seth bellowed, reaching for the wine glass instead of the coffee and knocking it over so that the dregs of red wine splashed over the white candle like a special effect in a gothic horror movie. 'Ouch, damn it.'

It took Jake a couple of seconds to register the red wine on Seth's hand wasn't wine but blood.

He stared transfixed. Completely unable to move as the ribbon of red oozed down his brother's arm to drip onto the table.

Chapter 26

Village of Stars

Emma

'Jake?'

As Emma reached over to hold Seth's hand up to help stop the flow of blood, she couldn't help but notice that as red as the trickle of blood dripping onto the table, Jake's face was grey. Really, completely, alarmingly, grey.

'*Jake*,' she called his name sharply again, and when that didn't produce a reaction she shouted, '*Hey, Commander Dixon! Eyes on me!*'

That seemed to get his attention.

'You're not going to faint on me, are you?' she asked him.

His gaze swung from hers to his brother's arm but seemed to realise that wasn't the best idea in the world, so bounced back up to lock onto hers again. Slowly he swallowed, then shook his head.

'Good. Because I need you to find a first aid kit.'

He nodded but still didn't move.

'It's really not that bad. Look,' she said, pulling on Seth's arm, 'it's stopped bleeding already.'

271

'Ow,' Seth grumbled. 'Have a care, Nurse Ratched.'

'You want your brother doing this?' she asked Seth. 'Because I'm happy to swap.'

'Definitely not. Carry on Nurse.' He looked perplexed for a moment and then said, 'Hey, you're not a nurse, aren't you an actress?'

She shook her head, grinned and answered, 'Maybe I'm a wrestler.'

'Seriously?' Seth looked particularly interested in this news.

'Did you come down with the last Delorean? No, not seriously,' Jake groaned, finally snapping out of it and moving to the cupboard under the sink and withdrawing a Tupperware box. 'Does she look all a-*GLOW* to you?'

'No, but then I sort of interrupted your moment, didn't I?' Seth said looking cheekily from Jake to Emma.

Emma laughed. 'I'm an ex-actress,' she confessed, not even thinking about how easy and natural it felt to admit. 'Nice to meet you, Seth – I'm Emma and I'll be running Cocktails & Chai when The Clock House opens.'

'Well, you can play nurse for me anytime,' Seth said.

'Leave Emma alone,' Jake advised, 'And don't even think about being sick in my kitchen.'

Seth nodded and then groaned. 'Can't make it work with Joanne, Jake. I've really tried. Just can't make it work.'

There was such sadness in his voice that Emma's heart went out to him. She let him talk as she gently cleaned the cut, making sure there was no glass in it, before applying antiseptic cream.

'Even with this place off my back, she doesn't want me,'

Seth rasped out. 'Maybe she really wanted this place? How would that be for karma? Your one didn't and my one did. If we didn't have dumb luck we'd have no luck at all. Although,' he smiled up at Emma as she popped a plaster over his cut, 'Looks like your luck's changed for the better.'

'Shut up, Seth,' Jake said, but his admonishment lacked heat as he cleared up the broken glass and stuck it in the rubbish.

'You're a good man, Jake.' Seth grabbed Emma's arm to get her attention. 'My brother's a good man,' he repeated.

'Yes he is,' Emma said, smiling at Jake, wondering why he looked uncomfortable with the compliment. 'So you'd better be up for listening to his lecture in the morning.'

'God, yes. The Jake Knightley lectures – if only they were as interesting as the Royal Institution Christmas Lectures,' he said, rising from the table on wobbly legs.

Quietly she passed Jake the mug of coffee in the hope he'd get Seth to drink some before he passed out.

With ease, Jake took the coffee in one hand and slipped his other under Seth's arms to help him out of the kitchen. 'Come on, then. Let's get you upstairs to your room.'

'Bloody hate being on my own, Jake. Maybe Emma will let me pitch a tent under the chandelier and I'll wake up Christmas morning with Joanne dressed in a sexy little Santa cosie.'

'Really *don't* need to hear about any Christmas cos-play scenario between you and your wife.'

'Soon to be ex,' Seth mumbled, '*Commander Dixon!*'

There was a small thud, presumably as Seth steered him

and his brother into a wall.

'Sorry. Might be a little hammered,' Seth slurred. 'Maybe I'll tell Joanne about the chandelier being up at Christmas. Rekindle the magic. Do you think it works twice?'

'It didn't even work once, Seth.'

'Course it did. Hope you fixed the hole in the roof coz you know this means the magic's already started.'

'It's a light fitting, Seth. It's not bloody magic.'

'Seriously, you know snow's coming, right?'

Emma heard Jake's deep sigh before he muttered, 'Et tu, Brute?'

Shaking her head at their weird conversation, Emma decided she may as well do a bit of bring-her-back-down-to-earth washing-up.

As her hands delved into the hot sudsy water, she allowed herself to think – to feel, for the first time since Seth had literally come crashing in on her and Jake.

Her kissing Jake had been pure supplication followed by holy-hell mortification.

Jake kissing *her* had been...

So good.

One touch of his lips against hers and, KAPOW.

A couple more kisses later and she'd been lost in him ... in them.

And then Seth had entered centre-stage and the moment had been lost.

From the instant Seth cut his hand and Jake's gaze had purposefully kept missing hers or only sticking for a second or two, she'd known he wasn't going to come searching for that moment again.

His loss!

A couple of soap bubbles exploded out of the bowl to hit her nose as she dumped the next pile of plates into the water with more force than strictly necessary.

Okay, she and Jake had gone from talking to library table in smooth and seductively scary-quick time.

And, okay, with all those journals under her, she'd practically lain on the history of the Knightleys not being 'great at love'.

But hadn't she assured him she hadn't had time for falling in love?

He probably thought she was feeding him a line.

She sighed.

She was so tired of people hearing her lines and not believing them.

No matter, she thought, as she scrubbed at a stain on a plate before realising it was part of the pattern.

She was hardly a stranger to rejection.

She'd do what she did after a failed audition. Smile and keep things light.

Should be simple enough to do and besides, she had enough going on with The Clock House and Jake had one foot out of the village already anyway.

'I can't apologise enough,' Jake said standing in the doorway watching her.

With only a little jump of surprise and a fierce warning to her insides to keep from curling at the sound of his voice, she turned around, reached for a towel and dried her hands. 'Don't worry about it. Family, huh?' she joked, hoping to lighten the mood.

He gave a grim nod and she noticed his hair was mussed.

Had that been from her hands earlier?

Or his hands when he'd realised his brother wasn't going anywhere tonight.

And that neither were he and Emma.

'Did you manage to get him into bed before he passed out?' she asked.

'Mmmn. I'm sorry he was so drunk. And he's the world's biggest flirt—' he broke off, and with a shake of his head, sighed. 'Sarah tried to tell me the separation was serious this time but I didn't want to hear it.'

'You can't blame yourself for your brother's marriage problems,' she said carefully, beginning to wonder if the whole family thought they were cursed in love or something?

'But I can blame myself for being too focussed on my own stuff and for making him feel he couldn't come to me unless he was so wasted I wouldn't turn him away.'

'He's going to feel rubbish tomorrow, but I expect he'll also feel grateful you didn't throw him out. Maybe he'll tell you more about what's going on then.'

'Maybe.' Folding his arms, he leant against the French dresser. 'So this evening didn't exactly go to plan.'

Embarrassed and needing to avoid picking it all apart, she said, 'Let's simply say it unfolded.'

As if aware he was leaning against furniture again and that last time he had she'd launched herself at him, he straightened and said, 'Unravelled more like.'

'No. Just unfolded. The more we make it into a thing...'

He nodded. 'I'll grab our coats.'

'And you really don't have to walk me home.'

'Of course I do. What if the bovine beast of Whispers Wood is on the prowl?' His smile was bigger this time as he attempted to match her light tone.

'My hero,' she called out as he disappeared to get their coats.

Left alone in the kitchen she stared down at her hands.

Don't go thinking of him in terms of a real hero, Ems. He might look after his family like he was one. He might be giving this house a heroic new lease of life. And he might kiss like the leading man in a Nicholas Sparks adaptation. But the way he's bringing this evening to an end? You were right. He's warning you good and proper he doesn't want to be placed in that role. And you need to show him you've received the message. That you're not one of those women who says one thing but wants another.

Like Alice?

Seth had said something about her not wanting this place.

Emma wanted to know if that was the only thing that had gone wrong between them... and she didn't.

Because she wasn't going to do this to herself.

Forget about the way he talked about the gardens. The way he'd cooked for her. The library. She shouldn't have allowed herself to be so charmed. So romanced. She suspected it had shown on her face just enough to have Jake dwelling on that now that he wasn't caught up in the moment.

Keep it light, she reminded herself.

She didn't need the complication.

And Jake?

Complicated in bold Times New Roman, 72 pt!

'I'm nearly used to seeing the bovine beast wander about the village now,' she said, joining him in idle conversation. 'Somehow knowing she's called Gertrude doesn't make her so frightening.'

'Gertrude just gets lonely sometimes,' he told her, coming back into the kitchen already wearing his coat.

As he held her coat open for her she bit back a laugh that they could go from deep discussion, to rolling across a library table, to mending his brother and tucking him up in bed, to talking about cows.

It had been quite the evening.

She shoved her arms through the sleeves of her coat and tried not to notice the warmth of his hands lingering on her as he closed the material around her.

'Emma—'

She thought she felt his head rest against the top of hers for a fraction of a second before he pulled away and as she turned she witnessed the conflict in him and only wanted to soothe. 'It's okay, Jake. As dates go, this isn't the worst one I've been on.'

'You're trying to be kind, and I'm making a hash of the end of a really nice evening.'

Nice? *Nice?*

He cleared his throat. 'If Seth hadn't walked in—'

'We probably would have come to our senses, anyway?'

she finished for him.

He hesitated, looking like he might want to say something else, but then nodded. 'Right.'

'So tell me your worst date ever and I'll tell you mine,' she said, walking through the kitchen to the hall, now just wanting to get home in as un-mortified condition as possible.

'Easy. I took Monica Drummond out for sushi and ended up in the hospital.'

'You got food poisoning?'

'Nope. The restaurant had a really great area set up for eating outside. I leant over a glass partition to see if the ophiopogons were real and sort of fell off the decking.'

'You didn't.'

'Needed three stitches.'

'Three. Wow. I guess you fainted and woke up in hospital with Monica beside you mopping your brow?'

'Fainted? No. Why would you think that?'

'There must have been blood. I assumed from earlier—'

He tensed. 'No—that was—I was reminded of something else.' Grabbing the torch from the shelf above the umbrella stand and checking it worked, he shoved it in his pocket and opened the front door. 'So come on, tell me about your worst date, then?'

She wondered what he'd been reminded of to turn him grey but one small glance told her he wasn't going to expand. Looping her scarf three times around her neck, she followed him outside.

It was freezing. The temperature had dropped dramatically and the path was hard and sparkly with frost under her feet.

'So my worst date,' she said, matching his hurried walking pace, 'would have to be getting stuck half-in, half-out of The Fluffy Duck's restroom window and having to call my flat-mates for help. Only instead of arriving and pulling me out, they told the manager who then called the fire service.'

'Your date must have been really bad to try the old fleeing-out-the-bathroom-window trick.'

Emma shuddered dramatically. 'Ate with his mouth open. Anyway he finished his meal and decided to see what all the fuss was about, and without even giving me time to squinch, took a photo and popped it on Instagram with the hash-tags #Avoid #SerialDateEscapee.'

'What?'

'I know. He didn't even have the manners to use a flattering filter!'

They walked a few steps in silence and then Jake shook his head again at the absurdity of her date and said, 'I should be thankful you didn't feel the need to escape Knightley Hall that badly.'

'And me already in my cat-burglar suit.'

'Next time—' he stopped. 'What I mean is—'

'What you mean is there's not going to be a next time and that's okay.'

He shoved his hands into his coat pockets. 'I'm going to have to keep an eye on Seth before I leave for Cornwall and, more importantly, Whispers Wood isn't anonymous like LA.'

'I guess,' she said, biting back the sigh that came with the truth. Whispers Wood wasn't a big city it was a small cosy village, where everyone knew your business. She wouldn't really be surprised if Trudie McTravers was phoning Cheryl Brown right this very minute to tell her the bartender had visited the garden designer, whereupon she'd taken a turn about the room, impressing him so much that he was now taking her on a perambulation through the woods.

'My family are already convinced that every woman I speak to for more than five minutes is going to be the one to help me run Knightley Hall.'

'Whereas you just want to be left alone to run it.'

'Right. Plus, you also have—'

'Too much going on,' she agreed.

'To start something—'

'That will only end up finishing,' she answered.

'Friends, then?'

'*Friendship is certainly the finest balm for the pangs of disappointed love,*' she quoted Jane Austen under her breath.

'What's that?'

'I said, oh absolutely.'

'Great. Nice and uncomplicated.'

'Yes. Nice.' She stopped at the edge of the green to look up at the stars and hopefully stem the silly tears that threatened. Focusing on the way they lit up the sky she was reminded that in the grand scheme of things she was really very small indeed. Her embarrassment would fade. In her experience friends stuck around for longer than lovers, anyway. And she needed friends if she was going to make her home in Whispers Wood.

'I keep getting caught out with how bright the stars shine over here,' she whispered, watching the trail of mist her breath made as it merged with the night air. 'Something about the lack of city lights, I suppose.'

'It is satisfying,' Jake murmured, tilting his head to look up at the sky too.

'Satisfying? It's sublime.'

'You're not going to burst into song are you?'

'Maybe ...' She met his gaze. 'Can you play the piano? Are you secretly really into jazz?'

'No and no.'

'Then I'm pretty sure we're not in La La Land anymore, Toto, so nope ... no bursting into song.'

At the beginning of the woods, Jake switched on the torch. There was light from the streetlamps at either end of the cut-through but the torch's beam shone on the bark of the silver birch, and the white trunks, so stark against the dark night gave the area an ethereal quality.

There was a special stillness to the night, and then it happened.

So soft she might have imagined it.

Until one landed on her cheek and nearly made her swallow her tongue at the wonder of it.

'Snow,' she squealed.

'Wow,' Jake put his finger in his ear. 'I think they heard you in Whispers Ford.'

Okay, so she hadn't swallowed her tongue. 'Snow,' she whispered reverently, hauling him to a stop and pointing up at the sky.

'It is not snowing,' he said, glancing up.

'There!' Emma said, jumping up and down, pointing to

where a snowflake fluttered to the ground. 'And there,' she said, grinning her head off and clutching her hands to her chest in excitement before whipping off her gloves, shoving them half into her pockets and holding her arms out palms up to catch the gentle flakes on her skin.

'It is not—' Jake broke off as a snowflake landed on his nose.

'Ha! Frozen fractals!'

'Okay so it's snowing. A tiny bit.'

'Do you think it will settle overnight?'

'Not if I phone Crispin now to alert the snowplough guy.'

She stopped twirling to look at him. 'You're being facetious?'

'How can you see to be sure, what with this snowstorm we're in the middle of?'

'Oh, I hope it does settle,' she said, pouting and then walking a few steps ahead of him so that he couldn't see her poking out her tongue to try and catch one. At the end of the cut-through she had more space to look up and twirl around again, catching more of the tiny flakes on her upturned face and giggling at the loveliness of it. 'I can't even remember the last time I saw snow.'

'God, Emma – you make it hard to walk away.'

Her eyes popped open and her breath got stuck somewhere in her throat. 'Thanks.'

'I wish—'

'It's okay. Besides, you're disappearing in a couple of days.'

'Yes.'

'I'll still be here when you get back you know.'

He didn't say anything and she was incredibly disappointed

to realise he didn't believe her.

He really thought she was using Whispers Wood to give her the space to discover her real passion all over again: acting. Whereas she'd been finally thinking she'd discovered her real one.

She looked at him as the snowflakes gently fluttered between them.

Jake Knightley couldn't possibly be her real passion.

He was gorgeous and sexy and kind and patient and, and, and ... yeah ... emotionally unavailable.

'Well, this is me,' she said outside the gate to Wren Cottage.

'Yes, this is you,' he said quietly and she wondered what he saw when he said that. 'I'll wait until you go inside.'

'Okay.'

'Goodbye, Emma.'

'Not goodbye – *au revoir*,' she insisted on replying, blowing him a kiss and turning around to hurry inside.

Chapter 27

Dashing Through The Snow...

Kate

'Have you seen Punxsutawney Phil around?' Kate asked Emma when she walked back into Cocktails & Chai and found her in exactly the same position she'd left her in half an hour before.

'Huh?'

'Easy Groundhog Day mistake. It's winter. There's a full centimetre of snow on the ground and I swear this is where I walked in thirty minutes ago.' Kate pointed up to the ceiling. 'What's with all the chandelier gazing?'

Emma swung around to face her. 'I was supposed to start bringing out the china, wasn't I? Sorry. I'll jump right on it – well, not *on it*, on it because then it would smash—'

'Okay,' Kate held up a hand to cut Emma off. 'Despite the fact Juliet's not due for another two minutes, I'm going to break with protocol, risk it for a biscuit, and without waiting for her, ask you how the date went, last night? I'm guessing that has something to do with,' she pointed back up at the ceiling.

'My date? My date was ... nice.'

'Nice? *Nice?*' Kate shoved her beanie back to expose more of her ears, thinking she must not have heard her correctly.

'I knew it,' Juliet said carrying empty plastic crates into the room, taking one look at Kate and accusing, 'I knew you couldn't wait until I got here to ask her. What have I missed? Tell me everything. No salacious detail is too small to leave out.'

'She just described the date using the four letter word,' Kate explained.

'Four letter word – oh my God, it was *nice?*' Juliet stood staring at Emma. 'I don't understand. How could it just be nice? It was Jake.'

'What was Jake?' Oscar asked, coming into the room with another two empty crates.

'It was Emma's date with Jake last night,' Juliet explained. 'And she's just declared it ... nice.'

'Ouch. Way to fell a man with one word. Do *not* tell him it was just nice,' Oscar advised.

'That was actually *his* adjective,' Emma declared, studying a list of inventory she'd printed out for the evening.

Kate shared a look with both Juliet and Oscar. 'I really didn't have Jake down as an idiot,' she murmured.

'Me either,' agreed Juliet. 'Plus, there was All The Sparks.'

'Emma, are you sure something wasn't lost in translation?'

'Mmm-hmm,' Emma said shoving a piece of foam into the bottom of one of the empty crates. 'Positive.'

Moving to stand beside Emma and help her stack china on top of the foam, she said gently, 'Why don't you tell us exactly what happened.'

Without looking at her, Emma carried on stacking. 'I met his sister and his nephew when they popped in. They're super-nice. Then we went on a tour of the gardens. He'd cooked me Thanksgiving dinner—'

'It was Thanksgiving yesterday?' Juliet made an 'eek' face as she came to stand the other side of Emma and help stack the crockery. 'Why didn't you tell us?'

Emma shrugged. 'I already knew you'd all been invited to Thursday night dinner for the Dinner That Wasn't a Big Deal.'

Sheila must have told her, Kate realised. They'd been at her mum's for their first weekly night dinner with special guest, Big Kev, and although no one had let on in any way that it was a huge deal, it had been.

'But Jake obviously knew what date it was, even if we're complete morons,' Juliet added with a nudge of Emma's elbow. 'That's more than nice, that's—'

'I might go and find Daniel,' Oscar inserted.

'Good idea,' Kate said. 'And then the both of you should go and find Jake and ask him why he thinks it's appropriate to use four letter words like 'nice' at the end of a date *he* asked for.'

'Oh my God, you can't,' Emma said, hugging her spread-sheet to her chest. 'You really, absolutely can't. I've already died of mortification around him at least twice now. I really don't think my heart can take a third time.'

Oscar smiled. 'Relax. There will be no questioning, infor-mation exchange or manly heart-to-hearts. Jeez, this is tree-lighting night, not poker night!'

As soon as Oscar left bearing two crates of china for the stall outside, Kate looked at Emma. 'So he cooked Thanksgiving dinner for you, you went on a tour of his gardens, then what? Did he start reeling off Latin names for plants and turn you off?'

'No.'

'Did you re-enact all of Shakespeare's soliloquies and accidentally send him to sleep?'

'No.' She held a cup to the light as if to check it for chips.

'So...?'

'We kissed.'

Kate leaned around Emma's back to catch Juliet's attention and mouth the word, 'Waaaahhh!' and once that was out of her system, returned to upright position. 'Please tell me Jake Knightley's kisses are a hell of a lot better than nice. It would be a crime for a man to look like that and not—'

'They were.' Emma licked her lips, frowned, and stroked a hand over the cup she was holding as she considered. 'They were pretty-darn fabulous, amazing, and mind-blowing.' Placing the cup inside the crate, she said, 'Huh. What do you know ... three words that are all much better than *nice.*'

Kate and Juliet both leaned back to silently communicate another 'Waaahhhh!' to each other.

'But then,' Emma added, reaching for her pencil and spreadsheet, 'Seth turned up drunk and so that put a stop to fabulous, amazing and mind-blowing, which gave Jake plenty of time to reflect on the date and decide that the best way to describe it was – you know – nice.'

Juliet laid a comforting hand on Emma's forearm. 'I'm sure

he was only—'

'Forget it,' Emma said, shaking off the sympathy, taking a full crate of crockery over to the door and picking up the last empty one on her way back. 'I just want to concentrate on setting up the best drinks stand at a tree-lighting ceremony in all the land.'

'But it's just so mystifying,' Juliet murmured.

'Or not,' Emma said with a small smile. 'He's just not that into me.'

'Again – mystifying. And not at all what was supposed to happen, given that it started snowing and you both stood under the chandelier.'

'This chandelier? What *is* the full story anyway? Jake told me some of it last night but it sounds as if there's more.'

Kate studied Emma for a moment. Perhaps if she learned of the folklore she might not be so quick to accept Jake's description of their date. 'Why don't you seek out Old Man Isaac tonight? I have a feeling he can tell it better than we could.'

At the sound of knocking on the open doors, all three raised their heads to find Gloria standing uncertainly in the doorway.

'Can I come in?' Gloria asked.

As if Emma immediately guessed Kate was going to pedantically ask, 'I don't know, can you?' she smiled at Gloria and said under her breath to Kate, 'Be nice.'

Be nice? To Gloria? But they weren't open yet!

'I wanted to have a quick word,' Gloria said, staring down Kate before her gaze took in the fact that Juliet was there as well and she paled.

'If it's to say you can't spare the hours to do the trial period after all, I'm afraid that's the only way you're making it onto the payroll,' Kate told her.

'I wanted to apologise,' Gloria said clearly.

'What?' This time Kate whipped off her beanie and shoved it in her pocket.

'I think she said apologise,' Juliet whispered.

'What have you done now?' Kate sighed.

Gloria blinked and then said, 'For before. For last year.'

Kate refused to let her mouth drop open. Instead she studied her and with a raised eyebrow, said, 'Okay, then.'

'Now?' Gloria asked looking uncomfortable.

'Were you thinking of a particular time?'

Gloria's lips thinned but she stuck to her theme. 'No. I can do now. Now is good. Can I have a drink?'

Kate rolled her eyes. 'If you need to be pissed to apologise—'

'I *meant* a glass of water.'

'Oh.'

'I'll get you one,' Emma interrupted kindly. 'In fact why don't you all sit down and I'll bring over some tea.'

'Shouldn't Daniel be here to receive his apology?' Kate asked. It was the very least he deserved after Gloria had so publicly humiliated him before the village fete in the summer.

'I already spoke with Daniel,' Gloria admitted, pulling out a chair and sitting down.

'What?' A disbelieving Kate sat down with a thud. 'When?'

'Yesterday. I saw him in Big Kev's. He was in there getting—'

Gloria suddenly shut her mouth with a snap but Kate's

dropped open in shock. She knew exactly what Daniel had been buying in Big Kev's at a quarter to eleven at night.

Gloria winced. 'Obviously you know what he was getting.'

'What was he getting?' Juliet asked, apparently consumed by the minutia of shopping at the local corner shop, late at night.

Well, they were all friends, Kate thought. With the exception of Gloria, that was. Folding her arms, Kate looked at Gloria to see if she would dare answer.

Gloria's gaze slid uncomfortably away from Kate's to answer Juliet. 'Condoms.'

Wow. It turned out she did so dare.

'Anyway, I saw him and apologised and he seemed to accept it.'

'Probably because he wanted to get as far away from you as quickly as possible.'

'No. I made sure.'

'You made sure? What did you do, follow him outside and demand he acknowledge your apology?'

A mutinous expression crossed Gloria's face. 'I realise I don't always choose the best words when I'm communicating.'

'He didn't say a word about this to me,' Kate accused.

'I expect he didn't want to spoil the mood.'

'Oh my God.'

Emma brought the tea to the table and smiled comfortingly at Gloria. 'Why don't you start your apology now?'

Gloria nodded and stood up.

'What are you doing?' Kate asked Gloria and then jerked her head to Juliet. 'What is she doing?'

But Gloria had already taken her phone out of her pocket. As she started scrolling through different screens, Kate lost what little patience she had left today and said, 'Or, we could all just play Pokemon Go, I suppose.'

'I'm looking for my apology,' Gloria told them.

'You're...?' Kate shook her head and then whispered to Juliet, 'Hands-down is this not the most bizarre turn of events ever?'

'Ever,' Juliet agreed.

'Right,' Gloria declared finally. 'Here it is. I wrote it down because—'

'You thought looking us in the eye would be a step too far?' Kate suggested.

'Because, I wanted to make sure I said everything. Ready?'

'Let's find out.'

Gloria cleared her throat and began reading. 'I'd like to tell you the behaviour I've exhibited over the last couple of years is not something you'd expect from me and that I could be forgiven because of the extenuating circumstance.' She looked up from her phone, straight at Kate and Juliet. 'But that would hardly ring true for either of you.' She stopped again. Swallowed thickly and then carried on, 'Yes, there were extenuating circumstances but let's face it ... my default personality has been "bitch" since I was twelve and we got evicted because of Mum's—' Gloria went beetroot red and started scrolling forward muttering under her breath about how she was going to skip to the apology proper.

Aw, man. Kate swore under her breath. Not because she couldn't stand to listen to any more of Gloria's apology but because she already found herself softening. You had to be in a pretty bad place to have to write down your apology. And it took serious guts to read it aloud to your audience. And she'd forgotten about her mum.

Still ... Gloria had, on purpose, hurt two people she loved, and she just couldn't bring herself to let her off mid-stride without hearing the full spiel.

'I think we're going to have to forgive her, Kate,' Juliet whispered out of the corner of her mouth a couple of minutes later when Gloria was still going. 'It's like she's been visited by Bob Marley.'

Kate tsked. 'And what, now she's all *One Love?*'

'Huh?' Juliet frowned. 'No, maybe it's not Bob. Who's that guy from *A Christmas Carol?*'

Emma, over-hearing, snapped her fingers as the answer, 'Jake,' came to her.

'Ha.' Kate pointed to Emma, as Gloria's voice tailed off. '*Jake* Marley? You're obsessed.'

'*Jac-ob,*' Emma said. 'Jacob Marley. He's the guy – I mean ghost. He's the ghost from *A Christmas Carol.*'

'Fine,' Gloria shouted over them, visibly counting to ten before dragging in a breath and saying, 'If you're not going to take a formal apology seriously, how about this: Whether it was the Ghost of Christmas Past or the Ghost of Christmas Future, all I really want is a fair-go helping Emma out at Cocktails & Chai. This place is firmly at the heart of the community and I want—' she blew out a breath and quietly admitted, 'I want to repay a little of the understanding everyone has given me for my ... for my—'

'Shitty attitude?' Kate provided.

'Yes. So, what do you say?'

Before Kate could confer with Juliet, Crispin's voice boomed out from the doorway, 'Well we might as well cancel the entire evening.'

'What? Okay, everyone stop,' Kate said, standing up.

'Collaborate and listen?' Juliet said under her breath.

'Gloria, save that apology as a memo because I find I do want to hear the whole of it uninterrupted. Now, Crispin, what, exactly, has you getting wiggy with it?'

'Wiggy?' Crispin's hand went straight to his head as if to check his wig was, in fact, on straight.

Damn it. It was because everything was going straight to Bizarro World in a sleigh that she'd slipped up about his wig. 'I mean jiggy ... I mean upset. What has you so upset? Why are you talking about cancelling the tree-lighting ceremony, which, by the way, we are *not* doing.'

'We'll have to,' Crispin said dramatically, stomping over to them. 'We need to call an emergency village meeting. Whispers Wood has been monumentally let down. Of course, I hold myself entirely responsible...'

'Hold it! I'm not sure the space time continuum can handle two Whispers Wood residents throwing themselves on the altar of forgiveness on the same day. Now who has let you down?'

'It's Raining Snow was supposed to be supplying the snow machines only now it's snowing here—'

'But it's not.'

'I told them that, but they're insisting it's going to, and have informed me an event-holder up the road from them has offered to pay twice their usual fee. And Reindeers R Us rang to say they can't get to us because—'

'Don't tell me. They're actually snowed in where they're based?' Kate supplied, finally considering joining him in full-on panic mode.

Crispin nodded. 'It's a complete disaster. Of course Whispers Ford put off doing their lighting ceremony until next week. Every year it's the same. Like they're ITV and we're BBC1, and we're forced into this battle to get the best date for the best show.'

'Crispin,' Kate admonished. 'I need you to focus. So, essentially all you're saying is that we're going to be missing snow and reindeer.'

'Yes.'

'Well, we'll have to cope. It's supposed to be all about switching on the Christmas tree lights and singing carols anyway. We'll still have the drinks stand. Mum's baked loads of treats to dunk in the hot chocolate. Felix is doing the hog-roast and jacket potatoes.'

'But what about the children?'

'Pretty sure we're not allowed to roast any of those.'

'They'll be so disappointed,' Crispin moaned, ignoring her.

'Mary will be handing out glow-sticks.'

'No candles this year?' Juliet asked.

'Health and safety,' Crispin explained. 'Trudie's been going on about how the children in the Christmas show have been turning up to rehearsals chatting about how they can't wait to have a sleigh-ride. She's never going to let me forget. She'll probably strip me of my robes.'

'Oo-er, let's not get carried away,' Kate said. 'Emma, why do you have your hand up in the air?'

'I have an idea? It's a bit out there but Crispin what would you say if I told you we could still put on sleigh-rides for the kids tonight?'

'I'd say, "It's impossible" you poor naïve fool.'

'How about if I told you that I know someone?'

Crispin gave her a bewildered look. 'But you've only been here five minutes.'

'Maybe that's why I can think outside the box. Will you trust me?'

'Even if she can't pull it off, we are not cancelling,' Kate insisted. 'When Daniel and I were competing for The Clock House this summer everyone realised it's good for the community to come together on a regular basis and celebrate Whispers Wood. That's what we're going to do tonight. And if Emma manages to provide sleigh-rides ... bonus.'

Crispin looked dubiously at them all.

'I bet Whispers Ford wouldn't lie down over a little hiccup like this,' Kate added.

He thought for a moment and then skewered Emma with a serious look. 'I'm placing my trust in you, young lady.'

'I won't let you down, sir,' she said with a salute.

'I suppose I'd better go and start checking Jake and the rest of the helpers have put the tree up securely.'

'Don't forget your clipboard,' Kate said.

As soon as he'd left, she turned to Emma and said, 'Right, what do we need to do?'

Emma looked around the table. 'I'm going to need every spare strip of battery-operated LED lights we can get our hands on. Felix must have a carriage, right? Do any of you have antler hair-bands? Juliet you must have a glue-gun, we'll need that. And oh, maybe a red nose – the kind they wear on Red Nose Day, and a few metres of elastic.'

'Are you thinking what I think you're thinking?' Kate asked.

'Is it too out there?' Emma asked, looking worried.

Kate shook her head and grinned. 'It's bloody genius. But it'll take a few hours to organise.'

'I can set up the drinks stall while you're doing that,' Gloria offered.

'Um...'

'No ulterior motive. Other than I'm eager to prove myself. And I can help run the stall this evening. It's vats of hot chocolate, tea and coffee. Seriously, how difficult can it be?' She stopped when she saw Kate's eyes narrow. 'Sorry. Sarcasm still stuck on eleven. Surely your mum knows how all the food should be set up? Phone her and she can supervise me.'

Chapter 28

Mistletoe and Whine

Emma

'You have to be joking?' Jake muttered as he walked around the tree inspecting it.

Emma waited for him to come full circle. She had to admit, walking out of The Clock House to see the Christmas tree already installed in the middle of the green, was impressive.

'Please Jake,' she begged, looking back to where Kate and Juliet were standing a careful distance away. Both were grinning and giving her the double thumbs up and she felt her chin tilt up determinedly.

'You'll have to get someone else,' Jake said, coming back to join her. 'I'm busy.'

'But friends are supposed to help each other out, aren't they? And that's what we are, aren't we? Friends?' she pouted, playing to the message he'd been so keen on delivering after their date. 'Crispin can finish off here. Felix is getting the food ready for tonight. Oscar and Daniel are getting the carriage ready. And you're the exact right man for this task. The *only* man.'

'How on earth do you figure that?' he muttered, before shouting, 'Okay guys, that's perfect, let's get the cherry picker ready for stringing the lights.'

'I figure it because the first time I met you, you were like the Christian Grey of cow whisperers.'

Jake dragged his gaze from the cherry picker being carefully driven along planks set out across the green, to stare down at her. 'Have you even checked what you want to do is legal?'

'Felix says she'll be fine with it.'

'Right. Because he had a full and frank conversation with her and she was all, "hey, exploit away".'

'Look, if she doesn't like it, we won't make her. But it's worth a shot at least. Think of the children...'

'That is so low.'

'So you'll do it?' Before he could say he wouldn't, she shouted to the girls, 'He'll do it.'

Jake sighed. 'I never stood a chance, did I?'

Pleased, Emma grinned. 'Oh, I should have said at the start ... your tree is massive.'

The side of Jake's mouth tilted up. 'As it happens that's not the first time I've been commended for the size of my,' he paused deliberately, 'tree.'

Emma giggled as Kate and Juliet approached.

'Gold star for you, Jake,' Kate said. 'Emma said you wouldn't let us down.'

Emma stared down at her feet at the outrageous fib. She really hadn't known whether he would help out or not.

'Oscar and Daniel are already at the farm rigging up the carriage with lights and some foliage to make it look all fancy.

Juliet's going to get glue-gun-happy joining Christmas head-band antlers together to get the proportions right. And I'm going to hunt up some blankets for the seats,' Kate finished.

'I may already have some you can use,' Jake said. 'Sheepskin, fake-fur and wool okay?'

'Perfect.'

'I bought a whole bunch of rugs and blankets this morning.'

Emma gasped, 'For the secret garden? You're going to set the scene like I suggested?'

'Couldn't say,' Jake responded mildly. 'On account of it being secret,' he added when the inquisitive stares obviously got too much. 'The blankets are in the kitchen at home if you want to collect them and cut the tags off. Seth will let you in. You might have to shout up at his window to wake him up. If he's in any fit state to, get him to help. Also, there's spare ivy behind the second potting shed. Use that if you want.'

'Brilliant.'

Emma felt a nervous flutter as she looked around the green at all the preparations for the evening. 'Are we crazy to try this?'

'Certifiable,' Jake answered.

'But it's going to work, right?' And before he could cough the word 'doubtful' she turned to Kate and Juliet and said, 'Meet us at the farm when you have everything ready. Text me if there's any problems. You,' she said, turning to Jake, 'can you officially hand over to Crispin? But, um, maybe don't tell him exactly, or in fact, anything at all about the plan.'

'He doesn't know?' Jake asked stunned. 'He'll have a coronary.'

'Nonsense. Think of the look of wonder on his face when he first sets eyes on—'

'That won't be wonder on his face, that'll be apoplexy.'

'I'm going to allow the cynicism,' Emma let him know, 'on account of knowing you're the kind of guy who will try everything to make this work out,' she paused and with an innocent smile, added, 'for the children...'

Jake stared at her for a full minute before he huffed out a breath and then turned, muttering about going to find Crispin and that he'd meet her down at the farm.

Having spent the walk to the farm lecturing herself on how it would probably be easier to relegate Jake to the friend-zone once he'd actually left Whispers Wood, and how as that was only one day away, she was just going to have to manage until then, she was feeling a lot more comfortable.

'You're going to do such a good job, aren't you girl?' Emma said, stroking her hand soothingly down the cow's neck, amazed at how un-scary it was to be in a field full of them when you had an emergency plan to save the tree-lighting ceremony. 'Everyone will be so happy to see you in your smart Christmas outfit,' she crooned.

'What are you doing?' Jake asked, climbing effortlessly over the fence with the harness Felix said would be best. 'That isn't Gertrude.'

'Of course it is.' Emma stepped back to stare at the cow she'd just been giving a pep talk to.

Jake threw back his head and laughed. 'Nope. *That's* Gertrude,' he said, indicating the cow next to it. 'You better hope your one doesn't understand English because if you've promised it the part and now you're taking it away...'

'Oh my God, Cow-With-No-Name I am so sorry,' Emma said, to the cow she'd been chatting to. 'But I'm afraid Gertrude is more experienced with crowds. What?' she said, tossing her hair back over her shoulder when she could feel Jake staring at her, 'It doesn't cost anything to be kind and I know what it's like to think you're in with a shot and then pffft, it's taken away from you.' Leaning forward she whispered in the cow's ear, 'It's not because you're not pretty, okay?'

Stepping towards Gertrude she reached out to carefully lay her hand against her neck while Jake started putting the reins on her.

'Just think,' Jake said, 'when you go back to LA you can put so many new skills on your Equity card application.'

'Hey Gertrude,' Emma said, ignoring Jake. 'Tonight, for one night only, you're going to be Rudolph. How does that sound to you?'

Gertrude looked very happy about the news. Emma refused to think about how Jake kept assuming she'd leave Whispers Wood.

'We're counting on you, Gertrude,' she soothed as Jake slowly and methodically buckled the harness and draped over the reins. 'We have a shiny, sparkly harness for you and a head-dress and everything. Oh, wow, look, your carriage awaits,' she said, looking up, as Oscar and Daniel drove up, the carriage secured onto the back of a trailer.

As they got out of the truck and started unloading the carriage, Emma said, 'Guys, it looks awesome!'

'You haven't seen the best bit yet,' Daniel added and with a flourish took out a control set and flicked a switch. The carriage lit up with Christmas lights and festive foliage.

'Where's the ivy I said you could take from behind the second potting shed?' Jake asked staring at the carriage.

'What do you mean?' Daniel asked, trying to adopt an innocent expression and failing miserably.

'What do you mean, what do I mean ... that is not ivy ... that's viscum album.'

'Hey, I'm not a garden designer. I attached the stuff that was handed to me.'

'Mistletoe,' Jake ground out. 'You've covered the whole thing in the stuff. Where the hell did you get it all?'

'It's all right, Jake, it can't hurt anyone, it's all plastic. Trudie gave it to us when we couldn't find the ivy. And we've got these too,' Juliet said, hopping out of the back of the truck and passing Jake the antlers and red nose to put on Gertrude.

'Oh, and Trudie also gave us these to give you,' Kate said holding out a large ball of red velvet until Jake reluctantly took it.

'Wait, what is it? Is it a Santa suit? Hey, where are you all going?' Emma said as the four of them jumped back in the truck.

'We need to head to the green to make sure Gloria and Mum haven't come to blows over the stall. You'll be all right attaching the harness to the carriage, won't you?'

The truck pulled away and Jake shoved the velvet suit at her. 'Well this is another fine mess, you've got us into.'

'I—Why are you expecting me to wear this?'

303

'Because it's freezing. Because it was your idea.' Jake started making sure the carriage was attached correctly. 'And because I'm definitely not.'

Shaking out the suit, she said. 'There are two here, one male and one female. And a bag of glow-sticks. I think we're supposed to hand them out to the kids?'

'If you wanted me to play Father Christmas, Hollywood, you should've been up front, straight from the start.'

'But I didn't know.'

'And then you would've known straight away that there was no—'

'Yeah, yeah, Mr Woulda Coulda Shoulda! Would it help you get into character if we renamed the trousers "whiny pants" and called you Father Eeyore?'

'Let me think,' he said, his head popping up from the other side of Gertrude. 'No. No it wouldn't. It's going to have to be enough that you got me to coax Gertrude into this ridiculous set of antlers and red nose.'

'She looks cute,' Emma said, pulling the thick red velvet cloak around her. At least it was warm she thought, shivering now that they'd got Gertrude all gussied up. 'You'll be fine, won't you girl? Saving the day. Getting to parade around the green. For the children...' she said, raising her voice at the last part and looking at Jake pointedly.

'Oh, good grief. All right,' he said with a disgusted sigh. 'Give me the bloody outfit.'

Without thinking she reached over to hug him and promptly froze when she encountered a ginormous bulge. 'What is that?'

'Damn, I forgot. I took a few baked potatoes off Felix's stall. I didn't have any hand warmers and I figured they'd keep us warm.'

'So that's a King Edward in your pocket, not a Prince Albert?'

'I thought we'd already agreed my tree is the biggest in all the land. Here, put one in each pocket. It's not much but it'll help with the worst of the cold. If we've really got to parade around in this stupid contraption handing out glow-sticks, then we're damn well going to be warm while we do it.'

She took them from him and glanced up at him. Her voice soft, she said, 'Jake, thank you for doing this with me.'

He looked at her with those dark and beautiful poet's eyes and then shrugged. 'Bah. I'm out of here tomorrow anyway.' Quickly he shimmied into the Father Christmas suit and hopped up into the carriage.

'Even with the snow?' she asked, clambering up into the carriage to sit beside him.

'It's going to be dicey no doubt, what with the weather forecast promising all of another two millimetres, but I think the Land Rover's going to be up for it. So how do you propose we get this thing moving, Calamity Claus?'

'I guess we pretend she's a horse? Hey, Gertrude can you act the part of a horse channelling Rudolph?'

Jake sighed and picking up the reins made a sort of clicking sound with his teeth and Gertrude started calmly walking forward.

Chapter 29

Pitch Perfect

Emma

Gertrude and her improvised sleigh was an overnight sensation!

By the end of her third turn around the green, she was trending on Twitter, had an Instagram account, and Crispin was tagging everyone he knew in Whispers Ford with questionable use of emojis.

The children had loved being driven around the green in a one-cow open carriage, wrapped in blankets, their bellies full of star-shaped Christmas spiced Churros, that Kate's mum was handing out from The Clock House drinks stall.

There wasn't anything much more fun – that Emma could think of anyway – than riding around with Jake while dressed in Santa costumes, handing out glow-sticks like they were going out of fashion. Except for maybe standing amongst the Whispers Wood community, a mug of hot chocolate in one hand, a song book in the other, singing Christmas carols while excitedly awaiting the big switch-on.

She scanned the crowd for Jake.

The hero of the hour. Not only had he steered Gertrude around and around the green, while listening to her going on and on about how fun it all was, he'd then taken Gertrude home to the farm for a well earned rest.

'Always leave them wanting more,' he'd said and promised to be back in time for carols on the green.

Mission accomplished, Emma thought as she searched the crowd for him. She craned her neck, but let's face it, at a smidge over five feet tall she needed everyone to be kneeling to see anything.

They'd made it all the way through *Away in a Manger*, *Ding! Dong! Merrily on High*, and *The First Noel* and she was beginning to worry Jake was going to miss the moment his tree lit up the green.

Then, as if she'd wished for him, there he was, standing opposite her on the other side of the circle, with an identical mug of hot chocolate, a songbook, and a smile that was a little, and for a little read *a lot*, swoon-worthy.

But why, if he'd known where she was, hadn't he come over to stand with her?

Maybe it was for the best, her brain sighed, even as the devil on her shoulder whispered, '*Maybe you should go to him. You've been so good, why not be a little naughty?*'

But then being a little bit naughty was what had got her into trouble last night, when she'd impulsively reached up to kiss him. As if to savour the memory she licked her lips and all the while the scales holding naughty and nice kept tipping one way and another, she sang, now quite determined to keep her gaze on anything and anyone but him.

307

When her willpower waved the white flag and she found herself once again watching him, she decided it would be better to move into a position where she couldn't see him at all.

She'd worked her way out of the crowd when she noticed Old Man Isaac making his way through the doors of The Clock House and on impulse followed him inside.

'Isaac,' she called. 'Is everything all right?'

'Yes. Nothing to worry about,' he called from the tearoom. 'I needed a bit of a sit down. I hope that's okay?'

'Of course,' she said, moving to switch on the main light. As soon as she could see with her own eyes that he was all right she relaxed. Pulling out a chair for him, she asked, 'Can I get you anything? A drink?'

'No, I'm fine. I had some of your fine hot chocolate off The Clock House stall. Gloria's doing a good job serving. She let slip that her being there was your doing.'

'That's kind of her but really I'm just pleased she's found something to help her feel more—' she broke off, pretty certain Gloria wouldn't appreciate having someone psychoanalyse her.

'She needs something at the moment,' Isaac said, letting the subject go with, 'I'm glad you noticed. And listened.'

'Comes with the territory,' Emma explained, indicating the bar. 'Can I sit awhile with you?'

'I'd be honoured. You can tell me how you're enjoying Whispers Wood?'

Emma leaned her chin on her hand and grinned. 'I love it. I love the sense of community. I love the characters. Sorry, I know they're people, not characters.'

'Oh, I think Whispers Wood has our fair share of characters. But I expect tonight our village green looks a bit like a film set.'

'With Trudie's singers all dressed up in Victorian costumes and Jake and I in our Santa suits, it really does,' she agreed. Was that why she'd felt so comfortable being part of it all?

'It's a very good thing you did tonight.'

'Thank you.'

'You and Jake.'

'Oh.' Emma could feel herself going red. 'We're not—'

'Of course it's not really so surprising,' Isaac said, looking up at the chandelier and then looking back at her with a warm smile on his face.

'Why does everyone keep saying that? And why does everyone point to that thing when they do?' she asked.

Isaac chuckled. 'Been keeping the plot-twists to themselves have they?'

'Kate mentioned you might fill in those gaps for me. I know your grandfather's friend – Jake's ancestor – commissioned the chandelier.'

'George Knightley? That he did. For his Anna-Rose.'

'Such a sad story.'

'Not when you realise it paved the way for the real love of his life.'

Emma sat forward, intrigued. 'I thought Lillian and George shared a marriage of convenience.'

'Is that what Jake thinks?'

'Yes.'

'Perhaps it's easier to believe that than believing two people from opposite sides of the world could meet under a chandelier and fall in love.'

'So they met under the very chandelier George hated being around because it reminded him of Anna-Rose?'

'It was Christmas 1927. A year after George had given William the chandelier so as not to be reminded of Anna-Rose. William kept it in the attics so George wouldn't see it. But his friend never visited anyway. He holed himself up in his big house, working on his gardens, day and night. Finally William decided to put the chandelier up in here, the formal dining room.'

Emma tried to imagine what the room would have looked like back then. The grandeur. The ambiance.

'Within days of the chandelier going up,' Isaac continued, 'the snow started falling and didn't stop. That Christmas it snowed and snowed and snowed. And then William's wife, Irene, had an idea. Why not have one big Christmas day lunch for the whole of the village? Anyone who was alone, or didn't have enough food, could come and share the day with them. William decided George had been allowed to mope around in his gardens for too long and dragged him from Knightley Hall. George and Lillian were the only two people unattached that day. They were sat next to each other for lunch,' Isaac paused and Emma enjoyed being made to wait for the rest of the story.

She smiled. 'Did they hate each other on sight?'

'I don't think they could have because they spent the entire day with eyes only for each other and were married the following year. The chandelier went back up into the Clock House attics when war broke out, but the story is always told that two unattached people, who meet under the chandelier at Christmas time, will bring romance and snow to Whispers Wood.'

'It's a magical story. But none of this proves Lillian and George were in love.'

'I guess that depends on whether or not you believe in magic,' Isaac commented, studying her intently. 'I rather think you do.'

Emma didn't know how to answer. She didn't want to disappoint him. He made it sound perfectly normal to believe in magic. More than that, he made it sound as if believing in magic somehow helped the world go round. She'd grown up in a land where movies were synonymous with magic and where the magic was supposed to happen every day.

And she'd tried every day for a lot of years to be part of that magic. To be positive. To be hopeful. To believe. But now she was supposed to believe everyone here assumed she and Jake were going to magically fall in love with each other because they'd been unattached when they'd stood under the chandelier?

'I can see I've left you with some things to think about,' Isaac said, getting slowly to his feet. 'How about we make our way back for the big switch on?' Isaac said.

'Sure,' she said, getting up too, her mind spinning.

'We always sing *O Christmas Tree* after the lights go on, so have your songbook to hand.'

By the time they rejoined the crowd outside, she'd managed

to get herself back in the moment.

'Isaac, Emma,' Kate greeted. 'Come and stand with us.'

Emma wandered around to stand with Kate, Daniel, Juliet and Oscar, and within seconds was unable to stop herself from scanning the crowd again for Jake.

He wasn't where she'd last seen him, between Trudie and Mary.

'Five, four, three—' Crispin bellowed from his podium.

What the hell was she doing, she thought angrily. It wasn't like this was New Year's Eve and she felt desperate in the countdown for a man – any man – to kiss.

'—two, *one*!'

She whipped her head around to the tree, and watched as pretty golf-ball sized lights bathed the branches in festive red, green, blue and yellow.

As the cheers went up, The Clock House lights came on, hundreds of tiny white lights illuminating the architecture and highlighting the clock face.

A second cheer went up and Emma could not have been more proud to be part of it all.

This was what she was in Whispers Wood for.

This was what she'd been missing out on for so long ... this sense of belonging.

'Right everyone,' Crispin said, all happy smiles now the evening had gone off without a hitch. 'If you'd all like to turn to the last page in your songbooks, although I'm sure you know all the words by now, Trudie will count us in...'

As the first line of *O Christmas Tree* rang out, Emma heard a distinctive male baritone sexy enough to send tingles up her spine.

Knowing before seeing, the smile had already formed on her face as she turned to see Jake standing about five people away from her, singing his heart out, looking proudly up at the tree.

His tree.

From his land.

'Why aren't you singing?' Kate whispered in her ear.

'I am.' Flustered, she turned to the last page in her booklet and stared down at the words.

'Why it's almost like you're specially attuned to one voice.'

'Stop that,' Emma hissed, and began singing loudly.

'You do realise you're dating Ryan Gosling,' Kate laughed.

'I am not dating Ryan Gosling. *Or* Jake Knightley.'

'Are you sure? You had a romantic dinner with him last night. And you took a romantic sleigh ride with him tonight. And he has a baritone to die for.'

'You're being ridiculous,' Emma said.

'Hey, Hollywood?'

Emma was pretty sure the crowd's singing drowned out her squeak as Jake appeared beside her.

'Ha,' Kate said. 'He might as well have said, "Hey girl". You are so dating Ryan-Jake-Gosling-Knightley.'

'O Christmas Tree, O Christmas Tree,' Emma sang, feeling the panic swell with the chorus, because Jake's voice wrapping itself around her made her want something he'd made clear he didn't think would be good for either of them.

And as her gaze slid inexorably to him once again, she thought of the snow, she thought of the chandelier, and forgot all about how he didn't want to start anything.

'Want to grab a hot chocolate, with me?' Jake asked as the last notes of the carol died out.

Emma blinked, her stomach fluttering as he smiled at her.

Her brain obviously interpreted grabbing a hot chocolate as code because as she fixed her gaze firmly on his chest and noticed the sprig of plastic mistletoe sticking out of his pocket, and felt herself nod in answer to his proposal, she had a feeling she was about to end up on the naughty list again.

'So did you have fun tonight?' Jake asked as they left the throng of people gathered around the tree and headed towards the cluster of tents that had been put up.

'The best,' she said, grinning up at him. 'It's not every day a gal gets to ride in a cow-drawn carriage pretending she's Mother Christmas to your Father Christmas.'

'No? You wouldn't do that in Hollywood?'

'I think it would depend on the leading man, and then I'd only do it if the scene really demanded it,' she joked back.

'You probably had a lot of leading men in Hollywood.'

'I beg your pardon?'

His expression turned horrified. 'No. Jeez. That's not what I meant. I meant, leading men over here are different.'

'What, they don't spout lines for a living?'

He frowned. 'Did you get a lot of that? Men feeding you a line?'

'Only from the ones not confident enough to emulate the blatant ones who only want something casual. But that's the harsh reality of the modern dating scene, is it not? It's probably no different to anywhere else.'

He slowed his pace. 'I'm not used to you doing cynicism.'

'Pretty convincing though, right?'

'Not really,' he replied, stopping to stare at her.

Had he just called her a crap actress? She stopped walking too.

'Hollywood—'

'I know,' she sighed because she recognised the look on his face. 'You think we'd be safer putting all the chemistry between us into a HazMat box.'

He ran a hand through his hair in frustration. 'It's just that—' he paused and she didn't want to hear another rejection.

She understood where he was coming from but she didn't want the last thing between them before he left for Cornwall to be that. Surely, just because getting involved might not be good for them in the long run, it didn't mean a little fun wasn't just what they needed now and reaching out she grabbed the mistletoe out of his pocket. Besides, maybe she'd got it wrong and his mouth on hers hadn't been the sexiest gift ever.

The air thickened tangibly and she knew he was staring down at her twiddling the mistletoe because as her gaze flicked up to meet hers she could see heat and desire and conflict.

'Emma.'

Her name on his lips, spoken like a prayer, was all she needed to hold the mistletoe over their heads, lean into him, reach up on tiptoes and whisper, 'It's just that what, Jake? It's just that, this?' She touched her lips softly to his. Inhaled his shaky exhale and stole the kiss she wanted – needed – in order to banish the rejection.

The whole of Whispers Wood faded away as she drank in the sweetness, the tenderness, the heat, the mastery and the seduction as his arms came around her and his mouth sought hers, over and over again.

There was no need for directing. No need to explain motivation.

There was only Jake and Emma, lost to everything as they discovered exactly how the chemistry between them raged.

Right up until the wolf whistling and the bellow of, 'Get a room, bro,' had them springing apart.

Dazedly, Emma looked in the direction of the interruption to see the grin slipping right off Seth's face as Gloria, looking unapologetic, poured the hot chocolate she was serving him onto his shoes.

Emma decided that wasn't near punishment enough and with a frustrated pout, turned to Jake and said, 'Would you mind awfully if you had one less brother by the end of the evening?'

Chapter 30

Miss Emma's Feeling for Snow

Jake

Jake could hear hammering and banter, which was confusing considering he was standing underneath a blanket of stars with a blonde wood-nymph in his arms, her face tilted up to his, her mouth begging to be kissed under the mistletoe.

Shaking his head to dispel the image, he opened his eyes to find his brother Seth standing over him with a hammer in his hand.

'What. The. Actual, Seth!'

'All right, Jakey,' Seth greeted, beaming at him. 'Glad you're awake. We could do with an extra pair of hands before you shoot off for Cornwall.'

'What the hell are you talking about?'

He wanted back in his dreams.

Where he could want Emma and Emma could want him. With zero complications.

Looking at Seth now, Jake decided he should have let Emma kill him last night. Instead Jake had been too busy taking the coward's way out, backing the hell away from the magic and walking over to his brother to make sure he was all right after Gloria had tried to melt his feet.

Hang on a minute?

'Who's "we"?' he grumbled. 'An extra pair of hands for what?'

'Emma—'

'Emma's here?' In an embarrassing show of modesty he pulled the super-kingsized royal-blue duvet up to cover his naked chest.

'No. Blimey. You need to start doing yoga or something, bro. Gardening's obviously not cutting it anymore.'

'No *you* start doing yoga,' Jake retorted like a child. Scraping a hand over his face, he considered why it was so very hard to be told what was going on. With a sigh, he threw back the duvet and got out of bed. 'Right. I am now awake. I think. Start talking.'

'Wow – you could warn a guy before you,' Seth pointed with his hammer and then made a show of looking anywhere else. 'I never figured you for the brother who slept in the nude. Marcus, maybe, but not you.'

'Oh, darn, I misplaced my designer onesie,' Jake answered dryly, running his hand through his hair and then walking over to the window. 'Aargh!' he exclaimed, rearing back at the view that greeted him. 'What fresh hell is this?'

'It's called snow.'

'But there must be at least a foot of the filthy stuff.' Walking forward, he peered out of the window again. It didn't make sense. Turning around he squinted at his bedside clock, the combination from the glare of the white snow and white sky making him see spots. Stomping over to his bedside table he picked up the antique carriage clock and brought it closer to his face. 'I've only been asleep a couple of hours.'

'Well that's not my fault,' Seth said.

To be fair it wasn't.

It was Hollywood's.

She kept pulling him in.

Getting him involved.

Making it harder for him to get in his car and leave.

God, those kisses last night.

He'd been so hyped ... so inspired by the time he got in last night he'd spent hours sketching designs, wondering where he could fit them in at Knightley Hall, knowing he wanted to create them here. Not save them for clients. He'd fallen into bed around four in the morning and it hadn't been snowing then. It was – he peered at the digital display – now seven. How on earth could the sky have dumped such a large amount so quickly?

'You said "Emma",' he growled. 'What did you mean?'

'When she realised how hard it was snowing and remembered you were off to Cornwall she phoned Daniel and Oscar and asked if they could come and fit the tarpaulin over the leaking part of the roof – you know, make sure it was secure – so that you could go away without worrying about it.'

Emotions, several, and each one stronger than the last, rushed to the surface.

Did she really think a few kisses followed by that magical repeat last night entitled her to muscle her way into his life and start giving orders about what was or was not to be done about his home?

'So, yeah, I have no clue what to get her,' Daniel said, as he hammered in a few more tacks. 'You know that saying: No question is too dumb? Apply that here as suggestions because there's only, I don't know, how many shopping days left?'

'Damned if I know,' Oscar said, 'But you can double the amount if you're buying online because of the whole twenty-four hour shopping thing. That's why you don't see me panicking about not finding anything that's quite right for Juliet, yet.'

Jake gritted his teeth and felt around in the tub beside him for a few more nails to secure the protective patch before they then tied down the tarpaulin. He didn't have time to calculate shopping days 'til Christmas. He'd done all his shopping weeks ago. Wrapped everything up and stored it round Sarah's so she could get it to wherever they were all going to be, come the big day. He didn't even have time to sit down with Seth and talk about what was happening with him and Joanne.

Not now he had to cover his roof because of the damn snow.

Every few minutes he found himself looking out over the edge of the roof, to the knot garden below, as if to check it really was covered in white. Then, he'd glance up at the sky and have to admit to himself all over again, that it did indeed look like it was going to dump a whole lot more.

And everyone would be going on about the bloody chandelier magically making it snow, which meant they'd then be going on about him and true bloody love, like it existed for the Knightleys for real.

Feeling the tension across his shoulders he tried to look on the bright side.

The sooner he got this done, the sooner he could get out of Whispers Wood.

Away from the snow.

Away from the gossip.

Away from the temptation of Emma.

'You two are lucky,' Daniel said, looking up at Seth and Jake, 'not having to interpret hints about the perfect Christmas present.'

'Here's an idea,' Jake said, 'you could always *ask* Kate and Juliet what they'd like.'

'Are you on something?' Seth asked, and Jake saw the apologetic look his brother threw his friends.

Oscar started feeding industrial string through eyelets in the tarpaulin. 'The other day a magazine was lying open to a house and for a moment I thought, wow, Juliet wants to move, but then I realised she already had, in with me, so then mostly I worried about what to get her again.'

'I still plan on giving Joanne a present,' Seth said.

That brought Jake's head up. 'You do?'

'Well, now I've lost my job as well as her, I can't actually afford anything so I—'

'You lost your job?' Jake put down the hammer in his hand, worried he might accidentally ram an extra hole in the roof.

Maybe he shouldn't be thinking about going away right now. Maybe he should suck it up and stay. The muscle ticked in his jaw and he swallowed back the panicky feeling.

'Don't go ape,' Seth yelled, holding out his hands. 'We're on a roof, it's not safe. Anyway because I can't afford anything, I made her something.'

'You want to get back with her so much that you made her a personal gift? With your own hands?' Oscar asked. 'Juliet would have my baby if I made her something. Which is ironic really considering—'

'You really want to get back with her?' Jake asked Seth, searching his face to try and get at the truth for once.

His brother stared down at the roof. 'I don't know. Yeah. Or maybe no. We can't keep doing this to each other, so maybe this time I should take the time to know for certain. I don't want to wade back into her life all John McClane at Christmas if we're only going to end up like *Die Hard 4.0* in the end. Being here and keeping an eye on the place while you're away,' he broke off to look Jake squarely in the eye, 'if it's okay with you, is going to give me some space to think.'

Jake didn't have the heart to leave his brother dangling. It was the first time Seth had ever spoken so seriously about taking the time to sort out what he really wanted. 'You can stay here for as long as you need. Wait,' something was just filtering through. He turned to Oscar, 'Why is it ironic?'

Oscar, looking shell-shocked, answered, 'Because I think Juliet might be pregnant.'

Weird that it was actually Jake who was the first to break cover. Standing up he carefully walked higher up the roof to hug his friend. 'Mate. Congratulations.'

As Daniel and Seth followed suit, Oscar laughed and admitted, 'Wait, I said I *think* she might be. At first I thought she looked tired because of all the hours she's been putting in to get the salon ready. But she's also been forgetful and emotional. When she saw you and Emma arriving with Gertrude yesterday,' he added, looking at Jake, 'she got *really* teary and don't take this the wrong way but happy-sad wasn't what first came to mind when you rode onto the green. Especially when I heard this one here,' he jerked his thumb at Seth, 'say it put a whole new meaning to John Wayne's "Get off your horse and drink your milk".'

'Because you could actually get off the cow and drink its milk,' Seth laughed, then realising they'd drifted off subject said, 'And I'll be shutting up now.'

'So anyway,' Oscar said, the stunned expression returning, 'I don't think the possibility has even hit her and I don't want to suggest it and spook her, I mean...' Oscar drifted off and then grinned and shook his head. 'I don't know what I mean, really.'

'But you'd be pleased if she was?' Daniel asked.

'I'd be over the moon.'

'Then I think I know what you could get Juliet for Christmas,' Jake said quietly.

'A pregnancy test?' Seth said.

'No,' Jake said, shaking his head and looking at Oscar. 'Didn't Kate get Melody that special necklace when she came back to Whispers Wood? The one that had Bea's birthstone and yours and Melody's on it? Why don't you get Juliet the same one but with her birthstone added – you know, to show her she's your family and then casually mention that anytime she wanted to add more birthstones to it would be fine by

323

you.'

Oscar considered for a moment. 'That's actually not bad. Clever. Subtle. Special. Romantic.'

'A baby,' Daniel whispered.

'Can you not say anything to Kate,' Oscar said seriously. 'I don't want her worrying about how the business is going to survive before it's even opened. And we don't know anything yet.'

'I'll keep schtum.'

'You think about having kids with Kate?' Seth asked.

'Sure. Further down the track. I'd like us to at least be living together first!'

'Again – you could always ask her,' Jake suggested, checking the cover was properly secured over the portion of roof they'd been working on.

'To live together?' Daniel checked his side was secure as well. 'It's tricky. Right now opening The Clock House is all-consuming. Add to that, she's only just settled into Myrtle Cottage. For a while everyone thought she was going to up and leave and she'd never admit it, but she's super proud of being comfortable enough in her own space to unpack and put the suitcases out of reach. Having her own place is a really big deal for her. Part of me knows she'd happily talk about moving in with me but where? We'd both have to leave the cottages we're renting and we'd need to be nearby for The Clock House. I love Mistletoe Cottage but it's too small for a family which would mean moving again.'

'You could always talk to Crispin about buying both the cottages and knocking them together,' Jake said, thinking aloud.

'Now that would be a Christmas present worth thinking about.'

'Lucky for you, you know a builder who could draw up some plans, right?'

'Jake, you old romantic fool, you,' Seth joked. 'Carry on like this I might be ready to declare you officially ready to reclaim the blouson shirt.'

Jake wasn't sure he'd ever totally surrendered it. Well, maybe for a while there last Christmas.

'That's us all sorted for presents then, what are you going to get Emma?'

'Nothing. On account of us not being a couple.' He wasn't oblivious to the looks the three of them gave each other and would cheerfully have been okay with a new hole in the roof opening up for him to fall through.

Kissing Emma on the green like that and getting so carried away, hell, it'd felt like he was claiming her. Like she was claiming him.

It was starting to feel more and more like he didn't have a choice when it came to wanting her and that scared him.

She deserved a leading man who didn't have this place for a mistress.

'How about a gift for saving the day last night then? You have to admit that was a pretty brilliant idea she came up with.'

'It was. But we'd still have switched on the tree lights and sung a few carols wouldn't we?'

'But would we have laughed as much? Would Crispin have

avoided bursting a blood vessel for another year?'

'And the looks on those kids' faces,' Oscar said. 'Priceless.'

All right. Damn it. They each had valid points.

'And last but not least,' Daniel added. 'There was the way she personally took the time to phone at ungodly o'clock this morning.'

'Yep,' Oscar joined in, 'to carefully point out that you were a friend in need.'

'And that as your friend,' Daniel added, 'we should leave our super warm beds and super hot girlfriends and report in for duty.'

'I would've called you myself once I'd heard the new weather forecast,' Jake said.

Oscar, Daniel and Seth burst out laughing.

'Hey, I ask for help when I need it,' Jake muttered.

Seth laughed harder. 'What can I say, guys? Deluded. This break's obviously going to do him the power of good.'

'Yeah,' Oscar said. 'You sit with your Christmas sea view and have a good think about what you *wouldn't have* done. At least now you know this place is going to be all right. And that we'll all look after Emma,' Daniel advised.

Emma didn't need looking after.

Emma looked after other people.

That was part of what he liked about her.

There was no tit for tat.

It came straight from the heart.

A generous heart.

Maybe he *should* give her a gift.

He had intended to stop by and see her today anyway

because he couldn't just disappear after all those kisses last night.

As the four of them traipsed back into the house and Seth offered to cook a fry-up Jake hung back. 'I'll be in the library for a while.'

'The library?'

Suddenly he knew the perfect thing to give her. 'I have an early edition of *Emma* there, I think.'

'Huh?'

'Not Emma, Emma. *Emma*, Jane Austen, *Emma*.'

'Huh?'

Bloody hell! *Of course* it didn't fit through the letterbox of Wren Cottage. Having lectured himself full circle about giving Emma mixed signals, and having had second, third, and fourth thoughts about giving her a Christmas present, he'd decided to post it through the letterbox and leave before he ignored everything he'd told himself and either stayed or invited her to Cornwall with him.

Casting a quick look to the heavens, Jake let out a sigh and pressed the doorbell. He would have head-butted the door in a proper vent but he didn't want to put his head through the giant wreath attached to the front and end up looking like he'd won a stage of a cycling tour.

The wait seemed interminable.

He should have realised she was probably at The Clock House getting ready for the opening tomorrow and was debating whether or not to swing by there before he left, when the front door opened.

'Hi,' he said quickly. 'I wanted to drop this off before—have you been crying?'

Her, 'Definitely not,' was followed by a sniff that very definitely suggested otherwise.

He felt a funny little pain in his chest. Instantly he wanted to fix what had upset her, or hurt whoever had upset her. A sudden awful thought swiped all others out of his head. 'Have you hurt yourself?' He took a step forward, his gaze going straight to her arms and realised he still had the present in his hands.

'I'm fine,' Emma said, automatically taking the present and staring down at it.

'Okay,' Jake swallowed. After last night, you'd think they'd find it easier to be in each other's company, not harder. 'Um, I wanted to say thank you for organising the help this morning. I appreciate it. And to also say, "Merry Christmas" and as a thank you, I got you a little something.'

Her silver eyes, red around the rims, got big as she turned the present over in her hands. 'You bought me a Christmas present?'

'Well,' his hand came up to swipe over the back of his head. 'Bought is such a strong word. God, don't open it now,' he said, reaching out to stay her hands, suddenly worried she'd take one look at it and think it stepped way beyond the realms of casual present and what did that mean, when he really didn't know what it meant. Probably didn't even have a chance of working out what it meant until he was hundreds of miles away. His fingers stroked over her knuckles and he felt the ridiculous rush of uncertainty. 'What I mean is, open it on Christmas Day.'

'I haven't got you anything,' she sniffed, her eyes filling with tears as she bowed her head.

'That's okay. Really. I—' he saw the packed bag in the hallway. Couldn't miss it really considering how small the hallway was. 'You're leaving.' The words emptied out of him, leaving him flat and wanting to snatch back his gift.

'I was, but I can't get out of here.'

Shock held him rigid even while he wondered why he was surprised. 'Lucky I caught you, I guess. Well, Hollywood, it's been nice.'

'*Nice?*'

'I hope you'll have fond memories of Whispers Wood.'

'Fond?'

'Mmmn. Have a safe flight.'

'Flight?'

'Home to Hollywood.'

'Hollywood?' Sudden understanding had Emma folding her arms. 'You thought I was leaving.'

'You just said so didn't you?'

'To Bournemouth. To see my dad.'

'Oh.' As her words and their meaning properly sank in so that his heart re-started, he could feel the heat suffusing his face. 'I feel like an utter dick.'

'Good. You should. It's totally uncool for you to think – this after me telling you I would still be here when you got back from Cornwall – that I would up and leave without saying goodbye after we've had our tongues down each other's throats. For the *second* time, I might add.'

'I'm sorry. Can I come in?'

'Why?'

'So you can tell me why you've been crying and I can figure out a way to help.'

'It's the snow,' she said on a sigh, opening the door wider for him to step through.

'I thought you liked the snow.'

'Not anymore I don't.'

He could hate the snow but not her. Somehow he'd got used to her obvious joy and enthusiasm and the minute it went missing it was like all the lights had gone out. 'What's the snow done to you?'

'To me? Try the whole country? Honestly, a teensy flurry and everyone comes to a standstill.'

'Not me, I'm still off.'

'Lucky you. The trains aren't.'

'Ah. Probably wrong type of snow.'

'Crappy snow.'

'Did you say your dad lives in Dorset?'

'Yeah. Funnily enough, it's not due to snow there until tomorrow.'

'So, problem solved, Hollywood. I can give you a lift.'

Chapter 31

Readers, I Drunk-Texted Him

Emma

They'd been in the car together for thirty minutes and even the soothing tones of the satnav couldn't reduce her heartbeat back to its regular rate.

Inside the Land Rover, it was warm and cosy and the scent of Jake's cologne was teasing at her, reminding her of last night.

If Seth hadn't interrupted the spell weaving itself around her and Jake, would they both have fallen all the way under?

She'd never met a man like him before. A man who knew who he was, what he liked, what he was tempted by, and what was good for him.

'It should only take about ninety minutes,' Jake said into the silence, 'everyone drives slower with the snow. You think you can stand being cooped up for that long?'

He must have noticed her clenched hands. 'Yes. Sorry. And thank you.'

'Here's a question that might relax you...'

Emma squirmed. She supposed the sooner they got this

Eve Devon

out of the way, the sooner she could relax. 'All right, yes,' she pre-empted, 'technically I *could* use the mistletoe as an excuse for last night, but honestly? I'd been thinking about kissing you for hours and—'

'Actually, I was going to ask you what made you want to become an actress!'

'Oh. My. God.'

'But I guess it would be good to try and, I don't know—'

'Draw a line? Re-establish boundaries?' Because clearly it hadn't been as good for him, and for good read: sexy, romantic, wonderful, *meaningful*, as it had for her – even with his reaction to thinking she'd been so scared by it, she'd packed up ready to fly out of Whispers Wood for good.

No, ultimately he'd decided she wouldn't be good for him. Whatever had happened between him and Alice had cut deep. So deep he was doing what he needed to survive and she could hardly blame him for that.

'I never had myself down as a rule-breaker, but you ... what I mean is, when I'm with you I seem to—'

'It's probably because of the chandelier.'

'*What?* No way.' His quick look of derision said everything he felt about magic, folklore and his real feelings about his own family history.

All of which only made it impossible to let the subject drop. 'Old Man Isaac says George and Lillian were in love.'

'Yeah? Who told him that?'

Hmm. Good point.

'Let me guess,' Jake added, 'you just have to "believe"?' He turned his attention from the road to her and then back again, as he added, 'I mean, why let a few little things like facts get in the way of a good story?'

Emma looked out of the window, staring at the way the snow was settling in drifts. 'Even if it's only a story,' she said gently, 'is it such a very bad one?'

'When you have a story told that affects generations of your family, that adds this ridiculous pressure, that makes half of them think they just have to pitch up and wait, and the other half feel like they have no control over their own destiny, let me know.'

Hmm. More good points.

'But just because they had a marriage of convenience,' she said, feeling the need to keep trying, 'doesn't mean it didn't grow into love.'

Jake sighed. 'Doesn't mean it did, either.'

'So what about your parents? You're saying they also have a marriage of convenience?'

Emma watched as his shoulders hiked up a couple of centimetres. 'It couldn't not be the way my father was only ever introduced to women from a certain social standing, who were only ever introduced to men like my father.'

Emma laughed. 'Yes, because in what world would it ever be okay for rich people to fall in love with other rich people! How very reverse-snob. So where did your parents meet, then? Were they introduced at some sort of society gala?'

'In a manner of speaking.'

Suddenly he was concentrating on the road ahead a little too conveniently. 'What do you mean?' she asked.

'The Clock House was having some sort of function, I

think. And before you ask, no they didn't stand under the chandelier. That chandelier has been safely tucked away in the attics for decades.'

'Well, I don't know, Jake,' Emma said sadly. 'I mean the way you tell it, it all sounds truly awful. How difficult it must have been to come from the same social standing and have so much in common. And what with them not even being formally introduced at a society gala full of weighty expectation, but meeting instead at a regular community event at The Clock House. And then, for them not even to be forced into marriage, but, it seems, being able to decide of their own free will?'

'Okay—'

'But here's the really despicable part: I mean being forced to create six children together. Presumably only out of duty? Really, it's incredible to me that you even know what love is.'

'Okay! *Maybe* there's more to my parents' relationship than Knightley Hall.'

'You think? Maybe you should ask them sometime?'

He was quiet for a few moments, and then graciously conceded, 'Maybe I should. So what about your parents?'

Emma put her head back against the seat and closed her eyes to think. 'I'm not sure they had one thing in common when they met. I suspect it was a case of opposites attract.'

'But you're not sure?'

She shrugged. 'They're super different. Mum's very outgoing and gregarious. Dad isn't. Mum's very "Try everything once, or even all at once". Dad's very single-minded and focused. Mum's very limelight. Dad's very behind-the-scenes.

Mum's not always very grown up. Dad's ... always ... very.'

'Did either of them remarry?'

'Mum's on permanent lookout. Dad remarried several years ago. I've spoken to her a few times but not met her.'

'You didn't go to their wedding?'

Emma brushed over the surprise in his voice with a casual, 'Apparently it was very spur of the moment.'

'That doesn't sound like how you just described your dad.'

'I know.' Emma turned her face to stare back out of the window, determined not to let the shadow of rejection cloud her day.

They rode along in silence for a while. The snowflakes that were drifting down got smaller until only a fine drizzle and the windscreen wipers kept them company.

'So you're incredibly nervous, I guess,' Jake eventually said.

'Oh, hardly at all.'

'Shame. I mean, if you'd have said very, I would have suggested stopping for a while to make snow angels but if you're only hardly at all nervous...'

She grinned. 'I'm not dressed for snow angels.'

Dressing for her date with Jake had actually been easier than dressing for today. In the end she'd gone with a fitted woollen dress in grey and periwinkle blue, with a cobalt winter wool coat for travelling in.

Not too 'try hard' she hoped and definitely not too Cinderella considering she was meeting her step-family for the first time.

'You need to get some cold-weather gear if you're staying,' Jake suggested.

'And work out how to fix the heating at Wren Cottage,' she agreed, ignoring the 'if' part of his statement.

'Why didn't you say? I'll take a look at it for you when we get back.'

She turned to stare at him. 'You're not coming back. You're going to the wilds of Cornwall. Remember?'

'Right. Wilds of Cornwall.' He cleared his throat and settled his hands more firmly against the steering wheel. 'Get someone to look it over when you get back. You can't have no heating in weather like this. Ask Daniel or Oscar. Not Seth.'

'Not Seth?'

'Of course you could ask Seth. I only meant – well, just make sure you get the heating fixed.'

'Yes, Dad.'

'Speaking of whom, what did you end up getting your dad for Christmas? You said you were going to think outside the box?'

'I'm having three patio roses delivered to his house.'

'Because two is too few, four too many!'

'Ha-ha. About the only thing I know about flowers is that you should go for an odd number. I know it's completely the wrong time to grow them but I figured it would be something they could all enjoy.' Because there was believing in magic, and there was not knowing your dad's family.

'In a hundred yards you will have reached your destination.'

The announcement from the satnav opened the flood-gates on her nerves.

As Jake parked up outside the modern town house, Emma took it all in.

It looked like the house in the photos he'd emailed her over the years, so that was good.

Crumbs, what if he didn't answer the door but someone she didn't recognise did? What did she say?

'You'll get a sea view,' Jake murmured.

'Huh?' she turned her face towards him, hating knowing her eyes were too large and showing too much.

'I thought you said you'd be coming back here for Christmas Day?' Jake asked and then cocked his head to indicate the view from the windscreen. 'You'll have a sea view the same as me.'

She looked out the window. Was he saying if she got nervous to look at the sea and think of him? 'I'm sure Dad won't mind if you come in for a coffee. You've driven all this way and—'

'Hollywood, you don't need me for this part. All you have to do is walk up to the front door and press the bell. Pretend you're in a film.'

'A film?'

'You know – where you're playing an uber-confident career woman who's flown in to spend the evening with her family.'

'Right.' She wasn't convinced she could put one foot in front of the other, let alone act her way through this situation.

'Plus, I really want to get to Cornwall before it gets dark.'

Oh. 'Okay. Thanks ever so much for the lift.'

He leant forward and brushed his lips against her cheek. 'Merry Christmas, Hollywood.'

'Merry Christmas,' she mumbled, her nerves taking an instant back seat to all the other sensations. While they were in the back seat, she figured she'd better see if she could leave them there, and hurriedly got out of the car. 'See you when you get back,' she called and hurried up the front path.

If she wasn't so tipsy, she'd be feeling really angry with herself for allowing herself to get so tipsy.

Obviously she should have thought this visit out way more.

Right now it didn't feel very polite to leave the TV on in the background while the daughter you hadn't seen in years visited. Or did her dad and his wife, Teresa, think it was okay because she was family?

It was hard to concentrate when *Jeremy Kyle* was about to announce paternity results.

She took another sip of sherry.

Sherry.

This was what it had come down to.

She felt like she'd stumbled upon some secret only old people knew about.

How easier life must be for them, sitting in their chairs, quietly sozzled, making it through awkward family visits, one bottle at a time.

She wasn't going to cry.

She was going to have another drink instead.

Jake was probably only about an hour away from his cosy retreat by now.

She wished she was sitting in the car beside him.

Everyone here was so polite.

Correction.

Her father and Teresa were polite.

Nicolette and Nicholas couldn't be bothered to meet their

step-sister.

Apparently they were both at Christmas parties they'd had booked for ages.

Maybe it was her. She wasn't trying enough.

'So, Dad, do you get out into the garden much?'

'I read the papers out there on a Sunday morning if the weather's nice, but other than that, I don't really have the time.'

'Oh.' Did he even remember the times he'd used to help her pick the rose petals? 'My friend Jake has the most amazing gardens.'

'In LA?'

'No. Over here. In Whispers Wood.' *Where I just told you I'd moved to.* She chewed on her lower lip. How was it going to help if she was rude? Lifting the glass to her mouth, she took another sip and wondered if she should cancel the order of patio roses?

'Did your father tell you,' Teresa said, moving to perch on the arm of the chair her father was sitting on, effectively presenting the two of them as a united front, 'We're off to Singapore for Christmas?'

'Singapore?' Emma's mouth dropped open so she shoved in some more sherry.

'Mmm. We have friends over there.'

'Oh.' Her heart threatened to beat straight out of her chest as she shifted her gaze to her dad. 'I assumed we'd be able to have Christmas together.'

'We'd have got you a ticket if we'd known you were staying rather than visiting. Your news has been quite the surprise,' her father explained. 'But perhaps it isn't too late? I can't

339

guarantee first-class seats will still be available,' he paused and looked a little embarrassed. 'That sounds terribly money oriented, but I wouldn't want it to come as a shock if you were sitting in another part of the plane to us.'

'But John,' Teresa said, placing a hand on his arm, 'how will we explain to Simon and Jayne that we're bringing another guest? Do you think they'll be able to fit Emma in at such short notice?'

The last thing Emma wanted was to be the cause of family stress. 'Actually I have to work over Christmas,' she managed to get out, rubbing her thumb up and down the stem of her sherry glass.

Her dad pursed his lips. 'Panto?'

'No, Dad. I'm a bar manager.'

'Bar manager?' He brought his steepled fingers together to rest against his chin as an aid to understanding. 'I thought you wanted to be an actress?'

'I did.'

'But not anymore?'

'No.'

'So how on earth did this bar manager job come about?'

'There's nothing wrong with being a bar manager,' she said defensively.

'Of course there isn't, Emma. I simply can't connect the transferable skills. They sound like chalk and cheese. What does your mother have to say about this?'

Emma couldn't believe that for the first time in years her parents might actually be in accord over something.

'I suppose you have to keep going until you find something

that sticks,' he said in the end.

'Sticks?'

'Now, John,' Teresa gave a nervous chuckle as she refilled all their glasses. 'We have to remember that this new generation doesn't get to do one job for life anymore.'

Emma pasted on a smile. 'Well, I *stuck* at acting for nearly twenty years so I guess you could call that a career.'

'But one you've now given up, it seems.'

Oh, bollocks to all this. Draining her glass of sherry, she picked up her handbag and asked, 'I wonder if I could use your loo?'

She swayed all the way to the downstairs cloakroom.

And as she stared in the mirror above the sink, shaking her head a little at all the matchy-matchy soap-dish, towels, lightshade, she realised how very drunk she was.

How long could she stay in here?

How long before she went back out there and faced the fact that the dream visit had been just that.

A dream.

How would she tell Kate and Juliet? How would she tell Jake?

Taking out her phone, she suddenly knew exactly how she could pass the time.

Carefully she started composing her thank you text.

Jake, I hope you got to your hideaway safely. I know we're both busy pretending there's nothing going on between us, but I wanted you to know that this thing that is definitely going on between us? Well, you can rest assured it has nothing to do with the chandelier. Because of course we didn't meet under the chandelier. Gertrude introduced us. Don't you feel better knowing the thing that started between us (the thing we didn't get around to really talking about) started before we even got to The Clock House and stood underneath the chandelier? Phew! I know I do!

I can't believe I admitted to thinking about kissing you for hours and you didn't say one thing about that. Did those kisses really mean nothing?

Or did you dream about me after last night?

I dreamt about you...

Sweet dreams, Jakey.

Hollywood xx

With a discreet hiccup she pressed 'send'.

Chapter 32

Driving Home for Christmas

Jake

Jake looked up as the front door opened. 'Mr Danes? Hi, my name is Jake Knightley. I'm a friend of your daughter. Emma?' he added, when there was no discernible change in expression.

'You're the one with the amazing gardens?'

Emma had been talking about him? 'Yes.'

Relief entered the man's eyes. 'You'd better come in. I'm afraid she's been at the sherry.'

Jake assumed that was some sort of euphemism.

But one look at the spacey eyes that lit-up to the size of saucers when she saw him, along with the way she plastered herself to his side and said, 'Jakey!' in a rather more outdoors than indoors volume voice and, holy Gertrude ... Hollywood was drunk!

He'd only left her alone for two hours.

What would've happened if he'd kept right on driving as planned?

If it hadn't started to snow again, he wouldn't have bothered listening to the weather forecast. And he'd only done that because the car had seemed empty without her. But as he'd listened, he'd known immediately Emma wasn't going to be able to get a train back to West Sussex that night and with The Clock House grand opening party tomorrow night she needed to be able to get home.

She hardly knew her dad. What if he was a really bad driver? Or didn't drive in snow?

So he'd sworn a bit.

Driven a few more miles.

Sworn a bit more.

Then turned the car around and headed back here, to her dad's.

She could always tell him thanks, but no thanks, couldn't she?

And if she'd happen to appreciate a lift back to Whispers Wood, well then the car wouldn't feel so empty.

And he wouldn't be forced into thinking about what she'd said on the drive up and how simple she'd made it seem to start a conversation with his parents about their relationship.

'Jakey,' she repeated, her hand sliding up his chest, her voice smoky and pleased, 'you got my text and understood the subtext and now you're here to take me away to your hideaway.'

'Um...' What text? What subtext? Looking at the baffled expression on John and Teresa's faces he tried a pleasant smile. 'She might have been a bit nervous so the alcohol's gone to her head.'

'Well, of course she was,' Teresa empathised. 'So were we. Hence the sherry.'

'Right,' he said, thinking what the actual, as his eyes slid to the large, empty bottle on the table. 'I don't suppose you could make her a large cup of black coffee?'

'Of course,' Teresa said, going straight into hostess mode. 'And for you?'

'Same.' He hadn't been drinking but he had been driving on not a lot of sleep. 'Emma? They're forecasting buckets more of snow.'

'Yay.'

'Yay, if I can get you back for the grand opening tomorrow.'

She nodded, already looking more sober. 'We should leave right away.'

'I think we have time for that coffee first.'

'I promise not to be sick in your car.'

'And that would be a "definitely have time" for that coffee,' he said aiming another smile at John and Teresa.

'You should stay for something to eat,' her father said quietly.

'No,' Emma shook her head, her hand clenching against Jake's chest. 'We should be getting back. But thank you for having me, though.'

Thank you for having me?

Ouch.

He watched Emma dutifully gulp down coffee and thought about the way his family just barged in and out of Knightley Hall and realised why she might not have had such a problem with it, if this awkward formality was the alternative.

And then he saw the way her eyes kept darting to the only colour in the white, modern kitchen. A multi-aperture, three-feet-tall photo-frame of the family.

He sat at the table and squinted at the pictures. He couldn't see Emma in any of the photos and with sudden under-standing, started drinking his coffee quicker.

By the time she'd finished her mug, barely fifteen minutes of pleasant small-talk had filled awkward silences.

As Emma got to her feet, everyone else at the table followed her lead.

'Well now,' her father began, 'Emma, you must come back and visit us after—'

'And you should come to Whispers Wood,' Emma rushed out, cutting him off.

Jake frowned. 'Won't you be coming back for—'

'Jake, if you could grab my bag?' Emma asked.

'Just a moment,' Mr Danes said, turning to his daughter. 'Emma, I'd be remiss if I didn't check you really wanted to go home with this man?'

Emma's nod was automatic. 'I really do.'

'Okay, well,' Mr Danes turned towards Jake and thrust out his hand, 'nice to meet you, Jake. Thank you for taking the trouble to come back for Emma.'

'Of course,' Jake said, feeling Emma's nerves as she tried to figure out whether to hug the man she hadn't seen for years, or shake his hand. Turning to run his hand reassuringly down her arm, and lightly lace their fingers together for a moment, he told her, 'I'll pop your bag in the car while you say your goodbyes.'

He'd only had the engine running a minute or so by the time

346

Emma opened the car door, eased herself into the passenger seat and smoothly snapped on her seatbelt.

'Thank you,' she whispered.

'Not a problem,' he told her, easing the car down the drive.

'It's really coming down now,' she said, staring out at the snow.

He waited a minute and then said, 'If it's any consolation I'd have been at the sherry too.'

'I can't believe I got drunk in front of my dad and his new wife. Way to go Ems, stellar performance,' she added under her breath and he hated hearing her so down on herself.

'Was it really that bad?'

'Yes—no—yes.'

'I guess this first visit was always going to be hard.'

She was silent a while and then out of the corner of his eye he saw her sit up straighter and drag in a breath. 'Yes. I'm sure next time won't be so bad.'

'Christmas Day, right?'

'Right,' she mumbled.

'Hollywood?'

'Maybe next Christmas.'

He breathed in deep. They hadn't invited her for Christmas Day? What the hell? The man's daughter was back at Christmas for the first time in years and he wasn't laying out the welcome mat? Wasn't throwing a party? Wasn't introducing or even including her in his life?

It was one thing to want to spend Christmas on your own like him, but to basically be rejected? He couldn't let that happen. He'd driven back to pick up Emma telling himself that as soon as the weather improved he'd be leaving Whispers Wood again. But now, before he left, he'd make sure that Kate and Juliet knew Emma didn't deserve to be on her own Christmas Day. Make sure they knew to spoil her as well.

After a few miles she broke the silence. 'So I have a question that might help you relax,' she mimicked his question from hours before.

Impressed with how she'd rallied, he smiled, wanting to pre-empt her question with his answer, like she'd done to him. 'Alice called off our engagement because she realised she couldn't hack the lifestyle.'

'I did wonder.'

'So had I,' he admitted. Along with realising how easy it had been to admit to Emma.

'It wasn't a complete shock, then?'

'Looking back, no. The manner in which she chose to tell me? Definitely. And that she left it so late in the day? I could really have done without that.' And what had come after, he thought, automatically shying away from sharing that particular memory.

'You didn't love her enough to try a different life with her? Sorry,' Emma added hurriedly. 'None of my business.'

'No. It's a fair point. The thing is I'd already led that different life with her. We'd done living in London. Socialising. Partying. Right from the beginning I'd said that that wasn't for me. Not for forever. I couldn't have been more clear that for me it was going to have to be Knightley Hall, and that if that wasn't for her, that was okay. She wasted two years convincing both of us that was what she wanted too. She must have been so unhappy. *Was* so unhappy, it turned out,' he said more to himself than to Emma.

'That's so sad.'

'Yep.'

He could feel her looking at him when she whispered, 'Did she break your heart, Jake?'

He thought about the last time he'd seen Alice and swallowed. 'Yes, but not for the reasons you think.' Before she could ask what that meant, he asked, 'So, tell me why you wanted to get into acting?'

'Oh,' she turned her head back to face forward. 'Doesn't every little girl?'

'So you wanted to be an actress ever since you can remember?'

'I think so. Books, plays, films. That ability to be whoever you want to be.'

Jake frowned. 'But it's not who *you* want to be though is it? It's who the person who wrote the book or the screenplay wants you to be.'

'I guess.'

'Why did you want to be someone else?'

'Who says I wanted to be anyone else?'

'That's what you just said.'

'No I—okay, I did. I guess I liked the costumes and the lights.'

'And you wanted to be famous?'

'No. I really didn't. I'd much rather be known for craft than face.'

'But it's such a beautiful face,' he quipped.

'Careful! You could really swell a girl's head.'

'And that's when I'm not even trying to make a girl fall in love with me!'

'Ha.'

'So was it a rebellious thing? Your mum and dad didn't approve?'

'Oh my mum more than approved. She took me straight to the source as soon as she and my dad separated. And, well, you've just met my dad.'

'It must have been hard on you being out there, with him here.'

'It was better than all the fighting,' she said quietly.

'So acting was an escape?' Just like the way he'd used gardening to escape all the endless arguments about Knightley Hall haemorrhaging money, he thought.

'Books were my first escape. I was convinced I wanted to be a storyteller of some sort. Acting seemed easier than writing. It's more physical.'

'You ever think about telling your own story?'

'Mine? It's way too boring. Yours though…'

'Oh, I think there's more than enough stories about the Knightleys in circulation.'

She laughed softly and then yawned, easing back into her seat.

'Hey, don't go going to sleep now, we're near Whispers Ford.'

'You know what?' Emma said, sounding as if she was trying to wake herself up. 'When I have kids of my own I'm going to make sure they grow up knowing without a shadow of a doubt that they're loved.'

Jake grinned as he drove through the village.

She made it so easy to believe.

So easy to see her with kids.

So easy to want...

Suddenly they were both leaning forward to peer out at the night.

'Why are there no lights?' Emma asked.

'Damn. I think the power's out,' Jake said, the only thing illuminating The Clock House as they drove past the green was the car's headlights bouncing light off the snow.

'You're kidding? Oh, snow, I so don't want to hate you, and yet, you insist on taking away the heat,' she moaned.

Jake was aware of dark silhouettes of cottages and trees. 'You could stay at Knightley Hall.' The words slipped out into the confines of the car and he found himself holding his breath, hoping she'd say yes.

What she actually said was, 'But you won't have electricity, either.'

'But I am man and I make fire,' he grunted.

She grinned. 'Sold.'

Jake shoved his phone back into his pocket as Emma came out of the bathroom holding the torch.

'You can use this room,' he said, nodding to the one opposite. 'I'll light a fire in there for you. Seth's room is in the other wing and my room is next door to this one.'

He saw her eyes go to his closed bedroom door as she took in the information, saw the way her fingers fiddled with the strap on her bag. 'So today was—'

'Quite the day off,' Jake said, watching her.

'Yes.'

'And tomorrow is your big night.'

'Well, The Clock House's at least. You could come to the grand opening now you're back.'

'I guess I could. If it keeps snowing I can't see me getting out of here tomorrow, and I do have a tux sitting in the wardrobe.'

'But after that...?'

'I can't stay here for Christmas, Emma. The snow will melt and I will want to leave.' It was important that he be clear, even as he wondered how he would leave her.

She gave a nod. 'Well, thank you for being my Mr Knightley-in-shining-armour today. Goodnight,' and stepping forward she rose up on tiptoes and brushed his lips with hers.

Before she could turn around and disappear into her room, he reached out to snag her free hand in his.

She glanced down to their joined hands and then sudden understanding crossed her face. 'Oh, right, the fire. I can probably light it my—'

He didn't let her finish the sentence. Instead he reached out, and sliding his fingers into the hair at her nape, lowered his mouth to hers.

She tasted the same yet different.

So incredibly soft and beguiling, but then as she nipped on his bottom lip, so incredibly hot and seductive.

The more he got to know her, the more he wanted to know.

The more his mouth explored hers, the more of her he wanted to explore.

The sound of the torch falling out of her hand had him lifting his head.

In the intimate light, their breathing more rushed, the sense of anticipation acute, he rushed out, 'Remember when I said you make it hard to walk away?'

'Uh-huh.'

'I *did* think about kissing you last night, Emma. It's why I kept a piece of the mistletoe.'

'What?'

'And I *do* think about kissing you. Pretty much all the time. Those kisses didn't mean nothing.'

'Wait,' she pushed him back to get some breathing space. 'You read my text.'

'Just now.'

'My *drunk* text.' Embarrassment flashed in her eyes and he lifted his hands to her face.

'Are you drunk now, Emma?' he checked, wanting them drunk on each other, not alcohol.

'Stone,' she said, her eyes sparkling, 'cold,' she added, as she placed her hand on his jumper, right over his abs, 'sober,' she finished, with a smile and then tugged so that he closed the distance again, tipping her head helpfully back so that his mouth could have access to her neck.

'You were in my dreams last night and this morning,' he admitted, enjoying her intake of breath. The way her hand tightened on him.

'You were in mine too.'

He lifted his head to stare down into her beautiful eyes. 'So here's the part where we could each go into our separate rooms and dream about each other, or—'

'Or,' she told him, opening his bedroom door and dragging him through into it. 'I choose "or".'

Chapter 33

Keep Calm & Jingle On

Kate

Was she the only one about to have a meltdown?

Daniel and Oscar were in deep conversation that sounded all very bonhomie.

She'd just left Juliet in her salon, singing along to the radio as she swept the already sparkly clean floor.

And whenever Emma thought Kate wasn't paying attention, she was grinning to herself like one of Juliet's Cheshire cats.

At least the power had come back on this morning, she supposed.

Of course it could just as easily go off again.

Whose bright idea had it been to open in the winter?

During a bloody blizzard.

Unable to stand still, she walked over to the window of Cocktails & Chai and stared out at the fluffy white flakes silently drifting down as if they didn't have a care in the world.

Kids had been out all day building snowmen. The green was now a mix of Antony Gormley-esque figures and Disney Olafs. 'I'm going to go outside and shovel the path again,' she

355

announced.

'What?' Daniel looked over to her. 'But it's still snowing.'

'I have to do something. We have guests coming in,' she opened the locket watch she never took off and glanced at the time, '*three hours*, people.' Her stomach lurched. 'How are they going to be able to get here if the snow is up to their armpits?'

'Relax,' Oscar said.

Kate watched Daniel give him the 'stop talking, idiot' hand-to-the-throat gesture.

'Oops,' Oscar added, his gaze swinging back to take in Kate's expression. 'Wrong choice of word.'

'Jake said he'll shovel the snow for us,' Emma said as she calmly lifted champagne flutes off a tray and held them to the light for inspection. 'He's going to get changed in one of the spa rooms afterwards.'

Kate felt her voice rise to a ridiculous squeak, 'But we'll all be using those rooms to change in ourselves. I can't just magic up another room for him. This wasn't on the plan.'

'Re—' Emma closed her mouth abruptly and then grinned. 'It's okay, I'm pretty sure I can share whichever room he's using.'

Kate stared at Emma. 'Oh my God,' she muttered as the light dawned, her nerves momentarily on hold as she called out to Juliet. 'Juliet? Juliet, get in here. Emma has had herself some sex.'

Emma's eyes went huge as Jake, who'd been coming through the doors came to an abrupt halt.

Kate saw Juliet bump right into the back of him before

she said, 'Did you call me?'

'I didn't say a word,' Emma, looking horrified, said to Jake, 'Not. One. Word.'

'You didn't?' Jake joked. 'First thing I did when I got here.'

Oblivious to his teasing because she was too busy looking like she wanted the earth to swallow her up, she gasped, 'You told *everyone?*'

'What,' Jake grinned, coming into the room fully, 'that you saw just how big my tree really is?'

'Oh my—' Emma put down the glass she'd been checking as if she was worried she was going to drop it. 'He's talking about his *bed*, guys. His bed.'

'Sure he is,' Kate snorted.

'He is,' Emma insisted, with a stamp of her foot. 'It's a four-poster carved out of wood like the branches of a tree.' She stopped when she saw the huge grin on his face and then with a playful punch and a quick shake of her head at discovering he wasn't angry their secret was out, she told him, 'You should definitely let the photographer take pictures of it.'

'What's that?' Daniel said, walking closer to make sure he'd heard right. 'You're going to let some stranger take photos of *his tree?*'

Emma gave a nod and grinned bigger. 'To advertise the gardens.'

'I am so completely lost in this conversation,' Juliet murmured.

Kate could hold the laughter in no more. As she let it free she felt some of the tension uncoil and it felt good. Better than good. For the thirty seconds' respite until the nerves came to clamour again. 'Guys, it's going to be okay, isn't it? People will come tonight? Please tell me people are going to come tonight? In their beautiful gowns. To celebrate us opening.'

'They will,' Emma assured her. 'Jake's going to shovel snow until there's a clear path.'

'Plus I have a system of pegs and Clock House business cards for staff to attach names to brollies and wellies, and a storage area all set up for them,' Juliet soothed.

Kate breathed a little easier. 'Now all we have to do is figure out what to do if the power goes again.'

'Candles,' Emma suggested. 'I have loads of spare for Christmas.'

'And I asked Crispin to put something on the *Whisperings* website asking guests to bring glow-sticks with them just in case,' Daniel said.

'And we have copious amounts of alcohol,' Oscar stated.

'Copious,' Emma confirmed.

'And, yay, for the backup generator,' Juliet declared with a triumphant grin.

'What a team,' Kate declared. 'Okay. Good. Great.' She'd just caught her breath when Sheila strode into the room with snow in her hair and lots of boxes in her arms. 'Mum! What are you doing here? You're supposed to be getting ready.'

'Relax.'

'Nooo,' Daniel, Oscar, Juliet, Emma and Jake all said simultaneously.

'I think they're all worried saying "relax" in a spa is like saying Macbeth at a play, or something,' Kate explained.

'Really Kate?' her mum said, setting down the boxes on the bar. 'It couldn't possibly be because you look like you're about to do a spot of projectile vomiting?'

Kate looked at her mum with a mixture of disbelief and awe. 'So happy you dropped by, Mum,' she mumbled.

Sheila smiled softly at her and walked over, grasped hold of her cold hands and gave them a quick squeeze. 'Bea would be so proud, darling. *I'm* so proud.'

'Oh.' Kate felt tears blind her.

'Now none of that or you'll ruin your makeup,' Sheila said with a sniff. 'Right then, I'm here to help Emma with that surprise for you, so Juliet? Kindly start on Kate's hair and don't let her in here until just before the party starts.'

Emma pouted. 'Last time I tried to tell Kate to keep out of this room, she engaged cohorts and blatantly disregarded my orders.'

'Last time,' Sheila said, 'you didn't threaten a visit from Crispin.'

'Crispin?' Kate looked around worriedly.

'I have him on speed-dial,' Sheila said. 'He's very worried you'll have overlooked something. I believe he's made a helpful checklist for you.'

Kate's chin came up proudly. 'I'd like to see him try and find something to fuss about,' she said and then had second thoughts because she had absolute faith in her team, and knew they could all do without Crispin being here early to inspect the place. 'Okay, everyone clear this room so Mum and Emma can work and no peeking.'

'Thank you, dear,' Sheila said as she started taking off her gloves.

As everyone started to disperse, Kate caught Emma's hand. 'Not so fast, you,' she said dragging Emma off to the side. 'I want to check something.'

'I won't start putting out the canapés until fifteen minutes before,' Emma said, going straight into work-mode. 'Gloria's getting ready now so she has plenty of time to start filling champagne glasses. I've double-checked with the catering company and they've promised they're turning up with at least three wait-staff. Let's see, what else? Juliet's going to do a simple top-knot hairstyle on me to go with the gorgeous Biba-meets-Studio-54 silver dress she's lending me so it'll take hardly any time for me to—'

'Never mind all that. Jake Knightley came to your rescue yesterday and as a thank you, *you slept with him?*'

'Well, no. I slept with him because I've been wanting to pretty much from the first moment I laid eyes on him,' Emma replied with a dreamy look on her face. 'You don't have to worry about me.'

Oh, but she did. Jake had told her how awkward Emma's meeting had been with her dad, and that was all very nice and protective of him, but, Emma didn't deserve to have thrown herself into a situation without thinking through the consequences. 'It's just that,' she chewed her lip, wondering how to phrase it. 'Jake's really intent on getting out of here for Christmas and how is that going to make you feel if at the first sign of snowmelt, he's freezing up again.'

'Relax. You're forgetting about the chandelier.'

'The chandelier?' Cripes. 'Emma, no, you can't go sleeping

with Jake because of some silly village folklore that doesn't take into account the real emotions of getting involved—'

'Joking!' Emma laughed. 'But it's super-sweet of you to worry.'

'You were?' She looked into Emma's eyes and along with a new depth of happiness she saw a spark of confidence she hadn't noticed before. 'You were. Oh my God. Are you *trying* to give me a heart-attack on the eve of opening my dream business?'

'Sorry. But seriously, whatever this thing between Jake and I is – whether we only need each other for right now – or whatever. I'm going in eyes wide-open. He's been nothing but honest with me the whole time I've been here. And if it turns out he and I are just for now, well, so be it. I'm a big girl.' She grabbed hold of Kate's shoulders and looked deep into her eyes. 'Okay?' And then her earnest expression transformed into a huge, lovely grin. 'Now let's get this place ready for a party.'

Two hours later, Kate was ready to wow guests.

She'd thoroughly inspected every inch of The Clock House except for, as promised, Cocktails & Chai and now she was ready for the grand opening.

Probably ready.

Her hand went to her locket watch and stroked over it reassuringly.

Definitely ready.

With the snow continuing to fall, she was going to have to trust that people were curious enough to venture out of their cosy homes to see what Kate, Juliet, Daniel and Emma had done here. Any problems after the party started and they'd simply have to fix them as they went along.

Running her hands down the black velvet, floor-length fishtail gown she'd poured herself into, she paused outside the doors of Cocktails & Chai and took a couple of shallow breaths while she waited for Emma to call her in. Breathing deep was a bit of an issue in the figure-hugging dress, unless she worked out how to breathe from her shoulders, because they were the only thing not being held in.

'I knew that dress would look gorgeous on you.'

Kate turned as Juliet stepped out of her salon.

'Right back at you,' Kate replied, taking in Juliet's 1950's cocktail gown in black and gold. In contrast to the plush velvet hourglass silhouette of Kate's dress, Juliet's dress had a scalloped lace neckline and a beautiful organza full skirt with gold overlay and with her hair up she looked like a red-haired Hepburn.

'I jumped a couple of decades and put Emma in a 1970's asymmetric silver lamé maxi-dress. She looks amazing.' Turning Kate gently, Juliet checked her hair. 'These Hollywood waves look good on you and it's a great way to advertise the salon. Maybe we'll do prom packages as well as weddings.' She gave an excited little squeal. 'God, Kate – I've been so, so tired – like wading through treacle tired. But now I can't wait to start.'

'Me too.'

'Me three,' Daniel laughed as he jogged down the stairs to stand with them in the foyer.

Kate smiled up at him and when he slid his hand around her waist, pulled her in close to his side, and whispered into her ear, 'You look beautiful,' her smile got even bigger.

'And look at you, all hubba hubba in your tux,' she answered.

The door behind them opened and Emma snuck through, quickly closing it behind her. 'Ready to see your surprise?'

'Before you do that,' Oscar interrupted, walking up to the group with Melody. 'I wanted to say a couple of words.'

Kate watched Melody automatically hug Juliet and thought about how much the three of them looked like a happy family.

'Hi, Auntie Kate, I'm so excited,' Melody said, moving to give her a hug and a kiss.

'Hello lovely.' Kate hugged her niece back. 'Me too,' she said watching Melody easily greet Daniel and Emma. Despite only recently turning nine, Melody gave every impression of, in fact, being nineteen. Bea would be so, so proud of her.

Oscar gave Juliet a quick kiss before handing each of them a small box wrapped in Christmas paper. Clearing his throat, he said, 'I realise I'm not officially a part of your venture here—'

'Your blood, sweat and tears are in this building too,' Kate insisted, feeling emotional.

'Thank you. I do consider myself an honorary part of team Clock House. The thing is,' he blew out a breath and stared down at the box he had in his hands, his fingers tapping against it a couple of times. 'You all know how much Bea dreamt of opening up this place. And I know she's up there,' with a gentle smile he pointed up at the heavens, 'looking down at all of this and getting such a kick out of it. Championing you all, waiting to see you smash it ... You've taken a dream and turned it into so much more and I've a feeling she's delighted about that too. I know The Clock House is yours now. All of yours,' he added, including Juliet, Daniel and Emma. 'But Melody and I were talking and we decided we wanted you all to have something – a way of remembering Bea's spirit. So,' he cleared his throat again as Melody slipped her hand reassuringly into his, 'um, yeah ... we had a little something made for each of you,' he gestured to the boxes they were all holding, 'and we thought you could wear them tonight.'

Wrapping paper was ripped off in seconds and somehow they were all opening their boxes at once, to find a tiny gold pin in the shape of a bee. Kate's fingertip stroked over the pin as warmth flooded her. Oscar had been looking after the bees that lived in the beehives behind the moon-gate, but everyone would always refer to them as Bea's bees.

She looked up to see Juliet hastily wiping away a tear as she mouthed, 'I love you,' to Oscar. Kate smiled as Oscar mouthed the words back, and then, so that she didn't blubber over them all, she concentrated on removing her little bee from its box and giving it to Daniel so that he could pin it on her, and then taking his little bee and pinning it to the lapel of his suit.

Oscar and Juliet followed suit, pinning their bees, followed by Melody and Emma.

'So,' Emma said, 'Kate, are you ready for your last surprise?'

'I don't know,' she answered shakily. 'I'm not sure I can

handle any more loveliness. I still have a speech to make.'

'Don't worry, all I've done is add a little extra something to the room,' and with a grin she threw open the double doors of Cocktails & Chai.

Chapter 34

'Twas the Night Before Opening and all Through The Clock House

Kate

Kate gasped and turned huge eyes to Emma. 'How on earth did you manage to do this?'

'Your mum is completely awesome. I wanted a way of showing off some of her baking so that guests would want to visit the tearoom during the day just as much as the bar in the evening. I gave her a tiny not-to-scale drawing and she did, well, this...'

In front of the Christmas tree Juliet, Emma and she had decorated, there was now a waist-height semi circular table covered in acres of satin the colour of the snow falling gently outside.

'Big Kev built the table,' Sheila said proudly as she came to stand beside Kate, looking very pleased at how it had all turned out.

'It's so beautiful, Mum,' Kate whispered.

'Magical,' agreed Juliet.

'It's Christmas on a table,' sighed Melody happily.

Along the table were stationed five different glass domes and inside each one was a complete scene from Whispers Wood made entirely out of gingerbread, and decorated with white icing and glitter. Her mum had recreated the row of cottages at the other end of the green with tiny roses climbing up the walls. Then there was the Welcome to Whispers Wood sign on the green with tiny woodland animals peeking out from the trees in the wooded area. Knightley Hall and its beautiful gardens took up another of the glass domes. She'd also recreated the tiny parade of shops on the other side of the green to the woods.

And right in the centre, in the largest snow-globe dome, Sheila had recreated The Clock House, complete with the courtyard, the moon-gate and Bea's beehives.

'It's absolutely incredible,' Kate murmured, taking in the exquisite detail as she tried to breathe past the lump in her throat.

'I know, right?' Emma smiled. 'And look,' with a press of a button, a miniature train puffed along the table.

'Each empty carriage is going to have a miniature Christmas treat that I've baked,' Sheila said. 'I thought Emma could announce a particular time each day during opening hours and the children could watch the train and line up to take one of the treats.'

'I can't believe what you've created,' Kate sighed and then swallowed, 'Actually I can. Maybe I get some of this from you.'

'The creativity and the drive,' Sheila said with a nod of her head, 'absolutely. The baking? Not so much, dear.'

'True,' Kate laughed. 'Okay, a few words before guests start

arriving.' Turning around she called out to her beauty therapists, Juliet's stylists and the wait-staff Emma had hired for
the evening to gather around. 'I just want to say thank you,
really. Thank you for being here tonight to celebrate what
we've all been working so hard to bring to life. I'm sure Daniel,
Juliet and Emma have all given you the same spiel I gave my
staff: tonight *is* for celebrating – but not too much. We all
need to bring our A-game to The Clock House tomorrow ...
when,' she grinned and with an almost can't-believe-we-made-
it-here shake of her head, said reverently, 'we officially open
for business.' Then, because she needed to release some of
the tension, she let out a, 'Waaah!' that had everyone laughing,
before she finished with, 'Right, stations everyone. Let's do
this.'

Music filled The Clock House, along with the sounds of
amiable chatter and glasses clinking, and whenever Kate had
a moment to think – which seemed only possible between
making sure everyone had a drink and trying to capture every
detail of the evening – that moment was spent making sure
her head didn't swell too badly from all the wonderful compli-
ments.

'Kate!' Juliet appeared through the crowd and grabbed her
arm as if she could barely contain herself. 'We have appointments in our appointment book at reception! People are
making appointments!'

Kate grinned. 'It was a good idea to have staff stationed at
reception, right? Daniel is a genius.'

'Who's a genius?' Daniel asked, smiling as he walked up

to them, cupping his hand behind his ear, to hear her say it again.

'You are,' she grinned. 'You are a genius.'

'Hubba-hubba *and* genius, you are so getting lucky tonight.'

'You hear that?' Juliet said to Oscar as he joined them.

'What?'

'These two,' she said, nodding to Kate and Daniel. 'They're going to have their own private party after this party.'

'Well, given that Melody has asked if she can stay over at Persephone's tonight,' Oscar said, with a waggle of his eyebrows, 'I was planning on the two of us having a party of our own as well.'

'How's it all going?' Emma said, squeezing through a gap in the crowd and holding out a honey martini for Kate. 'This is for you. I think it's going great. Isn't it going great? So many people have taken photos of your mum's snow globes, and they're already booking tables for afternoon tea tomorrow.'

'You having yourself a little Happy Dance, there, Hollywood?' Jake said, as he joined them. 'This is a party, you know. Show some respect,' he joked and then broke out into a strange sort of Running Man shuffle that had them all laughing.

'What on earth are you doing?' Gloria interrupted, marching up to them, and looking at Jake as though she was thoroughly embarrassed for him.

Kate had nearly got used to Gloria being around.

She was trying her hardest and to be fair, so was Gloria!

'Who have you come as tonight, Gloria?' Jake replied. 'A party pooper?'

'Try the dance police,' she shot back, 'because you just

violated every dance code possible. Speaking of codes,' she turned to look at Kate, her expression changing to awkward. 'You have a code red situation on the first floor.' Turning to leave, she threw over her shoulder, 'You're welcome.'

Kate stepped in front of her to prevent her from leaving. 'What the hell is a code red?'

'I would have thought that was obvious,' she smiled and then impatiently leant forward, 'You have a *situation*.'

Kate's gaze narrowed. 'A situation? What kind of situation?'

'An *au natural* situation,' Gloria advised.

'Au natural?'

'As in *sans apparel*.'

'Why do you keep speaking in French?'

'Oh for heaven's sake,' Gloria said, looking about nervously before gesturing with her arms for the group to move in much closer so that she could state in a low voice, 'Betty Blunkett is in Treatment Room 2 starkers. As in, in the buff. As in, *naked*.'

'What the what?' Kate said, unable to believe her ears.

'My eyes still hurt,' Gloria continued. 'You think a person can just unsee that?'

'You're sure it was Betty?' Kate asked, before urgently looking at Juliet who nodded and immediately left the group to go and check the room.

'Like I was going to ask for ID?' Gloria asked. 'I was showing a few people around, and thank God one of them stopped to answer their phone, which meant they all stopped – why old people move in packs like they do, I will never understand.'

Kate suspected it wasn't only the elderly that moved in

packs for protection from Gloria.

'Anyway I opened the door and there she was. I don't know which of us was more shocked.' Gloria put her hand to her chest. 'I quickly backed out then pretended the door was locked and sent the pack back down the stairs to look around Juliet's salon. And then I came over all duty-bound to tell you.' Gloria breathed deep and blinked a few times but she wasn't quick enough to mask the sadness. 'I guess she's having one of her episodes, or something.'

'You didn't lock her in the room, did you?'

Gloria looked thoroughly offended. 'I may be mean but I'm not cruel. Everyone knows you don't lock a confused and naked person in a room. I borrowed your 'Private' office door sign and swapped it with the Treatment Room 2 sign and hoped anyone else taking a tour would leave that room alone.'

'Good work.'

'Oh, how sweet. Are we doing peer review already? Thank you. I live for your positive encouragement.'

Kate didn't have time to count to ten. 'Aren't you still on trial here?'

'You're right,' Gloria nodded and smiled tightly. 'And this one is way above my pay-grade, so, like I said, I thought you should know.' And with that she sauntered off.

Juliet appeared back in the group's circle. 'I checked the room and the showers and she's not there.'

'Is it possible Gloria was spinning us a line?' Oscar asked.

'No,' Kate said, watching Gloria carefully. 'Look at her, she looks like she's scanning the room looking for Betty as well.'

'Okay. We should all split up and search,' Emma said.

'I have to do my speech in a moment.' Kate looked around the room nervously.

'Don't worry,' Daniel said calmly. 'We'll find her. You stay here and schmooze and then do your speech.'

'Fine. And if you find her—'

'We'll handle the situation sensitively,' Emma supplied.

'Thank you,' Kate told them all.

Halfway through her formal speech to all the guests, Daniel, Oscar and Juliet appeared in the doorway, shaking their heads helplessly at her.

Where on earth could Betty be?

Aside from the shock everyone would get if they saw a naked octogenarian wandering around, was the shock Betty was going to get if she suddenly encountered a crowd, or worse, Kate swallowed, the shock to her system if she wandered outside into the freezing cold night.

As she talked about all the different services the day spa was going to offer, she saw Daniel, Oscar and Juliet leave, presumably to re-search all the ground they'd just covered. They tag-teamed with Emma and Jake and right as Kate started talking about hot-stone massages, she saw a flash of pink.

With her heart beating wildly in her chest, she moved her hand up on the pretence of fiddling with her locket watch and pointed to her left while looking determinedly at Emma.

She saw Emma's head swing to the left and then saw the moment Jake realised Betty was walking bold as brass towards the kitchen at the back of the bar.

Eyes wide, she watched him hesitate and then start after

her.

Kate's gaze shot over the crowd to Emma who gave her a thumbs up, and then slowly, calmly, started walking after Betty and Jake.

Chapter 35

Opening Night Fever

Jake

For an eighty-seven year old, Betty Blunkett sure moved fast. By the time he'd opened the door into the kitchen and thanked the heavens the kitchen staff were listening to Kate's speech with everyone else, she'd opened the back door and disappeared on him again.

Quickly he scanned the courtyard and couldn't see any of the doors back into The Clock House open, but noticed the moon-gate was now ajar. Stepping out into the night, he crossed the courtyard patio, shrugging out of his jacket as he went.

He caught up with her in the meadow and automatically hung back for a second because she looked so fragile, slowly swaying back and forth as she quietly hummed to herself.

Not knowing any way around startling her, he made his voice friendly and calm as he said, 'Evening, Mrs Blunkett.'

Betty turned around, and quickly he stepped forward and wrapped his jacket tightly around her. 'Who are you?' she demanded. 'Get your hands off me.'

'Mrs Blunkett, it's me, Jake,' he said gently, struggling to make sure the jacket, which was, thankfully huge on her, stayed on.

'Who's Mrs Blunkett? I don't know who you are.' With panic in her eyes she tried walking around him.

'Hello, Betty,' Emma said cheerfully as if Betty wasn't standing naked under Jake's dinner jacket in a meadow covered in snow in the middle of the night.

'Lisa?' Betty squinted and moved closer to Emma. 'Is that you? This man was—'

'Offering you his coat, all gentleman-like,' Emma finished, giving Jake a reassuring smile. 'He's going back inside now, so there's nothing to worry about.'

'Are you sure?' Jake asked for her ears only as he stepped away from them.

'Absolutely. Betty and I are going to be right in,' Emma said, her smile bright and determined.

Thinking only to hurry back into The Clock House and grab coats for both Emma and Betty, he was surprised to find Old Man Isaac standing at the moon-gate in his coat, and holding one out for Jake.

'Wait,' Isaac said as instead of putting on his coat, Jake automatically went to take it to Emma. 'Not yet. You'll scare Betty.'

'They both need to be inside where it's warm,' Jake said.

'Emma will get her inside,' Isaac said watching the women. 'You just have to be patient.'

'Lisa, is it really you?' Betty asked staring at Emma.

'Who's Lisa?' Jake asked Old Man Isaac.

'Lisa was Betty's friend. They grew up together,' Isaac said quietly. 'But she died at least twenty years ago now.'

Emma avoided outright lying and said instead in a perfect British accent, 'And what's all this then?'

'Oh.' Betty looked around at their surroundings. 'I...'

'You always were the exhibitionist out of the two of us,' Emma said as if they were just chatting over a cuppa. 'Any excuse to dance.'

'Yes,' Betty nodded.

'But it's too cold to be flashing your bits for Derek,' Emma confided as she looped her arm briskly through Betty's and took a couple of steps forward.

'I'm guessing Derek was Betty's husband?' Jake asked as he and Isaac took a couple of steps back so that they weren't seen.

'Yes. He's been gone three years now.'

'Besides,' Emma said, pulling Betty across the courtyard and Jake was close enough to hear Emma's teeth beginning to chatter, 'It's Friday night and you know what that means.'

'Lock-in at the pub,' Betty said. 'They think we don't know about that.'

'I know. Men,' Emma said, pretending exasperation. 'It'll be different when you and Derek marry.'

Emma walked right past Isaac and Jake as if they were invisible. Her entire focus was on Betty and getting her back inside. Jake could only look on impressed.

'You really think Derek and me are going to get married?' Betty asked.

'Course I do,' Emma replied. 'He's going to pop an emerald

on your finger, Betty. I just know it.'

'How does she know all this stuff?' Jake asked Isaac.

'Besides the emerald on Betty's finger? She's a good listener, Jake. You've seen her in action, haven't you? You must have noticed.'

Yes.

He had.

There was something about Emma that had made even him entrust a few secrets to her.

Jake looked on as she headed for the closest door. Gloria was standing behind it and quickly pushed it open as they approached.

'An emerald?' Betty asked, caught up in the story. 'Do you really think so? Emeralds are my favourite. If he put one on my finger I'm not sure I'd ever take it off.'

'Well, let's get you inside then, where it's all nice and warm,' Emma soothed. 'And then we'll find your clothes and get you ready for the party.'

'Party? Will there be dancing?'

'Can't call it a party without dancing,' Emma confirmed.

Betty stopped and stared at Emma. 'And that's what you're wearing then?'

'Ah.' Emma looked down at her dress and then back up at Betty. 'It's fancy dress?'

'It's awful.'

Emma laughed.

'Who are you?' Betty suddenly said.

'I'm Emma, Mrs Blunkett. Emma Danes,' she replied, switching easily back from playing Betty's old friend to playing her new one. 'You're at The Clock House to celebrate it opening. Lots of friends of yours are here, so it will all start to feel familiar in a moment.'

'Use Kate's office,' Gloria said quietly. 'I've put all her stuff in there and you won't be disturbed.'

'Thanks Gloria.' Emma smiled her appreciation.

'I see Isaac,' Betty suddenly said, stopping inside the doors. 'Isaac, is it true? We're all here to party?'

'It is, Betty,' Isaac answered with a smile. 'Emma's going to look after you first. Make sure you're warm. And then, perhaps, you'll save me a dance?'

'All right then. I'll see you in a moment.'

'I'll look forward to it.'

Betty stopped in front of Jake and laid her hand gently on his cheek as if trying to capture who he was.

'Reminds me of my late husband,' Jake heard Betty say as she allowed Emma to steer her towards the lift.

Jake gave Gloria a nod of thanks as she silently moved past them to rejoin the party and then he turned to take the coats from Isaac. 'I'll hang these back up for you so that your hands are free to claim that dance with Betty.'

As he returned the coats to the coat-stand, he heard Isaac say, 'You know only a fool would pass up the opportunity of dancing the night away with Emma.'

Jake fussed with making sure the coats were hanging straight on the rail.

'And I never did have you down as a fool,' Isaac added.

'Well, then I might just have to at that – if only to protect my reputation.'

'Jake, Isaac, thank you,' Kate said as she walked over to them. 'Gloria's just told me Betty's okay.'

'Actually, it's all thanks to Emma,' Jake said. 'You should have seen her, Kate. She was incredible. The way she stepped in and looked after her.'

She'd gone from reality to pretence and then back to reality in her stride, which had to be down to her acting.

But also, he forced himself to consider the bigger truth; that it was down to her natural role of care-taking.

Because that's what Emma's greatest talent was, wasn't it? Care-taking.

In the same way she preserved a writer's words and kept care of their scripts, she took care of people.

She was able to put herself in other people's shoes and understand what was going on with them.

It was why she got living at Knightley Hall.

Alice had never understood that taking on Knightley Hall was about leaving a mark you could be proud of when the time came to pass it on.

Emma did.

The realisation made him nervous.

Because as much as he wanted so badly to trust it, he'd been wrong before...

'Didn't I tell you I always thought you were observant,' Kate said with a twinkle in her eyes and thankfully, before he could form a response, she was walking towards the lift. 'You two make sure you get yourselves a drink. I'm going to check on Betty and Emma.'

'Isaac?' Jake asked, as he accompanied him back into the

room, his glance automatically going to the chandelier. 'About George and Lillian...'

'Yes?'

'You must have seen them together. Did you think they were in love?'

'I was only a child, Jake. What did I know?'

'I guess.'

'You don't always have to look to your past to see your future, you know? Sometimes, you just have to leap,' Isaac said, and then held his hands out as if he had a dance partner in them as he danced over to the bar, leaving behind a knowing chuckle.

Jake knew the moment Emma walked back into the room.

His hand paused halfway to lifting his bottle of beer to his mouth and as her gaze found his, warmth flooded him and the nervous feeling came back, yet without hesitation he started weaving his way through the crowd to her.

'You okay?' he asked, unable to stop himself from reaching out to stroke a fingertip down her arm. Good. No hypothermia. Only skin as soft and warm as it had been when he'd traced it with his mouth last night.

'I'm fine,' she whispered back, her smile gentle as if a little surprised but pleased by his worrying about her.

He thought he'd shown her last night how much she meant to him, but then again, he hadn't said it with words so maybe she hadn't heard.

Or maybe she had and hadn't wanted to hear it?

'You did good, Hollywood. Better than good. You saved the

day.'

'If you hadn't got that jacket on her...' She shivered and he knew it wasn't leftover chills from being outside. She'd played a part to help Betty and she'd played it with skill and without artifice. And she'd done it because she could and because she'd felt for Betty.

But although she made it look easy, that didn't mean it had been.

'How did you know to say all those things?'

'I've got to know her during rehearsals for the Christmas show. Trudie managed to persuade her not to do the burlesque routine so she's going with reading a passage from *A Christmas Carol* instead. I've been helping her with her lines.'

He'd forgotten she was now part of the show.

More and more she was becoming assimilated into Whispers Wood's way of life.

'What did you decide to do for the Christmas show?' he asked.

'Tsk, tsk,' she grinned, wagging a finger at him. 'You'll have to wait until you come back from Cornwall and ask to watch someone's recording.'

So she *had* heard him. Had even believed him when he'd said he was leaving. He should be pleased about that.

So why wasn't he?

Why was he struggling to keep everything as light as she was?

'I haven't even had a chance to tell you how amazing you look,' he said.

'What, this old thing?' She glanced down at her gown and

grinned. 'Although I'm pretty sure Betty wasn't seeing this and thinking about the 1970s. I'm pretty sure she was thinking it would look better as a tin foil hat.'

'No way. In that dress you—'

'Should be, dancing ... yeah,' she sang, doing a quick Bee Gees disco move.

He looked around at everyone enjoying themselves and in an effort to match her lightness, he offered, 'Shall we, then?'

'Dance?' Shock entered those gorgeous silver eyes of hers. 'You and me? Together?'

He nodded and lifted the bottle to his lips to drink some down. 'Me and you.'

'Are you sure you can handle my moves?'

'I think I did all right last night.'

'More than all right,' she said, her eyes shining.

'You even let me take the lead for a while,' he grinned and taking her hand in his, moved towards the bar so that he could put down his drink, before moving into the centre of the room with her.

As soon as he took her in his arms, he felt better. Less nervous. Was that because in his arms was where she belonged, or because being in hers was the only place he wanted to be?

'Emma—'

'I like it when you say my name,' she said, pulling back a little to search his eyes. 'I don't mind you calling me Hollywood too much, but I do like it when you say my name.'

Last night had wiped away the distance that he'd held onto with the name and he found himself instinctively pulling her in closer.

'If I'd known you when Betty and Derek were our age,' he said into her ear, 'I wouldn't be spending my Friday nights in a pub lock-in.'

'Is that a fact?'

'I'd have taken you out dancing. Slow dancing. Like we're doing now. I'd have talked to you about earthy things that would have got you all stirred up.'

'Really? That's what you would have done is it?'

'Yes.'

'Tell me some more.'

'I'd have complimented you on what you were wearing while trying to figure out how to get you out of it.'

'Exciting.'

He swayed to the music with her, feeling one step away from his heart going out from under him.

'I'd have walked you home,' he whispered, feeling her shiver and knowing it was from him now and not from being outside in a dress as thin as the air.

'All gentleman-like,' she replied, her accent now her normal mix of American and British.

'And when we got to your door, I'd have offered to come inside and check your cottage was warm for you.'

She threw back her head and laughed.

'And I'd make sure the fire didn't go out all night.'

'I can't think of anything I'd like more than you walking me home tonight and making sure the fire doesn't go out.'

As they danced together under the chandelier, Jake's hands tightened reflexively.

Last night he'd thought he was simply surrendering to the

moment.

Now he realised it was more.

So much more.

He was falling.

Free-falling.

For Hollywood Danes.

On what would have been his wedding day!

Chapter 36

Badly Done, Jake!

Jake

Seven mornings in a row he'd woken up with Emma lying next to him.

Seven nights of keeping each other warm.

Seven days of sneaking moments to be together.

Moments that kept them eager for the end of a shift.

Seven days and seven nights and hundreds of moments where he'd kept putting off the knowledge that Christmas was creeping ever closer and he was still in Whispers Wood. Trying not to label what he and Emma had, but getting closer to needing to.

'I think I'll add some height with the roses on the far borders, maybe a deep blue salvia with spires of linaria purpurea to make a statement,' Jake said half to himself, half to Emma as he heard her padding back into the bedroom with the breakfast tray. 'And then for full out summer feeling I could block in some philadelphus. It's heavily perfumed but that might work well if I end up opening that area for weddings.' His heart gave a thwack against his chest wall as he thought about Emma still being here in summer and in his head he held up a yellow card for getting ahead of himself.

'Sounds perfect and dreamy,' Emma sighed as she set the tray on the end of the bed and went over to her dresser to check her phone.

Jake stretched and sat up in her bed. Tonight they were going to have to make it back to his proper-sized bed, if only to save his feet from getting frost-bite. 'Do you even know what those plants are?'

'Uh-huh,' she answered, eyes still on her phone. 'One's sort of blue and spiky and the other is a mock orange, isn't it?'

'Are you looking them up on your phone?'

She grinned. 'How do you spell linaria again?'

'I think we should discuss planting schemes back in bed.'

Her hand went to the top button of the shirt she was wearing. His shirt. She unbuttoned it slowly. 'I'm not sure. I mean I really enjoy talking planting schemes with you but don't think for a moment I haven't worked out you just want to put your big cold feet on me to warm them up.'

He smiled and snagged a piece of toast. 'I'm that transparent, am I?' As he chewed, his mouth got dry and worry scuttled across nerve endings. Were his feelings for her equally as transparent? He'd spent two years in a relationship with someone who he'd thought had felt about him, how he'd felt about her, and he'd been wrong.

'I love it when you talk Latin,' Emma said. 'So tell me more about what you want to plant in the borders—' she broke off as his phone started ringing and automatically reached for it to pass it to him.

He glanced at the caller display and frowned. 'Hold that thought,' he told her and into his phone, said, 'Felix? What's up?' He listened for a few minutes, and with a soft expletive got out of bed and started hunting around for his clothes. 'No. I'm sorry. You did the right thing phoning me, I'll come back now.'

'What's happened?' Emma asked as soon as he ended the call.

'Seth's left the bloody paddock gate open on the lower field and I now have a herd of cows heading straight for the gardens.'

'I'll come with you,' she said, immediately reaching for fresh underwear.

His hands paused on the button of his jeans. 'Don't be silly. You have to work.'

'My shift doesn't start for another hour and if we phone everyone on the drive over we can get them all to pop over and help. Have the herd back where it belongs super-quick.'

He swore again, this time silently at her automatic desire to help. Half of him wondered if it was desire to help or a much more deep-rooted *need* to help. The other half simply reminded him that he was supposed to be able to do all this on his own. 'Trust me this isn't going to be something you can fit in before your shift starts.'

'Then I'll be late for my shift. Gloria will cover for me.'

'Do you even know how to get cows to follow commands?'

'I can help, Jake. I want to,' she said, her voice determined as she whipped off his shirt to hand it to him to put on.

But what if she did help? What if she spent all day helping him and realised it wasn't what she'd signed up for? Even though, he thought, neither of them had got around to talking about signing up for anything together.

No. He couldn't risk it. He grabbed the shirt, gritting his teeth against the tease of her body heat. 'I know you do, but really, it's not necessary,' he said, buttoning the shirt up. 'I can sort this out myself. It doesn't need the whole village coming to my rescue when there'll be Felix and Seth already there.'

Emma stared at him like she was a crossword gal and he was a sudoku. 'It isn't rescuing you. It's helping.'

'Thanks, but I don't need it.'

'Don't need it or don't want it?'

He kept his eyes on the boots he was lacing. 'I don't have time to argue with you.'

'But you do have time to be a martyr? Because that's so much more attractive,' she finished sarcastically.

That earned her a look from under his lashes. 'Right now I don't have time to worry about what's attractive and what's not. And I don't have time to explain how to handle a herd of cows. You don't have the first idea about living in the country so don't even try to pretend that you do.' Getting to his feet he opened the bedroom door.

'Wow. Are you really that proud that not only can you not ask for help, you won't even take it when it's offered freely?'

At the front door to the cottage he paused. 'Let's not turn this into something it isn't.'

'Oh, I get exactly what it is, Jake. Careful you don't trip over your *cold feet* on your way to the car.'

'Seth, I'm not joking around. Phone me back as soon as you

get this message.'

Jake shoved his phone back into his pocket and stomped across the green towards The Clock House, where, he had a feeling, he was going to find his brother, propping up the bar.

At least that's where he hoped he'd find him.

Seeing him enjoy a drink would be the perfect excuse to let loose on the angry lecture that had been developing ever since he'd got home to find Seth AWOL and a couple of cows already in the rose garden.

'Jake?'

At the sound of Crispin calling his name Jake increased his speed. He knew it was rude, but the mood he was in? Chances were if he had to stop and listen to Crispin try and defend his friend of a friend's spurious claim about Jane Austen staying at the Hall one more time he'd probably blast Crispin so bad his wig would fall off.

He walked through the doors of The Clock House and if he'd been in a better frame of mind he might have taken a moment to enjoy the vibe. Might have thought about how it could be the same when he opened the gardens at Knightley Hall.

As it was he walked into Cocktails & Chai, shaking the snow from his head.

The endless bloody snow.

At this rate it would still be here come spring and he could kiss goodbye any work that was going to provide money to get the sodding hole in the roof repaired.

He walked up to the bar and scowled at Gloria. 'Seth not been in?'

'In the gents, I think,' she replied, considering him for a moment before fixing him a drink and presenting it to him.

'What's this?'

She tapped her finger against her nose and said, 'Giggle Water. On the house. You look like you could use one.'

'I'll be fine once I've had a word with my brother.'

Gloria didn't look convinced. 'Looks like you've got more than a word stored up in there, Jake. You sure a lecture is the right way to go?'

'Hi Jakey,' Seth said, from across the room.

Jake turned in his seat to regard him. 'Why haven't you called me back?'

Seth frowned and patted his pocket, and then, seeing his brother's expression, paled. 'Everyone okay?'

'Yes. But thanks to you I've—'

'Must have lost my phone,' Seth explained, cutting him off as he walked over to sit next to Jake and reach casually for his beer.

Jake felt the muscle in his jaw start to pulse as his teeth ground together. 'Lost it?'

'Seems like,' Seth said, finishing his beer.

'Well, really well done, Seth. Especially now you haven't got a job to pay for a replacement.'

'Perhaps I'll ask Santa for one for Christmas,' Seth returned and Jake heard but dismissed the warning note in his brother's voice and watched as Seth drained his drink and tried to catch Gloria's eye to signal for another. When that didn't work and he saw Emma walk into the room, he stood up and went over to her. Taking her in his arms he danced a couple of steps with her. 'Emma, dear heart, won't you fix me another drink? I have a feeling I'm going to need it.'

Emma laughed and playfully turned in his arms. 'Coming right up,' she said.

The red mist came down as Jake jerked up from his seat and strode over to his brother to grab a hold of him. 'What the hell are you doing? Get your clumsy, mauling hands off of her.'

Immediately Emma held her hands out to keep him and Seth separated and he had to admit he was impressed by her strength. 'Whatever you were about to say or do, don't,' she warned.

'Yeah,' Seth said, 'Watch your tongue, Jakey.' He lunged forward and to protect Emma, Jake lifted her out of the way and grabbed hold of Seth before he hit the floor.

'You smell like a brewery,' Jake accused. 'How the hell could you let him get into this state?' he asked Emma tightly. 'Why have you kept serving him?'

'Relax,' Seth said, 'I've only been here an hour. I've been at Joanne's most of the day. Probably where I left my phone.'

'You were at Joanne's all day?' Jake's hands tightened around his brother's shoulders and as Seth tried to shake him off, they merely tightened further.

'Look,' Emma warned quietly, 'if you're going to insist on playing out this whole Thor/Loki thing, take it outside. You're going to break something if you keep this up.'

'I'll clean up after,' Jake promised, as he stared his brother down. 'It's what I'm used to doing after all.'

'Here we go,' Seth said. 'Are you ever going to tell me what's got your tinsel in a tangle or are you only here to dish out a lecture?' Seth asked.

'The lecture comes free every time you say you're going to stick around and help, and then don't. Like I don't have enough to do at the moment. You left the paddock gate open this morning and I've had to spend the entire day getting cows out of the gardens and back where they belong.'

'Oh shit. I'm sorry.'

'You're always sorry.'

'Look, I've had a lot on my plate.'

'Oh, I can see that,' Jake said, indicating the beer. 'No wonder Joanne doesn't want to be with you. In the last few weeks I've seen you drunk more than I've seen you sober. That's when I've seen you at all, of course. All that, "I can be around to help out while I do some thinking". I should have realised it was more of your usual bull—'

'I haven't been around *because* I've been trying to do some thinking,' Seth replied. 'And I've been trying to do that away from where I might cramp your style.'

Jake's hands loosened their grip.

He supposed his not leaving for Cornwall had rather meant his brother didn't have time alone to think. Had Seth really been looking to stay out of his and Emma's way?

'Although why I bothered,' Seth laughed, shaking his head at Jake. 'You've already managed to stuff things up. Gloria told me how only this morning you managed to make Emma cry.'

Now his hands did leave his brother to hang at his sides as he turned to Emma, appalled. Unhelpful memories started intruding. Throwing him off course and making him feel helpless again.

'Don't be absurd, of course I didn't cry,' Emma replied, tipping her head up defiantly. 'Gloria must have used poetic licence.'

'So before you go lecturing me,' Seth said, poking him in the chest as if Emma hadn't spoken, 'Maybe you should explain how you managed to screw things up with Emma in a second of the time it took me to screw things up with Joanne. Come to think of it, it didn't take long for you to screw things up with Alice, too, did it?'

'I'm going to knock you out now,' Jake informed his brother. 'When you wake up, don't come anywhere near me or the Hall.'

'There'll be none of that. Here or anywhere else,' Emma advised. 'Seth, you can stay at mine tonight. Here,' she said, taking her keys out of her pocket and handing them to him. 'Take them and give Jake some time to cool down.'

'Helpful as ever, Emma?' Jake asked her tightly. 'And where will you be sleeping?'

'I'll be coming home with you.'

'Home? Did you just call Knightley Hall your home? What, you think if you find ways to make yourself indispensable you'll slot right in to life at Knightley Hall?'

'Get out.'

She said it so quietly that he had trouble believing he'd heard right. 'What?'

'You heard me. You're barred.'

'What for? Cruelty to cows? In case you haven't been

listening, I spent all bloody day looking after them.'

'You either take your foul mood out of here of your own free will, or I – not being too proud to ask for help if I need it – will get Gloria and whoever else I need to set you out on your ear. Don't think we can't do it.'

'She could,' Gloria said, 'she's got a black-belt in crumpet-wielding. Me?' She held her freshly manicured hands up. 'Not my circus, not my monkeys.'

'Like you could knock me out anyway,' Seth mumbled to Jake. 'You're more likely to send me to sleep with a lecture.'

'Maybe one of these days one will sink in. I take it from the fact that you're here and not at Joanne's, she didn't take you back this time.'

'And why would she,' Seth spat out, 'when I got round there to find she was moving the next guy in.'

'What?' All the anger drained out of Jake as he watched confusion, humiliation and helplessness cross his brother's face. 'Joanne has someone else?'

'For ages. Yeah. Don't I feel the man?'

'Shit. Seth—'

'Forget it – you're so wrapped up in not making any mistakes you wouldn't know the first thing about getting yourself out of one. I mean, do you even realise you're just like the rest of us?'

A screw up when it came to matters of the heart? Oh, it was entirely possible he had a Masters in it. 'You're right. Shall we not do this here, though?' He needed to get him on his own so he could talk about what had happened with Joanne. He needed to show him he was there for him.

'I mean, God forbid anyone find out you're human and stuff up occasionally,' Seth said, his voice rising. 'God forbid anyone find out about Alice and her cutting.'

Shock held him rigid so that he could only watch the instant Seth realised the words he'd uttered and how he wanted to recall them.

But it was too late.

As the hush descended on the room Jake felt the blood pound in his ears. 'You knew about Alice self-harming?'

'I'm sorry. I shouldn't have said that.'

He bowed his head. The silence sounded deafening. The guilt overwhelming.

'Jake?' Emma said his name gently.

Jake lifted his head, cleared his throat, and spoke to Seth, 'I'm sorry about you and Joanne. Truly. But at least she didn't hurt herself because she didn't want to be with you and didn't know how to tell you.'

'Jake,' Emma said again, reaching out to gently touch his arm. 'Let's go somewhere and talk.'

'So that you can help? Forget it. I'm barred. Remember?' and shaking her hand off, he walked out of the bar.

He couldn't believe Seth had known about Alice. Had the whole family? Is that why they hadn't quizzed him about disappearing on Christmas Day last year?

He'd made it halfway back across the green before the snowball hit him squarely in the back of the head.

He expected it to be Seth and was prepared to let him take a swing because for a family who'd been brought up not airing the family laundry in public they'd both done a passable job of hanging it all out on the line. He called himself a few names. He should have known Seth would have had his reasons for staying away.

Turning around, he managed half a, 'I'm so—' before he then got a mouthful of snow.

'Oops,' Gloria said, shaking snow from her hands, clearly not in the least bit sorry.

'Oops, my arse, Gloria. That was deliberate.'

'Nah. Well, not the second one in the mouth. I certainly hope there was no yellow snow in that one.'

'What the hell is wrong with you?'

'You are. The way you just treated Emma? Badly done, Jake. Badly done, indeed!'

He knew it. Knew it in the worst way. Didn't stop him from saying testily, 'It's none of your business.'

'As it happens it is. Since it was *me*, not Emma, who flirted with Seth from the moment he came into the bar looking like he'd been side-swiped.'

'You're living in Crazy Town if you think Seth is in the right place to be with anyone right now.'

At her raised eyebrow he thought, damn it, there he went again. Stepping in. Lecturing.

'Perhaps,' Gloria said as she buttoned her coat and popped her gloves on. 'But let's focus on you a moment. So you had an unpleasant truth come out and discovered it's not a very nice experience. You realise you still have to apologise to Seth and Emma anyway?'

'Stay out of it Gloria,' he muttered, starting to tramp through the snow.

'Why?' She asked, following him. 'Because I couldn't possibly know how it feels to have something you thought locked down and contained – something people can judge you for – out there?'

'Because you said this wasn't your drama.'

'You're going to have to let people judge you for someone else's actions for a while but you'll ride it out.'

She might know what she was talking about on that score, but if she was judging Alice she must know that that was part of the problem. 'Look, I know you're trying to help.'

'Don't be ridiculous. Of course I'm not. And if you tell anyone I was they'll never believe you. Look, it beats me how Emma gets to everyone, but she does. And what's more, she doesn't want anything in return. I can't pretend to be either seduced or impressed about that you understand, but for someone who's actually supposed to be into that – aka, *you* – you're making a really bad job of accepting it for the gift it is. Even when it's wrapped with a bow.'

'What makes you think that I'm into that?'

'Because I saw the way you looked at her on what was supposed to have been your wedding day to The Grinch.'

He stared down at his feet.

'Yeah,' she said. 'Someone noticed. Like you'd ever have been happy with The Grinch.'

'You don't know anything about what Alice went through.'

'You're right. And I'm sorry for that even as I can't help thinking she probably went a long way to making sure no one knew what she was going through. But, Jake, while I'm sure Seth is big enough to handle your cold shoulder, Emma isn't as tough as she likes to make out.'

What the hell did that mean?

Had she been acting her way through a relationship with him?

He pressed his hands to his eyes.

No.

She wasn't that person.

He sighed and looked at Gloria. 'By the time I go and find Seth and apologise, Emma will have probably packed and left.'

'Look around you, idiot. Nothing's getting out of Whispers Wood any time soon. Go find Seth, hug it out, and then work out how to apologise to Emma, because if you let her slip through your fingers, then really, I'm going to take every opportunity to call you the world's most ginormous arse.'

Chapter 37

Trying Hard Not To Show It

Emma

'It doesn't show any signs of stopping,' Kate said as she moved from the windows after restocking the little train that went around the Christmas tree with fresh baked miniatures.

'Are you worried about business slacking off because of it?' Emma asked her as she loaded empties onto a tray. Because to be honest, the busier Emma found herself, the less time she had for thinking about Jake, so she could have done with a few more tables being occupied.

'Not really. This close to Christmas we could all do with a rest anyway. I know you could.'

'Me? Oh, I'm fine.'

'Sure you are. You've only been working here every hour it's open and then helping out with the rehearsals for the Christmas show.'

'Speaking of the Christmas show, are you really okay with moving it to Christmas Day?' Emma asked.

'Since no one's going anywhere anyway because of the

snow, it makes perfect sense. How's it all coming together?'

'We had our dress rehearsal earlier. Don't tell Trudie, but it was really good.'

'I thought that was the whole idea?'

'Yes, but the rule is if you have a bad dress rehearsal it will go well on opening night. I had to ask some of the acts to go wrong on purpose, just to put her mind at ease.'

'Ah. You know, now that the show date has been moved, I've been thinking...'

'Mmn-hmm.'

'Why not have Christmas lunch here at The Clock House before it? You know, for everyone?'

'Everyone?' Emma turned to face Kate.

'That way anyone who was going to be on their own wouldn't have to be.'

Emma set the tray down behind the bar and popped a couple of mince pies on a plate and took them over to where Betty Blunkett was enjoying a pot of tea. When she'd proved her hands were steady, she faced Kate. 'Jake told you about my dad going to Singapore.'

'Yes.'

'Huh.' And he had the gall to bawl her out for being interfering and helpful.

'He did the right thing, telling me,' Kate said, 'because I'm not sure I could've taken the shame of finding out *after the fact* that you'd spent Christmas Day on your own.'

Shame!

That was the emotion Jake had on his face when Seth had let Alice's secret out. She'd been haunted by his expression and been trying to figure it out ever since he'd walked out on her.

Okay. Technically, she'd asked him to leave, but now it made sense. Or didn't. Not really. Was it shame for not being able to help his fiancée? Or maybe guilt for not realising what she'd been doing?

Either way her stupid big soppy heart wanted to let him know not everyone was talking about it. Not everyone was judging him. Not everyone was greedily demanding more salacious detail to feed off of.

'He must have thought the snow was going to clear and that he'd be out of here by then,' she mused, filling a tray with votive Christmas candles so that she could start setting them out for the evening.

'Well, he's definitely not going anywhere now.'

'I guess not.'

'So if you wanted to take off early and go and sort this all out with him, you could.'

'I don't actually,' she said as easily as she could manage. But when she felt Kate's assessing look, she added, 'I mean, at some point I know we'll get around to having a chat and clearing the air. But there's no need for a full post-mortem on a few nights in bed together. He was already getting cold feet about us and we'd barely started being an "us". And like I said, I'm a big girl. I can get up every morning, put one foot in front of the other and go about my day as if the world hasn't caved in. Because it hasn't.'

She stopped talking, afraid she was laying it on too thickly and shied away from looking at Kate as she busied herself

401

making sure the candles were exactly where she wanted them on each table.

Now was when she needed to act her socks off. Because she'd already said she wasn't leaving if things went south between her and Jake. Not that she'd be able to if she could anyway. But she'd said she wouldn't, so she was just going to have to brazen it out and get okay with seeing him around.

Get okay with feeling cold all the time.

Get okay with not laughing quite so much.

Get okay with not curling up on a library chair with him and talking into the night about anything and everything.

Get okay with feeling like her bed was the size of an ocean and she was a pea.

Last night, as she'd lain in that bed, freezing cold and a heartbeat from ringing Juliet and asking her to drop all her cats around for some company, she'd thought about how at least her mum would love it if she went back to LA. Her dad? She doubted he'd be shocked to discover she'd gone back on what she'd said she was going to do. He thought she was flitting from thing to thing anyway.

And Jake?

What would he think if she went back?

He'd probably be relieved.

On account of how he'd just been waiting for her to leave anyway.

That's what all the cold feet and the argument had been about: getting it in first before he thought she would.

Oh, yeah. She'd been a regular Sherlock, working it all out.

'So tell me more about having Christmas Day lunch here?'

she said, forcing some enthusiasm into her voice, determined not to think about Jake Knightley any more today.

'I was thinking it would work well as a sort of open house. We could put all the tables together in here.'

It made sense, Emma thought looking around the room. No way would Gloria or Old Man Isaac be able to get out of Whispers Wood with all the snow. Thinking about Old Man Isaac made her think about George and Lillian Knightley and automatically she glanced up at the chandelier.

And then Kate was furiously elbowing her in the ribs.

'Ouch,' she muttered looking at her.

Kate jerked her head to the double doors of the bar.

And Emma's eyes nearly popped out of her head.

Jake was standing in the doorway looking ... Looking ... she blinked a couple of times and realised Seth was standing right by his side.

'Kate?' Emma asked slowly, 'Kate what the hell are Jake and Seth doing standing in the door of my bar wearing mic packs?'

'*That's* what you notice here?' Kate asked, incredulous. 'Do you not see the dress whites and the aviator shades?'

This is not happening, she told herself even as her heart started pounding and Jake's gorgeous baritone started singing.

'*You never close your eyes anymore when I kiss your lips.*'

'Wow,' Kate murmured.

'*And there's no tenderness—*' Seth sang.

No, no, no, they weren't going to seduce her with appallingly good movie skits. Holding up her hand to silence them, she yelled, 'Stop!'

'Hammer-ed Time?' Seth asked, whipping off his shades.

'Trust me, already there.'

'Me too,' Jake said.

'You're here because you've been drinking?' Emma asked. 'Oh, really impressive, guys.'

'Have a heart, we're here to apologise. The jagerbomb was a necessity when Trudie offered to help us into our uniforms.'

'And I needed another to sing,' Seth said grinning from ear to ear.

'I take it you two have made up then?' Emma asked, knowing she should be looking from one to the other, but instead finding her gaze fixed on Jake.

'Yep,' Seth said and then nudged Jake who hadn't moved from the door. 'Jakey here has something he wants to say.'

Clearing his throat Jake walked slowly across the room to her. 'I'd appreciate it if you could spare me a few moments to discuss getting back that feeling we appear to have lost. You know, that loving one? I realise I've been a bit of an arse.'

'Oh you've realised that have you?'

'Well, I sort of had it pointed out to me.'

'You know none of this works when you can actually sing!'

'It doesn't work ... better?' he asked, looking hopeful with those intense dark brown eyes of his, making her insides jump about like a group of over-excited puppies.

'Nope.'

'Huh. So you can't spare me a few minutes of your time?'

'Sorry,' she said, indicating the only two tables that were occupied in the room. 'As you can see I'm flat-out here.'

Betty chose that moment to impart her own wisdom. 'It would have gone better if you'd walked in and simply swept her up into your arms and carried her out.'

'That's a whole other film, Betty,' Kate said with a grin.

Jake smiled. 'But if you'd find that more charming...'

'What the hell are you doing?' Emma shrieked as Jake lifted her into his arms.

'I'm borrowing you for a moment in a charming officerly-gentleman type way,' he said, carrying her out of The Clock House to shouts and whistles. On his way out he snagged a hat and coat from the nearest coat-stand. 'You'll need these.'

'You'd better put me down this instant, Jake Knightley.'

'Yeah, yeah, yeah. I know. You'll krav maga me, if I don't.'

She felt the cold air hit her face as he stepped out of The Clock House, crossed the gravel path and stepped onto the green. Slowly, he lowered her to the ground and with a sweeping gesture said, 'Ta-da.'

She followed his pointing finger and gasped.

On the middle of the green was a ten-feet-high snow sculpture of the word: SORRY.

'I wanted it to look like the Hollywood sign,' he said with a grin before his voice turned serious. 'I really am sorry, Emma.'

'For which part, exactly?' she wanted to know, unable to take her eyes off the huge sculpture.

'For backing away from us. For not letting you help. Either at Knightley Hall or in Cocktails & Chai.'

Now her gaze did swing up to meet his.

'I asked everyone who wasn't busy in the village to help me with this today.' He took off his glove with his teeth and fished in his pocket for his phone. Taking it out, he showed Emma the video of the construction. 'Crispin was artistic director so that's why the video looks like the making of the next supermarket Christmas advert.'

'It's impressive,' she said and then grinned up at him, 'and charming.' But what really melted her heart was that he'd asked everyone in the village to help him.

'Will you hear me out some time? Let me explain about Alice?'

'On two conditions.'

'Name them.'

'With a voice as good as yours, you have to be in the Christmas show.'

'Done.'

'The Christmas show that's now on Christmas Day.'

'I'd heard about that.'

'You won't be able to phone in your performance. You'll have to be here. In person.'

'I'm not going anywhere, Emma.'

'Neither am I. I know you don't really believe that or trust in that, but leaving is just not in my plan.'

'I want to. But after Alice—'

'What if I told you I'm not like the others?' she asked.

'Ah. Foo-fighting talk, huh?'

She nodded. 'I'm not Alice. I'm Emma.'

'I know.'

'Do you? I'm not asking for us to look years into the future and have it all nailed down.'

'But if we start this back up again you want me to trust that we're in each other's futures?'

'Yes.'

'I can do that. I want to do that. What's your other condition?'

'You have to let me do something for you at Knightley Hall.'

Chapter 38

Christmas Eve

Jake

'I need a hammer.'

Jake turned from the stove where he was making chilli to find Emma in the doorway, her woollen hat falling over her eyes and a big grin on her face. She'd been working outside in the gardens for the last three hours.

She didn't even look tired.

She looked beautiful.

Full of joy, enthusiasm ... *life*.

She also looked tempting. Very, very tempting.

If anyone had told him last Christmas that by the following Christmas Eve, he'd be snowed in, in Whispers Wood, with a beautiful actress from Hollywood – one who appeared to love the outdoors as much as he did – he never would have believed it.

'A hammer, huh?' he asked. 'Did you put it on your present list, because you know The Big Chimney-Loving Red-Suit-Wearing Jolly Guy on the Sleigh has probably already packed the presents for Whispers Wood?'

'Also, a cordless drill,' she laughed.

'Hmm. The chilli will be ready soon and the light's already fading.'

She batted those long eyelashes of hers and said, 'Come on, you've seen me handle a spoon like a pro.'

'I've seen you handle a spoon like a gun. Why exactly do you need a hammer and drill?'

'It's a surprise. Pretty please. Come on, you said you'd let me do this for you.'

'I did. Okay, one hammer and one drill coming right up,' he said, popping into the boot room to get the toolbox.

'I should probably take the whole box.'

He laughed and passed it over to her. 'You think you'll be finished before the food's ready?'

'Yep,' she said. 'Oh, I meant to tell you. It stopped snowing about an hour ago.'

'What, stopped completely?' His gaze went to the fogged up window. He hadn't even noticed.

All the while the snow had continued to fall, its soft blanket silencing the outside world, it had been so easy to focus not on the past as he'd worried he'd do the closer it got to Christmas, but on the present; being in Whispers Wood, and being here with Emma.

He hadn't had to think about what would happen when the snow stopped – had even forgotten it couldn't snow forever.

Even with a certain chandelier hanging in The Clock House.

He told himself that just because she hadn't been able to get out of Whispers Wood, it didn't mean she'd been feeling trapped and he allowed the hopeful breath in.

'I guess the weather forecast was right again,' she said. 'That's the last of the snow for a while.'

'Are you upset it's stopped?' he asked carefully, trying to take that breath in as deep into his lungs as he could and hold it there.

'It couldn't continue forever, could it? This is going to be my first ever Christmas with snow on the ground – for lots of other people too – which makes it even more special.' She did a little Happy Dance and when her hat slipped lower over her eyes, she pushed it back and headed for the back door.

'Hey, Hollywood?' he called before she disappeared back out the door. 'That looks good on you.' He nodded to the toolbox but really he meant the outside looked good on her.

As he went back to stirring his chilli, he grinned.

He'd promised her free rein in the gardens and the silly thing was he wasn't worried at all with whatever she was doing. He just liked the thought of her being happy out there.

This morning he'd helped her with an extra rehearsal for the Christmas show. Now that he'd agreed to sing, she'd informed him she had to re-block the second half of the show so everyone knew what they were supposed to be doing. It hadn't taken long to realise she'd taken over as director as well as performing some Jane Austen letters, which meant Trudie must be really impressed.

As Emma had talked him into entering from stage left – his other left, as she'd patiently explained when he'd gone the wrong way – he'd found Trudie back stage. Stationed at a mixing desk, she'd cued his backing track, quickly telling him that Emma had been born to do this.

He'd felt a jolt go through him.

If doing this was really what she was born to do, what if she came to realise choosing Whispers Wood had been a mistake?

And then he'd heard the kids in the big finale number all shouting 'Yes, Miss Danes' and following her instructions to the letter in a giggling mass of excitement, and he'd watched the pleasure dance across her features and he'd thought that what Trudie might mean was that it wasn't necessarily acting per se that Emma was born to do, so much as directing and helping bring people together.

The doorbell chimed and popping the lid back on the chilli he went to answer it.

'Crispin,' he greeted with surprise as he opened the door.

'Jake. I hope it's all right to stop by.'

'Of course it is, come on in.'

'Thank you,' Crispin said, following him into the kitchen. 'I won't stay long. I just wanted to tell you personally, that I've had some bad news on the Jane Austen front.'

Finally, Jake thought but instead said, 'Oh no, really?' and turned to flick the switch on the kettle, swallowing the smile on his lips.

'I'm embarrassed to tell you that it seems my source is … how can I put this delicately?'

'Unreliable?'

'Yes. Good word. Unreliable.'

'It's all right, Crispin. I would have found you tomorrow after the show anyway to tell you I've been through all the family journals and can't find even the slightest suggestion

Jane Austen visited the Hall. Coffee?'

'Perhaps a quick one.' Crispin whipped off his deerstalker hat. 'Seems this isn't the first time this person has claimed to have evidence that someone famous stayed at a stately home.'

'I'm sorry to hear that,' Jake said, putting two hot mugs of coffee down on the table and indicating the milk and sugar. 'If only because I know you just want Whispers Wood to be all that it can be.'

'That's kind of you to say. Mrs Harlow tells me at least once every evening that I get too excited, go in too quick, and end up having to pull out prematurely.'

Jake's coffee went down the wrong way and he shot up from the kitchen table to grab some kitchen roll. When he'd recovered coughing, he said, 'I'm going to have some photos taken of the gardens throughout the seasons to show progress before I open to the public. How about if we organise a blog for *The Whisperings* that details the progress I'm making?'

'Now that's a fine idea. Get the residents involved right from the go. Tease them with information and get them all fired up prior to opening. We could also have a look at—' he broke off, sighing as he saw Jake's expression. 'Well, thank goodness Mrs Harlow wasn't here to see that or tomorrow I might not get to unwrap the new set of golf clubs I spied hiding at the back of the wardrobe in the spare bedroom.'

'I won't tell her, if you don't.'

'So how are your parents? It'll be strange not seeing them at the Christmas show this year. Are they enjoying retirement?'

'I spoke to them last night, actually,' he said. He'd phoned before they left to go to his older brother Marcus's for

Christmas Day. He'd wanted to reassure them he'd look out for Seth and that they'd be having lunch at The Clock House.

He'd also taken the plunge and started that conversation Emma had suggested and it hadn't been so difficult after all. 'They're doing really well,' he told Crispin now. 'Mum wanted to know what plants would go well on their west-facing patio. I can't remember her ever being interested in gardening before.'

'You can't really blame her on that score. It's far easier to defer to the experts when you've got the main job of keeping an eye on six children. You have to admit if gardening isn't your forte the scale of the grounds here would be intimidating. They must be so much more relaxed knowing you're here to take over the mantle.'

'You know I think they are.' He hadn't even realised how much he'd been holding his breath ever since his parents' move to their bungalow in Hastings. But, as his mum had wasted no time pointing out, despite not making Knightley Hall a profitable home, they had loved it. The frustration of knowing they weren't doing a good job had taken its toll too often though and it was only now they were away from it they realised they'd allowed the helplessness they'd sometimes felt to overshadow the privilege of living there. They knew he was far better equipped to deal with the estate than they'd ever been but as his parents they hadn't wanted him to experience that helplessness, or if he did, certainly not to have to carry the weight of it on his own.

He'd laughed when she'd asked in a completely unsubtle way if that might be a worry she could cross off her list now that Sarah had told her about a certain 'charming Jane-ite' staying in Whispers Wood.

'Well, I'd better get back,' Crispin said, getting up and popping his deerstalker hat back on. 'I'm sorry I can't print your name in the Christmas show programme but your inclusion was a little last minute.'

'Oh, don't worry. I'm happy for my song to be a surprise.'

'Emma's the surprise. Don't you think? Breezing into Whispers Wood like a breath of fresh air.'

Yes. And hopefully staying too.

'I'll take that glass of wine now,' Emma said, her voice soft.

He turned the heat down on the chilli, noticing that her smile held a tinge of nervousness as she poured him a glass as well. 'We should take these with us.'

'Am I going to need a drink after I see what you've been up to?'

'No. Maybe. Oh and I need you to wear this scarf. As a blindfold.'

'O-kay,' he said slowly, taking it from her.

She took his free hand and led him around the back. He knew his land like the back of his hand but she was a good guide as she led them through the walled kitchen garden and through the archway into the rose garden. He could feel the snow underfoot and then the surface changed and he realised they were walking through the rose tunnel. At the end of it, she reached up and whipped off the blindfold. In a repeat of his words to her when he'd carried her onto the green, she said, 'Ta-da.'

He opened his eyes, blinked a couple of times and felt the

grin stretch wide across his face.

'This is incredible,' he murmured, looking down at her before his gaze went straight to the bricked up area he'd broken through.

Standing either side of the archway stood a full-sized knight in armour.

'Where on earth did you find those?'

'Believe it or not they were in the attics at The Clock House. Daniel found them when he was clearing out to prepare the office spaces. Old Man Isaac wondered if they'd originally come from here and had been used in a play or at a party or something. You have to imagine the brickwork eventually being covered with some sort of creeper or more roses.'

Behind the knights she'd installed wall sconces with torches and lit them.

'It's like a medieval entrance to a secret castle.'

'Would you like to go inside?'

'You've done more inside?'

'Uh-huh. You remember what I said you could do to the space to show the photographer when she came? Well, have a look and tell me what you think?'

He walked past the knights and poked his head through the gap in the wall.

'Wow.'

'Obviously, you can change it if you don't like it.'

In what amounted to no more than a ten foot by fifteen foot space she'd managed to create the perfect winter retreat.

'Where did you put all the snow?' he asked, looking down at the ground that was part compacted earth, part submerged brick.

'I didn't think you'd want it shovelled up in the rose garden so I wheeled it down to the copse.'

She must have been working flat-out the entire time she'd been out here.

As he looked up he saw hundreds of fairy lights criss-crossing their way across the open sky and she'd draped more over huge pots of box that she'd brought in and dotted about.

There was a wrought iron café table and chairs at the end nearest the extra wall sconces she'd installed. The chairs were covered in thick fur rugs and blankets that he'd ended up buying because he'd been so enthralled with the picture she'd painted.

The reality was even better.

On the café table she'd put a large clay pot filled with roses, hypericum berries and mistletoe, from the gardens. Huge storm lanterns had been lit and in the centre of the space was a fire pit she'd stocked with dry wood.

'Is it okay?' she asked, a slight breathless quality evident in her voice.

'It's pretty much the best thing anyone's ever done for me.'

'Okay. I thought if you wanted to grab a couple of bowls we could eat out here.'

'I love that idea.'

'There's one more thing...' she moved over to the wall by the open archway. 'This was what I really need the hammer and drill for. It's a sort of Christmas present. This whole space is, really. An area where you can chill while you work on getting the gardens ready to open to the public. I know you'll want to do your own design in here when the time is right, especially if you want to use it to do small wedding ceremonies, but I thought you deserved an area just for you. It'll be getting warmer soon and you won't want to sit in the library when you could be out here thinking and designing. Anyway, if you'd like to do the honours...'

He walked up to the makeshift curtain pole where she'd hung blue velvet curtains with little tiny silver stars on them which he thought he recognised as the same material Trudie used to make up her summer fortune teller's tent.

He drew the curtains open and when he saw what was behind them, burst out laughing.

Chapter 39

A Winter's Tale

Jake
  Behind the curtains, Emma had hung up a handmade blue heritage plaque saying:
JAKE KNIGHTLEY
Born 26th February 1986
Garden Designer
Sometimes Crooner
Possessor of the Certain Knowledge that Jane Austen Never Once Visited Here
  'You know,' he said, still laughing, 'Crispin popped in earlier to deliver the sad news that his friend of a friend wasn't exactly on the up and up.'
  'Did he?' Emma said, her eyes sparkling knowingly. 'He might have also delivered the lights and some of the pots before going back around to the front to ring the bell and tell you the news.' She pouted as she looked up at him. 'Poor Crispin, he was really worried about spoiling your Christmas.'
  'Don't worry I cheered him up by promising to do a blog on *The Whisperings* website about the gardens.'
  'You mean sort of like a journal about Knightley Hall?

Ooh, we could print them out and stick them in one of those leather journals and keep a copy in the library.'

He wondered if she knew she'd said 'we', not 'you'.

When the emotion of all that she'd organised and done for him clogged his throat, he clinked his glass against hers and took a healthy swallow of wine.

And when looking into her silver eyes produced more emotion, he smiled, and lowered his mouth to hers.

'Thank you,' he whispered against her lips and after he'd kissed her, turned to look around the room she'd created for him again.

'I'm glad you sorted everything out with Seth,' Emma mentioned later as they sat quietly chatting in the secret garden room.

With the heat from the fire-pit keeping them warm and the bowls of chilli long since eaten, he replied, 'Me too,' feeling mellow and happy and all without having put in a day in the gardens. 'He's not still in love with Joanne but I think it really shocked him seeing her with another man.' He looked up from his wine glass and caught Emma's gaze. 'I should tell you that the real reason Alice broke off our engagement was because she'd met someone else.'

'Oh.'

That was all she said.

No judgement.

No trying to coax out a few more details, or hurry his story along.

He watched the candlelight play in her eyes and wondered

how he'd ever thought her a chatterbox. She never did that waiting for someone to finish talking simply so that she could start talking again thing and he loved that about her.

Loved that she listened with her heart.

And by doing so, made it easy for him to tell his tale.

'I didn't actually discover that nugget until Christmas Day, which was a couple of weeks after she'd broken things off. I should go back a bit,' he said with a frown. 'Alice and I were supposed to get married last summer.'

'I thought your wedding date was the same day as The Clock House opening?'

'It was. But originally we'd planned to have a summer wedding. Three months before the big day though she asked to postpone it. There was a new contract her office had won and she wanted desperately to be the lead on it. I didn't see a problem. I knew how important her work was to her and to be honest it left me more time to work in the gardens.' He glanced up at her. 'Pretty awful, right?'

'I guess if you were both happy with postponing...' she said diplomatically.

'Yeah, I hear what you're not saying. And I agree with you. Once I'd had time to think about it, and realise postponing your wedding because of work opportunities wasn't what getting married was supposed to be about, I said I'd only be comfortable if we could name the new date there and then. Because there was always going to be work opportunities, right? A wedding shouldn't come second to that. I knew she loved Christmas so I suggested a December wedding.' He watched as Emma reached forward to top off her wineglass and waited until she'd taken a large sip before he continued, 'Other than asking if we could go somewhere hot for our honeymoon, she seemed genuinely happy with the new date. She worked crazy-hard on her new project and I did the same here. She had to miss a couple of wedding-planning things because of work but they were mostly family get-togethers to celebrate the upcoming nuptials, stuff like that. The village meeting last Christmas where I announced I'd be donating the Christmas tree for the green, she phoned to say she wouldn't be able to make and I was really disappointed because I'd told her family and friends would be coming back to the Hall to celebrate. She arrived halfway through the party, very upset, and almost as if she'd lose her nerve if she didn't just come out with what was on her mind, she told me in front of everyone that she couldn't go through with the wedding because she couldn't handle rural life and she knew I was meant to be here.'

'Wow, she said that in front of everyone?'

'Hmm. The thing is it was true. She couldn't handle the lifestyle. I knew it deep down but I ignored it. Alice and I used to ignore a lot of things. Most especially difficult conversations. So I didn't blame her for announcing it in front of everyone.'

'What did you do?'

'I think I just stood there.' His hand went to the back of his head as he confessed, 'It's hard to admit now but while everyone was thinking I was numb from my heart getting broken, I think I was just feeling incredibly sad to have let my family down. I knew how strongly they felt about having

421

someone at my side to share all this with.'

'So when did you find out she'd met someone else?'

'She called me on Christmas Day. I thought it was because she'd made a mistake and wanted to talk things through – maybe try again. So I left all my family who'd gathered to have a big day because they thought I needed cheering up, and I went to London to visit her.'

Now, with a trembling hand, he reached over to top up his own wineglass.

'When I got there she was in a really bad state. At first I thought she'd—' he broke off, unable to complete the statement. 'There was so much blood. I mean, I knew she'd self-harmed before but I'd never seen her get so out of control with it.'

'That's why you looked so upset when Seth cut himself,' Emma said almost to herself.

'Yes. Alice used to self-harm as a form of control. Not over me, but to help her deal with life getting too stressful.'

'That makes sense.'

'Does it?' He took another sip, grateful that instead of looking shocked and horrified she was sympathetic. 'I don't think it ever did to me. But then I guess I always had this place and design or gardening as an outlet. Somehow, I could put my hands in the earth, or my head into a design and the world and its problems could, if not melt away, at least quieten to bearable background noise.'

'For me it's reading,' Emma said, her smile gentle, as she leaned forward to rest her chin in her hand.

'No one knew, which I guess was a pressure-cooker waiting

to explode in itself, especially added to our lifestyle in London, which was too much about networking and not enough about simply enjoying each other's company. She held a senior position in her firm and she felt like she had to keep outperforming in her job in order to keep relevant. She was convinced if anyone ever found out she wasn't one hundred per cent in control, she'd be judged and sacked.'

'That's quite a heavy burden to carry around.'

He nodded. 'I thought when we came here to Knightley Hall that it would stop. I thought away from the rat-race she wouldn't need that kind of control or outlet. And then I found out that she was still doing it and I went ape and shouted, when I should have listened.'

'You shouldn't feel guilty for not reacting in the perfect way, Jake.'

'Why not? You are.'

'But I'm listening second-hand. I'm not hearing the person I love in pain and not knowing what to do to help. So what happened on Christmas Day?'

'She'd really scared herself and needed help. It took me a while to realise she hadn't called me because it was me she wanted. She'd called because I knew about the cutting and because I was dependable. It was so bad I had to take her to hospital. While she was being treated she finally told me all about the new guy at work she'd been seeing for months and begged me to phone him and explain.' He felt his molars grind together at the memory, almost as bad as when she'd opened her front door and he'd seen what she'd done to herself. 'It wasn't a pleasant conversation and let's just say he didn't want a bar of it. Bastard would have left her sitting there in that hospital getting stitched up all on her own.'

'So you stayed with her.'

'What else could I do?' He lifted his glass to his lips and drank the contents straight down.

'Nothing, Jake. You did the right thing. You were the friend she needed.'

He stared at the roses between them and bitterness was a chaser to the wine. 'When she realised the new man in her life had taken the first exit, she sat on that hospital bed asking if I would take her back.'

'You weren't tempted?'

He shook his head, adamant. 'She didn't love me and as bad as I felt for her, I knew then I wasn't in love with her. And I was so angry. Angry she didn't choose me until she felt all other choice had been taken away from her. Angry she would choose a life with me, a man who didn't make her happy, in a place that didn't make her happy, just so she wasn't on her own. And most especially angry that this place I loved so much couldn't console someone who could've done with somewhere peaceful, tranquil and inspiring to recover. But she was never going to see any of those things in Knightley Hall.' He swallowed and noticed some of the bitterness had subsided. 'So, yeah...' he dragged in a breath, 'I've been pretty angry.'

'Wait – I'm not sure I'm hearing you correctly – you're saying you were angry?'

His dark eyes flicked to hers in shock and then he saw the teasing glint in her eyes and shook his head that she could make him laugh after telling her all of that. 'I might have mentioned it.' He kept his eyes on her as he added, 'I'm not so angry now. This year, getting closer to finishing the gardens ... meeting a minx-like mixologist has made me realise ... I thought I needed to get away this Christmas to lay all the anger aside and let it go but I'd already let it go.'

'Do you still keep in contact with Alice?'

'Nope. We wasted all that time never properly talking and then we fitted in everything we needed to say to each other in one day. I told her I was going to visit her family and explain everything and she convinced me she'd get help. The last I heard she was doing well and after staying with her parents, ready to start looking for a place of her own again.'

'Well that's good. It sounds like she's getting herself happy and healthy again.'

He reached across the table to link his hand with hers. 'I needed you to know about Alice because I don't want this place to be a source of unhappiness for anyone else. I've seen it be a fear, a burden and an albatross. It deserves better now.'

Reaching out to lay her other hand over his she said, 'And so do you. I get it. I really get it.'

Jake looked at their joined hands.

This time last year no way would he have believed in magic.

But Emma being here...

She made him believe in it again.

He thought about the fact that tomorrow they'd be sitting under the chandelier in The Clock House.

Was it so inconceivable to think that this time next year there might be a wedding in Whispers Wood?

She'd done all this for him for Christmas.

Was he absolutely insane to be thinking about what he could get her for Christmas and wondering if a proposal would make a good present?

Chapter 40

On Christmas Day in the Morning

Emma

Emma Danes was in love.

Proper, grown-up, stuff-books-are-written-about love.

And not just with The Clock House, although she certainly couldn't deny the pride and the love she felt walking into Cocktails & Chai every day, knowing it was hers to run, to nurture, to grow.

No.

The person responsible for the truly, scary, crazy-wonderful state of being proper grown-up in love with, was Jake Knightley.

Releasing a happy sigh because she'd got to wake up next to him on the morning of her favourite holiday, she took the place-cards Juliet had plonked in front of her and started writing guest names on them. For an extra flourish, and because she was so happy, she drew a little holly leaf next to each name.

'Are you using the metallic pen to write the names?' Juliet asked her as she followed Kate around the long table, straight-

427

Eve Devon

ening the angle of every Christmas cracker Kate set down.

'Um ... sure,' Emma answered, immediately putting the three she'd already written in her bag under the bar and diving back into the box Juliet had given her to search for a gold metallic pen. 'So just to check I have everyone, I'm writing place-cards for Old Man Isaac, Gloria, Seth, and all of us?'

'Sounds right,' Kate said, counting on her fingers as she tallied names. 'But add in Betty. Daniel's going to go and pick her up when he gets Isaac so that neither has to trudge through the snow. Oh, and can you add my mum and Big Kev?'

'So with Daniel, you, Juliet, Oscar and Melody and then me and Jake, that's thirteen.'

'Nope, fourteen,' Juliet said, 'Mum said now the show is today as well, it wouldn't be fair to make Trudie cook for her too, so she's coming here instead. Besides, she's excited to see what happens about the snow and the chandelier.'

'It's already happened, hasn't it?' Kate said pointing to Emma. 'Where is Jake anyway?'

'He's with Oscar on the turkey transfer mission.' Oscar and Jake had both offered the use of their ovens to cook the four large turkeys and then bring them back to The Clock House to heat up in batches before serving.

'Remind me next time I open a business to put in extra large catering ovens in the kitchen,' Kate said.

'Ha. Remind me when you hear the timer start beeping in a minute, that that's when we need to start peeling potatoes,' Juliet said, and then giving up all pretence of subtlety, she snagged the box off Kate to put the crackers on the table herself. 'I don't know why it's so difficult for you to put them

428

exactly over the napkin, so that they line up nice and neatly.'

Kate grinned as if Juliet doing them was what she'd wanted all along and walked up to the bar where Emma had moved on to putting the finishing touch to three honey martinis.

'We've got time for a quick drink before your beeper goes off,' she told Juliet and then to Emma said, 'You'd think after being up for most of the night, she'd look completely wiped out, but of course she looks gorgeous.'

'Remind me what she was doing all night again,' Emma asked.

'I was "doing" reading,' Juliet said, bringing the empty box up to the bar.

'Reading,' Kate confirmed. 'All night,' she added in a sceptical tone.

'Hey,' Emma said, 'I love reading too. It's entirely possible to get the sort of happy, peaceful, completely content glow Juliet has from reading.'

'See?' Juliet said. 'You too could glow like us if you read more.'

'I read,' Kate insisted, taking a sip of her drink. 'I'm reading a book at the moment.'

'You're reading a book at the moment?' Juliet laughed disbelievingly. 'What's it called?'

'It has "girl" in the title.'

'Ooh, is it called: *Girl Opens Wildly Successful Day Spa?*' Emma teased.

'Or, *Girl in the Salon?*' Juliet said, picking up the theme.

'Or *Girl Walks Into a Bar?*' Emma asked.

Kate clicked her fingers. '*Girl on a Buoy,*' she said with a satisfied nod of her head. 'What?' she said as Emma and Juliet stared at her. 'Don't judge. It's a nautical thriller. Melody gave it to me.'

Emma's eyebrows shot up. 'I'm borrowing it after you, then. Hey, maybe we should start a book club at The Clock House?'

'That's not a bad idea,' Kate said. 'Could the reading part be optional though?'

Emma shook her head sadly and turned to Juliet, 'So you really think I'm glowing too?'

'You do seem to have got over being cold all the time.'

Emma blushed some more as she realised that despite the snow still being thick on the ground, she hadn't felt cold at all the last couple of weeks.

'Oh yeah.' Kate turned her head from Juliet to Emma. 'The blushing and sappy smiles are definitely down to reading. You going to drink that?' Kate asked Juliet, sliding the honey martini towards Juliet.

'Maybe later. We still have lunch and then the Christmas show to get through and if I start now I'll be asleep later.'

'Uh-huh,' said Kate, taking a sip of her drink. 'Because of all the *reading* last night.'

Juliet laughed. 'I had the best Christmas Eve ever. You know how Melody always has her head in a book?'

'#Rory,' Kate agreed.

'Right, well, to make this first Christmas special for us, she came up with this brilliant idea – actually the idea really came from Iceland.'

'The freezer shop?' Kate asked, tipping her head to the side at a 'does not compute' angle.

430

'The country,' Juliet replied with a roll of her eyes. 'Iceland has this tradition of giving books as presents on Christmas Eve. It's a really big deal over there. You exchange books and then stay up all night reading them.'

'Officially loving this idea,' Emma sighed and took a sip of her honey martini and before you could say 'We all want some figgy pudding', she was thinking about *next* Christmas Eve and being with Jake in the library at Knightley Hall. There would be a fire lit and mugs of mulled wine and plates heaped with mince pies and chocolates and there would be her and Jake curled up together on one of the armchairs. Just the two of them and their books. And maybe a dog. She'd always wanted a dog. She could see a wise and wily Irish wolfhound affectionately named Sir Wolfie Knightley snoozing in front of the fire and—

She took another hasty sip of her cocktail because ... getting carried away, much?

Kate laid her hand over Juliet's and this time there was no teasing in her voice as she said, 'Seriously, how clever is that niece of mine that she thought to start a new tradition this year for just the three of you on your first Christmas together.'

'I know,' Juliet said, fanning her face as her eyes got watery. 'I'm so damn happy. Honest to goodness I cannot process how blessed I am. And apparently we're doing some more presents later. After we finish up here and get back home.'

'We're doing our presents after we lock up here later, too,' Kate said.

Emma took in the secret smile on Juliet's face and wondered if it was because she, like Emma, knew Oscar had been asked by Daniel to draw up plans to knock Mistletoe Cottage and Myrtle Cottage into one bigger cottage for him and Kate to live in together. Or, whether it was because – judging from the way Juliet hadn't touched her drink yet – one of her presents to Oscar and Melody might be a positive pregnancy stick!

And then turning her attention to how Kate's fingers were tracing a pattern in the marble of the bar top, she asked, 'So what did you end up getting Daniel?'

'Oh, I got him an envelope of dirt.'

'An envelope of dirt? Um ... have you heard of re-gifting? Because I'm pretty sure both Juliet and I have something we could give you to give to him that's better than a bunch of dirt.'

'Trust me it's going to be perfect. I've got it all worked out. We both promised each other we wouldn't spend any money because we've had zero spare cash after setting up this place and zero time to get all flashy. So, the envelope is my way of asking him to move in with me. It's to represent us knocking our cottages together, because no matter how I try and work it, there's just not enough room to grow in a place the size of Mistletoe Cottage. So tonight, when we have our chat over the garden wall, because that's our little way of debriefing our days, well that's when we're going to exchange presents and that's when I'm going to ask him.'

'Wow,' Emma whispered. Finding out that Kate and Daniel had essentially chosen the same gift for each other made her heart melt.

Her gaze went to the chandelier.

Technically, she and Jake hadn't met for the first time under it, but they were going to be sitting underneath it on Christmas Day, celebrating.

Could there be another celebration at Christmas time next year?

One that saw her dressed in an empire-line Regency styled dress of white and gold, standing opposite her Mr Knightley?

Chapter 41

The Ghost of Christmas Future

Emma

Emma looked around the dining table, and allowed the sounds of everyone chatting together as they finished their Christmas lunch, to sink in and fill up her senses.

In her wildest dreams she never would have thought that this winter she'd embark on an adventure that would sweep her up, carry her across an ocean, and set her down in a community that welcomed her wholly. And definitely not an adventure that would place a man directly in her path and have her fall in love with him.

But from the moment she'd opened up Kate's email with the offer to come and run Cocktails & Chai, that's effectively what had happened and truthfully? She wasn't sure life could get better.

'Top up?' Jake said, waving a bottle of wine in front of her.

Dragged from her philosophising she shook her head, smiling at him as she put her hand out to cover the top of her glass. 'No way. We've still got the Christmas show to get ready for.'

'Well, I need one more glass if I'm to get up in front of everyone and sing. I'm no longer sure how you got me to agree to this. Must have been some tricksy magic. There's still time to back out, right? I mean, sleeping with the director must get me some perks.'

She grinned. 'Sleeping with this director is perk itself. Besides, you have to do it,' she leaned closer to him and putting on her most plaintive expression, said, 'you know, for the children.'

'Wow. You're good.'

'You know it.'

'What if I forget the words?'

'I'll get someone to write them out on giant cue cards for you. You wait; two lines in and the audience will have fallen in love.'

He bent his head and made his voice low. 'What if it's only one person I want falling?'

Her breath caught and her heart started hammering. 'I—I think that would be absolutely fine – as long as you were there to catch her.'

Jake grinned outrageously, curled his arm and bent his head to kiss his bicep. 'Then I think we're all good.'

Emma burst out laughing. 'My hero.'

'My Emma,' he said, quietly, simply and lovingly, so that her heart went from hammering against her insides to sort of melting through them.

'Hey, you two,' Seth said from across the table. 'Try and show a little restraint, some of us are still eating.'

'You're just jealous,' Gloria told Seth, poking her tongue

out in jest.

Emma looked at Seth looking at Gloria ... and noticed Gloria looking right back at Seth.

Interesting.

And then she looked up at the chandelier, realising that technically, Gloria and Seth were the only two sat at the table who were unattached.

'Just because Jake's officially back to owning his billowy romantic shirt,' Gloria announced, stealing a parsnip off Seth's plate and grinning as she bit into it.

Even more interesting, Emma thought as Seth's gaze narrowed on Gloria's mouth.

Hiding her grin Emma wondered if perhaps after Christmas she might flex her matchmaking muscles again.

'He told you about the shirt?' Jake asked Gloria, looking incredulously at his brother. 'Well, that's you disinvited to poker night.'

'Oh, let him play,' Daniel said. 'I could do with winning. Again.'

'Are you seriously trying to claim that out of the three of us,' Oscar piped up from the other end of the table, 'you win the most hands?'

'Fighting talk,' Big Kev stated, 'but you know very well that if *I* was invited I'd be walking away with the pot.'

'You can take my place at the table,' Seth replied. 'I'm not exactly flush right now.'

'Please,' Cheryl said, 'As if you *boys* don't already know that if I was there I'd wipe the floor with you all.'

'Don't pander to their sexist poker night, ladies,' Sheila said,

'We have much more fun things to do.'

'Yes,' Juliet agreed, announcing to the table, 'We're starting a book club.'

'Where *everyone* will be invited,' Kate said, before leaning across to say to Emma, 'because it was actually a really good idea and it would be lovely to hold something here for the community.'

Emma laughed and impulsively launched to her feet, tapping her knife against the glass to get everyone's attention. With everyone's gaze on her she tried not to get flustered and remembered sitting in Jake's car outside of her Dad's and him telling her to pretend she was a confident character from a play or a film. 'I'd like to say a few words and then propose—' she got no further because suddenly Jake fumbled his wine glass, splashing the contents over the tablecloth.

'You all right there, Jakey?' Seth asked, and Emma couldn't even begin to guess at the grin playing across Jake's brother's face.

Several hands reached for their napkins to help mop up the stain and after a moment, Jake was waving his hand, having composed himself to look up at her and say casually, 'Carry on.'

'—propose a toast.' She shot a quick look at Jake but his expression was inscrutable and then she realised everyone was waiting to hear what she had to say. On a deep breath, she said, 'I guess I really wanted to thank everyone for welcoming me so fully into the community here. When I arrived, the only person I knew was Kate, and well, she's great and everything.'

Kate bowed and said, 'I really am.'

'And so humble,' Emma teased. 'Anyway, you're all the absolute best and well,' feeling tears of gratitude fill her eyes, she charged her glass, and said, 'To Christmas at The Clock House.'

'Christmas at The Clock House,' came the cheer back as everyone raised their glasses in toast.

Everyone was settling back down with their drinks when Gloria said, 'Okay, whose ring-tune is *The Big Bang Theory*?'

'What?' Emma looked up and realised she recognised the sound. 'Oh. That's me. I mean, that's my phone.' Getting up from the table she dived behind the bar to retrieve her phone from her bag and answer it. 'Penny?' she said excitedly. 'Penny, is that you? Oh my God, I can't believe it's you. Happy, Happy Holidays. How's it going over there? You're never going to believe this but it's snowed here. *Snowed!* It's like something out of a movie! Wait—I'm going to take a photo and send it right to you. You will not believe how beautiful everything looks.'

She looked around the room grinning at everyone and saw Jake mouth the words, 'Who's Penny?' and she laughed and said to the room, 'My agent. Penny is my agent. Penny say hello to everyone ... what? Hang on a moment, I can't hear you,' and popping her finger into her ear to deafen out the sound of chatter resuming around the table, she said, 'Say that again.'

'I *said*,' said Penny, 'How fast can you pack your bags because I got you the best Christmas present ever.'

'I don't understand, what do you mean best present ever?'

'The part is yours, Soy Bean.'

'What part is mine?'

'*The* part. The one you wanted. The Jane Austen-esque rom-com. They phoned me yesterday and told me they made a mistake. The other person isn't going to work out.'

'*The part is mine?*' At some level she realised her voice had risen a few decibels but it wasn't until she was actually lapping the room, screaming over and over, 'The part is mine, the part is mine,' that she realised she might have deafened not only Penny but also everyone in the room.

The Cocktails & Chai room.

Of The Clock House.

Where she worked.

She stopped her crazy happy dancing and froze, except for her eyes, which tracked to each individual in the room but Jake's.

'I don't understand,' she said now, her voice barely a whisper. 'They were so sure.'

'They want you. *You*. They released her from her contract *before* they phoned me – that's how much they want you. I've been trying to call you since yesterday.'

Yesterday, Emma thought.

When she'd spent the day preparing Jake's Christmas present.

'Is it my fault you don't answer your phone?' Penny was saying. 'Anyway the part is yours, now get your skinny finest actor's ass back here so we can start work. They want to start shooting straight after Christmas. Read-through in the studio and then they'll send the travel schedule. So great that you're already acclimatised to English winter because you'll be back there filming within the month. Phone me back with your flight details, okay?'

'Okay.'

'Happy Christmas my little Adzucki Bean.'

'Happy Christmas,' she said into the phone. She hadn't failed? She'd got the part? She stared at her phone for several seconds before she remembered where she was.

'What was that all about?'

And now she did look at Jake.

And he stared back at her.

Waiting quietly with about a thousand questions in his eyes.

'Um, so, that was my agent Penny. She's been trying to call me since yesterday to let me know that the lead part in a movie I thought I'd lost, is actually mine again. If I want it,' she tacked on.

Suddenly her sightline to Jake was blocked by Kate throwing her hands up in the air and with an excited 'Waaah,' rushing in to hug her fiercely. 'Oh my God, Emma. Well done. That's amazing news. Right?'

'Right,' she said trying to find Jake in the crowd of hugs as everyone now got up from the table to offer their congratulations.

'Best Christmas *ever*,' Kate told her, hugging her fiercely.

'Ever,' she replied, her voice dull, her body feeling numb.

'So what are you going to do?' Gloria's voice cut through the cheers.

'Do?' Emma blinked, trying to get her brain to work.

'Yes. Do you want to accept?'

'If I accept I need to go home and pack like right now because I'd need to be on a plane ASAP.' Taking her courage in her hands she lifted her head to seek out Jake.

'Wow. They don't hang about, do they?' Juliet said quietly.

'At least it's stopped snowing,' Jake said.

All heads turned to look at Jake who had now stood up from the table and moved to stand opposite Emma.

'Stopped snowing?' she asked with a frown.

Clearing his throat, Jake nodded. 'They'll be clearing all the roads. You'll be able to get a lift to the airport. Planes will be taking off.'

Ask me to stay.

But he didn't.

She waited some more.

But he said nothing. Merely shoved his hands into his pockets.

Whipping her head around to find Kate, she said, 'I can't possibly go.'

'Why not?' Kate asked.

'Well what about my job here? I've made a commitment.' She could feel her breath getting shaky. 'I can't possibly leave you in the lurch.'

'Sweetheart if it's something you want we'll manage. I could even get Gloria to take over, seeing as she's not, like, you know, totally useless.'

'I bask in your praise,' Gloria said, looking at Kate like she was mental for encouraging Emma to go.

'But what about the play?' she said stupidly.

'Oh yes, because in comparison, the Whispers Wood Christmas show is not only equal to, but seen as better than a Hollywood movie,' Kate said. 'You've worked towards this all your life, haven't you? If you want it, take it.'

No.

This was silly.

She lived *here*.

She worked *here*.

She was in love *here*.

She couldn't make that work elsewhere.

Her gaze swung back to Jake and she licked her lips. 'Jake?'

'What they said,' he answered, looking back at her like she was the only person in the room. 'You can't let this slip through your fingers if it's what you want.'

'What if it's not what I want?' she said bravely. Hopefully.

'What if you're just too afraid to say that it is?' he asked, walking slowly towards her. 'What if I say it for you?'

'What if you tell me to stay?' she countered, tears clogging her throat because he was really telling her to go? Rejecting a future together? Rejecting her?

'I can't do that, Hollywood.' He reached for her hands.

'I'm not Alice,' she whispered. She knew he'd been hurt. Knew he didn't trust easily. But did he really believe she'd be happier in Hollywood, than here with him?

'I know that.'

Ask me to stay. Why won't you ask me to stay?

'The chandelier,' she suddenly said and that was when everyone else must have sensed her desperation and that this was a conversation they shouldn't overhear because they began

442

leaving.

'Is just a chandelier, Hollywood,' Jake said gently, reaching up to tuck her hair back behind her ears.

'But what about Sir Wolfie?' she whispered, seeing her dream of next Christmas disappear.

'Hollywood, I have no clue who Sir Wolfie is, but I do know that if you don't go, you'll never know for certain—'

'Stop calling me Hollywood, I know you only do it when you're—'

'Ho Ho Ho,' Trudie interrupted in her cheerful, booming voice, as she made a grand entrance, oblivious to the undertones as she sprang into action, rolling up her sleeves and heading over to the table to start clearing it. 'Had a good lunch, did we? Fandabbydozy. Right then, let's start moving the tables out of the way.'

'We'll talk later,' Jake said, stroking his fingers over her cheekbone, and then he was stepping back and turning around and reaching for a stack of chairs.

'Yes,' she whispered, taking a step backwards too. 'Later.'

'Give me a hug then, Jakey,' Trudie said.

While Trudie reached forward to give Jake a Christmas hug, Emma slipped quietly out of The Clock House doors.

Chapter 42

A Blue, Blue, Blue Christmas

Emma

Emma ran through the snow.
Damn it.

She'd just allowed that to happen?

She hadn't thrown back her head, opened her mouth, stuck her hand down her throat and grabbed hold of her heart so that she could rip it out to offer to him?

What the hell was the matter with her lily-livered self anyway?

Call herself a woman?

She should turn around right now and march right up to him and tell him that she – that she...

He didn't want her to.

The knowledge crept painfully up her throat waiting to sob itself out in the privacy of Wren Cottage.

He wanted her to go back to Hollywood.

She wasn't good enough.

Not at showing him how good they could be together.

She thought she had, but he would have fought for her to

444

stay if she had.

Would have told her to stay here in Whispers Wood.

For him.

Why hadn't he?

How could he have just stood there while everyone celebrated?

Watched her without passing comment while she accepted everyone's congratulations?

And watched her still as the most horrible chill invaded her person, turning the blood running through her veins icy and setting her teeth achatter.

By the time she let herself into the cottage she'd thought of as home for the past few months she was shaking from head to foot.

Bloody heating still wasn't working properly, she thought, pacing back and forth across the lounge carpet trying to get warm, trying to thaw out, trying to think.

After a few moments mostly what she thought was that she couldn't wait to get out of here.

As if she needed a Viking Jane Austen hero with a super sexy British accent anyway?

She had the part of her dreams to fall back on.

Slipping her phone from her pocket she looked up flights out of Heathrow and wondered how much a taxi to the airport would cost on Christmas Day.

Probably like a gazillion dollars.

Or pounds.

She could Uber it.

Running up the stairs to the bedroom she pulled her case

out from under the bed and threw it on top of the beautiful white duvet and blankets.

Flinging open the wardrobe doors she started pulling out clothes and squishing them into her case.

No time for the life-hack packing tips she'd tried out to save her clothes from creasing on the way over.

Of course why she was bothering to pack anything to go back to LA with, she didn't know.

She was going to have to go on a diet the minute she landed anyway because she'd been eating, well, like a normal person, all the time she'd been here.

Maybe instead of stupid starvation, she'd hit the gym instead.

Do some actual krav maga classes.

Throw in some yoga for good measure.

She'd need the meditation because she could already feel the familiar tension cracking her spine at the thought of going back to it all.

Zipping up her case she was surprised she didn't have more stuff, but then when you left to go on an adventure, you never took all your belongings with you, did you? You didn't want anything too comfortable with you in case it held you captive. Held you back.

If she left her heart in Whispers Wood at least it would be one less thing to carry.

It was all such hard work, she thought.

This going backwards simply to start going forwards again.

But as soon as she started filming, well then, she'd be so excited, wouldn't she?

Before she knew it she'd be so caught up in it all, she'd be happy again.

Yep.

Hands down, doing this film was going to be her greatest adventure yet.

She should start packing her bag – purse – she'd need to start calling it a purse again.

And then she'd call Penny and ask her to email over the script. She could read it on the plane. Get a head-start. Or at least catch up.

The tension ratcheted up another notch and yet as she descended the stairs her legs felt like lead.

In the lounge she picked up her bag-purse and half-heartedly started dropping things into it.

She absolutely did not want to go.

There.

She'd said it.

Acknowledged it.

But she couldn't stay here.

She'd said if things didn't work out between her and Jake then she would stay anyway.

But that had been when she was feeling smug.

Now, she was just feeling defeated.

Emma sunk down onto the sofa.

She so didn't want to feel defeated again.

She'd felt that when she'd slipped into bed the first time Penny had told her she hadn't got the part.

To feel it now though, after she'd been so happy, was so much worse.

Choking back another sob, she reached for her phone and called Penny who answered on the first ring with a, 'Hi, you want I should email you the script? Good idea.'

'Penny, I'm not coming back.'

Wait—what?

Emma blinked and looked around to check someone else hadn't uttered the words.

'We seem to have a bad line. Did you say you weren't coming back?'

'I don't want the part, Penny. I don't want *any* part,' she offered truthfully. 'What I want – what I *choose* – is to stay here in Whispers Wood. I've—' she stopped talking as her gaze fell on the Christmas present lying on her coffee table. The Christmas present Jake had dropped off for her the day after the tree-lighting ceremony. 'Penny, I'll call you back, 'kay?' and without waiting for an answer she hung up and reached for the gift. She'd been saving opening it until today but because she'd stayed at Knightley Hall last night she'd forgotten about it.

Now she remembered on the day he'd stopped by, before he'd given it to her, he'd rushed forward asking if she'd hurt herself when he'd seen she was upset. After his experience with Alice he must have assumed the worst and she felt sad for all he'd been through.

Had he not asked her to stay because he'd been doing what he did with Alice and avoiding the difficult conversations?

She held the gift in her hands.

The present was book-heavy and book-shaped.

He'd given her a book.

With trembling hands she started to unwrap it and the second she saw the leather binding she knew.

Another sob slipped out of her throat as she stared down at an early edition of Jane Austen's *Emma*.

He'd given her something he knew she'd love.

Because he knew her.

Cared about her.

She was being given the opportunity here to choose.

Not to go from opportunity to opportunity because it got her out of a hole, or a rut or because it effectively got her out of having to make a decision about what she really wanted.

She knew what she really wanted, didn't she?

She'd been happy for weeks.

She didn't feel like she was hanging on, waiting for the drop, like she so often had with acting.

Being at Cocktails & Chai – being with people, helping them, looking after them – made her feel like she was connected to something real.

Being with Jake was real.

And it made her happy.

The happiest.

With a giant sniff, she sat up and reached for her phone.

'Penny, I'm so sorry to keep phoning you on Christmas Day, but the thing is, I've met someone and—'

'Well this isn't the twentieth century, Cannellini Bean, bring him with you.'

'That's not going to work. He has responsibilities here. *I* have responsibilities here,' she added, thinking that she really did like Gloria, but she wasn't ready to let her run Cocktails

& Chai just yet. 'And, besides, I really don't want to act anymore.'

'Is this all just because of a man?'

'It is, but it isn't. There are other things here that I love too. And I'm not with the man.' Her gaze strayed straight to the book. 'I mean, I hope to be. If I can get him to listen.'

'I have to tell you, Lima Bean, this guy is sounding less and less of a prize.'

'Oh, he's being a complete and utter idiot, but I love him.'

'You—well, look at that, your British accent came back.'

'I'm sorry I won't be putting it to proper use in the movie.'

'Just go and tell that complete and utter idiot that he's what you want and you're not taking no for an answer.'

'Penny, you really are the loveliest agent a person could ask for.'

'So go get your man, Twinkie.'

'No beans now I'm off the books?'

'I'm swapping to cakes now I know I'm going to get to come to the UK one day and meet your guy.'

'I'll talk to you soon, just because I want to, okay?'

'Okay. Happy Christmas, Cupcake.'

Putting down the phone, Emma picked up her book but when she felt the tears welling up again she put it back on the coffee table to protect it.

She knew the text of the book inside out but she would treasure this copy. Because it was the first Christmas present Jake had given her.

Reaching for a tissue she blew her nose and sank back onto the sofa, forcing herself to think about what she was going to say to Jake.

She'd never felt so unscripted in her life.

Maybe if she acted the confident brook-no-argument woman in love, he'd finally believe her. Or at least find the act sexy for long enough to distract him while she came up with another plan.

She stared at the book, hoping for inspiration and then suddenly she was frowning and sitting up to grab the book off the table and inspect where the pages weren't lying flat.

Curious, she turned the book upside down, and shook it lightly.

A piece of paper slipped out and seemed to float midair until she reached out to catch it.

A letter?

Slipped inside the book, either as a bookmark, or so that it could be treasured?

She turned the paper over and on the front she saw written, in bold precise handwriting, *Lillian*.

With a pounding heart, she unfolded the letter and began to read.

Five minutes later she was crying again as she shoved her feet into boots that were two sizes too big for her, but at least not freezing cold.

Wrenching open the front door of Wren Cottage, the letter tucked safely in her pocket, she set off through the snow for The Clock House.

Chapter 43

The Show Must Go On

Jake

How stupid could he get?
    Jake couldn't believe he'd been thinking about proposing to Emma and now he was standing at the side of The Clock House stage in a tux, waiting to do his song in the Christmas show and she was back at Wren Cottage probably packing.

Earlier, when he'd looked up from the chairs he'd been setting out and spied her through the window, running across the green like she was running to a better life, he'd felt as if his heart was being ripped out.

He was so used to being dealt the hand of something or someone 'better' coming along but now he knew he'd started believing that *they* were each other's 'better' coming along. Poking his head around the curtain at the side of the stage, he looked out past the audience, and as his gaze caught on the chandelier – that bloody chandelier – he cursed. Could not have been more wrong, could he?

'Did you just use a profanity in the presence of a minor?'

Startled, Jake looked down at his side to see a boy about the age of eight or nine dressed as an elf.

The sight made him want to swear again. The last thing he was in the mood for was company.

Biting back another curse, he admitted, 'You're right, I did. And that was very wrong of me. Very wrong indeed.'

'It's all right.' The boy grinned up at him. 'I'm an elf anyway, so I'll let it pass.'

'Right.'

Jake went back to staring at the chandelier. He had to do the show … for the children, as Emma loved to say. But the end of this show – the end of this Christmas – now couldn't come soon enough as far as he was concerned.

'So have you got stage-fright?' the elf whispered. 'Is that why you swore?'

Jake gritted his teeth and said under his breath, 'No, I swore because I let the love of my life slip through my fingers.'

He should have told Emma he loved her before practically shoving her back in the direction of Hollywood, shouldn't he?

Should at least have given her the choice and given himself the chance of her choosing him.

'That was pretty careless. Why didn't you hold on tighter?' said the boy, like he had the wisdom of Solomon or at least Old Man Isaac.

'*Because*,' Jake answered testily, 'if you love someone you're supposed to set them free.'

'Huh?'

He'd wanted her to be happy.

And she'd been rejected for part after part yet every time she'd risen back up, all Terminator like, to brush off the hurt, and put herself out there again.

Someone who showed that much resilience deserved their happy ending.

'Why don't you just go and catch her again?' asked the boy.

'Because you can't catch people who don't want to be caught.'

'Except for if you're the police.'

Jake's mouth formed a half-smile at the faultless logic and then found himself sighing again when his shadow said, 'So you seriously let the love of your life slip through your fingers? Just like that?'

Jake looked down to find the boy shaking his head sadly at him and adding, 'Because even I knew at age five when I asked Poppy Druthers on a play-date and she said no, that I should ask her if that was her final answer.'

'And was it?' he found himself asking.

The boy rolled his eyes. 'You know I'm beginning to worry there's not enough time between acts to tell you all the things you should already know by now – what with you being the adult here and me being *an elf*.'

'Interesting. I'm not sure where a sarcasm act fits in a Christmas show,' Jake said, looking behind him for the boy's parents and thinking that possibly Gloria Pavey had a son walking around Whispers Wood that she didn't know about.

'Good job my act is comedy then,' replied the elf.

'Comedy? You're sure about that, are you?'

The elf huffed out a, 'Suddenly everyone's a comedian,'

454

then said, 'I'm a last minute stand-in ... I'm guessing for The Love of Your Life?'

Not wanting to be reminded of how stupid he'd been, Jake said, 'Unless you get a lot funnier, and a lot taller, I'm not sure you're going to be *anyone's* love of their life.'

'First the swearing, then the elfism ... I sincerely hope *your* act isn't comedy.'

'It's singing.' And he was carrying on this ridiculous conversation, other than the fact that it stopped him dwelling on how this was possibly – no, definitely – worse than last Christmas ... because? 'Look, do you absolutely have to stand next to me? Shouldn't you be off practising your act or something?'

'I'm checking the audience vibe. If my material goes down well, I'm thinking of applying for *LGT*.'

'Don't you mean *BGT* – *Britain's Got Talent*?'

'Hello?' The elf rolled his eyes and indicated the clothes he was wearing, '*LGT* – *Lapland's Got Talent*.'

'Funny guy.'

'Elf,' the boy corrected. 'Funny elf. Boy, you're hard work, but I guess if you've just had your heart broken, you're not really my core audience,' and then as if feeling sorry for him, he muttered not so softly under his breath that Jake couldn't hear him, '#concerned.'

'And is that,' Jake made the hash-tag sign with his fingers, 'concerned for my heart or for your act?'

'Hey, us broken-hearted have to stick together.'

Ah. So Poppy Druthers had given him her final answer then. 'She probably wasn't sophisticated enough to understand the elf thing,' he consoled.

'Yeah, but back in '13 I mostly dressed as Batman.'

Jake laughed and said with commiseration, 'Girls!'

'Unfathomable,' the boy replied.

Yeah. He should have talked it out with Emma then and there, he thought. Why had he thought giving himself time to collect his words was a good thing?

Because she mattered and he hadn't wanted to stuff up.

Hadn't wanted to hear her argue on the side of going back to Hollywood and then hear himself lecture as he started to panic.

Adrenaline rushed through him as the knowledge that he should have thrown everything he had at trying to persuade her that she should stay slapped him about the face.

'Hey, kid,' he said, suddenly knowing what he had to do.

'*Elf!*'

'Right. Elf ... How's your singing voice?'

'Not too bad. If the comedy doesn't work out I've been thinking I could go the Zayn route.'

'Okay, I kind of think the girls would be into that, but first, you want to sing my song for me?'

'What's your song?'

'*I'm Dreaming of a White Christmas.*'

'Definitely not.'

'It'll make the girls go crazy.'

'I couldn't just do my comedy act?'

'That would work too. I have to be somewhere. Tell Mrs McTravers something came up but that you're taking my spot as well as The Love of My Life's spot.'

He turned to go and there she was.

The Love of His Life.

Standing right in front of him.

She was breathing hard like she'd run all the way from Wren Cottage and his heart started beating really, alarmingly, fast.

Elf tugged on his sleeve. 'Is this her?'

'Yes,' Jake replied, hating that he could see that she'd been crying but also thinking that she'd never looked more beautiful.

'I'm no expert yet,' Elf said, looking up at him, 'but don't you think you should do something other than stand here?'

'Yes.'

As soon as he could get his act together he was going to drag her into his arms and tell her he loved her and ask her to stay and—

'Jake? Oh, there you are sweetie,' Trudie said. 'Two minutes until you're on—' she stopped abruptly when she saw Emma standing in front of him. 'Wow. Okay, well, um ... yay,' she said, lifting her hands in a sort of cheer as she stared at them uncertainly. 'Um ... so this is your two minute warning.' She made hurrying motions with her hands. 'Life's short, talk fast.'

'I choose you,' Emma stated loudly.

'I said talk fast, not talk loudly,' Trudie whispered, pointing manically towards the act on stage.

'Sorry,' Emma whispered. 'I choose you, Jake Knightley. I know you feel as if you don't get chosen – that you didn't get chosen to run the Hall and well, Alice...'

'Who the—'

Jake put his hand over Elf's mouth to stop the words and explained, 'As a wise elf just taught me: Let's not with the profanity when there's children around.'

Elf gave a thumbs up and Jake removed his hand.

'I know what it feels like not to get chosen, Jake, and I'm telling you that I choose you and Knightley Hall.' She looked at him and when he didn't speak, tossed her hair determinedly back over her shoulder, licked her lips and repeated, 'I choose both – if you'll both have me.'

'You know it's actually okay to choose everything,' Jake finally answered. 'If doing the film is really what you want ... you'll always have a home here ... with me. You could fly back on weekends. I could fly to you.'

She shook her head. 'Acting isn't what I want to do. I didn't really choose it – it chose me. When I was too young to really understand the spell I was casting and I clung to that magic because it was too scary to choose something real and I was too proud to let go. I'm not letting you go, Jake, so if you really don't want to be with me, you're going to have to do some pretty hardcore convincing.'

'Don't take his final answer unless it's a "yes",' Elf helpfully asserted.

'So,' Trudie said, brushing away tears, 'this all seems like it's going really well but it's time for you to get on that stage and sing your heart out, Jake.'

He had so much he wanted to say to Emma. So many kisses he needed to give her but Trudie was literally pushing him towards the stage now.

'Stop,' Emma insisted. 'Don't sing the song. Read this letter out instead.'

'What?' he looked down at the letter she thrust into his hand.

'Trudie,' Emma pleaded, 'don't cue the song. Let him read the letter, okay?'

'Okay, but get on that stage now so I don't have to fill.'

In a daze Jake walked to the edge of the curtain and stopped as Elf came up beside him, slipped his hand into his, and tugging him onto the stage, announced to the crowd, 'Ladies and gentlemen, a guy in a tux and an elf walked into a bar...'

Chapter 44

The Big Finale!

Emma

'Trudie,' Emma called, reaching out to grab her arm and prevent her from disappearing. 'I have one more change I want to make to the show. Is that okay?'

'But the big finale is coming up after Jake, it's all the year 2 children singing *We Wish You A Merry Christmas.*'

'That's fine, but the bit after that, I want to make a change, can I have a quick word with them?'

'All right. But don't get them over-excited. We don't have time for a wee break.'

Giving Trudie a big kiss on the cheek, she whispered, 'Break a leg,' and headed into the kitchen area to talk to the children.

By the time she made it back into the room, the funny little kid dressed as an elf had the audience eating out of the palm of his hand.

'You're back,' Kate said softly as she walked up to stand beside her.

Emma turned and grinned at her. 'I never left.'

'You're certain this is what you want?'

'Oh, I'm so positive, I'm about to bring this house down.'

'I love it,' Kate said and then leaned in closer, 'cute little elf is going to be a big act to follow though.'

'... So, while my friend here gets over his stage-fright,' Elf said as Jake walked over to sit down on the stool and open the letter she'd given him, 'Let me take this opportunity to remind you that after Christmas comes January. And we all know that the deadline for tax self-assessment is the thirty-first, right? Not mine – well, the date's the same but mine's called *elf* assessment.'

The audience laughed and Emma watched Jake's face as he realised who the letter was addressed to. She saw him glance up at the chandelier and swallow back some emotion.

'You ready, there?' Elf asked Jake as the laughter died down.

'I'm ready,' Jake's deep voice spoke out across the audience as the elf sat down cross-legged to hear his new friend read. 'This letter that I've been asked to read out is dated the twenty-first of July, 1928,' he cleared his throat and began, '*My dearest Lily,*

This morning as I watched you in the rose garden, carefully selecting and then cutting the Albertine and Dainty Bess for tonight's centrepiece, there was such a delightful secret smile on your lips that two things occurred to me...

Firstly, you obviously find the Rosemounts as dreadfully dull as I – their company only tolerable if you can see your favourite roses on the table! Perhaps, as your smile suggested this morning, you will look at the roses this evening and think about after-wards, when I pluck one from the rose bowl and follow you up to bed...

Jake stopped reading and reached out to cover the elf's large pointy ears.

Elf shook him off and said, 'Please, that's probably just old-speak for saying they were going to go to their room to chill and watch Netflix.'

Emma, along with the audience, burst out laughing.

'Who do you think this elf belongs to?' Kate asked.

'Richard Curtis?' Emma replied.

'*Perhaps that certain smile is playing across your beautiful face as you read this,*' Jake continued. '*I'm coming to know your smiles, my dearest Lily.*

Favourite is the one you graced me with on our wedding day. When I lifted your veil, my hands so clumsy, my heart so happy and your eyes met mine with such sweetness, such humour, such joy and your smile full of reassurance and tipped up at the edge with the suggestion of adventures to come.

It's the same smile you smiled when you told me we were to have a little George or a little Lillian running around the house and gardens by Christmas.

Will they have your many smiles, my Lily? Your temperament, your strength, your sense of humour and your sense of adventure?

I cannot wait to find out.

I thought when we married at Christmas last year, that you being my bride was the best Christmas present I could ever have asked for, but this … this surpasses even that.

How blessed we are to count William and Irene as our good friends. Magic was on our side the day William dragged me to The Clock House two Christmases ago. And magic played its part in me being seated next to you.

I feel blessed every day that you had the good manners to haul on the reins of my ill-mannered demeanour and correct me on a couple of things – namely that I was stupid to think that a woman in want of a husband was really only in want of a rich husband, and also that I was stupid for thinking I must be on my own forever and that together you had decided we would make an excellent team.

Which brings me to the second thing that occurred to me as I watched you cutting the roses...

I think I will put a secret door into this part of the rose garden and create a space just for us. I know that it is hard to create a home in a house this size, but you have done us proud. With the house and grounds needing to provide more and more, how nice it will be to have an area just for us, Lily.

A place for you to know how loved you are.

Because you are so loved, my dearest Lily.

Even though it's July, it feels like Christmas. Christmas in July, what a perfect idea! "Merry Christmas", my love,

Yours forever, George xx'

There was a moment's silence and then the audience started clapping.

And while the crowd were still applauding him, Jake rose to his feet, met her gaze and said, 'I love you, Emma Danes.'

Her heart feeling like it was going to burst out of her chest, she walked up onto the stage and said, 'I love you, too.'

'You've given me a piece of my family history I never believed existed.'

'She kept the letter tucked between the pages of *Emma*.

The copy that you gave me for Christmas.'

'I think George did finish the room. I think he put in a door and that I just didn't realise it was a door. I thought it was bricked up. Kept away. Kept secret.'

'When really it was just a secret for them.'

All of a sudden the stage was invaded by singing children.

'Hey, I'm in the middle of declaring my love here,' Jake said.

'Sorry,' Trudie said, poking her head around the curtain. 'But these kids have been waiting for hours to do their song and have I mentioned they've been drinking orange juice all afternoon?'

Emma laughed and grabbing his hands pulled him to the side of the stage and said, 'This is actually for you, anyway. Okay, kids, hit it...'

As the class sang *We Wish You a Merry Christmas*, Emma kept her hand in Jake's.

'You wanted them to sing to me?' Jake said out of the side of his mouth as the notes of, 'And a Happy New Year,' died out.

'No. It's the next bit. Watch,' and stepping forward, she said, 'Right, remember what we talked about? Okay, everyone with a letter sign step forward.'

Jake and Elf, along with the entire audience at Cocktails & Chai watched as thirteen children stepped forward holding up giant letters stuck to broom handles, spelling out *Merry Christmas*.

'Now,' Emma said, clutching her hands together and shooting Jake a nervous glance before looking back at the children, 'Switch,' she instructed.

There was a bit of a kerfuffle as seven children with signs suddenly stepped forward again.

Emma turned to Jake. 'Surprise!'

Jake looked at the signs and then looked back at Emma. 'Misty Me?'

Elf slapped a hand over his face.

'What? No,' and turning to face the kids she muttered, 'Oh my God.'

Elf stepped forward and said, 'Allow me,' and as he sorted the children out, turned to the audience and said, 'It's really apparent that we need to work on our education system, people.' To more laughter he finally turned the reordered children around.

'Ta-da,' Emma said.

Jake looked at the new order. '*Marry Me?*'

'Okay,' Emma answered, her nerves rattling as she took in Jake's shocked face. 'I mean not like right now,' she gabbled. 'Obviously. Way to jump on everyone's Christmas celebrations.' She laughed nervously. 'But maybe next year? That would give us plenty of time to date properly, to work everything out. I mean you have the gardens to work on and I have this place to run, so...' she ran out of words.

'Say "yes, final answer",' Elf helpfully suggested.

'Yes,' Jake said, stepping forward to take Emma in his arms. 'Final answer,' he whispered to her.

'Now do you need me to fill,' Elf said, 'while you kiss the love of your life or do I have to do everything for you, because you know, she is really pretty,' he said, waggling his eyebrows.

'Elf, where are your parents?' Emma asked, 'Because I actually know a good agent they could talk to.'

'Please,' Elf replied, 'you think the couple in the red suits don't deserve a little sleep the morning after the night before?'

'I'm going to kiss the love of my life now,' Jake said, laughing as he lowered his mouth to Emma's.

Elf moved in front of the kissing pair. 'Ladies and gentlemen, that completes the entertainment portion, aka our Christmas show.' And with The Clock House chandelier twinkling down over the room, he bowed and said, 'Merry Christmas to all, and to all a good night.'

Author Letter

Dear Reader,

Merry Christmas! I hope you've enjoyed returning to Whispers Wood for some festive feel-good fun. I've loved writing another Whispers Wood book about some of my favourite things: Christmas, Jane Austen, Vikings, snow, roses, chandeliers, and, of course, top of my 'favourites' list ... romance ☺

While researching for this book I came across the most wonderful thing: Jólabókaflóð. This Icelandic word loosely translates as "Christmas Book Flood" and relates to the country's publishing industry releasing all its books during the Christmas season. A tradition born from that has lots of people exchanging gifts of books on Christmas Eve and then staying up all night to read them. The partaking of hot chocolate while reading is also heavily encouraged!

Well, I have to tell you that right away I fell head over heels in love with this tradition; I mean, if you love books and you love Christmas, how could you not fall hard for this, right? I've always believed that choosing a book for someone special in your life is one of the most personal, most thoughtful, most romantic presents you can gift because it requires forethought and knowledge of that person. For me, un-wrapping a book at Christmas and diving right in is:

#PureMagicAndBliss.

So guess which Christmas tradition went straight onto my 'favourites' list? Yep!

There's no doubt my list is both eclectic and ever-growing, but confession: getting to combine my favourite things into a romantic comedy, while sometimes challenging, is also the absolute bestest fun ever and I wanted to send out the most mega-ginormous Thank You to you all for buying the first book in the series and making it into a supermarket bestseller.

If this is your first visit to The Clock House, you can read all about Kate and Daniel, and Juliet and Oscar's adventure in the first Whispers Wood book: *The Little Clock House on the Green.*

And if you've read both the Whispers Wood books now, you'll know that falling in love is only the beginning...

I've enjoyed adding to Kate and Daniel's and Juliet and Oscar's stories alongside sharing Emma and Jake's in this book, so it's only fair to continue that with the third book in the Whispers Wood series.

With Jake working on the gardens at Knightley Hall as well as the courtyard at The Clock House, and Emma managing Cocktails & Chai as well as writing a screenplay, it's no wonder plans for their wedding are being neglected.

Calling in a favour and asking Gloria Pavey and Seth Knightley to help them seems like the perfect solution – if the two of them can put aside their deep mistrust of all things matrimony *and* stop striking sparks off each other for long enough to help put a wedding together, of course.

If you love your books to come with a helping of humour, a touch of quirk, lashings of romance, oh, and this time ... a film crew arriving in the village, **then make sure you Save the Date for a Whispers Wood Wedding!** The only question is ... whose will it be?

Love and little clock house kisses,

Eve xx

Acknowledgements

The biggest thank you to Kimberley Young and the HarperCollins HarperImpulse team. In the year that HarperCollins celebrates its two-hundredth year – with all the wonderful stories that have gone before and all the wonderful stories yet to come – I am so, so proud to write for you.

Huge heartfelt thank you to Charlotte Ledger, my gorgeous editor extraordinaire, who not only continues to champion all my ideas for *The Little Clock House*, but this year, has been so supportive when Life threw curve balls at my writing schedule.

Hugs to my beautiful friends Suzi and Rachel. Not only do you get it when I disappear into the writing cave, you reward me afterwards with excellent *Gilmore Girl* chats! So many fab catch-ups soon, my lovelies.

Thank you to my brother, Gavin, for just being an excellent brother, really!

And, as always, hugs and a big soppy thank you to my gorgeous husband, Andy, who knows that the only thing to do when life is all a very lot is to tilt your face to the sun and put your best foot forward.